𝒯RUE
ℒOVE

THREE
NOVELS

Lurlene McDaniel

TRUE LOVE

THREE NOVELS

Don't Die, My Love

I'll Be Seeing You

A Rose for Melinda

DELACORTE PRESS

Don't Die, My Love copyright © 1995 by Lurlene McDaniel
I'll Be Seeing You copyright © 1996 by Lurlene McDaniel
A Rose for Melinda copyright © 2002 by Lurlene McDaniel

All rights reserved. Published in the United States by Delacorte Press, an imprint of Random House Children's Books, a division of Random House, Inc., New York. This omnibus edition comprises *Don't Die, My Love; I'll Be Seeing You;* and *A Rose for Melinda*, originally published separately in paperback in the United States by Bantam Books, an imprint of Random House Children's Books, a division of Random House, Inc., New York, in 1995, 1996, and 2002, respectively.

Delacorte Press is a registered trademark and the colophon is a trademark of Random House, Inc.

Visit us on the Web! www.randomhouse.com/teens
Educators and librarians, for a variety of teaching tools, visit us at
www.randomhouse.com/teachers

ISBN 978-0-375-86148-2

Printed in the United States of America
10 9 8 7 6 5 4 3 2 1
First Omnibus Edition

Random House Children's Books supports the First Amendment
and celebrates the right to read.

Contents

TRUE LOVE

THREE NOVELS

Don't Die, My Love

"I'll get the door!" Julie Ellis called, bounding down the stairs from her bedroom. She yanked open the heavy front door to see Luke Muldenhower on her front porch. He grinned as she pulled open the glass storm door and threw herself into his arms. "I've missed you," she cried, snuggling against his chest.

"Blame your father," he said, kissing her. "He's the one who made the team stay for the championship game. It wasn't fun watching the finals, feeling like it should have been us playing for the state title."

Indiana's Waterton Warriors football team, whom Julie's father coached, had made it all the way to the state football finals in their division. On Thursday, the school had shut down. Buses were chartered and most of the town had taken the trip to Indianapolis for the playoffs. Waterton had lost in the semifinals, and while the students and fans, including Julie and her mother, had returned glum and deflated, the players had remained behind until Saturday night to watch the game for first place.

Her father had returned only hours before. And Julie had been waiting anxiously for Luke to drop his stuff at his house, then come see her. She was sorry they'd lost, not only for the sake of school pride, but because she knew how much winning meant to both Luke and her father.

She led him into the living room, where a fire crackled in the fireplace, warding off the late-November chill, and sat him down beside her on the sofa. "Believe me, Mom and I've heard every detail about how bad things went for us. If only time hadn't run out . . . If only Bobby Spencer had hit his man in the end zone with ten seconds left on the clock in the third quarter . . . If only the referee hadn't called a holding penalty on the final play . . ." Julie ticked off the reasons she knew by heart. "Dad's been over every minute of that game and why we lost it."

She gave Luke a pouty look. "But enough

about the game. This is our first date in months that doesn't revolve around football, and I don't want to talk about anything except us and how wonderful you think I am."

He laughed and hugged her. "You're wonderful."

"And?"

"And I love you like crazy." He pressed his forehead against hers and kissed the tip of her turned-up nose.

"That's better," she said with a sly smile. "Forget about football tonight. Next year, *you'll* be the senior quarterback, and you'll take us to the state finals. For now, the season's over. Let's talk about the Christmas dance. It's only three weeks away. Do we want to double with Solena and Frank? You know how they're always fighting with each other."

Luke didn't have a chance to answer, because Bud Ellis, Julie's father, walked into the living room. "I thought I heard you come in," the coach said.

Instantly, Luke was on his feet, his hand outstretched. "Hey, Coach. Sorry about the game."

"Not your fault," Bud Ellis insisted. "I should never have pulled you out and put

Spencer in. You were doing great, but you looked tired."

"It's this flu. I'm having trouble shaking it."

"You look like you feel all right now," Coach said, his gaze flitting between Luke and Julie's radiant face.

"Julie's good medicine," Luke said, taking hold of her hand and pulling her up alongside him.

"We've got a date," Julie told her father. "No more football season. No more curfews."

"*You* have a curfew," her father reminded her.

"Curfew, shmurfew." Julie put her hands on her hips. "Tonight we're going bowling and then we're going to eat a goopy, gooey hot fudge sundae, and since tomorrow's Sunday, Luke can sleep in 'til noon before he has to come take me out to the mall."

"Hot fudge sundaes! Sleeping 'til noon!" Her father looked horrified. "Don't go spoiling my prize quarterback and making him soft, Julie-girl."

Julie knew that would be impossible. Luke had a muscular physique to die for, made harder by the playing season plus hours of daily weight training in the gym. "The only soft thing about Luke is *me,*" she said with a flounce of her blond hair. "And whose side are you on anyway? *I'm* your flesh and blood."

Her father grinned and chucked her under the chin. "Yeah, but you can't play football. And you throw like a girl."

She knew her dad was teasing, but still his remark stung. She was her parents' only child. And a daughter at that. She had never doubted that her dad loved her, but Luke was clearly the son Bud Ellis had always wished he had.

Luke reached his arm around her waist and pulled her next to him. "And I, for one, wouldn't want it any other way. Julie's just about perfect, I'd say."

She felt gratitude for his gentle defense of her. "We're supposed to meet Solena and Frank at the bowling alley in fifteen minutes," Julie said, glancing at the antique clock on the fireplace mantel.

Luke helped her with her coat, and they'd gotten as far as the front door before her father said, "Some college coaches are sniffing around about you already, Luke."

Luke stopped and turned. "They are? Who?"

Inwardly, Julie groaned. It was unfair of her father to hold out this carrot when he knew they were in a hurry. "Can't you talk to Luke tomorrow about this?"

"I could," her dad said.

But Luke wasn't budging. "Tell me, Coach . . . Who's asking?"

"Ohio State for one."

"No lie?" Luke broke into a grin. "One of the Big Ten's asking about me?"

"You're good, Luke; they *should* be asking. And you've still got another year in high school. They'll be on you like white on rice after next season."

Julie refrained from rushing the discussion even though they were going to be impossibly late. Football was Luke's *only* chance to make it into college.

"So what did you tell him?" Luke asked.

"I told him to stand in line!"

Both Luke and her father burst out laughing. Julie smiled and shook her head. "You two are totally weird." But she was glad for Luke. She loved him and wanted him to receive every break he deserved.

Once outside in the crisp November night, Luke took her in his arms and kissed her long and hard. She felt her knees go weak. "I guess you really *did* miss me," she whispered when he released her.

"Now that the season's over, I've got to make up for lost time. You know I love you, Julie."

"I know. But it's always nice to hear you say it."

He opened the door of his car for her. The vehicle was old, but clean and well maintained. Luke had worked long hours the summer before to earn the money to buy it, and when he'd turned seventeen in October, his mom, who worked at the steel mills, had gotten it painted a deep navy blue. The car caught the color of the pale full moon in its shiny finish.

They drove to Waterton's lone bowling alley, parked, and went inside. The sounds of balls striking pins punctuated the air. Frank sauntered over. "Sorry we're late," Luke said. "Where's Solena?"

"In the bathroom sulking."

"Don't tell me you two have had another fight," Julie said in exasperation.

"She's impossible, Julie. Why's she so jealous?"

Julie shot Luke a look that said, *Let me go see what I can do,* and headed for the rest rooms. She found Solena inside, dabbing her eyes with a paper towel. "Now what's wrong?"

Julie asked, none too patiently. She'd been looking forward to an evening of fun, not of refereeing her friends' spats.

"I caught Frank talking to Melanie Hawkins."

"It's not a federal offense."

Solena threw down the wadded towel. "It might not seem like any big deal to you—you've got Luke, who's never even so much as looked at another girl since he fell for you in fifth grade. But out here in the *real* world, it's pretty grim. Girls are always coming on to Frank. And he likes it!"

"Frank likes you, Solena. How many times do I have to tell you? And I know girls are waiting to snake away guys like Frank and Luke, but give your guy some credit. If he wants to date Melanie, he'll tell you."

"Oh, you just don't understand!" Solena stamped her foot.

Julie was trying to be sympathetic, but it was difficult. It was true that Luke had hung around her since he was ten. Of course, then, she couldn't see him for dust. In fact, she'd found it annoying to have some skinny, scrappy kid with shaggy black hair following her everywhere. But when he was twelve, he joined one of the football teams sponsored by the YMCA that her father coached and she learned more about him.

She learned that Luke's father had died in a steel mill accident when Luke was only eight and that his mother was struggling to raise him alone. She learned that he was always in trouble and solving his problems with his fists. Football and her father's belief in Luke as a player had saved him from growing up in the juvenile detention center.

On her fourteenth birthday, Luke had shown up on Julie's porch holding a fistful of flowers, and when she'd taken them and looked into his dark brown eyes and seen absolute adoration for her, something inside her had melted. They'd been dating steadily for the past three years and everyone knew that Julie and Luke went together like ice cream and cake, sunlight and summer.

"We're going bowling," Julie told Solena firmly. "And if you don't join us, Melanie really *will* have an opening. Is that what you want?"

Once she'd coaxed Solena out of the bathroom and they'd found Luke and Frank setting up in one of the lanes, Julie felt better. Solena sulked for a while longer, but soon she seemed like her old self. Julie sat nestled against Luke's side while Solena and Frank took their turn at the pins.

"Glad you could soften her up," Luke said, tugging playfully on Julie's blond hair.

"I wasn't about to let Solena ruin our evening. Besides, I have plans for you later, buster." She pressed her lips against his neck.

"What plans?" he asked, a smile in his voice.

She pulled back, looking puzzled. She reached up and pressed her fingers along the side of his jaw. "Luke," she said. "What's this lump?"

2

Luke pulled away, his expression self-conscious. "Swollen gland, that's all."

"Did your doctor see it?"

"Julie, it's nothing. When a person gets the flu, glands swell."

She frowned. "Is the one on the other side swollen too?"

Luke stood and picked up his bowling ball. "Are you going to hang out your shingle?" He held up an imaginary sign. " 'Julie Ellis: Medicine Woman.' Come on, it's our turn. Bet you a buck you can't make a strike."

She leaped to her feet. "You're on, buster."

The rest of the evening passed quickly, and by the time Luke drove her home, Julie was feeling content. She hooked her arm through Luke's once he stopped his car in front of her house, then leaned her head against his broad shoulder. "I had fun," she said.

"Me too. But then I always have fun when I'm with you."

She felt a tingling sensation along her skin. Luke said romantic things without calculation. Which was one of the reasons she cared for him so much. "I think you should sleep in tomorrow," she told him. "You need a chance to recuperate."

He didn't argue. "I am feeling pretty lousy. Maybe some extra sleep will help. I'll call you after you get home from church."

She raised her face and received his long, lingering kiss, then got out of the car. "I can make it up the walk by myself. Go home and get to bed."

He smiled, but even in the faint glow of the lights from his dashboard, she thought he looked weary and pale. She squeezed his hand through the open passenger window and dashed up the sidewalk and into her house.

"Is that you, Julie?" she heard her mother call.

"No, Mom. It's a burglar."

Her mother came into the foyer, her terry-cloth robe wrapped around her slim figure.

"Cute," she said, without humor. "Come sit down and visit with me."

"I'm tired. Can we talk tomorrow?" Julie was certain she knew what her mother was going to say, and she wasn't in the mood to hear it. Especially after the good time she'd had with Luke and her friends.

"You'll be too busy tomorrow." Her mother led her into the living room, sat, and patted the sofa cushion beside her. "Come on. It won't take long."

Julie sighed and scrunched herself into the corner of the plush rose-colored sofa. She hugged a throw pillow to her chest. "So, what can't wait until tomorrow?"

"Julie, I'm concerned that you're not sending out applications for college."

"Oh, Mom—not this again." Julie groaned.

"Listen to me. I'm a guidance counselor, for heaven's sake. I know what I'm talking about. The freshman classes for all the really top colleges fill up fast and you're too bright, your grades are too good, for you not to get into any college you apply to. I've already talked to dozens of kids in your junior class, and they're sending off forms right and left. You should be too."

"Mom, I've got tons of time to think about

college. I won't even take the SAT exam until next fall, and those scores are what colleges really consider."

"Naturally the SATs are important, but you won't have any trouble with them. You should start applying now to the colleges you're truly interested in."

Julie struggled to keep from losing her temper. She knew her mother was trying to be helpful, but all Julie felt was unnecessary pressure. "Can't I just enjoy high school? Good grief, it's not even Christmas yet! I don't want to deal with college now—especially when I have over a year of high school left." She got up from the sofa.

"It's because of Luke, isn't it?" Her mother's voice was low, but it stopped Julie in her tracks.

"I don't know what you mean."

"You're so busy thinking about Luke that you don't think about yourself. You spend more time with him than with anything else."

Julie clenched her teeth, hating that her mother was partly right, yet not wanting to admit it. "Of course I like Luke. But I do plenty of things with my friends. And I've never once let my grades drop, have I?"

"Julie, I'm not trying to be a nag. It's just that I want so much more for you."

Julie spun and peered down at her mother on the sofa. "More of *what?* Why shouldn't I have a boyfriend and have fun with him? What have you got against Luke?"

"I haven't got anything against him. He's a nice boy. But I want to see you go to college. I want you to get out of this smelly little steel town. Have a career. See the world."

Julie rolled her eyes. *The same old argument.* "Mom, just because you hate Waterton doesn't mean I do. Daddy and I both love it here." By bringing her father into the discussion, Julie felt a sense of leverage. It was true that her dad liked the small steel town where he'd grown up and where he now held the job of athletic director and football coach for northwest Indiana's top-rated high school.

"And don't forget," she added hastily, before her mother could react. "Luke's going to get a football scholarship and be out of here in two years. So, based on your logic, why would I even want to stay if he's gone?"

Her mother's hands, folded in her lap, appeared rigid, as if she were gripping something so tightly that she couldn't let go. "I wasn't badgering you, Julie. I only want you to think about *your* future. Not Luke's."

"I do think about my future. I'll go to college, Mom. And I won't end up at any 'Podunk University,' either." She bent and kissed her mother quickly on the forehead. "Now, I've got to get to bed. It's late and I promised Mrs. Poston I'd help her with Sunday school class in the morning."

Julie breezed from the room and up the stairs without giving her mother a chance to stop her. And once safely in her room, she flopped on the bed and exhaled deeply. She'd heard her father say many times, *"The best offense is a good defense."* And that was what she'd offered her mother tonight—a great defense.

Julie wasn't fibbing when she'd said she wanted to go away to college. But what she hadn't said was that she wasn't about to choose a college until she knew where Luke was going to attend. Hadn't her father said that college coaches were already lining up to offer Luke athletic scholarships? Well, once Luke got down to serious negotiations, Julie would begin to apply to those colleges.

She knew her mother wouldn't like her plans, but right now, Julie didn't care. She wasn't about to spend four years apart from Luke Muldenhower. Besides, her mother was right about one thing: Julie Ellis was smart, and as long as she kept her grades up, she figured she could get into most any college she wanted.

And Solena was right about something too: the world was full of girls waiting to steal a guy like Luke. "I won't let that happen," Julie said out loud. "Not in a million years."

She loved Luke with all her heart. And she wasn't about to let him get away.

"I think you have a fever, Luke." Julie pressed her hand on his cheek as she spoke. Automatically, she moved her hand to the side of his neck, to where she'd first felt the swollen gland the night before. "And your gland doesn't seem any smaller."

It was Sunday afternoon and he'd come over to study with her. Their books were strewn across the dining room table, but Luke had spent most of the past hour resting his head on the book in front of him.

"I'm fine," he said, not too kindly. "You're not my mother, Julie—get off my case."

"Well, excuse me for being concerned." Julie shoved her chair backward and stood up.

"Wait a minute. I didn't mean to snap at you. I didn't sleep good last night, and today I've got a pounding headache."

Instantly, she was sorry for being cross with him. "Why don't you go back to your doctor?"

He shrugged. "I just don't want to. What's he going to do? Give me another prescription for antibiotics? The last prescription didn't help."

"Then that's all the more reason to go."

Pale November sun shone through the window and shimmered in waves across the table. "Office visits and prescriptions cost money," he said. "Things are tight with Mom this month. She doesn't need any extra expense."

Julie knew it was hard for Luke to talk to her about his poverty. Ever since his father's death, his mother had worked full-time and he had worked summer jobs, but there still never seemed to be enough money to go around. "She has health insurance from her job at the mill," Julie said. "She'll get reimbursed."

"Yeah, but she has to pay up front, then wait for the insurance company to reimburse her."

"So what's your point?" Julie crossed her arms, refusing to back down.

Luke tossed his pencil on the table. "My point is that I don't want Mom to spend the money for some stupid flu bug that will eventually run its course."

"That is *so* dumb, Luke Muldenhower. Tell my dad and he'll see to it that you get to the doctor. And it won't cost you a thing!"

He shoved away from the table and stood. "I don't need charity, Julie. It's my flu, you know. And I don't want your daddy to foot my bills."

"That's the *dumbest*—"

She got no further. Luke stepped around her and headed out the door. She called for him to return, but all she heard was the slamming of the front door behind him.

3

"What's all the noise about?" Julie's father sauntered into the dining room, part of the Sunday paper in his hand, his reading glasses pushed down his nose.

"Nothing," Julie said. Suddenly, she realized she sounded just like Luke, saying things were fine when they weren't. "We had a little disagreement and Luke left."

"He'll come back when he's cooled off," her father said. "But don't be hard on my man, Julie-girl. Luke's had a rough season. He doesn't need hassle from his girl."

"Well, thank you, Dad, for your support. Did it occur to you that Luke might be the one in the wrong in this?"

Her father threw up his hands, the paper dangling limply. "Hold on. I'm not about to get in the middle of some lovers' spat. I was just wondering why the door slammed so hard."

Julie thought it ironic that her father could be so high on her relationship with Luke and her mother so down on it. Traditionally, such things tended to be the other way around, but her father had always had a soft spot for Luke and Julie had often felt that he'd take Luke's side against anyone—including his own daughter. "Next time Luke leaves in a huff, I'll tell him not to slam the door," she said.

He started to say something, but the phone rang and her mother called, "Bud, it's for you."

"Back in a minute," he said to Julie. "And we'll discuss what set Luke off."

Julie didn't want any discussion. If Luke wanted her father to know how bad he was feeling, he'd have to tell him. She wasn't about to after the way he'd carried on over a measly doctor's visit.

Twenty minutes later, her father was still on the phone when the doorbell sounded.

Luke was standing on the porch, looking contrite, his hands behind his back. "Can I come in?"

Julie pushed open the door, turned on her

heel, and headed to the dining room, with Luke tagging after her.

"Here. These are for you." He held out a small bouquet of flowers. She recognized them as the kind sold down at the Kroger grocery store, yet they conjured up memories of bouquets from the past he'd given her. It was his favorite means of communication.

"Do you think you can solve every problem with flowers?" She took them and buried her nose in the petals of the yellow and red mums.

"Can't I?"

He looked so cute and apologetic, she had a hard time not smiling. "Yes," she admitted. "You know how I feel about flowers."

He grinned. "And me? How do you feel about me? Am I forgiven?"

"I wasn't trying to tell you what to do," she said, returning to the topic of their disagreement. "I'm worried, that's all. You've been sick for weeks and you don't seem to be getting any better. I guess I can't understand why you don't go back to the doctor and demand he make you well. The football playoffs are over with now, so you really should go to the doctor. And money's no excuse."

He had sat down in a dining room chair while she talked. His long, lanky body drooped, reminding her of a balloon that was losing air. She thought he looked thinner than usual, but she wasn't about to mention it to him. "I know you're right," he said quietly. "I've been putting it off because . . . because I'm worried too."

"You are?"

"Other glands are swollen—the ones under my arms. And at night I get these terrible sweats. I mean I wake up and the sheets are soaking wet. I've been changing them every morning so Mom won't know."

Julie felt her stomach constrict. "This doesn't sound right to me. Maybe it's more than the flu."

"I guess I thought it would eventually go away."

"But it hasn't."

He shrugged. "Look, I'll go back to the doctor, but not until Christmas break."

"That's another three weeks!"

"I'm drowning in schoolwork. What with the playoffs and all, I really fell behind."

"But—"

He placed his fingertips across her lips to silence her. "Julie, I'm not smart like you. I have to work hard for my grades, and I can't slip up. Football scholarships to the best colleges mean you have to be a good athlete *and* a good student. The better my grades, the better my chances."

"But you have a whole year before you have to choose a college. Why not concentrate on your health now and work on your grades later?"

He shook his head and flashed a winsome smile. "Maybe you should be a lawyer. You're worse than a bulldog when you get hold of something. You just won't let it go, will you."

She felt her cheeks color. "I'm worried about you. Don't go brushing me off."

He got to his feet and wrapped his arms around her. She started to tug away, but his arms were strong and made her feel warm and safe. In his arms it didn't seem like anything was overly important, or frightening. "Besides," he said, "I've got to take my girl to a big formal dance. What if the doctor puts me on bed rest or something? How will I take her to the dance then?"

"I don't care if we miss the dance." Julie said the words, but knew it wasn't true. She really did want to go to the dance. She'd already bought her dress.

"Well, I care," Luke insisted. "It gives me another excuse to bring you flowers."

She pulled back and stared up into his face—the face she'd grown to love so much. "But the minute Christmas break starts, you'll go to the doctor?"

"Yes."

"Promise?"

"Unless I'm well, of course." He kissed the tip of her nose. "But you'll have to go with me. I really don't want to bother my mom with this. Not with Christmas and everything."

"You bet I'll go with you," Julie said. "In fact, I'll drive you personally."

He bent his head to kiss her mouth, but just then Coach Ellis came through the dining room doorway. Luke let Julie go. "Guess who I've been on the phone with," Coach said, looking excited. He didn't wait for their guesses. "The head of the school board. It looks as if those funds are going to be allocated for Waterton High to build that new football stadium."

Luke gave a high five. "All right!"

Julie knew how important the project was to her father. He'd been trying to push it through for over three years, but had met with steady setbacks. The present stadium was inadequate, since the number of kids attending the high school had grown so large. The often overflow crowd had to be accommodated on makeshift benches along the sidelines and the present bleachers were rickety, even hazardous. "That's great, Dad."

"I guess our being runner-up in the state made an impression on the board," Coach Ellis said, rubbing his hands together gleefully. "I'm going to get a jump start on this. I'll have an architect draw up some blueprints and be ready to lay them out for the board at their meeting in January."

"A new stadium." Luke's brown eyes gleamed. "When will it be finished?"

"If all goes according to my timetable, you could start your senior season in it."

Luke looked surprised. "That's not even a year from now."

"If it gets hustled through, we could break ground this spring. But it's not the construction that takes so long, it's getting the turf ready for play. It's possible that it could be ready by fall."

Luke shrugged. "Even if I can't play on it, the next class will. I'm just glad we're getting it."

"I want you to play on it." Coach Ellis sounded so adamant that Julie half believed he could have the grass grow on a schedule that met his demands.

Once he'd left the room, Julie turned toward Luke. "Dad sure doesn't let much get in the way of his goals for his football team, does he?"

"He's a great coach, Julie."

"He's the only coach you've ever had."

"No matter. He's a great coach by any standard. He doesn't teach you what to think out on the field; he teaches you *how* to think. I've learned everything I know about the game from him, and it's going to be my key for getting into college. And who knows—maybe even someday, the pros."

Julie felt a twinge of jealousy over the prominent place football held in Luke's life. Sometimes it seemed that the game was more the center of his world than she was. The feelings were childish, but that didn't stop them from coming. She wished she was as focused on something as Luke was on the sport of football. Maybe someday she would be, but right now, there was only Luke. "Well, if you go to the pros, I'll take out a franchise on you. How's that sound?"

"If I go to the pros, you're coming with me."

"Really? And what will I do? Organize your social calendar and commercial endorsements?"

"Not to worry—I'll find something for you to do." He plucked up one of the bright golden mums from the bouquet lying on the table and poked the stem through the silky blond hair above her ear. "I'll cover you in flowers someday, Julie-girl. And you won't be able to refuse me anything."

She laughed. "For every flower, you'll get a kiss."

"Promise?"

"Promise."

4

"Your dress is awesome, Julie, and it really looks *great* on you." Solena was stretched across Julie's bed while Julie modeled for her. The dress's full taffeta skirt made a swishing sound as she pivoted toward the full-length mirror mounted on the back of her bedroom door.

She admired her reflection and the way the black fabric shimmered in the pale winter light coming through the windows. "You don't think it's too plain?"

"No way. It's elegant. And I love the way it falls off your shoulders. Pretty sexy."

The bodice fit perfectly and the neckline scooped downward and out to expose her creamy white shoulders and the swell of her breasts. "It cost me every penny of my Christmas gift money, plus a month's worth of baby-sitting funds, but I just fell in love with it. I had to have it."

"Wait 'til Luke sees it. He'll positively drool."

Julie smiled, imagining the look in his eyes when he saw her in the dress. "I like your dress too," she said, catching her friend's gaze in the mirror. "The color's perfect with your dark hair." They had come from Solena's house, where Solena had shown off her new dress.

"Next to you, I'll look like a frump tomorrow night."

"That's not true!"

Solena waved aside Julie's protest. "I can live with it. Just so long as I look better than Melanie."

"Are you still worried about her and Frank?"

"Maybe not worried . . . but I do want to be prepared." Solena scooted off the bed. "Let's run up to the mall and look for a new perfume. Frank needs an excuse to nuzzle my neck, don't you think?"

"I'd love to, but I can't. Luke's mom invited me for supper tonight."

"But it's only one o'clock. Supper's hours from now."

Julie didn't want to tell Solena the whole

truth, but this was the afternoon Luke was supposed to go to his doctor for another checkup. School had been out for a few days, but it had taken until today to get an appointment with the doctor. Half the town was down with the flu and Luke's doctor had been booked solid. "I promised him I'd come early," Julie told her friend.

"I'd say this qualified as early," Solena grumbled.

"We can go to the mall tomorrow. I still have some Christmas shopping to do and we can look for perfume then. And if we get there when it opens, it'll be less crowded. I mean, can you imagine how busy it is this time of day?"

Solena fumbled in her purse for her car keys. "Okay, but I want to be there when they open the doors tomorrow."

"I'll pick you up," Julie said, seeing Solena off.

Once Solena was gone, Julie changed into jeans and a sweater and grabbed her coat. "I'm out of here, Mom," she hollered, banging the storm door as she left.

It had snowed the night before, but the plows had cleared and salted the streets and traffic flowed smoothly. Julie drove across the railroad tracks that divided the city of Waterton and soon reached Luke's neighborhood. The houses were older and smaller here, clumped together, so that there were almost no side yards between them. The homes were close to the mill and changed owners frequently as the mill hired and laid off through the years.

Several homes were in need of repair. Luke's house needed a coat of paint, but still it looked tidy and neat compared with that of a neighbor, who had old cars partially torn down in his front yard. In the cool light of winter, the block seemed shabby and dismal.

Julie parked in the driveway and Luke met her on the porch. He gave her a quick kiss. "Mom took the afternoon off from work and she's cooking up a feast."

Inside, the smell of bubbling spaghetti sauce made Julie's mouth water. She followed Luke into the kitchen, where his mother was stirring a pot on the stove. "It smells wonderful," Julie exclaimed.

Nancy Muldenhower put down her wooden spoon, wiped her hands on a dish towel, and hugged Julie warmly. "I'm glad you could come for supper. Although it won't be ready for another three hours." She shot Luke a glance. "He insisted that you had to come this afternoon so that you could drive him somewhere. Why isn't Luke driving? What's going on with you two?"

Her lively brown eyes, so much like Luke's, caused Julie to grow flustered. "He's keeping a promise to me," Julie said hastily.

"What promise?"

"We'll tell you at supper," Luke interjected, getting Julie off the hook. Looking at Julie, he said, "Let me get some things out of my room and then we'll split."

Julie sat in a yellow kitchen chair to wait. The kitchen table looked scarred, battle-weary from years of service.

"Luke says you two are planning to stop by tomorrow night before the dance so I can see your dress."

"Yes . . . on our way to pick up Solena and Frank."

"It's nice of your father to lend Luke his car for the evening. Mine's not much newer than Luke's."

Julie's dad had made the offer weeks before and Luke had been thrilled over the prospect of driving the sporty auto. Julie would have been just as happy in Luke's car, but no one had asked her opinion. "Well, you know how Dad feels about Luke."

"He's been very good to my boy, and I'll always be grateful for the way he's taken him under his wing. It's not easy raising a boy without a father—especially in this neighborhood. I'd have moved years ago if I could have afforded it."

Julie thought Luke's mother was attractive, even if she was on the heavy side. Luke had always been protective of her, careful not to cause her worry or problems, which was part of his refusal to keep returning to the doctor for his unremitting flu bug.

"I like your house," Julie said. "It's cozy."

"It's old." Nancy stirred the sauce again and tapped the wooden spoon on the side of the pot. "We're putting up our Christmas tree next week. You will come and help decorate it, won't you?"

"Of course. How else can we keep Luke from slinging the tinsel on it?"

The two of them were laughing when Luke came back to the kitchen, ready to leave. "Why do I get the feeling you're laughing at me?"

After Nancy and Julie had poked some more good-natured fun at him, Luke promised his mother to return by five and he and Julie left the warm kitchen. Julie drove and Luke stared pensively out the window. "It's only a follow-up visit to your doctor," she chided, knowing instinctively how keeping the appointment was bothering him.

"I think it's a waste of time and money. I've been feeling better, you know."

"But you're not completely well." She thought he still looked thin, and she could see his gland protruding from beneath his jaw. "Maybe you have mono," she suggested. "You know—the 'kissing disease'?"

He grimaced. "That would be terrible. I'll have to give up kissing you."

"I haven't caught anything from you yet. If it's mono, I'll wear a mask." She grinned. "Come on, lighten up. This'll be over in no time. And tomorrow night we go to the dance and I'm going to look so good, it'll blow your socks off."

"Too late—you already blow my socks off."

The doctor's waiting room was crowded with sniffling kids and crying babies. A few adults sat with their heads buried in their hands, looking feverish. "If you're not sick, you will be by the time you're done sitting around this place," Luke grumbled.

"Stop grousing," Julie said. "Be a good sport."

Julie flipped through magazines while Luke fidgeted and watched the clock. Over thirty minutes passed before he was finally called into one of the waiting rooms. Another forty-five minutes passed and Julie grew restless herself. She imagined Luke forgotten in some cubicle, getting angry while he waited. Forty minutes later, the outer door opened and Luke's mother hurried inside.

"Nancy! Why are you here?"

"The doctor called and told me to come. I didn't know you were taking Luke to the doctor, Julie. Why didn't either of you tell me?"

"Luke didn't want to worry you."

"What's wrong with Luke? He wasn't sick when he left home."

At a loss for words, embarrassed, Julie shrugged.

An inner door opened and a nurse called them in. Quickly, they followed the woman down a narrow hall and into an office where a doctor sat behind his desk, writing in a file folder. Luke sat stiffly in a side chair. "Luke, are you all right?" His mother rushed toward him. Julie followed, hanging back slightly.

"I don't know." Luke sounded sullen. "Ask him."

The doctor stood and nodded. "I'm Dr. Portage."

"I'm Julie Ellis, his, uh . . . friend."

"I'm his mother. Where's Dr. Simms?"

"He's taken me on as his assistant."

"Tell me what's wrong."

Dr. Portage sat and steepled his fingers together. "I've checked Luke over, listened to his symptoms, and done some preliminary blood work. As I told you on the phone, I'm concerned about his elevated white blood count."

Julie felt her heart pounding and reached for Luke's hand. "Luke, he's scaring me."

Luke looked away. His hand felt cold as ice.

"I don't mean to alarm any of you," Dr. Portage said. "But I don't like what I'm seeing. I suspect Luke has some kind of infection. According to his records, he's been treated with antibiotics, but he hasn't responded as he should have."

"Are you saying you'll have to run more tests?" Nancy asked.

"Yes. And he needs to be in the hospital in order to run them. I've got a call in to St. Paul's Hospital in Chicago."

"Why Chicago? What's wrong with Water-ton General?"

"They don't have the equipment and staff I want for Luke."

Julie and Luke exchanged glances. His dark eyes bored into her, making her even more afraid. "What do you mean?" Julie asked. Her voice quivered.

Dr. Portage looked directly at Luke. "I want you to go home, pack a bag, and drive straight to St. Paul's."

5

Luke jumped to his feet. "Right now? You want me go check in right *now?* No way!"

"The sooner the better," the doctor said.

"Now, Luke, we should do what the doctor says," his mother added.

"But the dance is tomorrow night."

"I don't care about the dance," Julie interjected.

"Well, I do."

The doctor's phone rang. He spoke quietly into the receiver, hung up, and told Luke, "That was St. Paul's. It's all arranged. You're to check in this afternoon, as soon as possible."

The remainder of the afternoon passed in a surrealistic blur for Julie. And while she would not recall later the exact sequence of events, she'd never forget the cold, snakelike fear that clutched at her insides and numbed her soul. She cried when she called her father on the phone from Luke's house. She found comfort in his absolute refusal to believe that the doctor was anything but "an incompetent fool who's allowed Luke's flu to get out of control and now has to cover his mistakes by subjecting Luke to useless testing."

"I'm going with them to St. Paul's, Dad."

"Maybe I should drive over too."

She knew he was preparing his presentation for the school board about the new stadium. "Why don't I call you from the hospital once I find out what's going on."

"All right. You stay with Luke's mom. She'll need someone."

Afterward, Julie watched Luke and his mother pack a duffel bag, her hands stiff with concern, his jerking with pent-up anger. Julie rode with them on the sixty-mile trip from Waterton to Chicago, and once inside the mammoth hospital, she sat with Luke in the patient admitting room, listening to Luke's mother answer countless questions and watching her fill out long insurance forms.

Julie took the elevator with Luke, his mom,

and a nurse to the sixth floor and accompanied them to the hospital room, where two beds, two bureaus, and two nightstands filled the space. All that separated the beds was a thin, pale green curtain. Luke was the only occupant, but the nurse told them that another patient could be checked in at any time and become Luke's roommate.

The nurse chattered cheerfully—Julie assumed to make them feel at ease. She told about the hospital routine, meals, TV, visiting hours. She said lab technicians would come to draw blood and do simple routine procedures. She told them that Dr. Portage would be in later that evening to see Luke and that he'd have a colleague, Dr. Sanchez, with him.

The nurse gave them more forms and instructions on how to find the nearby Ronald McDonald House, the facility where families of sick children could stay to be near their kids. Luke said, "I'm not a child. And I don't plan to be here too long."

And the nurse replied, "I'm just giving information."

"How long will he have to stay?" Nancy asked.

"That's up to his doctors."

Julie's head swam with information, jumbled emotions, the foreign smells of antiseptics, floor wax, and antibacterial soaps. She felt like a bird pushed helter-skelter by some strange air current. She felt so sorry for Luke she wanted to cry, and her eyes burned with unshed tears.

"I'm sorry about the dance," he said when his mother had gone with the nurse to take care of more details.

"The dance is nothing. All that matters is you getting well."

"There's nothing wrong with me except that I'm run-down. It's all some stupid mistake. Dr. Portage just got alarmed because he didn't cure me the first time."

"That's what Dad says. He wants to come see you."

"Not tonight. He's my coach, Julie. I don't want him to see me like this."

"I won't be able to keep him away."

Luke twisted his bedcovers, wadding them in his large fists. "Will you make sure Mom gets home all right?"

"I'll watch out for her. And I'll come back with her tomorrow."

He stared out the lone window. Night had come, and the darkness looked cold and brittle. "I hate this, Julie. I really hate this."

"It'll be over soon." She wanted so much to cheer him up. "You'll be back home and it'll be Christmas and New Year's and then school will start again. Everything's going to be okay."

She hugged him, locking her arms around his body. They held on to each other until his mother returned. She hugged him too and said she'd be back first thing in the morning. Julie and Luke's mother walked to the doorway, where they turned and waved. Julie's gaze lingered longingly on Luke's face. He smiled and flashed them a thumbs-up.

His expression was confident, identical to the one he wore during a football game against a superior foe. Julie had seen such bravado in his eyes a hundred times. Yet this time, she saw one more thing in their dark depths. She saw fear.

"There's no way I'm not going to spend the week over there with Luke's mother, Mom." Julie stood facing her mother defiantly in the middle of the kitchen floor, two days later.

"But it's almost Christmas, Julie, and we haven't even put up our tree."

"How can I think about Christmas with Luke going through all those tests in the hospital? Mrs. Muldenhower and I can stay together at the Ronald McDonald House and be with Luke every day. And that's where I want to be."

"Honey, I'm concerned about him too, but it's not like he's family. . . ."

Julie felt anger, hot and violent, simmering in her blood. She wanted to scream at her mother.

"Calm down," she heard her father say. He turned to his wife. "Be rational, Patricia. Of course Julie wants to be with Luke. That hospital is the pits for an active kid like Luke. And the tests they're fixing to give him could make a grown man cower."

Patricia Ellis stamped her foot. "Stop ganging up on me. I know he's your prized player, Bud. And I know he's Julie's boyfriend. But it's Christmas, for heaven's sake. Julie should be here with us."

"By Christmas Day, Luke will be home," Julie insisted. "And until he is, I'm packing some things and staying with him. And you can't stop me!" She spun on her heel, but her father stepped into the doorway, blocking her way.

"Watch your temper," he warned. He looked over her head at his wife. "You're wrong on this, Pat. Julie should be with Luke and his mother. And I'll be going over most days for visits, so I'll keep a check on her. Luke's a fine kid, and he shouldn't have to go through this by himself."

With her father's help, Julie had won the battle, and when Luke's mother arrived an hour later, Julie was packed and waiting by the front door. In Chicago, they checked in at the Ronald McDonald House, a modern facility with beautiful sleeping rooms, a huge living room and TV area, a modern, fully stocked kitchen, laundry facilities, and a large playroom for younger brothers and sisters of patients at St. Paul's.

Julie and Nancy unpacked quickly, then hurried the two blocks to the hospital. They arrived at Luke's room in time for his return from radiology. "What did they do to you?" Julie asked anxiously.

"A CT scan," he said.

"Did it hurt?"

"Not a bit. They shoved me inside this huge machine and took an X ray of my entire body. The worst part was having to lie perfectly still while they did it."

"What's the X ray for?"

"To see my glands on the inside." He gave

her a sidelong glance. "Maybe I'll start glowing in the dark."

"Very funny."

His mother kissed his forehead. "One of the nurses said Dr. Sanchez was on the floor. I'm going to find him and talk to him. Be right back."

When she'd gone, Luke opened his arms and Julie leaned over the bed to receive his hug. "I've missed you," he whispered against her ear.

"Oh, Luke, I've missed you too. I wish I could take you home with me right now."

"Why don't we make a dash for it? They won't notice until suppertime."

She laughed. At least he was in better spirits.

"Any feedback about the dance from Solena?" he asked.

"She and Frank missed us going with them."

"You didn't get to wear your new dress."

"I'll wear it to the next dance for you."

"Maybe we can go someplace special New Year's Eve. Would you like that?"

"Sure. But before we make any plans maybe we'd better see how all these tests come out."

He looked downcast. "I just want my life back."

She quickly searched for a way to distract him. "Did Dad tell you that the school board put off their vote on the new stadium until the middle of February?"

"He mentioned it when he was visiting yesterday. He was mad about it, wasn't he?"

"You know my dad," Julie said. "He doesn't *wait* too easily. He wants that stadium and he wants it *now!*" She banged her closed fist on the bedside table in an imitation of her father. "He says that if the school board doesn't get cracking, they won't break ground for it this spring."

"It'll get built," Luke said.

"I know. But he has his heart set on you playing in it your senior year."

Luke sighed. "Right now, I feel too weak to *pick up* a football, much less think about playing a *game.*"

"You'll feel better soon."

"I hope so." He held up his hand, which was fastened to an IV line. "They're pumping me full of antibiotics, but they don't seem to be helping much. I feel like a pincushion. Every day the lab takes blood. This is a real drag, Julie."

While Julie was trying to think of something to say to cheer him up, Luke's mother returned. Her face looked calm, yet Julie suspected she was upset. "I cornered that doctor of yours, and he said that they're going to take you into surgery tomorrow and do a biopsy on the gland in your neck."

"Surgery?" Julie felt her knees go weak. "You mean they're going to operate on Luke?"

"It's only a biopsy," Luke's mother said, trying to make it sound like a simple routine. "They'll take out some of the cells and send them to the lab for analysis. And they'll do a bone marrow biopsy at the same time."

"What are they looking for?" Luke asked the question without emotion.

"I'm not certain," Nancy said. But Julie could tell by the look in her eyes that she had a suspicion. One that she wasn't about to reveal. And one that, whatever it was, frightened her very much.

6

The biopsy procedure was indeed simple. Luke went down to the surgical floor at seven the next morning and was back in his room by nine. Both Julie's parents drove to Chicago to wait with Julie and Nancy, and afterward they all trooped in to see Luke as soon as he was brought up from recovery.

"You don't seem groggy from the anesthetic," Julie's mother observed. "When I had Julie, I was sick for three days from the stuff they gave me to put me to sleep."

"The anesthesiologist said that I would come out of it pretty fast, and he was right. I feel pretty good. Except that my neck hurts. And my hip's sore too." He touched the large white bandage taped to his neck and patted the covers atop his hips.

"That's because of the bone marrow aspiration. They inserted a syringe into your bone marrow and drew some out for testing," his mother explained. "Do you need some pain medication?"

Bud Ellis announced cheerily, "Luke's no *wimp*. He's used to taking hard hits on the football field, so a little slice out of his neck and a sore spot on his body won't set him back much."

"I only take hits if my defense fails to block their tackles," Luke said, making light of his discomfort.

It bothered Julie that he had to put on some macho act for her father, but she didn't say anything because she didn't want to embarrass him. As soon as her father left, she'd make certain that he got a pain pill from the nurse.

"What's next?" Coach Ellis asked.

Nancy responded with, "The full pathology report on the lump will be available in a couple of days; then Dr. Sanchez will know what we're dealing with."

"So, you'll probably be home for Christmas after all," Patricia Ellis said. "That'll be good." She paused, then added, "You know, I was wondering if the two of you might like to come over for Christmas dinner."

Julie was positively shocked. Her mother had never issued such an invitation before. Of course, Luke had eaten with her family on occasion, but never with his mom as a guest too.

"Are you sure?" Nancy asked, looking hesitant. "I've been so preoccupied with all of this that I haven't given Christmas a second thought. It would be very kind of you to have us."

"We're absolutely sure," Coach interjected.

"No need for both of us to cook," Patricia added.

Julie wondered if this was something her mother had come up with on her own or if her father was responsible for the invitation. At the moment, she didn't care. The thought of having Luke at her family's table for Christmas dinner would help her get through the ordeal of the hospital.

"Thanks, Mrs. Ellis," Luke said. He always called her "Mrs. Ellis" because she treated him rather formally. It irked Julie that her mother didn't adore Luke the way she and her father did, but she'd learned to live with it.

"I know it can't be fun being stuck in the hospital all during your holiday break," Julie's mother said.

"As word's gotten around, some of the guys on the team have called me. A few are going off on skiing trips with their families and staying at fancy resorts. I tell them that this is my resort for the holidays."

The adults laughed and the coach tapped Luke's shoulder. "That's the spirit. I knew they couldn't keep you down."

Later, when he and Julie were alone, Luke confided, "I wasn't exactly honest with your father. All this stuff *is* getting me down."

"It's okay to tell him. You don't always have to act as if you're in complete control."

"No, it's not okay. He expects me to blow this off and not get depressed."

"I know he does. And it makes me mad."

Luke looked surprised. "Why?"

"Because you shouldn't have to hide what you're really feeling for fear that it might disappoint someone."

"Don't be mad."

Unexpectedly, tears sprang to her eyes. "Well, I am. I'm mad because this is happening to you and you didn't do anything to deserve it. And I'm mad because people— especially my father—are acting like you shouldn't be too bothered by any of it. That's so lame! If it were me, I'd be throwing things at everybody who stuck his head in the door. Nurses, doctors, lab techs—everybody."

Luke grinned and took her hand. "Don't think I haven't wanted to. But I figure they're all only doing their jobs. Besides, don't forget—I'm a lover, not a fighter." He winked and she returned his smile. He said, "I got you a present."

"Me? But when, and how?"

He opened the drawer to his bedside table and extracted a long-stemmed red rose, wrapped in cellophane and tied with a bright green Christmas bow. He handed her the flower. "When I was in the recovery room, I begged one of the nurses to buy it for me in the gift shop and put it in my room so I could give it to you."

A lump of emotion clogged Julie's throat. "You're the one who's sick. *I* should be buying *you* flowers."

He shook his head, looking pleased by the reaction his unexpected gift had caused. "I'd rather have tickets to the Super Bowl."

She hugged him, holding him tightly and with great feeling. "Oh, Luke, I can't wait until all this is over."

"Me too," he said into her ear. "The only thing that's made it halfway tolerable is that you're here with me. Just a few more days, honey. Just a few more days."

The afternoon Dr. Sanchez came to discuss Luke's diagnosis with Luke, his mother, and Julie, the nurses were decorating the floor for the holidays. The scents of pine and bayberry filled the halls and each door was garnished with colorful ribbons. But when the doctor came inside the room, he closed the door and shut out the noise of Christmas preparations. The sun slanted through the blinds, casting patterns across Luke's bedcovers. The doctor, his hands full of charts and papers, pulled a chair to the side of the bed. Nancy sat near the doctor and Julie remained in her perch on the bed, her fingers laced through Luke's. The adjoining bed was still empty, so there was no one to overhear, no one to shut out with the flimsy green curtain.

"You're not smiling, Doc," Luke said. "Did the nurses forget to invite you to their Christmas party?"

"No way. Who do you think plays Santa Claus for the pediatric ward?" His banter was easy, but Julie saw that his eyes weren't smiling.

"So, what do you have to tell us?" Luke's mother asked. "What's wrong with my son?"

The doctor flipped open the manila folder on his lap. "I'm going to give this to you straight, Luke, because you asked me to."

"Yes, I did."

"And because it's the only way I deal with my patients. I talk straight."

Julie's heart began to hammer and her fingers tightened around Luke's.

"The official name for what you have is Hodgkin's Lymphoma."

Julie heard Luke's mother gasp and saw her shake her head. "What's that?" Julie asked, not one bit embarrassed by her ignorance.

"It's a form of cancer that develops in the lymph system, which is part of the body's circulatory system. Right now, you're in an early stage and your prognosis is good."

Cancer! Julie felt as if someone had hit her hard in the stomach and knocked the wind out of her. Maybe she hadn't heard Dr. Sanchez correctly. "But Luke's so healthy," she blurted. "He plays football."

"Hodgkin's is rare—it accounts for less than one percent of all cancer cases. Unfortunately, when we see it, it's in young people between the ages of fifteen and thirty-five. Basically, as in all cancers, the cells of the lymph system go crazy and start dividing at will. This breaks down the immune system—your body's infection-fighting machine—and it can spread to other organs."

Luke's face looked impassive, as if he were listening to a weather report. Julie wanted to scream, *No! No! You've made a mistake!*

"He never complained of any pain," Nancy said.

"His symptoms were classic—swollen, painless nodes in his neck, night sweats, fevers, weight loss. But those symptoms could be ascribed to any number of illnesses. That's why we ran so many tests." Dr. Sanchez removed several papers from the file folder.

"Your pathology report shows that the cells in your neck were positive for cancer. But on the good side, your CT scan showed that your lymph network looks clean. And your bone marrow biopsy was negative also. In other words, the cancer hasn't spread yet."

" 'Yet'?" It was the first time Luke had spoken.

"Untreated, it will spread."

"How do you treat it?" Luke asked.

"We start with chemotherapy."

Julie felt sick to her stomach. She'd heard about chemotherapy and its side effects.

Dr. Sanchez continued. "I'm moving you up to the oncology floor and assigning you another doctor. Paul Kessler is one of our top oncologists—a big football fan, too. He played for Duke University as an undergraduate. You'll like him."

"So I won't be home for Christmas." Luke's voice sounded flat. "You told me I'd be home for Christmas."

"You might be," Dr. Sanchez said. "Chemo patients are given their initial doses in the hospital to see how they tolerate the drugs and to work out the best combination. We'll insert a Port-A-Cath here." He touched an area near Luke's collarbone. "It's a tube gizmo surgically implanted under the skin so that your chemo can be administered without having to stick you all the time. The catheter's opening will be on the outside.

"Medications will be inserted every three weeks for six cycles, for a total of eighteen weeks. At that rate, you'll be through chemo by April."

"I've got to walk around with a stupid tube hanging half out of me? I've got to take all these weird chemicals? What about school? What about my *life?*" Luke's voice rose.

"Dr. Kessler will answer all your questions. Chemo is his specialty. But you'll be able to return to school once you're on the program. And after you adjust, you'll resume regular life. The chemo treatments will eventually be over, Luke."

Luke's face had become an angry mask and his hand in Julie's felt icy cold. "And then what, Doc? Will the cancer be gone forever? Will I get to pick up where I left off? Or is this thing going to hang over me for the rest of my life?"

"I can't answer that, Luke. I don't know."

"Well, maybe I don't want to go through chemo and all. Maybe I just want to pack up and go home and forget the whole mess."

"Luke, you can't—" his mother began.

The doctor interjected, "You have the right to refuse treatment, Luke, but it wouldn't be wise. With it, you at least have hope for recovery. Without it, you will most certainly die."

7

Nothing had prepared Julie for Luke's diagnosis. She moved through the next day in a numbing fog of disbelief. She sobbed into the phone when she told her father and felt an odd kind of comfort in his display of explosive anger. Her mother was sympathetic, and sorry, but she wanted Julie to come home—Christmas was only a week away. Julie refused, becoming adamant about staying with Luke's mother at the Ronald Mc-Donald House. She couldn't leave Luke. She simply couldn't.

He was started on chemo, and the side effects were immediate. He began vomiting continually. "It takes some adjustments to arrive at the right combination," Dr. Kessler said. "The important thing is, Luke has to keep eating."

His advice seemed stupid, since Luke couldn't keep anything down. Luke begged Julie to go home. "I don't want you to see me like this," he moaned. His skin looked ashen.

"I'm not leaving," Julie insisted. Yet, the weekend before Christmas, she decided to return home long enough to replenish her wardrobe—and to appease her mother. She rode the high-speed train from Chicago to Waterton, where her father picked her up at the station.

"You look thin," he said.

"I'm fine," she told him.

Walking into her house, she felt like a stranger. The decorations were up. It was the first time in all of her seventeen years that she hadn't helped with the festivities. She went quickly to her room, and felt like a stranger there too. Everything was familiar, yet alien. She'd grown used to the hospital smells and sparse furnishings. Her room seemed too colorful. Too cluttered.

Julie kept a tight rein on her emotions as she dumped the contents of her suitcase on the bed and started toward her closet for fresh clothes. Midway, she stopped. Draped on a hanger from atop the molding of the closet door, exactly where she'd left it, was the black taffeta dress she was to have worn to the school holiday dance.

The dress looked beautiful and pristine. It reminded her of a simpler time, a throwback to days of unhurried sweetness when nothing was more pressing in her life than studying for a test. Or talking on the phone with Solena. Or making plans for a date with Luke. She felt a catch in her throat.

Slowly, she approached the dress and fingered the satiny material. How foreign it felt. Her hands were used to touching hospital sheets, hospital-issue pajamas, and cotton blankets. The dress's elegant fabric no longer belonged in her world. She wondered if there would ever be room for such an extravagance again.

Tears slid down her cheeks, wetting her skin. She felt her shoulders begin to shake as sobs, unchecked, poured out of her. *Luke, Luke . . . What's going to happen to us?* She couldn't stop crying. Couldn't stop aching inside. Julie buried her face in the dark fabric and felt the dampness soak into the material. She could almost hear her mother saying, "Be careful. Water will stain taffeta. It's not a very practical dress, you know."

But Julie only wept harder, not caring.

Somehow the tearstains seemed appropriate. The dress would wear the watermarks forever, a symbol of the lost innocence of her life. Of the cruel and bitter upheaval in Luke's. The dress was fantasy. The heap of practical clothing on her bed was real life.

Quickly, Julie jerked open the closet door and, with muffled weeping, began to repack.

On Christmas Day, Luke's hair began to fall out. "Ho, ho, ho," he said without mirth, holding up the wad of hair left on his pillow.

"It's only hair," Julie said. But inwardly, she was shaken.

At her mother's insistence—as well as Luke's and his mother's—she had gone home Christmas Eve and spent Christmas morning with her parents. Then, bringing gifts, she and her family had driven over to Chicago to visit Luke.

The hospital staff had done its best to make the day festive for the patients on the oncology floor, wheeling them out of their rooms to gather round the decorated tree in the rec room next to the nurses' station. They had bought and wrapped gifts for all their regulars, which Julie found touching. It struck her that in a weird way, they were all part of a family, one held together by the disease of cancer. Many of the patients were worse off than Luke, but he was the youngest one on the floor, and clearly a favorite of the staff.

Coach Ellis brought him a football signed by the players on the Indianapolis Colts, and she had given him a baseball hat, a sweater, and a glamorous color photograph of herself. He sat holding it, staring down at her smiling face. "You're beautiful, Julie. You look just like Marilyn Monroe."

"Oh, stop it," she chided, embarrassed by his compliment. He'd been a fan of Marilyn's for years; posters of her hung in his room beside posters of NFL superstars. "You told me once that you wanted a good picture of me, so I had it made for you. It's nothing special."

"It is to me." He looked into her eyes, and in spite of his gaunt face, his thinning hair, and his sallow complexion, she still considered him handsome. "I bought you this last October. I've been paying it off a little at a time. Mom got it out for me last week when she went home for the day." He handed her a small, wrapped box.

Inside was a gold bracelet, the chain thin and delicate, with tiny pearls set like staggered snowdrops along its length. She thought it was the most wonderful gift she'd ever received from him and told him so by kissing him in front of the entire assembly. Everybody clapped and Luke blushed. "I got you this too," he said, and produced a rose, which gave her another opportunity to kiss him.

That night, Julie and Luke's mother returned to their room at the Ronald McDonald House. Nancy put away her few gifts. Julie's parents had been generous to Luke's mother, buying her a stylish cable-knit sweater and a gift certificate to a Waterton area department store, which Julie had brought to Chicago.

"Being stuck in the hospital is a crummy way to spend the holiday," Julie announced as she climbed under the covers. "And I know the hospital kitchen tried, but my mom's Christmas dinner is so much better."

"Perhaps she'll give us a rain check on that dinner."

"I know she will."

"I can't thank you and your parents enough for all you've done for Luke and me. When Luke was younger, I was so afraid he'd take up with the wrong crowd. But then football came along, and with it, your dad. He's treated Luke like a son."

"Luke's never talked much about his father.

Not even to me. I guess he misses having one more than ever now."

"I don't think he remembers Larry very well."

"He died in a fall, didn't he?"

"Yes. He was walking the steel riggings. He'd only been on the job for a few months. The company paid his funeral expenses and I was lucky enough to be hired on as an office worker."

"Well, you're the office *manager* now," Julie said.

"It's taken me seven years of hard work to get there. That's why I want Luke to go to college."

Although Julie believed Nancy accepted the way she and Luke felt about one another, Julie also knew Nancy had dreams for her son. She prized education and always urged Luke to get good grades so that he could have a better life. In that respect, Nancy and Julie's mother thought alike. They equated getting out of Waterton with optimum happiness.

"You're lucky to have such a nice family, Julie. I wish I had more family around me. Especially now."

None of Luke's grandparents was living. "Luke's uncle Steve knows what's going on, doesn't he?" Steve was Luke's father's only brother.

"Yes, but he's all the way out in Los Angeles. Except for phone calls and cards, there's nothing he can do. We haven't seen him for years. He's a bachelor with a job connected to the movie industry. He has a life of his own out there. No . . . I'm afraid all Luke and I have for support is each other. And your family, of course. Your family has made all the difference in our lives, Julie."

Julie wondered if Nancy would be so comfortable if she understood how much Julie's mother wanted Julie and Luke's relationship to cool off. "I'll always be here for Luke," Julie declared. "No matter what."

Nancy smiled. "Right now, you're the only thing holding my son together. This chemo business has knocked him for a loop. Kids—boys especially—think they're invincible. Why, I can count on one hand the number of days Luke's been sick in his life. When he gets sick, he doesn't mess around with the small stuff, does he?"

Tears filled Nancy's eyes and Julie thought she might break down. "The chemo treatments won't last forever," Julie said hastily.

Nancy sniffled hard. "And he isn't nearly as sick as he was in the beginning."

"Still, it's a crummy way to spend Christmas."

"A crummy way," Nancy echoed.

Their conversation had come full circle. They gave each other a good-night hug, turned off the lights, and went to bed. Julie lay in the dark staring at the window. Even though the curtains were closed, she could see the faint outline of Christmas lights aglow in nearby buildings. Their soft colors reminded her of her tree back home and filled her with longing to be a kid again. To be exhausted from getting up too early to see what Santa had brought. To be full of Christmas dinner and too much candy. To be snuggled in her own bed, in her own room, with nothing to think about but playing with her new toys when morning came.

But she wasn't a little girl anymore. And this Christmas, she was miles from home, in a rented room, with a hospital a block away. With Luke, the only boy she'd ever loved, receiving chemo for a rare and deadly form of cancer. She fingered the bracelet on her wrist and stuffed her fist into her mouth, so that Nancy wouldn't hear her cry herself to sleep.

8

Dr. Kessler allowed Luke to return home New Year's Day. Luke was to remain on chemo for another week, then go off treatment for two weeks, then begin the process all over again.

"The county can get you tutors so that you can stay on grade level," Julie heard her mother, who had brought a casserole to Luke's house for dinner that night, tell him.

"I might want a tutor," he said. "I'd really like to stay caught up with my class."

Until then, it hadn't occurred to Julie that Luke might not go back to school. The term started the next day and she had to return. "You should come to school," Julie said once her mother was gone. "Everybody's asking about you. You'll feel better seeing the gang."

"I don't know," he said. "I look pretty

grim." He wore his baseball cap all the time to hide his bald head.

"Not to me."

"Then you'd better get glasses." He sighed and flopped back against the couch. "I look like a freak, Julie. And I feel like one too." He pulled the neck of his sweater up higher, making certain it covered the catheter near his collarbone.

"You can't stay out the entire term," Julie insisted.

"When I'm off chemo, I might consider going back. But once I start treatments again, I'll have to drop out. I don't want to start barfing in the classroom."

"Not even in Ms. Tyler's?" She named the most formidable English teacher at the high school.

He ignored her attempt to be funny. "Don't pressure me. This isn't something I can decide now. Will you come over tomorrow afternoon and tell me about your day?"

"Sure," she said, but she was disappointed. Somehow, she'd assumed that once he got out of the hospital, he'd act more like his old self.

Julie returned to Waterton High and was bombarded with questions about Luke all day long. Students, teachers, even the principal and office personnel queried her. In the cafeteria with Solena, she could hardly get her lunch down for the interruptions.

"Frank says that the guys on the team want to do something for Luke, but they don't know what," Solena said after the crowd momentarily cleared away from the table. "Some of the guys are weirded out about it. They think Luke hung the moon and they can't imagine him being sick this way."

"Then fire up your imagination—he really is."

"But *cancer!* It—it's so *unfair!*"

"Please, Solena, don't talk about it. I know it's unfair, and I get mad whenever I think about it. So why don't we just change the subject, all right?"

Solena looked contrite. Julie heard the drone of nearby voices, the clatter of silverware, the clack of plates being scraped and stacked. After a few minutes of awkward silence, Solena said, "Frank's taking me into Chicago Friday night for a concert. I wish you and Luke could come with us. We haven't doubled in ages—it would be like old times."

"Well, we can't." Julie hadn't meant for her voice to sound so sharp, but Solena was getting on her nerves.

"What are you going to do with yourself?"

"What do you mean?"

"Will you . . . you know . . . date any-body else?"

"How could you suggest such a thing? I would never run around on Luke. Especially now."

"I—I didn't mean get *serious* with anybody else, but golly, Julie, what are you going to do Friday and Saturday nights? Just sit at home? Or go over to Luke's all the time?"

Julie hadn't thought that far ahead, but all at once she saw the weeks stretching in front of her in one long, monotonous string. With Luke sick and not willing to come out of his shell, there'd be no dates, no special events in their lives. The thought upset her. And she was upset with Solena for making her think about it. "He won't be sick forever," Julie snapped. "As soon as he's finished with his chemo treatments, he'll be well and he can pick up his life again."

"That's good. I was hoping everything would get back to normal for the two of you."

Normal. After so many weeks of being in the grip of crisis, Julie had forgotten what "normal" felt like. Suddenly, she felt de-pressed. But she also saw that she couldn't allow Luke to retreat from the world, for both of their sakes. If she loved him, she'd do her best to help him resume a normal existence. And if he loved her, he'd do it.

She discussed it with her father, and two days later Julie was at Luke's watching an afternoon TV game show with him when her dad arrived carrying a large box.

"What's up, Coach?" Luke asked as Bud Ellis set the box in the center of the floor, right in front of the television screen.

"I brought you a little present." He proceeded to open the box and to lift out shiny new barbells and weights. "You know that the guys on the team are hitting the weight room regularly."

"Sure. We—they do every year."

"Well, I figure you won't be going to the gym right away for workouts, but I don't want my number one quarterback turning into a glassy-eyed wimp." He cast a disdainful glance toward the TV. "I want you on a weight-lifting program, Luke."

"Gee, Coach, I don't know . . ."

Julie held her breath. She saw the struggle Luke was having stamped visibly on his face. He didn't want to let her father down. But he was also very unsure of his abilities.

"Luke, I don't expect you to bench-press two hundred pounds the way you were when the season ended. This stuff is just to get you started, keep you from falling too far behind. Start slow. Do arm curls with low weights." He fitted five-pound disks onto a set of barbells as he talked. "Do three sets of twelve four times a day until you feel stronger. I'll work with you."

Julie could see the muscle along Luke's jaw working and knew he was clenching his teeth. "Don't you want to play next season?" she asked.

"I haven't thought about anything else," he said quietly. "Football means everything to me."

"Then let's get you started on a program to build you back up," Bud said.

"I feel pretty lousy, Coach."

"I know, son." He reached out and gripped Luke's shoulder. "But you will feel better. You're going to lick this thing, Luke. You're going to get well and you're going to play football in your senior year. And every college coach in the country is going to sit up and take note."

Julie saw the fire of longing flicker in Luke's brown eyes. It caused a lump in her throat as she realized how long it had been since she'd seen it there. She was grateful to her father for igniting it. "I'll help, Luke," she said. "When you're strong enough to run laps, I'll clock you. I'll even run with you."

He gave her a partial smile. "What if you beat me?"

"I can keep my mouth shut. I won't blab it around."

He reached down and gripped the thick steel middle of the bar, and slowly, he lifted it, curling it up to his chest. "Man, I'm weak as a kitten."

"But the muscle's still there," Coach said. "All you have to do is tone it, build it up. You can do it, Luke. I remember that scrawny little kid who first reported to the Y locker room when he was twelve. Why, I was sure a big puff of wind would blow him over."

Luke smiled. "I wasn't much, was I?"

"What you lacked in build, you made up for in determination. I never saw a kid as determined as you. You spent months in the weight room bulking up. And more months practicing throwing the football."

"You still think I'll have what it takes to play?"

"You've always had what it takes: determination plus hard work."

"Lots of guys work hard at the game. And you're a good coach."

"But you've also got talent, Luke. I can't put into any player something God left out."

Luke's gaze skimmed the weights strewn around the carpet. "I guess I could give it a try. The days get pretty long with nothing to do but feel punk and do schoolwork."

"That's the spirit," Coach Ellis said, beaming him a smile. "After I wrap up my duties at school, I'll head over here and we'll get to work."

"I do want to play again," Luke said wistfully.

"And you will," Julie's dad insisted, giving Julie a sly wink.

She smiled, feeling optimistic that Luke would soon get his zest back. She was appreciative of her father's actions and saw with clarity one of the reasons he was such a good coach: he inspired and motivated a person; he didn't threaten and intimidate.

And she made up her mind that she wasn't going to sit around feeling sorry for herself because she had to stay home on a Friday or Saturday night. As long as Luke was sick, she'd be there for him. By spring, this whole chemo business would be behind him and they could get on with their lives. And she was now more positive than ever that whatever Luke Muldenhower did with his life, she wanted to be right by his side doing it with him.

She reached over and laced her fingers through Luke's. "If you're going to pump iron, I will too."

Luke and her father glanced at each other.

"I'm serious," Julie said. "What's the matter? Can't stand a little competition?"

Luke tweaked the muscle in her upper arm and rolled his eyes.

"Very funny," Julie sniffed.

But her father broke out in a roaring laugh and Luke's smile lit up his face. Julie thought the sight so beautiful that she didn't mind one bit being the focus of their joke. No, not one tiny little bit.

9

Eventually, Luke decided to return to school. Julie was proud of him, for she knew it wasn't easy. He'd always been admired at Waterton High and looked up to by both students and faculty. He was handsome, the star quarterback, a good student, and an all-around nice guy. But cancer and chemotherapy had left their mark.

There were those who whispered about the change in him. The girls were the worst. Julie would swing into the bathroom between classes and conversation would stop as all eyes turned toward her. She'd know they'd been discussing Luke, and she disliked them for it—would glare at them, daring them to continue with their gossip.

His baseball hat became a familiar sight in the halls and classrooms. No teacher ever asked him to remove it. Often, because he was so tall, Julie could see the hat bobbing above the crush of bodies passing from room to room between classes.

In a show of camaraderie, the players on the football team bought matching baseball hats and wore them every day. Even Julie's dad wore one, and one day the local paper came out and did a story about Luke and the symbol of the hats.

On the weeks he was on chemo, Luke wore bulky sweaters to hide the black pouch he strapped around his torso that controlled the flow of medications into the Port-A-Cath in his neck. If he felt nauseated in the classroom, he simply edged out the door and into the bathroom. He never had to ask permission. It was simply understood that if Luke needed to leave for a while, he was free to go.

He continued his weight regime, and slowly his muscles began to strengthen. He took special vitamins, protein powders, and high-energy drinks to maintain proper nutrition levels. He insisted on going to a tanning salon to give his sallow complexion a more vibrant and healthy look. One day Julie teased, "You'd better be careful, Beach Boy. The girls are starting to look hard at you, and I can't stand the competition."

"You have no competition," he said. "Never have. Never will." And to make his point, he had flowers delivered to her in the middle of a morning class.

By April, the last of the snow had finally melted and flowers had begun to bloom, first crocuses and jonquils, then tulips and lilies. Julie often found Luke after school sitting in the old bleachers overlooking the football field. She would climb up the weathered wooden slats and sit beside him, bringing him sometimes a candy bar, other times handfuls of foil-wrapped candy kisses. Chocolate seemed to be the one thing he could always keep down, no matter how sick the chemo made him.

"So what are you thinking about?" Julie asked as she settled next to him late one afternoon. A cool breeze was blowing. She hugged the letter jacket he had given her when they were freshmen tightly to her body.

"I'm thinking that spring's my favorite time of year," Luke told her. He was gazing thoughtfully out across the field. The grass looked hopelessly brown, but a few hardy dandelions had begun to dot the ground like bright yellow exclamations points.

"I don't believe it. You love football, and that's in autumn."

"Yeah, but before now, I took spring for granted. Everybody does, you know. They figure that it'll just wander in. But this year, it's extra special to me. And extra pretty."

"Why, Luke—you almost sound like a poet." She linked her arm through his.

"I'd write a poem if I could." He tossed back his head and breathed in deeply. "Everybody's always rushing around, Julie. They never stop and look around. They never see the new green color of the trees. Have you ever noticed how bright that shade of green is? And the flowers . . . flowers always seem to know when it's time to start growing. One day the ground is flat, and the next day little green stems are poking up. I've watched them for a week, so I know. They're asleep under the ground all through winter. Then they pop up."

She'd never heard him be so contemplative. "I guess we all take such things for granted. We figure, 'Spring came last year; it will this year too.'"

His gaze swept the area. "I'll never take it

for granted again. I'll always be grateful to see every spring that ever comes along."

She shivered, not from the cold, but from the tone of melancholy in his voice. "I will too."

He looked down at her. "So maybe this whole experience has made me more sensitive. What do you think?"

"I think I'd rather you not have had the experience and be less sensitive."

He laughed, and the sound thrilled her. He was beginning to seem so much more like his old self. "I start the final round of chemo next week. I didn't think I'd ever get to this point."

"And next Saturday is the sports banquet," she reminded him. The year-end awards banquet for the athletic department was to be held at Waterton's only resort hotel, built on the shore of Lake Michigan. Every athlete in the high school would be honored and over two hundred people were expected to attend. "Dad's talked about nothing else for days. You are taking me, aren't you?"

His expression clouded. "Julie, I don't know how I'll be feeling—"

She interrupted. "Poor excuse. We missed the Christmas dance and the Valentine's dance. We have to go to the banquet. I won't take no for an answer."

He was quiet.

She asked, "Luke, what's wrong? Why don't you want to go?"

"It's hard to be around the team, that's all."

"You see the guys every day at school. What's the difference?"

"The difference is I'll be on display. At school, I can just blend into the crowd. But the banquet will be full of parents and news people. I hate people staring at me, Julie . . . feeling sorry for me."

"People can't help but feel sorry. What happened to you stinks. But look how far you've come! People want to be happy for you too. They want to see you be the winner that you are."

He cocked his head. "Do you really believe I'm a winner?"

"I don't hang with losers."

"I love you, Julie."

She grinned. "Then I'll take that as a yes. You'll take me to the banquet?"

He slumped, feigning defeat. "Do you always get your way?"

"Of course—I'm Coach Ellis's daughter."

She looked at her watch. "Now let's get you home. It's time to begin your workout."

Hand in hand, they descended the bleachers and headed for the parking lot.

Julie had never seen her father so nervous as he was the night of the banquet. He kept tugging at the neck of his rented tux. "For heaven's sake, Bud, stop fidgeting," Julie's mother said. She wore a filmy black dress that Julie thought made her look sophisticated and pretty. "We've been going to these banquets for years. This one's no different."

"It is for me."

Julie was aware that something was going on. Her father had been acting secretive for days.

Patricia Ellis asked, "Do you have to wear that baseball cap tonight? It looks silly with the tux."

Julie butted in. "The whole team's wearing their caps, Mom, because Luke has to wear his. I think it's sweet." She smiled at her dad.

Her mother sighed. "Very well. Let's go. We promised Nancy we'd pick her up at five-thirty."

Julie's parents left and minutes later, Frank, Solena, and Luke drove up to her house. "You look good enough to kiss," Luke told her when she slid into the backseat of Frank's car.

"I'm puckered up."

He kissed her lightly. "I'm nervous," he confided. "People have been acting strange around me. Especially Frank." He nodded toward the back of Frank's head. The customary hat was pulled low over Frank's ears.

Solena glanced back and rolled her eyes. She was clearly disgusted with Frank, but Julie didn't care. She was glad the guys were wearing their matching caps.

The dining hall of the luxury hotel was packed with tables and crowded with people. Each sport had been granted a specific area of the great room. Football took up the largest space and was up front, near the podium. At the speakers' table, stretching across the front of the room, special dignitaries were seated. Julie waved to her parents, who were seated between the principal and school superintendent.

All through the meal and award presentations, Julie held Luke's hand under the table. She realized it was difficult for him to sit through the ceremony, knew that every award, every word of praise reminded him of the "before time"—before he got cancer. Luke was showered with certificates and trophies, including the prestigious Player of the Year, an award that usually went to a graduating senior, not a junior. But there was little doubt that he deserved it. Leading the team to the semifinals of the state championship was something no athlcte from Waterton had done in over twenty-five years.

"We'll win it next year," Julie's father said into the mike as Luke made his way back to his seat carrying his trophy. The room erupted into cheers and shouts. Coach Ellis held up his hands for quiet. "I have a little something I want to show all of you," he said.

A curtain parted and two waiters carried out an easel. On it was a large, flat object covered with a velvet drape. "Ladies and gentlemen," Coach Ellis said with little fanfare, "I want to present the final drawings of the new Waterton Warriors football stadium."

He pulled off the drape and exposed a gorgeous artist's rendering of a brand-new stadium. The crowd applauded wildly. "We'll break ground this summer," the coach said. "And although it won't be completed until the following fall, it will be the best stadium with the finest playing turf in the state. In fact, we may play the state championships here in the future."

Again, wild applause. Julie squeezed Luke's hand. The stadium would not be ready in time for him to play in it, but it was still nice for her to see one of her father's dreams come true.

"Uh—Coach . . . ," Frank called, then stood up, walked swiftly to the front, and spoke into the mike. "The guys would like to say thanks for a great year." He handed Julie's dad a long white envelope, which Julie knew contained tickets for a night on the town in Chicago.

"And one more thing," Frank said.

In unison, the players stood. Mystified, Julie gave Luke a questioning look. Equally baffled, he shrugged.

"This is for you, Luke, buddy. It's a little present that the guys and Coach want to give you."

One by one, the team members removed their baseball caps to expose heads shaved perfectly bald. Every one of them, even her father, had shaved his head clean. People gasped, then began to applaud. Then they stood and looked toward Luke.

Julie rose to her feet, her gaze locked on

Luke's face, a lump the size of a fist lodged in her throat. She saw tears shimmering in his eyes. Then he too stood, swept off his hat from his smooth head, and bowed in tribute to the sacrifice his coach and friends had made in his honor.

10

J ulie celebrated the completion of Luke's chemo by throwing a party, and she gave it the night her parents were to go into Chicago to use their banquet gift certificate.

"I'm not sure, Julie," her mother said when Julie told her the plans. "I hate to leave you and your friends unchaperoned."

"Mother, please." Julie sighed dramatically. "My friends know how to act. Most of them are Daddy's players; they're not going to get crazy or anything. Daddy would make their lives miserable."

"*No* alcohol," her mother said emphatically.

"Not to worry. Everybody wants Luke to have a good time and so I know they'll be on their best behavior."

"Is Solena going to help you?"

"Solena and a couple of others. We'll clean everything up. Don't worry."

So, her parents left in the early afternoon and Julie and her friends baked pizzas, made tacos, whipped up batches of chocolate chip cookies, hung lights on the back patio and deck, and set up two sets of stereo speakers—indoors and out. Just before six o'clock, the girls went up to Julie's room and got ready.

"Hair spray!" Solena shrieked. "I forgot my hair spray."

"Put a lid on it," Diane called. "Use mine."

Julie watched her friends running around and felt satisfaction. She thought back to those long days when Luke was in the hospital and recalled how much she had missed this kind of activity. One thing about the whole experience—it certainly made her more appreciative of everyday life. And grateful for life's "little things."

Although it was May, the evenings were still cool. Julie wore a dress and a lightweight sweater the same color as her eyes, and when Luke arrived with Frank, his expression told her that her choice had been perfect.

"Look at this," he said, and sweeping off his cap, he bent to show her the top of his head.

"There's black fuzz," she exclaimed.

He grinned. "I figure it'll soon be long enough for you to run your fingers through."

"Why wait?" she asked, and brushed her palm over the downy growth.

Frank was dancing past with Solena. "Make a wish," he called to Julie.

"I wish it'll grow so long so fast, he'll have to wear a ponytail to the first football practice."

"If any of us come to training camp next August with ponytails, your father will personally shave our heads again."

They laughed, and Julie leaned forward and placed a kiss on top of Luke's head. Her bright pink lipstick left a perfect imprint of her mouth.

"Oh, man!" Frank groaned in protest. "Wipe it off."

"Not a chance," Luke said. He took Julie's hand and led her out onto the deck, where music was playing and a few couples were slow-dancing. He took her in his arms. "It feels so good to hold you like this," he whispered in her ear.

A tingle shot up her spine as she realized how much she'd missed him. True, she'd been with him every day, but not like this. Not with him feeling well and wanting to act like a boyfriend again. "I promised my parents there wouldn't be any trouble," she said softly.

"What kind of trouble could this lead to?" He nuzzled her neck and her heart thudded expectantly.

"The kind where I lose my head and leave lipstick marks all over your body."

He chuckled. "Promises, promises."

"Don't test my patience, buster."

"How about if I test your endurance?" With that, he kissed her, holding his mouth to hers until she was dizzy.

The slow-dance music ended and another, faster song began. He broke the kiss and grabbed her hand. "Come on. Go for a walk with me."

They strolled down the sloping backyard, through the tender green shoots of new grass, until they reached the huge oak tree at the far end of the yard. He leaned against the tree and pulled her against him. She felt his hands smooth her hair and heard him breathe in its fragrance. "Oh, Julie . . . I'm so glad it's all over with."

She knew he was referring to his cancer treatments. "Me too."

"Of course, I still have to go for blood work

every six weeks for a while. And Dr. Kessler wants another CT scan the first of June."

"I'll go with you."

"I'll never forget the way you've stood by me."

She pulled away and realized he was being sincere. "Luke, I could never have left you alone in all this."

Doubt flicked across his face. "Sometimes, I was afraid you would. It couldn't have been much fun skipping stuff at school—the dances . . . basketball games. Guys would line up if they thought you were free of me, Julie."

"Line up for what? A rejection slip?" She reached up and traced her fingertips along a carving in the tree. "Remember doing this?"

He glanced over his shoulder and read, " 'LM plus JE.' I remember. I was twelve and I saw you out here with Tommy Fischer one afternoon. I got so jealous that late at night I sneaked into your yard and carved this into the tree."

"And when Tommy saw it, he knew immediately who LM was and he got so scared you'd beat him up that he ran off and never came over again." She poked Luke's chest and teased, "That wasn't very nice."

"You were so mad, you threatened to have your father throw me off his team." Luke grinned, remembering.

"And then you showed up on my porch holding that wad of flowers and you looked at me with those big brown eyes and I melted."

He grinned more broadly. "Once I discovered your weak spot, I never forgot."

She snuggled close again. "Lucky for you I'm not allergic to flowers."

She heard him sigh, heard the rumble of his heart against her ear, and thought she'd not been so content since before Christmas. "Did I tell you Uncle Steve called me?" he asked.

"When?"

"Last night."

"All the way from Los Angeles?"

"He was checking on me and Mom. He's a nice guy." Luke paused. "He's invited me out to visit him this summer."

"Really?" She was half glad, half sorry. "What did you tell him?"

"I said I wasn't sure. Of course, Mom wants me to go. You know how she feels about Waterton and getting out of this town."

"You should go," Julie said halfheartedly.

"I don't want to leave you."

She was touched, but thinking about all the

misery his illness had caused him, she knew she couldn't allow him to forgo the trip on her account. "You couldn't stay long anyway," she said. "Dad will expect you to show up on time for fall practice."

"What will you do this summer?"

"Mom's got me a job with her friend Mrs. Watson to help down at the public library." Julie wrinkled her nose. "She wants me to *work.*"

"That's a pretty good job." Summer jobs in a town the size of Waterton weren't plentiful, and Luke and Julie knew she was lucky to have one. Luke added, "Just think, you'll have some money to take me out."

"I'll have money to buy school clothes," she corrected.

"I'm wounded."

"Get over it." She patted his shoulder, then sobered. "Actually, I'm kind of provoked with my mom. She committed me to the job without even asking me first. But that's her style—jump in with both feet and make excuses if you have to back out."

"But you won't mind working there, will you? I mean, it beats schlepping groceries or baby-sitting."

"I guess not. Anyway, if you can go visit your uncle, you should."

"Will you write me?"

"Every day."

He rested his chin atop her head. "I'm going to start working out at the gym after school with the guys. I've got a lot of body-building to catch up on. Uncle Steve says he belongs to a gym and I can work out whenever I want if I come. I have to be in good shape by fall."

"If you're worried about losing your starting position, don't be," Julie said. "Dad's counting on you to lead the team."

"Maybe that's what's got me worried."

"How so?"

"He expects so much of me, Julie. I—I don't how much this problem's affected my game."

She understood his fears. Her father had a subtle way of applying pressure, of placing a mantle of expectation on his players that weighed heavily. No one ever wanted "to let Coach down."

Her mother often tried similar tactics on her, but she was not very subtle and usually it led to friction between them, rather than compliance. "You'll get your game back," Julie assured him. "My dad will see to it."

Luke grinned. "You're the only person in the world who can twist your father around her little finger."

"Don't you believe it. Daddy loves me, but we're both stubborn."

Luke looped his arms around Julie's waist. "You know what I think?"

"What?"

"I think this conversation has gotten too far afield. I brought you out here, away from all those partying people, to get your undivided attention."

"You've got it. What do you want?"

"This." He lowered his head and skimmed her mouth with his lips. Again, her knees went weak. "I love you, Julie."

"Talk is cheap," she whispered.

He straightened, reached into his jeans, and pulled out a pocketknife. "Then let me spell it out for you."

He dug the tip of the knife into the bark of the old tree, and soon, under their initials, symbols emerged—the letter I, a lopsided heart, and the letter U. He stepped back. "Now it's in writing for the whole world to see."

She draped her arms around his neck, rose on her tiptoes, and kissed the end of his nose. "For the whole world to see," she echoed. "The whole, entire world."

Julie, Luke, and his mother rode the train into Chicago the first Friday in June for testing. They had to take the train because Nancy's car was in the shop and Luke's was too old for such a trip. "I like the train," Nancy insisted.

Julie didn't mind it because she could cuddle with Luke while watching the scenery zip past. Eventually, trees and countryside gave way to buildings, parking lots, and malls.

At the hospital, Julie waited with Nancy while Luke went into the radiology department for the test. She tried to read a magazine, but couldn't concentrate.

When Luke came back, he told them, "Dr. Kessler wants us to wait while the radiologist reads the scan. He says it'll save us a trip back."

So they waited another hour, until Dr. Kessler's nurse called them up to his office on the seventh floor. They rode the elevator, Julie feeling as if her stomach were twisted in a knot. Perhaps it was just being back in the hospital that was making her nervous; she wasn't sure. All she knew was that she wanted to see a smile on Dr. Kessler's face and hear him give Luke a clean bill of health.

"The last time your scans were negative," Nancy said. "No reason they shouldn't be the same now."

But when they walked into Dr. Kessler's office, he wasn't smiling. Behind him, X rays were mounted on a light board so that they glowed clearly in dull gray and white.

"Is that me?" Luke asked.

"That's you," Dr. Kessler said. "And I'm afraid there's a problem. There's a mass in your chest."

11

"A mass?"

"A growth—a small tumor," the doctor said, tapping Luke's chest. "It's here on your left side, between your lung and your heart."

Instantly, Luke was on his feet, rage registering on his face. "What do you mean 'a tumor'? Are you saying that I'm not well? Are you telling us that after all that stinking chemotherapy, I still have cancer?"

"Hodgkin's is a tricky beast, Luke. Your lymph system networks your whole body. All it takes is one maverick cell to escape and settle elsewhere." The doctor's voice kept calm.

Nancy looked so pale, Julie thought she might faint, and Julie felt as if she herself might throw up. "I don't believe it. I don't believe that after all Luke's been through, he isn't cured of this thing," Julie cried.

"He's been in remission," the doctor said. "And when caught early, seventy-five percent of all newly diagnosed Hodgkin's *is* curable."

"But not Luke," Nancy said. "Not my son."

"This is a setback," Dr. Kessler conceded. "Usually remissions last longer."

"I don't want to go back on chemo," Luke shouted. "I don't want to take that stuff again."

Dr. Kessler stood and took Luke by the shoulders. "You won't do chemo again. At least, not now. I'm going to put you into radiation treatments."

"Radiation?" Nancy asked.

"Radiation will shrink the mass so that we can remove it surgically. It might possibly eliminate it altogether."

"I can't miss any more school." Luke sounded distraught. "I'm already behind and I don't want to be sick and throwing up like before."

"Radiation's not like chemo. And you won't have to come here to get the treatments. You can go to Waterton General. A friend of mine, Dr. John Laramore, is a radiation oncologist there, and he'll be handling your case."

Julie felt as if they were trapped in a bad dream, one that was circular and kept coming back to the same starting place. Why couldn't Luke get out of this nightmare?

Dr. Kessler made several phone calls and gave Luke fresh assurances. Then Julie, Luke, and his mother left and caught the train home. The very next day, Luke was to start his radiation therapy. He had planned to go to the gym and begin his weight-lifting schedule, but instead he would report to Dr. Laramore to begin another journey into the unknown.

Julie's father refused to believe the news when Julie told him. He ranted and raved, hopped into his car, and tore over to see Luke. Depressed and morose, Julie flopped on the sofa and flipped through the TV channels without pausing.

Her mother watched her for a few minutes, then came and took the remote control from her hand and turned the set off. She said, "I'm sorry, Julie."

"It isn't fair, Mom! Luke did exactly what the doctors told him to do—*everything!* And now he's right back at square one."

"Maybe not. Maybe the tumor is a freak thing that the radiation will clear right up."

"Well, I'm going with him tomorrow and I'm going to ask this new doctor a million questions."

"Julie . . . I—um . . ."

Julie looked up at her mother, who was chewing her bottom lip and looking perplexed. "What is it, Mom? What do you want to say to me? Don't tell me not to go. Because I *am* going."

Her mother sighed and sat down on the outermost edge of the sofa cushion, her hands folded neatly in her lap. "I wouldn't ask you not to go. I know how involved you've been in Luke's illness."

"So what's your point?"

"It's just that it *is* Luke's illness. You've gotten awfully wrapped up in this thing. Don't forget that you have a life to live too. You shouldn't let his health problems take over your whole existence."

"I can't believe you're saying this! You know how I feel about Luke. I can't abandon him."

"Don't be so dramatic. I'm not asking you to abandon him. I'm simply asking you to step back and get some perspective. You've gotten so wrapped up in this whole business that you've lost sight of your own goals and plans."

Fuming, Julie asked, "And what goals might those be?" How could her mother be so insensitive?

"You haven't done a single thing about college since our discussion last November. I'm telling you, Julie, now is the time to start applying. All the really top colleges fill up fast. If you aren't careful—"

Julie propelled herself off the couch. "I can't believe you're hounding me about something as unimportant as a college application! Don't you understand, Mom? Luke's cancer is back. He's not rid of it and . . . and . . ." Her voice began to waver.

"I didn't mean to upset you," her mother said in her most soothing tone. "I thought perhaps thinking about college would take your mind off Luke. Thinking about your future should be a fun thing."

Julie shook her head, and hot tears stung her eyes. "My future? You still don't get it, do you, Mother? Without Luke, I don't *have* a future. Without Luke, I don't even want one!"

She spun, ran from the room, and raced up the stairs, where she slammed her bedroom door hard behind her, then threw herself across her bed and sobbed.

As soon as school was out on Monday, Julie and Luke headed to Waterton's hospital, where Nancy joined them from her job at the mill. Dr. Laramore worked in an adjoining office building, on a floor named the Wilson Cancer Center. His suite was spacious and well decorated, with stacks of magazines, tables containing half-completed jigsaw puzzles, and, in the reception area, a desk that held a coffeemaker and ice-filled bowls with cartons of juice. "Help yourself," a nurse said. Luke declined.

Dr. Laramore was a pleasant-looking man, trim and well built, with a mustache. He ushered Luke, his mother, and Julie into his office and sat down at his desk. Julie took a deep breath, reached for Luke's hand, and thought, *Here we go again.*

"I've been over your records," the doctor said after introductions. "And I've studied your scans carefully. There's a growth in your chest and another, much smaller one in your groin."

Julie felt Luke's hand tighten around hers. "Dr. Kessler didn't mention that one."

"It wasn't as easy to detect. Besides, that's my job—to go over your scans with a magnifying glass." He paused, letting the news sink in.

"What will you do about it?" Nancy asked quietly.

"What we're going to do is bombard both areas with a mantle of radiation to damage these cancer cells and stop their growth. You'll be given a total of twenty treatments—five a week for a month. Nothing on the weekends."

Luke looked surprised. "That doesn't seem like much time. I mean compared with the chemo."

"You'll be receiving very high doses of radiation, and while it will be painless, there are side effects."

"Such as?"

"You'll be unusually tired. And the skin in the treated area will redden, as if you've gotten a mild sunburn. Apply no lotions or creams, though, unless I okay it. And because the treatments will be on your chest area, you may have a sore throat and difficulty swallowing . . . some loss of appetite is normal. You may develop a dry cough too."

Luke shook his head in disgust. "And the other area?" he asked.

Dr. Laramore steepled his fingers together and let his gaze bounce between Luke and Julie. "Often, both Hodgkin's and the treatments for Hodgkin's can cause fertility problems." He paused, waiting for their reactions.

"Are you saying my son might never have children?" Nancy's question brought the problem into sharp focus for Julie.

"It's a possibility. Although," he added quickly, "young men are more likely to regain their fertility than older men."

"Any other little tidbits?" Luke asked, his voice crisp, sarcastic. He did not look at Julie, but kept his eyes riveted on the doctor.

"That's about it." Dr. Laramore stood. "I'd like to get started as soon as possible. The first thing we'll do is define the exact area we're going to treat. We'll go back to one of the radiation rooms, where my technicians will measure, calculate, and mark you up. From the information, I'll create a graph to program the computer for your specific needs, taking into consideration your body density and the position of the tumors."

" 'Mark me up'?"

"With the help of lasers, we'll literally draw lines with a marking pen in a grid pattern on your body that I'll use to determine the exact spots that will receive the radiation. Try not to wash these lines off, because we'll use them every day."

"Can I shower?"

"Yes, but no soap on the marks until you've completed your treatments. The technicians will redraw the lines as they fade."

He walked them down the hall to a room where a large machine stood in the center of the floor, a bedlike table positioned under it. There were computers in the room and outside the door, which looked heavy and strong. "It's solid steel," one of the nurses said as Julie studied it. "Can't have any radiation leaking out."

Julie thought, *It'll be leaking into Luke's body,* but she didn't say it. Signs on the walls read: "Caution. X ray machines in use." She felt as if she'd stumbled into some sort of high-tech nuclear time warp. The machines looked cold and menacing.

"The two of you will have to wait in the lobby," a nurse told Julie and Nancy. "This will take about an hour."

"An hour?" Nancy sounded dismayed, and seemed hesitant to let her son remain inside the steel-lined room without her.

"The calculation part takes the longest,"

Dr. Laramore said kindly. "From now on, Luke will have a standing appointment to come in and be treated. The actual treatments take no more than a minute or so. And they're painless."

Julie and Luke's mother returned to the spacious lobby and took a seat. They didn't speak. Julie felt overwhelmed, imagining Luke being marked up like a piece of wild game after a kill. The doctors were going to shoot massive amounts of radiation into him in the hope of destroying the cancer cells that had invaded him. They were going to subject him to nuclear medical technology. And possibly rob him of his ability ever to have children.

"If it saves his life, it's a small price to pay," Nancy said quietly, as if she'd read Julie's mind. "His life is worth *any price.*"

12

"Are you sure it didn't hurt?" Julie asked Luke afterward when they returned to his house.

His mother had insisted Julie stay for dinner and was downstairs in the kitchen. Upstairs, in his room, the delicious aromas of browning hamburgers and sizzling onions permeated the air. Luke's bedroom was small, and the heavy oak furniture that had once belonged to his grandmother seemed too big for the space. Football trophies lined a shelf hung over his bed, while books had been stacked along a wall between his stereo and a study desk.

Large posters of a youthful Marilyn Monroe smiled beguilingly from his walls. Julie used to tease him about his "Marilyn fixation," but today she hardly noticed the pictures. She was apprehensive about his radiation therapy, and not hiding it.

"Didn't hurt a bit," Luke said. "I just had to lie really still while they drew on me." He lifted his shirt, and Julie saw bright blue lines on his skin that disappeared below the waistband of his jeans. "Actually, it sort of tickled."

She leaned in closer, squinting. "What are those little dots between the blue lines?" She followed the small dots down his chest with her eyes.

"Tattoos," he said. "Permanent marks so that the technician can always line up the machine perfectly. If the radiation beam is even a tiny degree off, the wrong part of my body will get the radiation."

"So they play connect-the-dots on your skin every time?"

"That's right." He pulled his shirt down to cover the blue lines. "Personally, if I got a tattoo, I'd have picked something more exciting—like a mermaid, or a heart." He patted his upper arm. "It would read 'Luke loves Julie.' "

She appreciated his trying to lighten her mood, but she didn't like this radiation business one bit. "I want to go with you for your treatments. What time's your next appointment?"

"Every day at three-thirty, but I don't want you to come."

"But why?" His response surprised her.

"I've been thinking about it, Julie, and there's nothing for you to do but sit in the lobby. I'd rather go on in by myself, get my treatment, then head to the gym."

"The gym? But the doctor said you'd be tired."

"I don't care what the doctor said. So long as I'm able to function, I'm going to stick with my normal routine."

"But there's all that juice to drink and all those puzzles to work at the radiation center." She hoped humor would persuade him to let her come along.

"Sitting around waiting is boring, Julie. I don't want you to do it anymore."

"But—"

"Please," he interrupted. "It's what I want."

She was frustrated, but she didn't argue.

Every afternoon that week, Luke left school as soon as classes were dismissed. He didn't change his mind about Julie accompanying him to the cancer center; in fact, he kept to himself even at school, telling Julie that he didn't have much of an appetite and that he was skipping lunch. And in the evenings, he told her he was cramming for finals and thought it best he do it alone.

On Friday, he insisted he was tired and wanted to turn in early and that she should make other plans. Confused by his behavior, but determined not to let it dishearten her, Julie invited Solena to spend the night.

"I don't get it," Julie told her friend as they sat on her bedroom floor, sorting through old photos and nibbling on popcorn. "Why is he shutting me out this way?"

"It *is* kind of a mystery," Solena agreed. "I mean, the whole time Luke was in the hospital and even when he went through chemo, he wanted you with him. Frankly, I can't see the difference between radiation and the other."

"Me either. I don't understand him these days. He's so moody. I can't figure out what he wants from me."

"Did you do something to make him angry?"

"Like what?"

"Like flirt with another guy."

Julie rolled her eyes in exasperation. "Grow up, Solena. I haven't *thought* about anybody but Luke since he got sick. And even before that, I didn't want to date anybody else."

"Sorry . . . I lost my head. I know you and Luke are number one with each other." Solena grew silent, contemplative. Finally, she said, "You know, what's happened to Luke has brought Frank and me closer."

"How so?"

"If something like cancer could happen to a guy like Luke, it could happen to any of us."

"Nobody gets to pick what life gives them," Julie said, toying with a photo of her and Luke from their ninth-grade dance. They both looked so young. And so happy. She sighed and tossed the photo aside.

"Frank's gotten a little paranoid," Solena continued. "Every time he feels a bump or lump, or even if he has a headache, he gets squirrelly. He says, 'Solena, look at this. Do you think it's anything serious?' As if I'd know."

"He can't live his whole life thinking he's going to get some dread disease."

"That's what I tell him, but he still worries. He's always popping vitamins and eating health foods—as if that will keep him from ever getting sick."

"It can't hurt. Luke's doctors have said that

his good physical condition helped him recover so quickly from chemo and the biopsies.
And I know he's working hard to get his fit-
ness back so he can play ball next year."

Solena began absently to arrange kernels of
popcorn in a straight line on the carpet. "Can
I ask you something?"

"Ask."

"Did you and Luke ever talk about getting
married someday?"

"He asked me to marry him in the sixth
grade."

Solena made a face at Julie. "I meant sometime more recent."

Julie wasn't sure how to answer. Sure, she'd
been secretly planning to attend whatever college Luke chose, but she knew he wanted a
shot at a career in professional football, and
she wasn't sure whether marriage and pro ball
would mix. "You know my mother would
croak if I got married before I climb some
corporate ladder."

"But do you want to marry Luke? Would
you if he asked you?"

Unwilling to answer, Julie decided to go on
the offensive. "You must be curious for a reason. Are you and Frank thinking about marriage?"

"Not exactly, but he's been awfully nice to me lately."

"You're usually worried about him dumping you and dating someone else."

"I told you this whole business with Luke has changed him."

"Seems like a good change to me."

"In some ways it is. But in some ways it's scary." Julie looked quizzical, and Solena hastened to explain. "It's like he suddenly got old. Like life is serious business and he shouldn't have fun anymore. As if having too much fun is something taboo."

As Solena struggled to express her thoughts, Julie nodded. "You mean, if his best friend has to suffer then he should too."

"Yes!" Solena cried. "That's exactly what I mean. He feels guilty because he's healthy and Luke isn't."

"Luke's going to get well."

"I know he is," Solena said. Yet her tone wasn't as convincing as her statement.

"And when he does then everything will be like it used to be. And everybody will act like they used to act."

"You think so?"

"Absolutely." Julie waved her hand and scattered the line of popcorn Solena had so carefully arranged. "Hey, let's say we sneak downstairs and watch a movie. My folks should be dead to the world by now."

"Good idea." Solena rose and scooped up the bowl of popcorn. She paused, saying, "I'm glad we talked, Julie. I didn't have anybody else to tell about Frank, and I knew you'd understand."

"Once Luke recovers, Frank will be his old self. Wait and see."

"One more thing," Solena added. "I'm glad you invited me over tonight. I've missed you. I know how involved you've been with Luke and that's okay, but still, I miss the stuff we used to do together. Not just you and me, but you and Luke and Frank and me. We sure had some good times."

"I've missed the old days too."

Solena sighed and shrugged. "Oh, well, I don't mean to be a party pooper, but I did want you to know how I feel."

"Thanks." Julie gave her friend a quick hug.

They pattered down the stairs and into the family room, popped a tape into the VCR, and settled down to watch. But Julie could hardly follow the story line because her mind kept wandering back to Luke. The cool way he was treating her had her mystified—and worried. She didn't understand why he wasn't letting her remain close to him. Or why he insisted on going through his latest series of treatments by himself. It wasn't like Luke. He *always* wanted her with him.

The next day she casually asked her father how he thought Luke was behaving.

"Like he wants to put this whole mess behind him and get on with his life," her father told her with a pleased smile. "He's working hard in the gym. I'm impressed at the way he's making a comeback."

"Well, maybe he should be taking it easier."

"Aw, Julie-girl, don't go trying to turn Luke into a wimp. He's doing just fine. No need to hover over him like some kind of watchdog."

"Really, Dad, that's not what I'm doing. I'm just questioning if he's overdoing it or not."

"No way," her father said with a wave of dismissal, but Julie wasn't so sure. She also didn't know whether Luke's new attitude came from a genuine desire to refocus his attention onto football or from a desire to back away from her. But she was determined to figure it out.

13

Luke was halfway through his radiation treatments when school let out for the summer. On the last day of classes, Julie found him down at the construction site of the new stadium. Bulldozers were moving dirt and the rickety old bleachers had been partially torn down to make way for the new. "Hi," she called over the noise of the big yellow machines.

"Hi yourself."

"Looks like real progress, doesn't it?"

"It's going to be a great stadium."

She gazed up at him longingly, wishing he'd take her in his arms the way he used to do. She recalled her vow to figure out what had gone wrong between them and realized that she was more perplexed than ever. Luke rarely asked her out these days, keeping to himself, shunning contact with almost everybody. "So, what's on your agenda for your first week of summer vacation?" she asked brightly, hoping to draw him into conversation.

"I'm doubling my efforts in the gym."

"Can you do that?" She thought he looked tired.

"Dr. Laramore says I can do whatever I feel like doing, and I want to get back into shape as quick as I can." He sounded cross with her for even asking.

They listened to the roar of the machines while Julie racked her brain for another topic. "I start my job at the library Monday."

"I hope you like it."

If this had been a normal summer, he'd be taking her to the library and making plans to pick her up afterward. If they'd been spending their spare time together, she wouldn't feel so awkward around him. They'd be talking all the time and would know what was going on in each other's lives. "Once the radiation's over, what will you do?"

"I'll have to go into Chicago for a day or so of testing."

"Do you want me to come with you?" she asked anxiously, hoping he'd say yes.

"No. It's not a big deal. Just all those boring tests and scans again."

"I don't mind."

"Forget it. Mom and I'll trudge through it."

Again, the roar of a bulldozer broke into their conversation. Julie felt grateful for the interruption. His rejection stung, and she didn't trust her voice. "And then?" she asked when the noise died down and she'd regained her composure. "Do you think you'll take a summer job?" He had always worked summers to help out his mother.

"Who's going to hire someone like me? I could get sick again."

He sounded bitter, and she felt sorry for him. "So you won't do anything?"

"Remember me telling you about Los Angeles?" She nodded. "Uncle Steve called and said he'll send me a plane ticket the minute I agree to come."

"So you're going?"

"I'm going."

"How long will you stay?"

"About a month. I'll be home in time for August practice."

"Of course." Her stomach knotted. She remembered telling him to take the vacation, and after all he'd been through he deserved to go somewhere and have fun. But she knew she'd miss him terribly, and that it wouldn't be easy seeing him leave when she wanted to be with him so much. "I hope you have a good time in L.A. Do you still want me to write you?"

"If you'd like . . . but I won't be leaving until July."

Julie decided to try one more time to lure him out of his shell. "How about us doing something with each other tonight? Solena's having a party to celebrate the end of the school year. Why don't you take me?"

"Um—I don't think I feel up to it. You go on without me."

"But you feel good enough to go to the gym this afternoon?"

She'd tripped him up, and his face flushed red. "Julie . . . I never know exactly how I'm going to feel. . . ."

"No problem," she said, backing away. "I'll go without you."

"Julie, I—" He looked troubled, but she brushed it aside, suddenly wanting to get as far away as possible from the noise of the machinery and the pain Luke was causing her.

"I've got to go." She turned and darted off.

"You'll let me know about your first day of work?" he called as she fled.

She felt like saying, *Fat chance!* But she didn't. Because no matter how badly he was hurting her, she knew she couldn't hurt him. She couldn't because she loved him. She couldn't because something deep inside her kept saying that he still loved her too. And it was that ray of hope that she clung to.

The golden sunshine of Monday morning did little to dispel Julie's gloom. The weekend had been long and difficult. She'd reached for the phone many times to call Luke, but each time she'd pulled back, telling herself that if he wanted to talk to her, he would call. Except that he hadn't.

She left for her new job at the library, entered the hushed building, went to Mrs. Watson's office, and knocked on the closed door. She was ushered inside by a heavyset woman with graying hair and lavender-framed eyeglasses.

"Julie! So glad you'll be working with us this summer," Mrs. Watson said with a smile as she pumped Julie's hand.

" 'Us'?"

"Yes. Meet my nephew, Jason Lawrence."

She gestured to a tall, slim boy with blond hair and green eyes. "Jason's a sophomore at Ball State University in Muncie and he'll be living with me this summer, and working here too."

"Hello, Julie Ellis," Jason said with a grin that sent her a message of approval.

She smiled politely, but coolly.

Mrs. Watson went on to discuss their respective duties. The work seemed simple enough to Julie, and by lunchtime she had begun to catalog a stack of new volumes while Jason manned the front checkout desk. He asked her to lunch, but she told him no. By the end of the workday, Julie could barely keep from dashing out the door. "Take you home?" Jason asked as she hurried past. "Maybe you could show me around town."

"Can't tonight," she told him. All the way home, she pondered her situation. Julie had gotten a plum of a job without any effort. She was working with a good-looking college boy who was going to be around all summer. She was to be working with him all day, every day, for three solid months.

Grimly, Julie pulled into her driveway and hurried into her house. Her situation looked like a setup. And it had her mother's fingerprints all over it.

She found her mother in the den, sorting through piles of papers. "How was your first day?" Patricia Ellis asked cheerfully.

"Did you know Mrs. Watson's nephew is working at the library too?" Julie asked without preamble.

Her mother's gaze avoided Julie's. "I think she mentioned it to me. Is he nice?"

"I think he wants to date me," Julie said boldly.

"Well, that might be fun. I'm sure he'd like to make friends—"

"Mother!" Julie interrupted. "How could you? Did you think I was going to fall into some other guy's arms just because we were working together every day?"

Her mother looked startled. "I don't know what you mean."

"You don't let me drive to the mall without a third degree and yet when I told you some stranger you've never met wants to date me—which, incidentally, I made up—you say, 'That might be fun.'"

Color stained her mother's face. "Well, of course, I'd have expected you to bring the boy to meet your dad and me. What do you mean, you 'made it up'?"

"I mean that I'm not interested in anybody

but Luke. No one is going to come along and make me forget him."

"I never expected you to stop dating Luke, but I have noticed how things have cooled off between the two of you, and when Mrs. Watson told me about her nephew and about how he's a journalism major at Ball State, I thought that maybe you'd like to get to know him. He can tell you a lot about college life, Julie. Ball State is a fine school, one you should apply to this summer."

"I don't believe this." Julie felt furious. "I don't believe you're trying to sabotage my life."

"Oh, really—"

"No, it's true. Please hear me, Mother, once and for all. I don't want to date anyone else but Luke. I *will* go to college and I *will* start applying in the fall. But this is summer vacation and Luke is sick and he needs me."

"He certainly hasn't acted much like it," her mother fired back. "You sit home most of the time waiting for him to call."

"Well, that's about to change," Julie said. She grabbed her purse from her mother's desk and fished out her keys. "I'm going to Luke's. Don't wait supper for me."

"Julie!" Her mother called.

But Julie wasn't listening. She rushed out the door, jumped into her car, and sped across town to Luke's house. She pounded on the door until he opened it. He looked shocked at seeing her. "What's wrong?"

"That's what *I'd* like to know, Luke." Julie brushed past him and planted herself in the center of his living room floor. She crossed her arms and leveled her gaze at him.

"Nothing's wrong," he insisted.

"Guess again."

"I don't know what you want me to say."

She rolled her eyes in exasperation. "You sound like my mother."

"What do you mean?"

"Never mind." She glared at him. "You've been ignoring me for weeks, Luke."

"No," he said quickly. "I've just been giving you space."

"Space for what?"

"*Space*. You know, breathing room."

"Did I ask you for breathing room?"

He raked his fingers through his hair, which had grown to over an inch. "I don't want to fight with you, Julie."

"Good, because I don't want to fight with you either." She took a deep breath and held it. Finally, she said, "My new job is going to work out fine. There's a college guy working with me who's really nice. He wants me to go out with him."

"Are you?"

"I'm considering it."

A flood of emotions crossed Luke's face. "Please don't." His voice was scarcely a whisper.

"Why shouldn't I? I mean, you're giving me all this *space*. I can't sit around doing nothing with it."

He came to her in one long stride, threw his arms around her, and crushed her against his body. "Don't, Julie," he pleaded, sounding tortured. "Don't leave me. I can't make it without you."

14

After the way he'd been acting toward her during the past weeks, Julie was caught off guard by his impassioned plea. She said, "You *have* been avoiding me, Luke. And it hurts." Tears welled in her eyes. Her anger was gone, but not her frustration.

Slowly, Luke released her. He took her hand and walked her to the sofa, where he sat her down and studied her face with his dark brown eyes, so intently that she thought she might drown in them. "Staying away from you hasn't been easy for me."

"Why would you do it in the first place? If you're miserable and I'm miserable, why would you continue to ignore me?"

"That's not what I was trying to do, Julie." He sat next to her without releasing her hand.

"I—I really don't know how to explain what I've been feeling."

"Try."

"It really bummed me out when the cancer flared up again and I had to start radiation. After I went through chemo, I thought it was finished. Instead, I discovered it had just begun. Dumb of me."

"But this could be a fluke. Once you complete radiation, it'll be gone for good. You've done it all—chemo and radiation. What's left?"

"If this doesn't do the trick," he said quietly, "I'll need a bone marrow transplant. If the cancer spreads to my bone marrow, there's no other treatment."

A chill frosted her heart and made her stomach tighten. She'd read enough and seen enough on TV to know that bone marrow donors were scarce, mostly because it was so difficult to find a compatible match. "You aren't there yet," she said emphatically. "And I don't think you ever will be. Chemo and radiation will do the trick. You'll see."

"A lot will depend on how the tests turn out in Chicago. The scans and bone marrow aspiration will tell the story."

"I know." She squeezed his hand. "And

speaking of the hospital, why won't you let me come with you? Why are you shutting me out?"

"Maybe because I'm worried the scans won't be all right."

"Don't you want me with you if the news is bad?"

He looked vulnerable and terrified. "Yes. More than anything."

"Then let me come."

"I want you to have a regular life, Julie. You shouldn't have to sit around hospitals and doctors' offices waiting for me. Waiting to see if my life's going down the toilet or not."

"Luke, tell me, what's a 'regular life'? Dating someone else?"

He answered her question with one of his own. "Do you like this guy from the library? Do you really want to date him?"

"No way. But *you're* not dating me either."

"It's because I hate tying you down." He glanced at the floor, looking ashamed. "If I love you, I should want what's best for you, and you didn't sign up for having a sick boyfriend. You're beautiful, Julie, and you should have more than I'm giving you. You should be going to parties and doing stuff that's fun."

Her heart went out to him as the reason for

his actions became clearer to her. "So you thought by avoiding me, I'd get interested in somebody else."

"Yes."

"But when I told you I might date somebody else—"

"I couldn't stand it," he blurted. "I love you so much it hurts. So you see, I'm not only sick, I'm a coward too."

She eased off the couch, knelt on the floor in front of him, rested her palms on his thighs, and gazed into his face. "I hate what's happening to you, Luke. I think it's gross and unfair and horrible. But it doesn't change the way I feel about you. I still love you, and the feeling isn't going away."

The look he gave her reminded her of a drowning man miraculously thrown a lifeline. He caressed her cheek gently and she turned her head and kissed the inside of his palm. "I'm sorry, Julie. Sorry if I hurt you in any way. I only want what's best for you, and sitting around waiting for me to get well doesn't seem like something you should have to do."

"But it's what I *want* to do. And this time next year, when this is all over, being with you is still where I'll want to be. This time next year, you'll have a college all picked out, and wherever you go, I'll go."

"But your mother—"

"Will live with it. I figure you'll only take a scholarship to a great college, so she'll be happy when I choose the same great college. No matter how you look at it, everybody wins."

"*If* I get offered a scholarship." Luke's face clouded. "Who'll want me, Julie? What college coach is going to take a chance on a quarterback who has cancer?"

"You'll be well by then. And remember, my father's on your side. He won't allow anybody to reject you because of possible health problems."

"You have more faith than I do."

She patted his hand and rose. "One of us has to."

He stood and took her by the shoulders. "When I go for my testing in two weeks, will you come with me?"

"Absolutely," she said with satisfaction.

"And this guy at the library who wants to date you?"

"Is history."

A slow smile spread over Luke's face, making Julie's knees go weak and her pulse flutter.

"Let's go to a movie, and afterward get ice cream to celebrate," he said.

"I'd love to. I missed dinner tonight."

"Then I owe you," he said. "I owe you big time." Luke swept her into his arms and buried her mouth in a kiss.

Julie, Luke, and his mother made the trip to Chicago one warm morning during the last week of June. Julie held Luke's hand while he stared pensively out the train window. She knew he was worried. The last time they'd made the trip they'd expected everything to be fine, but things hadn't been fine. And now, after weeks of radiation, Luke had no assurances that he was rid of his cancer.

At the hospital, Julie and Nancy followed Luke from department to department throughout the long day of testing. They sat in cubicles and lounges, flipped through magazines, watched dull afternoon TV. The three of them ate lunch in the hospital cafeteria amid the clank and clatter of trays and silverware. No one ate much.

In the late afternoon, Dr. Kessler ushered them into his office. Julie's palms were sweating and she felt sick to her stomach, remembering the last time he'd spoken to them and dropped the bomb about the tumor. But today, he was all smiles.

"You're looking good, Luke."

"Really?"

"Thank God," Nancy whispered, her voice trembling.

The CT and bone scan films were spread across the light board hanging on the wall behind his desk. "We won't have the results of the bone marrow aspiration for a few days, but I don't expect any surprises."

Luke rubbed his hip, which was still sore from where the needle had been inserted to extract marrow for the test. "So I'm cured?"

"I didn't say that."

Julie's elation did a stutter-step. "But if there aren't any bad cells? . . ." she began.

"I prefer to think of your disease as in remission," Dr. Kessler explained. "No two cases of cancer are alike, but the longer you remain in remission, the higher the probability that you'll recover completely."

A grin split Luke's face. "I don't care what you call it, I just want to be rid of it."

"What do we do now?" his mother asked.

"Go home and have a great summer. I'll see you in three months."

Luke fairly sprang out of his chair. "Let's

get out of here," he said to Julie and his mother.

After good-byes to the doctor and staff and the scheduling of another testing day in September, they headed for the train station. This time, the ride back passed in a state of euphoria. This time, even though dusk was falling, the world zipping by the window looked bright and beautiful.

Once home, they decided against a party. But Julie's father insisted on celebrating and took all of them out to dinner at a fancy restaurant on the outskirts of Chicago.

The dinner was perfect and her father couldn't stop grinning and slapping Luke on the back and toasting him with pitchers of iced tea. Julie's mother seemed equally happy over the news and Luke's mother couldn't take her eyes off her son.

"I knew you'd lick this thing," Coach Ellis kept saying. "Can't keep a good man down for long."

Under the table, Luke slipped his hand into Julie's, and when they returned to Waterton that night, he gave her six long-stemmed red roses—one for every week he'd isolated himself from her. She put them in a vase and fingered the petals tenderly. "You always can get to me with flowers, Luke Muldenhower. They're beautiful."

"So are you."

"I'm going to miss you when you go off to Los Angeles," she confessed.

"I want to talk to you about that."

She noticed that his eyes were glowing and realized he'd been guarding a secret. "What about it?"

"I called my uncle and told him that as much as I appreciated his offer, I couldn't come."

"No, Luke—"

"Just listen. I told him that I couldn't stand to be away from you, not even for a free month in California."

She shook her head, thrilled in one way, sorry in another. "You call him back and tell him you're coming."

"Well, that's just it." Luke brushed her long blond hair off her bare shoulders. "He called me last night and said that if you were that important to me, then he'd send you a ticket also."

Her mouth dropped open. "You mean he wants us to come together?"

"And to stay at his condo and to show us the time of our lives." His face clouded momentarily. "Do you think you can come, Julie? I know you have a job and all, but if you can't come with me I don't want to go."

She nibbled at her bottom lip, contemplating the situation. "The job's nothing. Solena can take it over."

"But your parents . . . what will they say?"

More than anything, Julie wanted to go with Luke. She wanted to spend as much time as possible with him. The need to do so felt compelling and urgent. She couldn't be separated from him, not even for a month. Steely resolve stole through her. "I'm going, Luke," she said. "And don't worry, I'll persuade my parents."

"But your mother—"

"Leave my mother to me . . . I'll handle her. I promise." Julie was thinking about the way her mother had manipulated the job so that Julie could spend time with the librarian's nephew. "Believe me, Mom owes me this one," Julie added. She slipped into Luke's arms and sealed her vow to him with a kiss.

15

The plane descended through a bank of thick white clouds tinged in pink, and aimed for the long runway of Los Angeles International Airport. Julie pressed her nose to the small, oblong window, peering down at the cityscape spread out below. She clutched Luke's arm. "My gosh, look. There's civilization as far as I can see."

Luke craned his neck to peer past her shoulder. "It's sure nothing like Indiana. And look at the expressways!" Superhighways looped like broad, flat ribbons through the concrete maze of buildings. In the far distance, foothills, looking brown and parched, rolled across arid stretches of ground.

They had left Chicago's O'Hare Airport at 7 A.M. and chased the rising sun westward. Because of the time change, the plane would land close to the time it had departed Chicago. "How will you know your uncle?" Julie asked.

Luke extracted a photograph from the pocket of his shirt. "He sent Mom this last Christmas." A tall man with brown hair, broad shoulders, and a winning smile stood beside a petite red-haired woman. Both were wearing hiking gear. "And of course, he has a picture of me."

Once the plane landed, Luke grabbed up his backpack and Julie her satchel, and they deplaned, walked through a doorway, and found themselves in a throng of people. Julie caught her breath. She'd never seen such crowds.

"Luke! Over here!"

Julie and Luke turned to see a man waving from his position beside a round white pillar. A red-haired woman, who looked to be in her thirties, held his other hand. After hugs, Luke introduced Julie and Uncle Steve introduced the woman as Diedra O'Ryan, his "significant other."

Steve insisted on first names and Julie liked the idea. She felt awkward calling him "Uncle" when he wasn't kin to her. "Trip okay?" Steve asked.

"Perfect," Luke said.

Steve studied him. "You look so much like my brother."

"Mom's showed me photos of Dad, but I don't see the resemblance," Luke replied.

"Trust me," Steve said, still studying Luke's face. "You're the image of him at seventeen. It's like seeing a ghost."

"Are you tired?" Diedra asked, interrupting the bittersweet reminiscing.

"Not really. We got up at four to catch the limo bus to O'Hare," Julie answered quickly. "But I've been so excited about the trip that I hadn't slept all night anyway."

"I'm glad your parents let you come," Steve told her.

"After you called and talked to them, and after Luke's mother assured them that I'd be safe with you in L.A., and after I whimpered and whined for a week, they had no choice," Julie declared with a satisfied smile.

They laughed. Julie didn't add how tough the sell had been or how she'd brazenly pitted her parents against one another to get her way. In the end, her father had come over to her side, and although her mother hadn't been happy, she had resigned herself to Julie's making the trip.

"We've got a ton of things planned to do while you're here," Steve said.

"We want to do it *all*," Julie said.

By now they'd entered the baggage claim area, and Steve and Luke went to retrieve his and Julie's luggage. Diedra asked, "How's Luke feeling?"

"Really good. Planning this trip was fun and gave him lots to think about besides cancer."

Diedra nodded. "Steve's been worried sick ever since he found out. We would have come to Indiana, but Steve didn't want Luke to think that the family had been called in for a bedside vigil."

"Luke wouldn't have wanted Steve to see him following chemo anyway. He lost all his hair and got really ill. And then the radiation made him so tired, he wouldn't have wanted his uncle to visit then either."

"Steve figured a vacation in L.A. would be much more healthy than a race to Luke's bedside."

"Good choice. Luke's over the worst of it now, and this is the way he wants his uncle to see him—not sick with cancer."

"I understand." Diedra's green eyes

clouded. "My mother died from cancer five years ago. It was hard watching her suffer."

Julie tossed her long blond hair. "Well, that's not going to happen to Luke. His last checkup was perfect, and now all he wants is to get on with his life."

"And with you cheering him on, I'm sure his life will be interesting." Diedra's eyes sparkled mischievously, and Julie blushed. "I told Steve that the time to go east for a visit is when Luke's healthy and playing football again."

Julie nodded. "Good idea. With Luke, our high school has a great shot at going to the playoffs. At least that's what my father says."

"You make Luke sound like a true hero."

"Okay, so I'm his biggest fan."

"Good for you." Julie's gaze connected with Diedra's, and she knew she had made a friend.

The ride to Steve's condo community took them down expressways with names on exit ramps that Julie had only read about or seen in movies and music videos. At one point, high on a hill, she saw the tall white letters of "Hollywood" spelled out. Steve promised them a day of touring the famous area.

Steve's neighborhood contained rows of town houses that looked alike—white stucco walls, red barrel-tile roofs, and red-painted doors. Some homes had wrought-iron grill-work over windows and Spanish-tile walk-ways. Clumps of hibiscus bushes and vines of bright fuchsia bougainvillea lined medians and gateways.

Steve's three-story town house was spacious, built so that all the downstairs rooms looked out onto an inner courtyard with a tiled gar-den and a bubbling fountain. "Beautiful," Julie cried.

Upstairs, Julie's and Luke's room each had its own bathroom. "I saw a place like this once in a magazine," Julie told Luke when they were alone. "What's your uncle do for a job, anyway?"

"He's a cinematographer. Far cry from the steel mills, don't you think?"

Julie recalled the cornfields of her home area, the towering grain silos, the smoke-belching stacks of the mills. "It's different, all right. Maybe some college out here will want you."

Luke shrugged. "This is a long way from Indiana."

"Thanks for bringing me, Luke."

He pulled her into his arms. "I couldn't have come without you."

Diedra called to them from the bottom of the stairs. "You two want some chow?"

In response, Luke's stomach growled, sending Julie into a fit of laughter. They bolted down the stairs and Diedra took them through sliding glass doors and into the courtyard, where a table set with platters of fresh fruit and sandwiches stood waiting. Steve was on a portable phone, but he signaled them to sit down. Julie sat facing the fountain, a large concrete pedestal holding a boy riding a dolphin, studded with colorful tile. Water bubbled into a basin where lily pads and pale pink lotus flowers floated. Sunlight dazzled Julie's eyes and flecked off the dancing water.

"Do you want to rest?" Steve asked as soon as he was off the phone.

"No way," Luke said, biting into a thick sandwich. "I spent months resting. All I want to do now is *go.* "He paused. "But what about your work?" At the mills back home everyone worked shifts.

"I'm taking some time off," Steve said. "I've earned it. And besides, how often does my brother's kid come to visit me?"

"What about you, Diedra?"

"I work with Steve," she said. "We have a

two-month hiatus before we start our next film. So, I'm coming along for the fun."

Julie was glad. And very impressed by Steve and Diedra's glamorous profession. All at once, she began to get a glimmer of what her mother kept harping about when she said that the world was a big place and that Julie owed it to herself to check it out. Still, for right now, her world was high school. And Luke. Always Luke. She couldn't forget that. But perhaps, together, the two of them could discover the rest of the world and find a place in it for themselves, the way Steve and Diedra had.

"So what would you like to see first?" Steve wanted to know.

"Hollywood," Luke said without hesitation.

"And that sidewalk with all the movie stars' handprints," Julie added.

Steve grinned. "I figured you'd want to go there, so that'll be our first stop. I've made reservations for dinner at Planet Hollywood . . . unless you'd rather go to the Hard Rock Cafe."

"Let's go to both," Luke said quickly, making them laugh.

"You do have a whole month out here," Diedra teased.

"We'll go to Universal Studios, Disneyland, visit a movie production set, take a hike up in the hills—"

"How about Rodeo Drive?" Julie blurted out the name of the most famous shopping area in Beverly Hills. "I promised Solena I'd buy her something from there."

"What?" Luke asked. "A pack of chewing gum? That place is expensive."

"I know a few stores we can shop at," Diedra assured them. She glanced at Steve, who cleared his throat.

"But before we take off, there is something very special I want you to plan on doing with me and Diedra while you're here."

"Name it." Luke tilted his head, his expression curious.

"It's a big favor," Steve said. "And we need both of you to help."

"Count me in," Julie said, also curious as to what she could possibly do for them.

Steve reached over and laced his large fingers through Diedra's small, delicate ones. "While you're here, Diedra and I want to get married. And we want you two to be our best man and maid of honor. What do you say?"

16

"Married?" Luke's face broke into a grin. "That's cool. You bet I'll be your best man."

Julie felt less enthusiastic. She'd only just met them and didn't feel qualified to be a maid of honor. "But what about your family? And how about your best friends? Won't any of them want to be in your wedding?" Personally, she couldn't imagine getting married without Solena standing with her.

"I'm the only one left in my family," Diedra said. "And Steve's my best friend." She patted his hand affectionately. "And we made up our mind that we want the wedding to be very small and very intimate. We just want the two of you there."

"And I was the best man at your parents' wedding," Steve said. "If my brother were still alive, I'd ask him, but you're his son and that's the next best thing to his being there."

"When are we going to do this?" Luke wanted to know.

"We were thinking about the week right before you go home. There's this little chapel up the coast and that's were we want to do the deed."

"The chapel's beautiful," Diedra added. "And quite old. The Spanish settlers built it in the 1700s and monks still take care of the place."

By now, Julie too was caught up in the excitement. It all seemed so romantic. "I didn't bring anything very dressy."

"Rodeo Drive, remember? My treat," Diedra said with a wink.

Steve groaned. "Dress shopping?" He glanced at Luke. "While they shop, we'll knock some golf balls around."

"Suits me," Luke said.

After more discussion, more food, and two quick phone calls to Indiana so that Luke and Julie could tell their parents they'd arrived safely, the four of them headed for Hollywood. On the way to the car, Luke plucked a bright red hibiscus flower and tucked it behind Julie's ear.

"Pretty," he said gazing into her eyes, and she caught the double implication of his compliment.

Hollywood's Walk of Fame was a long sidewalk teeming with tourists, where star shapes had been set in granite and concrete, each bearing the name of some famous screen personage. At Grauman's Chinese Theater, signatures were scrawled in the cement, accompanied by handprints. Julie and Luke shouldered their way through throngs of tourists, exclaiming over names they recognized, pausing to ask about names they didn't. Steve knew a great deal about the silver screen and kept up a running commentary. "He's better than a tour guide," Diedra confided.

The names rolled past Julie's vision, and sometimes she hesitated even to step on a particular slab, as if it might desecrate the person's memory. The sun beat down on her back and shoulders, but she was so immersed in stargazing that she barely felt its heat. All of a sudden, Luke stopped and pointed down.

There in the concrete was the signature of Marilyn Monroe, her handprints above her name. He whipped off his baseball cap and placed it over his heart. "A moment of reverence, please."

"You an MM fan?" Steve asked.

"She's the other woman in his life," Julie explained. "But I've learned to live with it."

Luke paced around the square bearing Marilyn's name and handprints. Tourists streamed by them, snapping pictures and exclaiming over other names. "You know what, Julie? I'll bet your hands are the same size."

"I'll bet not."

"Only one way to find out."

She glanced at all the foot traffic. "I'll get stepped on."

"We'll protect you," Steve said. He and Diedra and Luke formed a circle around her.

"Are you kidding?" But a glance at their faces told her they weren't.

"Come on," Luke urged. "What can it hurt? Don't you want to know?"

She sighed, dropped to her knees on the hot concrete, and carefully placed her hands into the mold of Marilyn's. To her astonishment, it was a perfect fit. "I don't believe it."

Luke whooped and his face split into a grin. "I knew it! I knew your hands would be the same size. This is so cool."

Julie stood. "That's about all of me that's the same size."

Luke seized her around the waist and lifted

her off the ground, laughing. "I have a living duplicate of Marilyn. Does life get much better than this?"

Julie blushed furiously. He was causing a scene and a small crowd was looking on with curiosity. "He's crazy," she mouthed apologetically to the onlookers. "Heat stroke."

Luke bent her backward and kissed her soundly on the mouth. The crowd broke into applause.

"Luke! This is *so* embarrassing," Julie hissed.

"So what? We'll never see these people again. Besides, life is short."

Steve and Diedra stood to one side and laughed. When Julie was finally able to regain her composure, they headed off to other attractions. She pretended to be in a huff, but of course she wasn't. If anything, she was more in love with Luke than ever. Not because he'd kissed her in public, but because he wasn't afraid to show his feelings for her to the whole world.

Yet his statement, "Life is short," haunted her the rest of the day. She'd heard the phrase many times, but when Luke said it, it took on a deeper, more profound meaning. *Life was short.* And only a person who had looked death in the face could understand how very short it really could be.

The days passed in a whirlwind of activity and blended into one another like colors flowing across the sky at sunset. Julie fell in love with California. Steve took them on some great driving tours. Julie thought the city of Los Angeles too large, too busy, too filled with smog and exhaust fumes. But in the valleys, where farmers grew lush green crops, and in the foothills, where cactus and jagged rock formations looked wild and untamed, and on the beaches, where ocean waves rolled in timeless swirls, she lost her heart. And because she could share it all with Luke, the beauty and grandeur of the state took on an almost hallowed meaning for her.

"Promise me you'll bring me back here someday," she said to him one starry night when they were alone by Steve's courtyard fountain.

"You mean leave Indiana?" His eyes danced mischievously.

"I could be persuaded." She dipped her hand into the cool water, where golden fish swam lazily beneath lily pads.

"But remember the smell of autumn—of

woodsmoke, and how the leaves change colors. Can you leave all that for this?"

Memories of chilly nights and football games and the thrill of the year's first snowfall came to her. She felt a twinge of homesickness. "But don't forget there aren't any flowers half the year. And you know how much I like flowers."

"Well, I like it here too." His voice sounded low and soft in the velvet night. "It's hard to think about going home."

"Then don't think about it. We've got two more weeks."

He leaned back against the bowl of the fountain, rested his elbows on the lip, and gazed up at the glittering stars. "Sometimes, the past six months seem like a bad dream. Like they never happened to me. I wish I didn't have to go for testing ever again."

A chill coursed through her as the memories flooded back. "The testing's routine. The results were fine last time and they'll be fine next time too. I'm telling you, Luke, it's over. You've licked Hodgkin's." Suddenly, a new fear seized her, and she leaned toward him. "You are feeling all right, aren't you?"

"Me? I feel great. I'm sorry, I didn't mean

to alarm you. I was just thinking out loud, that's all."

She sighed with relief. "Good. We've been so busy and you've seemed so energetic—what with working out every day—that sometimes I forget . . . you know . . . about your health."

"I forget about it too." He stood and drew her up into his arms. "And I didn't mean to bring you down by talking about it."

"No problem." She rested her head on his broad, hard chest and heard the rhythm of his heart.

"Will you promise me something?"

The rumble of his voice tickled her ear. "I'll promise you anything," she answered.

"Promise that with or without me, you'll come back here someday."

She pulled back and gazed up at him, at his strong jawline, at his dark eyes, now even darker with only stars to light his face. "Sorry . . . I can't promise you that. Without you, I won't want to come back here. This place is wonderful, but only because you're here with me."

He kissed her then, drawing her mouth to his, and suddenly it felt as if all the stars in the sky above had sprinkled themselves upon her. "Luke . . . ," she whispered.

"My love," he whispered back.

Julie and Diedra shopped for dresses on Rodeo Drive for the upcoming wedding. Julie couldn't believe the prices, or the rows of limousines parked in front of the stores. "I never knew there were so many rich people in the world," she told Diedra as they sat in a trendy restaurant having lunch.

"Out here, you get a warped perspective of wealth and material things. Don't let it dazzle you."

"I won't. But if Luke gets to play for the NFL someday, he'll be rich."

"Is that what he wants to do?"

"Yes—although his illness sort of side-tracked him. But now that he's well, I think he'll start wanting the things he used to want again."

"Does he talk about it much? About how having gotten cancer makes him feel?"

"We're both angry about it. It isn't fair, you know."

Diedra set her fork down. "Life's never fair. Sometimes we're lucky enough to find someone to love and who loves us, but 'fairly' isn't the way God runs the world."

Julie nodded. "Still, Luke gets down. I think he's afraid his cancer will come back. I tell him he's well, but still he gets depressed about it."

"You should let him talk to you," Diedra said, sipping her water. "I remember how much my mother needed to talk to me about her dying."

"But Luke's not dying."

"It doesn't matter—he still needs to get out his feelings, and because he loves you, you're the one who needs to help him talk about them."

"It's depressing for me too. I don't want him to talk about dying."

"I'd never tell you what to do, Julie, but think about it. Think about listening, really listening to his heart."

Julie pondered Diedra's advice long and hard, and two days later, when Steve and Diedra were called in for a planning session on their upcoming film project, Luke suggested he and Julie strike out on their own.

"Where are we going?" she asked as he started up Diedra's sports car. She had lent it to them for the day.

"You'll think I'm nuts, but more than anything, I want to visit Marilyn Monroe's grave."

Julie gulped, then said cheerfully, "If that's what you want to do, let's go."

"It's what I want to do." Luke put the car into gear and they drove off into the hot Los Angeles morning.

17

Julie juggled a map of Los Angeles while Luke piloted the car out onto the expressways. "Do we know where we're going?" she asked.

"I think so," he said. "I asked Steve for directions before he left."

The overhead sun blazed down and the wind blew over the open convertible, tangling Julie's hair.

"You're beautiful," Luke yelled above the roar of the engine. With his free hand, he touched her blond hair, struck golden by the rays of the sun.

"You're prejudiced," she countered.

He got off the expressway and drove down a busy thoroughfare. Eventually, he turned and stopped the car near a small, neatly kept church. He opened her door and led her through the church's parking lot, along the side of the building, through a wrought-iron gate, and into a small cemetery. The grounds were neat and well maintained, with walkways that led in orderly directions.

"Are you sure this is it?" she asked. Somehow, she had expected Marilyn Monroe to be buried in some soaring mausoleum of marble and whitewashed granite, not off some side street in the middle of a business district.

"I'm sure," Luke told her. He stopped in front of an above-ground crypt.

Carved in the stone, along with the dates of her birth and death, was Marilyn's name. The letters looked stark and surreal to Julie, and she felt goose bumps rise along her arms. She thought of all the posters she'd seen of the famous movie star, even movies she'd watched with Luke starring Marilyn, yet those images seemed far less real than her name etched in granite—perhaps because, Julie mused, behind the wall of the enclosure lay her mortal body.

Julie touched the letters gingerly. "These are different from the letters in the sidewalk," she said.

"These are final," Luke observed. "When you see somebody's signature, you expect them to be alive. But these are carved out for a person. The person doesn't have any control over these."

"Why did she get buried here? Her grave seems so ordinary for someone so popular."

"Joe DiMaggio, one of her ex-husbands, arranged this. He decided that since her life had been so public, her death and burial should be private. He loved her, even though they were divorced."

Julie honestly didn't want to be discussing death with Luke, but she recalled Diedra's urging her to listen if Luke ever wanted to discuss his feelings. And she realized that his need to see Marilyn Monroe's grave was somehow connected to his feelings about what was happening to him. "I wonder if he still loves her."

"It's hard to say. I do know that after she died, a red rose was put on her crypt every day. Every day for twenty-five years."

"Wow . . . that's awesome." Julie thought about how much she loved receiving flowers from Luke. "Too bad Marilyn couldn't let the sender know what it meant to her."

"Julie, do you think when people die they can communicate with the people they love who are still alive?"

She considered his question, then said, "I

don't think so, Luke. I think death takes people out of this world forever and that there's no way back. But I do believe in heaven, a place where souls go and where people meet again after death. Don't you believe that?"

His eyes clouded. "Sometimes I believe it. But other times, I'm afraid it's not true and that death is the end of ourselves. That we just stop existing. And we're gone forever."

She shook her head. "I'd rather not believe that way. If that's true, then why do we ever get to live? Why even *bother* to live? I like to think everybody gets to meet up again in heaven."

"I hope you're right."

She could tell he was troubled by questions he couldn't express, by mysteries he couldn't understand. She wanted to help him, but didn't know how. She didn't want to think about death and eternity, and she didn't want him thinking about it either. Regardless of what Diedra said, he was too young to talk about dying, and according to his doctors, his cancer was in remission, so she couldn't see the necessity.

She touched his arm, half to reassure herself that he was still flesh and blood. "Enough of this talk, Luke. Why don't we talk about lunch instead?"

He grinned. "Okay, so I got a little heavy. But I've been thinking more and more about things I never thought about before I got sick. I don't mean to be gloomy or to scare you."

"No problem. I guess it's only natural to think about this stuff when you've had a close call, or a serious illness, but you're fine now and so I think you should be considering next football season and how hard my father's going to be pushing you. Now *that's* scary."

"True. He's expecting me to take our team to the state finals. I hope I can."

"I know you will." She offered him a dazzling smile and took his hand. "Why don't you say good-bye to Marilyn and let's blow this place. Steve and Diedra promised to be home in time to take us to the Hard Rock Cafe for supper."

He draped his arm over her shoulders and, without so much as a backward glance, he led her away from the grave of Marilyn, away from the cemetery, and away from all the images of death that haunted him. Julie felt relief. For now, it seemed that he had closed the book on his shadowy thoughts of nonexistence and was content to walk in the light of the sun.

That weekend, Steve and Diedra took them hiking in the foothills. They left the city before daylight and were on the trail as the sun began to rise. Eastward, the indigo-blue sky faded to a paler shade of blue and streaks of pink heralded the dawn. Stars began to disappear, and slowly light reached brightening fingers across the rugged landscape and lit dark rock formations, one by one, like candles on a cake.

Julie was cold, but in an hour, as the day chased away the night, warmth spread over her like butter on warm toast. "I'm hungry," she announced finally.

"We're just about to stop and fix breakfast," Steve said, removing his backpack. "We'll need some firewood. Diedra, Luke, fan out and collect some sticks."

Wearily, Julie sat on a nearby rock. "What are we going to eat? Roadkill?"

"Bacon and eggs," Steve said, taking utensils out of his knapsack.

"You're kidding!" Julie exclaimed, pleased.

"*Powdered* eggs," Diedra said. "Sometimes not as good-tasting as roadkill."

"Do you doubt my culinary skills, woman?"

"Never." Diedra winked at Julie and Luke, who had dumped an armload of sticks and twigs at Steve's feet. "Actually, he's fed me before, and he does a passable job."

"I hope so," Luke said. "I'm hungry enough to eat the dirt off my boots."

"Which is one of our chef's most famous delicacies," Diedra joked. "And one of his best-kept secrets as to how he makes people believe he's a skilled chef. He allows his guests to get so hungry that no matter what he serves, they think it's wonderful."

"Talent such as mine doesn't need your grief," Steve announced, feigning hurt.

"Just cook," Diedra said.

In no time, Steve had the fire built, fresh coffee boiling, and bacon frying. Julie never remembered anything smelling so delicious, and she cleaned her plate greedily once breakfast was served.

"Where do we go from here?" Luke wanted to know as they put out the fire and packed up the utensils.

Steve pointed toward a flat stretch of land. Beyond it, rocks rose in jagged patterns. "In those canyons is some of the most beautiful wilderness on the face of the earth. We'll spend two hours going in, two coming out. Then back to the Jeep, and home."

The Jeep was parked at a communal parking area, miles away. "Why don't you go on and pick me up on the way back," Julie said with a yawn.

"This from a female who practically walked my legs off on Rodeo Drive," Diedra teased.

"That was different."

Luke grinned. "Yeah . . . out here there aren't any 'Sale' signs."

"Very funny." She rose to her feet. "All right, I'll show you all how tough I am." She marched off toward the canyons. Luke followed.

An hour later, she was very tired, but the stark beauty of the terrain held her interest. The four of them began to climb. The going was slow and the footing difficult, mostly because the ground was loose and Julie's boots kept sinking. Pebbles splattered behind her with every step.

"The view at the top is worth it," Steve insisted.

Winded, Julie muttered, "It had better be."

Luke, obviously in good shape again, didn't seem to mind the climb one bit. When at last

Julie hoisted herself onto level ground, she heaved a breath, then stared at the view below. Gullies and ravines wound through magnificent rock formations as far as her eye could see. In the bright sunlight, the rocks looked gardenlike, blooming in red and gold and white. Purple shadows cut swaths along the ravines and faded to black when the sunlight failed to penetrate the twists and turns.

"Wow," Julie said.

"Unbelievable," Luke said, standing next to her.

Wind, moaning in the ghostly gullies, was the only sound.

"If a person got lost in there, how'd he ever find his way out?" Luke asked.

"He might not," Diedra said. "That's why it's safest to climb up and look down on it."

"Shout something," Steve said. "Go ahead. Don't be shy."

Luke stepped forward and, cupping a hand around his mouth, yelled, "Luke loves Julie!"

The sound bounced off the canyon walls, reverberated, slid into the ravines, and finally evaporated into the air. Julie smiled at him, stepped closer to the rim, and shouted, "Julie loves Luke!"

Again, the words ricocheted back, rolling

waves of sound on a river of wind. "Julie and Luke forever!" Luke yelled. The words leaped back toward them, loud, then soft, then softer and softer before fading away.

"One more time, together?" Luke asked, taking her hand.

They lifted their arms and shouted "I love you" in unison, blending their voices and words until the two became as one. And they listened as their words returned to them, until the echoes of their words became as embedded in the memory of the canyon as the colors of the sun.

18

When Luke and Julie were four days away from leaving Los Angeles, Steve and Diedra made the final preparations for their wedding. The day before the ceremony, the four of them drove north along the coastal highway, toward Monterey and the centuries-old chapel that Steve had reserved for the wedding.

The road hugged the shoreline and, from the backseat of the Mercedes, Julie watched the ocean sweep across coarse-grained beaches of sand and, where there was no beach, watched the salty water smash into soaring, craggy cliffs of rugged granite. Steve turned east, into the hills, and drove over a ridge into a sunny, sleepy valley, seemingly untouched by time, that cradled a quiet town.

The chapel, in the center of the town, was a

rectangular adobe building with a bell tower and an ancient mission bell that monks rang every morning and at twilight. There was a single main street, lined with boutiques, gourmet food shops, and colorful craft stores selling Native American and Mexican artwork.

Steve had arranged for two rooms at a quaint bed-and-breakfast inn—Julie and Diedra in one room, he and Luke in another. They ate supper on the back patio, under trellises draped with night-blooming jasmine and moonflowers. A man playing a Spanish guitar strolled among the tables, serenading the diners.

They ate leisurely, lingering over coffee and dessert, enjoying the balmy night breeze that gently stirred the petals of the flowers and sent sweet, subtle scents across the patio. Julie kept gazing up at the stars, which were spread out across the sky like jewels on black velvet. She could hardly believe that in two days, she and Luke would fly back home and California would be only a memory. She heard Luke ask, "You two going to go on a honeymoon?"

"We head for Europe at the end of next month for our next film project," Steve replied. "We thought we'd grab our honeymoon before we have to start work."

"Where?" Julie asked, thinking how romantic it sounded to honeymoon in Europe.

"London, first," Diedra said. "Then Paris and Madrid. We'll be filming in Spain, so that's where we'll end up."

"How long will you be gone?" Luke asked.

"Almost four months," Steve said. "We've got to hunt out locations before we start filming. And once we wrap up the European project, we head on to Japan for the next one. We probably won't be back in the States until next spring."

Julie sighed. "High school sounds so boring by comparison."

"It's a long time to be away from home," Diedra said. "Especially when all we really want to do is settle down and have kids."

Steve took her hand. "And that's just what we're going to do once the Japanese project is over."

Diedra smiled at him and, sensing their tender bond, Julie reached for Luke's hand. She was surprised to see Luke studying his uncle with an expression of sadness. She wondered what he was thinking and feeling, but she didn't get the opportunity to ask because as soon as dinner was finished, she and Diedra returned to their room amid talk of tomorrow being the "big day."

While Diedra took a shower, Julie lay on her bed staring moodily into space, wondering about Luke. The phone rang and she grabbed the receiver. Luke's voice said, "Julie, meet me in the chapel tomorrow morning at ten."

"The wedding's not until one."

"I know, but I want to talk to you before the wedding. And I don't want to be rushed."

The inn wasn't far from the chapel. According to local legend, in olden days a bride would walk barefoot from the center of town to the church, where her groom would be waiting. "Is something wrong?" Julie asked, feeling a flutter of fear.

"I just want to talk to you," Luke said. "Please. It's important."

Wild horses couldn't have kept her away. And so the next morning, promising a nervous Diedra she'd be back in time for lunch, Julie hurried down the quiet street to the chapel. She pushed open the timeworn wooden door. Inside, the air was cool, candles glowed on the altar, and small rectangular windows allowed sunlight to filter into the darkness. She waited for her eyes to adjust and saw Luke sitting in a pew near the front.

She slid in beside him. "Hi," she whispered, for although they were alone, she hesitated to break the reverent quiet. "What's up?"

He turned to her and took her in his arms. "I wanted to be alone with you here, before the wedding and all."

She returned his hug and felt her anxiety evaporate. "Well, here I am."

Luke shifted in the pew, and Julie could tell that something was troubling him. All at once, he asked, "What if you could never have babies, Julie? Would that make you not want to marry someone?"

Caught totally off guard by his question, Julie fumbled for an answer. "Gee, Luke, I haven't even decided what college I want to attend. It's hard to think about having babies and what I might want years and years from now."

"But it's important. I—I need to know."

"Did all of Steve's talk about kids make you think too much about your future? You know, like the day we went to Marilyn Monroe's grave?"

He shook his head. "It started me thinking about what my doctor told us about the radiation possibly making me sterile. It made me wonder if getting married knowing I might not be able to give a woman kids would make her not want to marry me in the first place."

"If having kids is the most important thing, then maybe it would make a difference. But no one knows if they're able to have kids until they start trying. I guess if babies are *that* important to a couple, and they can't have their own, then they adopt. It seems like the world's full of unwanted babies."

"That's true, but I want to know how important having children is to *you*."

"Why?"

"Because I love you, Julie."

"I love you too."

"Because I want to marry you."

The atmosphere in the chapel became charged, and Julie could scarcely hold in her breath. Her heart hammered against her rib cage. "Didn't you ask me that in sixth grade?"

He smiled at the memory, easing the tension. "Yes, and you said, 'Get lost, bozo.' "

"Ouch! Was I that mean?"

"You've made up for it."

"So is this a bona fide marriage proposal?"

He took her hand. "There's never been anybody else for me except you, Julie Ellis. And there never will be."

Her heart melted. "And you're afraid I

might not want to marry you if I know you might not be able to have children?"

"You should have a choice."

"You're my choice," she said softly.

A smile of joy and relief lit his face. "That's what I wanted you to say. You already told me that the cancer didn't matter to you, but I had to know for sure how you felt about this baby thing."

"Now you know."

He straightened his leg, dug in the pocket of his jeans, and withdrew a small box. "This is for you."

Heart pounding, she opened it and saw a ring of fine silver, intricately carved, with a turquoise set in its center. "It's gorgeous," she whispered.

"It's Mexican. According to folklore, long ago, before soldiers went off to war, they gave this kind of ring to their special girl as a signal to others she was taken."

"So is this my engagement ring?"

"It's a promise ring." Luke removed it from the box and slipped it onto the third finger of her left hand. "It's a promise that someday I'll buy you a diamond engagement ring, when I can really plan on marrying you. I know you have college ahead and I know your mother will kill me if you don't go."

Tears filmed her eyes as she held out her hand to stare at the ring. "We both have college," she reminded him.

"Well, the jury's still out about my future."

"Don't say that!" Her tone was urgent. "You can't promise to marry me and then say you might not have a future. I won't hear it."

"Knowing that you want to marry me someday gives me more to look forward to than anything else ever could," he said in an attempt to calm her.

"Even more than playing football?"

"Football's only a game. *You* are real life." He leaned forward and, in the quiet sanctity of the chapel, he kissed her lovingly on her lips.

Hours later, Julie returned to the chapel with a nervous Diedra and Steve. Since the ceremony was to be small and unattended, Diedra didn't walk down the aisle. She joined Steve at the altar in front of the priest while a guitarist played haunting Spanish music.

Julie thought Diedra looked beautiful in a simple white summer dress of eyelet lace. A white-lace Spanish mantilla covered her head and flowed down her shoulders. Her bouquet was made up of lilies mixed with pale purple orchids. Steve's eyes shone as he gazed at her, reminding Julie of candles alight with fire.

Julie wore a sundress in the palest shade of butter yellow, carried a bouquet of daisies and gardenias, and quivered with excitement and anticipation. Someday, *she* would be the bride, and Luke her groom.

Luke stood beside Steve, looking lean and fit in a navy-blue suit. The family resemblance between nephew and uncle was striking. During the speaking of the vows, Luke caught Julie's eye, and it was as if every word the priest spoke was meant for them also: ". . . *for richer, for poorer, in sickness and in health, 'til death do us part.*"

The words took on new meaning for Julie. Getting married was a serious business—a life-and-death commitment. A pledge to be joined with one other person for all of earthly time. And when the person you loved, as she loved Luke, already had a life-threatening illness, the promise seemed even more profound.

She locked gazes with Luke and saw his love for her shining in his eyes. She smiled, hoping to communicate that she was willing to make such a commitment to him. That she was willing to stand by him no matter what his future held.

She fingered the silver and turquoise ring on her finger—his promise ring. Silently, she promised to love and stick by him until they could say their vows before God and formally pledge their love for all time.

19

Julie and Luke returned home to a crowd of family and friends waiting for them at the airport. Everyone was glad to see them and everyone started questioning them at once about their trip. Julie's father reminded Luke about upcoming preseason practice, Luke's mother eagerly sorted through photos of Steve and Diedra, and kids from school wanted to know who they'd seen who was famous.

The hawk eye of Julie's mother fell on the ring, which Julie brushed off as a souvenir, but when Solena came over to her house the next morning, Julie told her the truth.

"A promise ring! Oh, Julie, that's so-o-o romantic."

"When he gave it to me in that chapel, my heart almost stopped." Julie held out her hand, allowing the ring to catch the light of the morning sun coming through her bedroom window. "I'm never going to take it off."

"This means you're practically engaged. Are you sure you can wait to get married until you're out of college? That's years from now."

"I know, but Luke should have a chance to play college ball and I really would like to have some kind of career. If you could have met Diedra and seen how cool she was, you'd understand. Besides, now that Luke and I are sure that we want to get married, we can take our time about it. But you're right—it *is* going to be hard to wait," she added wistfully.

"Well, I don't think it's fair for one person to have so much going for her. But"—Solena smiled—"if it has to be somebody, I'm glad it's you."

"Thanks. What's hard for me now isn't thinking about college, but thinking about high school. I'm bored already, and my senior year hasn't even started." She hugged her knees to her chest and rested her chin on them. "So how was your summer? And how'd the job go? What was Jason like?"

Solena wrinkled her nose. "Waterton is mega-boring—the armpit of the Midwest.

And as for the job and Jason, well, the best I can say about the whole experience is that I got a regular paycheck."

"Pretty dull, huh?"

"Jason discovered Melanie Hawkins and spent the whole month of July trailing after her. It was disgusting! Don't guys have any self-respect?"

Julie giggled. "Well, at least that kept her away from Frank, didn't it?"

"Yes, but . . ." She jutted her lip in a pout. "It sure didn't give me a chance to have an adventure like you. And Jason is going home soon, but Melanie will still be here. So, I guess it'll be another year of keeping her away from Frank."

"You can do it, girl."

Solena made an outrageous face. "Okay, tell me more about California."

"It was the most wonderful place in the world. I never had so much fun, and because I was with Luke . . . well, that was the most special part of all."

"How's he feeling?"

"Fine. He worked out at his uncle's gym to stay in shape."

"Seeing how good he looked at the airport, it's hard to remember how bad he looked during chemo. I'm sure this whole mess is behind him."

"Me too," Julie said. She gazed down lovingly at the ring. "Especially now, when we have so much going for us."

On Friday, Luke and Julie had Solena and Frank over to her house for an all-night video movie marathon. "Your last all-nighter," her father told the boys. "Once practice starts, it's back to hard work and regular hours."

In a way, Julie resented the imposition of the schedule, but with Luke looking forward so to resuming play, she kept her feelings to herself. Practices were called for three hours each morning and two hours each afternoon at the nearby middle school field, which would be their temporary home field for the fall season. In the grueling August heat, Luke was so exhausted he fell asleep early each night, leaving Julie to spend her time hanging out with her friends and getting ready for the start of the school year.

On Labor Day, her father had his annual barbecue bash for all the players on his team. He fired up a massive grill in the backyard and fed over thirty guys, from incoming freshmen to seniors. Luke was clearly the hero of the day. A newspaper reporter showed up, interviewed him, took pictures of Luke and the team, and told Luke there'd be a front-page story in Sunday's sports section.

Late in the afternoon, Luke whisked Julie away to the high school and the football stadium, which was still under construction. They climbed up a new set of concrete bleachers and settled on the highest tier. Below, the field appeared green, with wispy strands of grass, but the underground sprinkling system had yet to be installed and the final sod hadn't been put down. Since the growing season was all but over, it would be spring before the new turf could be installed.

"Too bad I won't get to play here," Luke said.

"This time next year, you'll be throwing for some college. Daddy says the Tulane coach has contacted him about you."

"Tulane and Ohio State. I wish I could play for both of them."

"I've never seen Dad so eager about the start of a new season. He's driving me and Mom crazy with football talk."

Luke puckered his brow. "Everybody's counting on me, Julie. I hope I don't let them down."

"You'll do just fine. Just make sure you don't get hurt."

He grinned. "Frank's my main man up front, and he says he'll take off anybody's head who sacks me."

"And if he doesn't, he'll have Solena and me to face."

"That'll keep him scared enough to do his job."

"It better." She twined her fingers through his. "I got a postcard from Steve and Diedra in Paris."

"Me too. They sound like they're having a ball."

"Diedra says that she wishes we were with them and that when we take a honeymoon, we have to include Paris on the tour. What do you think?"

"I think we'll be lucky to afford Parris Island, South Carolina."

"Are you kidding? By then, you'll be a Heisman Trophy winner and a first-round draft pick for the NFL."

"I like the way you think, Julie," he said with a laugh. "I've dreamed about playing pro ball since I was a kid."

"You still should."

He shrugged. "Let's face it, I may not be

anyone's first choice anymore. Cancer has a way of scaring pro scouts off."

She linked her arm through his. "You're *my* first choice."

He leaned over and kissed the tip of her nose. "Then get a good education, in case you end up supporting me."

She grimaced. "Isn't it enough I get this from my mother? Do I have to get it from you too?"

"She on your case again about picking a college?"

"She's never gotten *off* my case. So give me your top three choices and I'll tell her and she can start sending off for applications."

"You're really serious about going wherever I go?"

"Of course. Unless you want to be separated for four years."

"Not hardly." He studied her face. "It's just that I want you to do what you really want—not feel tied down by promises you made to me."

She held out her hand. "Then this ring doesn't mean anything?"

"It means I love you and want to marry you."

"That's what *I* want. And so going to a college far away from you isn't likely."

The sky was darkening, threatening rain. "We'd better head for home before we get drenched," he said, pulling her to her feet.

They hurried down the steps and onto the field. The ground was lumpy and hard. Julie jogged ahead to the center of the field, stopped, and tried to imagine what it would be like to play a game with hundreds of people cheering and yelling her name. She couldn't. Yet for Luke, she knew, it was a common occurrence.

Luke came alongside, picked up a stick, tossed it high in the air, and caught it while she cheered. "Our first game is against Hammond next Friday. Your father thinks we'll wipe up the field with them."

"One thing my father knows is football," Julie said. "If he thinks we'll win, we probably will."

Luke gazed over the field, letting his vision sweep from one end to the other. "Yep, this is going to be one fine field." He took the stick and scrawled symbols in the dirt. He made the letter I, drew a heart, and then scrawled the letter U. It was the same "I love you" message he'd carved on Julie's backyard tree the previous May.

"Don't let my dad see you marking up his field," she teased. "He'll have a fit. Football players are supposed to be tough, not sissies who fall in love."

His eyes twinkled. "Is that what I am, a sissy?"

"A wimp," she said, as large drops of rain began to splat against the ground.

"You call me—a guy who's going to be on the front page of the sports section—a wimp?"

Playfully, she stuck out her tongue and darted off.

He chased her down and began tickling her sides. "Who's a wimp?"

Julie shrieked with laughter and fell to the ground, rolling every which way to evade his fingers. Rain fell in sheets, stinging Julie's skin and soaking them both. In minutes they were streaked with mud, but Julie didn't care.

Pressing her to the ground with his body, Luke pinned her arms over her head. "Beg for mercy," he said above the sound of the pouring rain.

"Never," she cried.

Water streamed off him and his eyes looked like glowing coals. Julie felt a surge of fire course through her body and was surprised that her skin wasn't sizzling with the heat. "Then suffer the consequences," he said.

He lowered his mouth to hers and kissed her long and deep while the rain washed over them and thunder clapped in the sky.

20

By the end of September, the Waterton Warriors were 5 and 0 and ranked number one in their division in the state. Luke got most of the credit for team leadership, while being lauded for keeping a cool head under pressure and for his golden throwing arm, and Julie had never seen her father more excited about a team. "This is it, Julie," he'd say each morning after a victory. "I've waited for this team for over twenty years. They're the best. And Luke is absolutely the finest player I've ever coached—one in a million."

"I agree, Dad," she'd reply. "He's one in a million." But for Julie, his stellar status had little to do with football. She loved him so much it was becoming increasingly difficult to think about waiting until they both finished college to get married.

Meanwhile, her mother never let up on her about college. To appease her, Julie sent off for applications to Tulane and Ohio State. "Why Tulane?" her mother asked.

"Why not? You said I should get away from this area."

"Well, what course of study are you interested in taking? Some colleges concentrate more on one area than another. If I know what you're interested in, I can do a computer search for the schools that offer your area of interest and you can apply to them."

"I'm not sure. Isn't it enough I'm picking some colleges without having to determine the entire course of my college career before I even begin?"

"That's not what I mean."

"Can we just drop it, Mom?"

Her mother studied her thoughtfully, and said, "I'm not stupid, Julie. I know you're ambivalent because you want to wait and see where Luke chooses to attend."

Julie saw no reason to argue about it. "So what? Only the best colleges are recruiting him, so it's not as if I'll pick a bad one."

"You need to choose a college based on your needs—not Luke's."

"Mother, please, stop it. I'm doing the best that I can."

Frustrated, her mother turned her back and swept from the room.

Julie was at the mall one Saturday afternoon when she ran into Luke's mother. They went to the food court, ordered frozen yogurt, and sat together to eat it. "I don't get to see much of you anymore," Nancy said between bites. "If it weren't for home games, I doubt I'd see you at all."

"I miss coming over. Blame my dad. He's so fixated on this season, he practically keeps the team under lock and key. It's so-o-o frustrating."

Nancy smiled. "You think you're frustrated. You should see Luke pacing the floor wishing he could be with you."

The news thrilled Julie. She liked knowing Luke missed being with her. "He has a lot of pressure on him."

"That's true, and I've mentioned to him that he shouldn't be too intense, that the entire fate of the football season doesn't rest on his shoulders. It looks to me as if he's losing weight, and I'm afraid he's worrying too much about the season."

Julie set down her spoon. "But he's feeling all right, isn't he?"

"He says he is."

Seeing Nancy's concern upset Julie. "He told me his checkup went fine. It did, didn't it?"

"I haven't heard otherwise."

Ironically, on the day Luke had been scheduled to go into Chicago for testing, Nancy had had an office review by the corporate bigwigs and Julie had been scheduled to take her SAT exams. Luke insisted that he could go through the routine without them and that if there were any problems with his blood work or bone scans, he'd be notified. The day after, the Warriors had played one of their top rivals and Luke had led them to another victory.

Julie picked up her spoon and dug into her frozen dessert. "Well, I'm sure that if anything were wrong, you'd have been notified by Dr. Kessler."

"You're right. Luke says I shouldn't obsess about every little lost pound or sniffle he has." Nancy smiled wanly. "I know he's right, but it's hard for me not to. Last winter and spring were the longest days of my life. I just couldn't believe Luke was having such problems. He's always been perfectly healthy."

"We shouldn't think about those bad times. The important thing is that he's fine now and on the way to the rest of his life." Julie smiled. "And I'm glad to be going along for the ride."

Nancy laughed. "I don't know what he'd do without you, Julie. He's been crazy about you since he was just a little kid."

"That's nice of you to say. I'm crazy about him, too."

The food court tables had filled with the lunch crowd while they'd been talking, and the smells of fast food hung in the air. Nancy glanced nervously from side to side. "Um—I don't mean to pry, but I am curious about some things."

"Ask me."

"You and Luke have discussed marriage, haven't you?"

Now it was Julie's turn to cast a nervous glance. "I suppose we have."

"Don't be concerned: I'm not against it. But I really do want Luke to go to college."

"He'll go," Julie assured her. "How could he not go with all these college football coaches after him?"

Nancy smiled and relaxed. "How indeed!

I'm glad, Julie. I want so many things for Luke, and he's so close to getting some of them."

Julie understood, and only wished her own mother could be as flexible as Luke's. "I won't take his dreams away," she said.

"Please don't think I'm prying or trying to tell you what to do. One of the things he wants—that he's always wanted—is you. And I won't interfere with any plans the two of you've made."

"It's all right," Julie insisted. "Luke and I plan to have it *all.*"

Nancy's round face broke into a broad smile. "And you will. I'm positive of that. With all that the two of you have going for you, you'll have everything life has to offer."

Julie basked in Nancy's approval, only wishing that Luke were there to share it. That night, the Warriors would play their homecoming game, and afterward, there was to be a dance in the gym. Luke would be taking her and there'd be no early curfew, so she could spend hours with him. Snapping out of her reverie, Julie said, "Sit with Solena, Mom, and me at the game tonight."

"I'd love to," Luke's mother responded.

"After all, this one's against the Trojans,

and I think we should all be together when
Luke hands them their first loss of the season."

That night, the air was crisp and cold, perfect
for playing football. The middle school stands
were packed to overflowing, as the Warriors-
Trojans game was one of northwest Indiana's
great rivalries. TV cameras and newspaper
photographers had special field passes and
crews were set up along one end zone.

In the stands, behind the Warriors' bench
on the fifty-yard line, Julie watched Luke
warm up on the field throwing passes as her
father paced furiously along the sidelines.

"So where do you think they are?" Solena
asked, craning her neck at the crowds sitting
behind them.

"Who?"

"The college scouts! Frank said the stands
would be crawling with them for tonight's
game."

Julie's father had told her the same thing.
But Julie wasn't interested in talking about
scouts. She kept her gaze on Luke, who
seemed to be having trouble with his passes.

Following her line of vision, Solena said,
"I'm sure he's just nervous. Wait 'til the game
starts."

Yet, when the game started, Luke didn't improve. Only a clever play by the defense kept the Trojans from going out in front during the second quarter. Julie anxiously twisted the blanket across her lap. Luke couldn't blow it now. Not with so many important people watching.

She saw her father call Luke to the sidelines and lecture him sternly. Luke had ripped off his helmet and Julie could see that he was grimacing and sweating profusely. "I wish Daddy would get off Luke's case," she said to her mother irritably.

"Never tell your father how to coach a game," her mother said. "One way or another he gets the best from his boys. And Luke's his pride and joy."

Her mother's words didn't comfort Julie, whose mood only darkened when Luke took a hard hit minutes before the half ended. "Where was his protection?" she shouted, springing to her feet. She glared down at Solena. "Frank's supposed to cover him!"

"Don't yell at *me*," Solena exclaimed.

Angry and agitated, Julie sat down, only to watch Luke being helped off the field and taken to the locker room. The announcer commented about Luke being shaken up on the play, and Julie's anger turned to anxiety. She longed to rush off to the gym, but knew she'd never get inside. "He'll be all right," she heard Nancy say.

Mercifully, the half ended and Coach Ellis jogged with his team off the field. The roar of the crowd dropped to a lull. "Popcorn?" Patricia Ellis asked.

Julie shook her head and snapped, "How can you ask about popcorn when Luke's hurt?"

"I'll go with you," Nancy said, heading off an argument.

Julie's mother and Nancy stood, but didn't leave, because someone called their names. Julie turned to see Brett Carney, one of the new freshmen on the team, hurrying toward them. He was in his uniform, but because he hadn't played, his jersey was clean and unmarked. "Coach sent me," Brett said, climbing up the few rows to where they sat.

"What's wrong with Luke?" Julie asked as her heart thudded rapidly in her chest. "I know something's wrong. Tell me."

Brett's eyes were wide as saucers and his skin looked pale, as if he'd had a great fright. "Luke collapsed in the locker room," Brett said. "He's being taken to the hospital."

"Which one?" Nancy asked.

"Waterton General."

Julie grabbed for her purse and car keys, but her mother pulled them from her hands, then took both Julie and Nancy firmly by their elbows and said, "Come on. I'll drive."

21

"Why is it taking so long?" Julie paced the floor of the emergency room waiting area like a caged cat.

"I'm sure the doctors have to check him over completely," her mother said in an attempt to calm her down.

Even Luke's mother hadn't been allowed behind the doors to the room where Luke was being examined. She sat tight-lipped on the edge of a chair, clutching her hands nervously in her lap.

"Don't they know we're worried? Don't they know how hard it is to wait and wait?" Julie continued to pace. Her hands felt clammy and cold and her heart raced. "I wish Daddy were here."

"You know he'll be here as soon as he can get away from the game."

"That stupid game is the cause of all this," Julie cried.

Solena, who'd insisted on coming to offer Julie whatever support she could, said nothing and watched Julie pace.

A doctor emerged from behind the treatment room doors. "Are you with Luke Muldenhower?"

"I want to see my son." Nancy hurried to the doctor's side. "What's wrong with him? How is he?"

"He has a concussion," the doctor said. "He's alert, but extremely fatigued, and we want to hold him overnight for observation and keep a check on his vital signs. He's being moved upstairs to a room. Dr. Portage has been notified and will be here soon to check on your son."

Julie remembered the doctor who'd first treated Luke for the infection that had become Hodgkin's. At least he was familiar with Luke, and she was glad that Luke would be with a doctor he knew. "Where's his room?" she asked.

When they were allowed to see Luke, it was all Julie could do to hold back until after his mother had fussed over him. When it was Julie's turn, she put her arms around him and buried her face in his neck. "Oh, Luke, I've been so scared."

"I got hit, and then I got dizzy and fell in the locker room. I don't remember much, except that I was playing lousy."

Julie thought he looked pale, and in spite of the coolness of the room, he was perspiring. "Just so long as you're all right."

"We're going to lose the game because of me."

"Forget the game. It doesn't matter now."

"It matters to me."

They stayed with him until her father arrived. He barreled into the room and tore to Luke's bedside. Julie saw worry lines etched in his brow. "Got here as soon as I could. How're you doing, son?"

"Did we lose?" was all Luke wanted to know.

"Hey, you win some, you lose some. That's the way the game goes."

"So we lost." Luke turned his head toward the wall.

"Don't worry about it. We'll meet them again in the district playoffs and we'll kick butt."

Luke didn't seem mollified. "And how about the scouts? I guess they saw me play the worst game of my career."

"One game won't make or break your future, Luke. They'll be back."

"They'll say I blew it when it mattered, when I was under pressure."

"No they won't. Stop stewing about it. Get some rest, and as soon as the doctors say you can go back to playing, you will. You might miss one game at the most."

"I'll miss more than that," Luke said enigmatically. His dark eyes looked so unbearably sad that Julie felt cold fingers of fear squeeze her heart.

"Not because of a little bump on the head," Bud Ellis said. "Wait and see."

"Sure," Luke answered. "Whatever you say, Coach."

"Something's come up in Luke's blood work," Dr. Portage told Luke's mother the following day when she and Julie had come to visit Luke. He'd caught them just as they were about to go into Luke's room.

"What do you mean?"

"I'm having his radiologist look over some

X rays and test results, and I've ordered a bone marrow aspiration."

Julie felt sick to her stomach, as if someone had punched her. She heard Nancy say, "But he just had that battery of tests at St. Paul's in Chicago last month."

"No he didn't." Dr. Portage closed the chart he'd been holding and looked at Luke's mother gravely. "I called and asked for some of his records to be sent over. His last checkup at St. Paul's was in June."

Julie reeled at the news. That was before she and Luke had gone to Los Angeles. "But he said he'd been checked," she blurted. "He told me he'd gone by train and gotten his checkup."

"Well, he didn't," Dr. Portage said. "According to their records, he never went."

"Why did you lie to me, Luke?"

Julie watched Luke's face as his mother asked her question. He looked ashamed and pale. Ghostly pale. "I rescheduled my appointment, that's all. I was feeling good and so I figured I could postpone it for a while. I would have gone as soon as football season was over."

"Football season! Since when is football more important than your health?"

He looked helplessly at Julie, who struggled to hold back tears. "Everybody was expecting so much from me. I—I didn't want to let them down."

"Who would you have let down? Everybody knew you'd been sick. Nobody held you accountable."

"Mom, please, I'm not up to fighting about this. I feel awful right now."

Nancy's expression didn't soften, but before she could speak, Dr. Portage called her out of the room and Julie found herself alone with Luke. She crossed her arms and dabbed at her eyes. "I would have skipped my SATs and gone with you, if you'd asked," she told him. "Why didn't you ask me?"

"I told you, I would have gone later."

"Did my dad put pressure on you? Because if he did—"

"Julie, stop it. Everybody put pressure on me! Don't you understand?"

"*I* didn't pressure you. I only want you to play football because it means so much to *you.*"

Luke pulled himself up and hoisted his legs over the side of the bed, grunting in discomfort. He took a few deep breaths and stared at Julie, his dark eyes made darker by the paleness of his skin. He looked miserable. "It's true you never pressured me to play ball, but you put plenty of pressure on me to be well."

"How? When? I never did."

"You tell me all the time, 'Now that you're over cancer,' and, 'You're fine . . . time to get on with your life.' "

Stricken by his words, stunned by his accusation, Julie began to recall all the times she'd said such things. "But I was only trying to be positive. I was only trying to encourage you."

"Don't you think I want to be well, Julie? Don't you think I want to be rid of this and be normal? And play ball? And marry you? Don't you think if being positive would make me well, I would be well?"

Tears spilled down her cheeks as his words fell like blows. "But the tests—"

"I had one good checkup after my radiation treatments. Then I had the best summer of my life, with you, and then I had to face going back for more testing and maybe hearing that I was sick again. And everybody wanted me to be well so much. And *I* wanted it so much." He hung his head and took deep breaths before continuing. "'So it was easy to put off going for the testing. Maybe I figured what I didn't know wouldn't hurt me."

She ached for him, for herself. "Oh, Luke . . ."

"I told myself there'd be time to get check-ups after the season was over. After the team went to the state finals. I wanted that so bad, Julie. So, I kept playing, kept ignoring what was happening, even when the symptoms started coming back."

"You've been sick?"

He shrugged, refused to meet her gaze. "First it was the fatigue. Then the night sweats. I washed my sheets so Mom wouldn't know. I knew I was in trouble, but I kept pushing myself. I didn't want to let anybody down. I didn't want to find out the truth."

"That you're out of remission," she finished flatly. She felt as if someone had pulled a plug on her emotions and drained them all away.

"Yes."

"Do you know it for sure?"

He looked up and held her blue eyes with the dark pull of his own. "I know how I feel, Julie; I've been here before. And in ER, once they read my chart and saw that I'd been treated for Hodgkin's, they wanted to do a bone marrow. That's not a routine test for a head injury, you know."

She looked at her hands, at the promise ring that now seemed to mock her, to ridicule all it had stood for between her and Luke. "I'm sorry if I caused you any harm by insisting that you be well. I didn't mean to make you skip your testing."

For the first time since they'd been talking, Luke reached out and touched Julie. He smoothed her hair and ran his fingers tenderly along her cheek. "I'm not blaming you. I would never blame you. It was my choice. Coach always taught us to take responsibility." He offered a humorless chuckle. "No, I knew the chance I was taking; I knew the consequences. All testing would have done was confirm what I already knew."

Fresh tears spilled from Julie's eyes, and slowly Luke took her in his arms, where she sobbed, soaking his hospital shirt. "I love you so much," she managed between sobs.

"Loving you was all I had to hang on to sometimes. When I'd wake up at night, sweaty and nauseous, I'd remember L.A. and that church, and all the fun. It got me through."

Julie didn't know how long she had been clinging to him, but when Nancy and Dr. Portage returned to the room, she was still in Luke's arms. She pulled away reluctantly.

"Luke, we need to talk," Dr. Portage said.

The expression on Nancy's face told Julie what he was going to say before he spoke.

"There are cancer cells in your bone marrow," he said.

Luke's emotion could be seen only in a tightening along his jawline. "So where do I go from here?"

"Back to St. Paul's. They'll start looking for a compatible donor via computer in the national marrow registry. Unfortunately, the task is complicated because you have a rare blood type."

Luke didn't flinch. "Is that it?"

"They'll put you back onto chemo maintenance to inhibit the spread as much as possible until a donor's found."

"So, I guess this means that I'll be out for the rest of the season."

Luke's attempt at humor brought a thin smile to the doctor's lips. "Shall I write a note to your coach excusing you from play?"

"How about if you write one to God instead? Tell him to find me a donor." Luke pulled Julie closer to him. "Tell him I don't want to die."

22

Luke went back to St. Paul's long enough to have his chemo device implanted and his dose regulated. Upon returning home, he doggedly started school again, and his baseball hat once more became a familiar sight in the halls and classrooms.

News of his need for a bone marrow donor made the front page in the local paper and was picked up by the Associated Press national news service. He got calls, offers of money, requests for TV interviews—everything except a compatible donor. He asked for nothing, preferring to stay out of the limelight. By fielding calls and running interference, Coach Ellis saw to it that Luke and his mother weren't hounded.

At school, Frank rallied the football team, as well as the student body, and he and Solena initiated a bone marrow testing day. A doctor and three nurses came from St. Paul's with syringes and vials for blood samples, along with permission slips. Most of the students lined up after school to have their blood tested for a possible match.

Coach Ellis was first in line. Julie was second. It touched her, seeing the support and caring Luke inspired in their classmates. The paper covered that event also, but she couldn't bring herself to read the stories. They left her sad and depressed. And scared. For she knew that a bone marrow transplant was Luke's only hope for survival; he was getting sicker and balder and more gaunt from the chemo and the relentless advance of his cancer, and time, Julie knew, was running out for him. A donor had to be found—and found soon.

As October faded into November, Luke was able to attend school less and less. On the days he did come, Frank picked him up and Julie drove him home. Yet he rarely wanted to go home until they visited the new stadium, which was now almost fully constructed. Even on cold, blustery days, he insisted on going. Julie would take his hand and they'd slowly climb the new bleachers, sit, and gaze down at the field.

"I sure wish I could play football again," Luke said wistfully one November afternoon.

"If those doctors find a donor in time, you will," Julie answered.

"Don't you ever give up?"

"No. And neither should you."

He entwined his fingers with hers. "When you're up against a superior enemy, sometimes it's okay to bow out gracefully," he said quietly.

She whirled to face him. "I hate it when you talk so negatively. A donor *will* be found. And you *will* go to college and play football."

"Come on," he chided. "I don't like arguing with you." He managed one of his endearing grins. "I'm a lover, not a fighter. Remember?"

She returned her gaze to the barren, muddy field, where large clumps of dirt were riddled with bulldozer tracks. It looked brown and ugly, making it hard for her to imagine the field flat and thick with a carpet of grass. "Yes you are too a fighter. I've seen you fight to win in many a football game. And to me, your life is much more worth fighting for than any game."

"I *am* fighting for my life, Julie. I fight for it every day."

"But you talk about losing the fight, and that really scares me."

"I can't win every game I play."

"It's being on the chemo, Luke. It's getting you discouraged. Once you're off it, you'll feel better about everything."

"I promise: I won't give up." He toyed with a strand of her long hair.

Thoroughly depressed, Julie changed the subject. "Our last home game's in two weeks. Will you come? Dad wants you to."

"I'm coming," he said. "I started the season with the team, and I want to finish with them."

Without Luke, the Warriors had lost their heart to win and had quickly slipped from their number one ranking as what had been their most brilliant season turned to dust.

On the night of the game, Julie and her family picked up Luke and his mother in a specially equipped van. Too weak to walk, Luke had been given a wheelchair. "Are you sure you're up to coming?" Coach asked.

Luke settled his baseball cap and told him, "Yes. I want to go." Luke's clothes hung on him. His once-powerful physique had melted away and his body had turned skeletal as the war against cancer raged within him. Julie re-

minded herself that he'd regained his form after his first bout with chemo was complete
and that she should have every hope it would
happen again.

They drove in silence to the game and, once
there, Coach Ellis positioned Luke on the
field, along the sidelines, at the end of the
Warriors' bench. When the team filed onto
the field, each player stepped in front of
Luke's wheelchair, removed his helmet, and
shook Luke's hand. Julie watched from the
stands, a lump in her throat, as Luke gave
every player a high five, a smile, a few words.

And at halftime, she watched her father
push Luke's wheelchair out to the middle of
the field while the announcer recited his football exploits and the bright field lights glinted
off the polished metal of his chair. Cameras
flashed as the mayor and superintendent of
schools stood with him. The mayor made a
brief speech about how much honor Luke had
brought to Waterton with his talent. He gave
Luke a plaque and then announced, "In your
honor, the new high school stadium will be
called 'Luke Muldenhower Stadium,' and will
be formally dedicated as such come spring."

Julie heard Luke's mother gasp when the
announcement was made and felt Nancy reach

for her hand. Tears were all but blinding Julie, but she held her head high, feeling more pride for Luke than ever. His talent might have brought him fame, but his courage in the face of cancer had brought him honor.

Spring. Julie wondered if Luke would still be waiting for a donor or if his bone marrow transplant would be history by then. *Spring.* The season of flowers and fresh green grass seemed so far away. They still had the long, harsh Indiana winter to endure. She bowed her head and whispered fervently, "Hurry up, spring."

"Julie, we need to talk." Patricia Ellis came into Julie's room, closing the door behind her.

Julie didn't mind the interruption. She'd tried valiantly all evening to study for her upcoming finals, but had been unable to concentrate. She turned down the Christmas music playing from the radio on her desk. "What's up?"

"What are you doing about your acceptances to Tulane and Ohio State?"

"What do you mean? I'm not doing anything about them."

Her mother looked confused. "You've got

to choose one of them. After all, you're graduating in six months and—"

"Mother!" Julie stood. "What are you thinking? I can't go off and leave Luke. What if he gets his donor marrow? I need to be here for him."

"Julie, are you serious? Are you telling me you're not going off to college just because Luke isn't?"

"Of course I'm serious. I wouldn't dream of leaving Luke."

A worried frown creased her mother's brow. "You can't put the rest of your life on hold for Luke's sake. I'm sure if you ask him, he'd want you to go ahead with your plans."

"My plans are to stay with Luke until he's well. If that means postponing college for a year, then that's what I'll do."

Her mother didn't back down, but her expression grew pensive. Haltingly, she said, "Luke's gravely ill, Julie. What if . . . what if a donor can't be found?"

"I think one will be found."

"But honey, what if—"

"Stop it!" Julie stamped her foot. "I won't hear all this horrible talk. Luke's *got* to get well again. I can't even think about going through the rest of my life without him. I wouldn't even *want* to!" She held out her hand. "Remember this ring? It's more than just a souvenir from my summer vacation. It's a 'promise ring.' Luke gave it to me. It's his promise that someday we'll be married."

Her mother looked dumbstruck and Julie felt a thrill of triumphant satisfaction. "I had no idea the two of you were that serious," Patricia Ellis said slowly.

"Well, we are. And as long as I can be here for Luke, I will be." Julie was amazed that she could have lived so long under the same roof with her mother and still feel so far apart from her. The woman didn't understand, and she never would.

"We need to talk more about this, Julie."

"No we don't. I've made up my mind. I'm not leaving Luke." Julie crossed her arms in stubborn defiance, all but daring her mother to argue with her.

She never got the chance. The phone on Julie's desk rang and when Julie grabbed the receiver, she heard Nancy's anguished voice say, "I just called an ambulance to come get Luke. He's bad off, Julie. Really bad. And I'm scared. Can you meet me at Waterton General right away?"

23

At the hospital, Julie and her mother learned that Luke was having difficulty breathing and that his mother had called the ambulance in a panic. "You did the correct thing," Dr. Portage assured her after he'd examined Luke.

"Will he be all right? Can I take him home?"

"He's still in respiratory distress, so I'm admitting him. I've put him on a respirator."

Nancy cried out and Julie felt wobbly on her feet.

"It's only temporary, simply a way to help him breathe more easily for a spell. I'm ordering X rays to find out why he's in trouble." As an afterthought, Dr. Portage added, "As long as he's on the respirator, he won't be able to talk, so I'll keep him sedated too."

Numb, still shaking from an adrenaline rush of fear, Julie sank slowly into a waiting room chair. Her mother said a few words to Nancy, then headed for the phone, saying, "I'm calling your father." Bud Ellis was at a meeting.

He arrived to join them in less than thirty minutes. "What now?" he asked.

As Luke's situation was explained to him, Julie watched his shoulders sag and heard him mutter, "Poor kid."

The lobby of the hospital had been decorated for Christmas, which was only two weeks away. A feeling of déjà vu slid over Julie: Luke had spent the previous Christmas in the hospital. She remembered the sense of determination they'd all felt about him getting well and the almost childlike naïveté with which they'd faced the future at that time.

"It's not going to go away, is it, Daddy?" she asked. "It's not ever going to leave Luke alone."

"It does seem relentless." Her father sighed and shook his head. "This makes no sense to me, Julie. Why should a kid like Luke go through this when he's got so much to live for? I've talked to him about it."

His admission surprised Julie—Luke had

never mentioned it to her. "We've talked too, but we never came up with any answers."

"There aren't any. It's just . . . *life*. But going through something like this sure shows what a person's made of, and in my book, no one is made of finer stuff than Luke."

Julie saw a film of tears swimming in her father's eyes, and the sight rattled her. In all the years she'd lived with him, she'd never seen her father cry.

He cleared his throat. "He's like a son to me."

"Don't give up on him yet. He's still got plenty of fight left in him."

And sure enough, by the next day Luke was breathing easier and had been taken off the respirator. He looked very pale, but he gave Julie a smile and a thumbs-up when she came into his room. "We've got to stop meeting like this," he said in a hoarse whisper.

She'd been warned that the breathing tube they'd inserted in his throat would affect his voice. "Let's go back to L.A.," she said, taking hold of his hand.

"If only we could."

They were alone, but Julie didn't know how long the time would last. Nurses breezed in and out of the room regularly and his mother could pop in at any time. An idea had been forming in her mind for days, and suddenly this seemed like the perfect time to present it. She studied the ring on her finger. "Did you mean what you asked me in L.A.?"

"About marrying you?" His gaze also fell on the silver ring. "I meant it." A shadow of doubt crossed his face. "Are you having second thoughts? Do you want to give the ring back?"

"No way." She seized both his hands and pressed them against her breasts. "Why should we wait to get married, Luke? Why, when it's what both of us want?"

"What do you mean?"

"Let's get married now. It doesn't have to be a fancy ceremony . . . and we can do it here in the hospital if we have to. Your mother, my parents, Solena and Frank, Steve and Diedra—if we can get them here quickly. These are the only people who matter in our lives, so they're the only ones we should invite."

She talked rapidly, hardly breaking for a breath, spilling her long-pent-up emotions. "I don't need a fancy dress . . . why, the one I bought for the Christmas dance last year will do nicely. Oh, I know it's not white, but who cares? You and I know we've never messed around. And the hospital is all fixed up for Christmas, so the ceremony could be really festive. Besides, don't you think a Christmas wedding would be fun? Every anniversary we'd have *two* reasons to celebrate.

"We don't have to have a reception or any-thing, either. Heck, some cheese and crackers is fine with me. Your mom could whip up one of her fancy cheese dips and my mom could do some kind of cake. Not a wedding cake." She made a face. "I've always thought the ic-ing on those things was too sickly sweet. And once you're out of the hospital we could take a little honeymoon to—oh, anyplace—I don't care—"

Luke freed one hand from her embrace and placed his fingertips against her lips to silence her. "Julie, stop."

She stopped, and the silence in the room was deafening.

"I can't marry you now."

She felt a sinking sensation. "Why? I know you love me, and I love you. What else mat-ters?"

His gaze roamed her face as if absorbing it. "I love you all right. And because I love you, I can't make you a bride and a widow in the same month."

"But the doctors are going to fix you up and you'll go home and wait for a donor. You can't give up, Luke. You can't."

He looked at her so tenderly that she almost started crying. "I know why I'm having trouble breathing, Julie."

She couldn't force herself to ask why. Because not knowing served as a protective shield, and so long as she didn't know, she could hold off the finality of what was happening to him.

"I have a tumor in my lung, Julie." He touched his chest. "And the chemo isn't stopping it from growing. They want to cut it out."

"Operate?" She said the word as if it were alien.

"It's located here"—he pressed his palm against the left side of his chest—"very near my heart. It's compressing my heart and taking over my lung. Surgery's my best hope."

"When?" She felt icy cold and stiff, and forming words took great difficulty.

"Day after tomorrow."

Too soon! her mind cried, but her voice said, "But it will make you better, won't it?"

"They think so."

"Will you do it?"

"I talked it over with Mom and my doctors, and it's what I want to do."

She had fears and doubts. She had a host of reasons why he shouldn't, but she saw his steely look of determination and knew he would do what he wanted and that nothing she could say could dissuade him. Not that she was sure she should try. If surgery offered hope and made him more comfortable during his wait for a marrow donor, perhaps it was worth doing. "I'll be here for you," she said.

He smiled. "The first thing I want to see when I get out of recovery is your face." He rested his palm on her cheek. "And when I close my eyes on the operating table, the thing I'll see inside my mind will be your face."

Tears swam in her eyes. "After this operation is over, after you get your strength back, promise me you'll reconsider marrying me right away."

"We'll talk about it after the surgery." He smoothed his thumb across her lips. "Of course, if we do get married soon, your mother will kill us both and the surgery will have been for nothing."

She gave a short laugh. "I don't care what

my mother thinks. I want to be with you, Luke, for the rest of my life."

His gaze caressed her face. "That suits me fine."

The day before Luke's surgery, Steve and Diedra flew into Chicago, rented a car, and drove over to Waterton, lifting Julie's spirits immensely. When they walked into Luke's room, Steve held up his hand and said, "Now don't panic, nephew. We're only here because word got around that you were driving the doctors and your mother nuts. Besides, we were sick of sushi—that's fish you eat *raw*, in case you don't know it—and your mother promised us a good home-cooked meal."

Luke was all smiles. "You came all this way to see me?"

"You and Julie," Diedra said. Julie had seen the expression of shock that crossed Diedra's face when she'd first seen Luke and how she'd quickly suppressed it. Diedra gave him a hug. "We've missed you two."

"Did you bring pictures from your honeymoon?" Julie asked.

"An albumful," Diedra said.

They spent the afternoon looking through the photos and talking, and later, when Julie and Diedra went down to the snack bar for ice cream and Steve stayed behind with Luke, Julie told Diedra that she and Luke might marry as soon as he recovered from his surgery. "Would you stay for the wedding?" she asked.

"Of course we would." Diedra tipped her head thoughtfully. "After you're married, where will you live?"

"With his mother, I guess. She's a lot more sympathetic about me and Luke than mine. And once he's gotten his new bone marrow, he can finish high school. Then, I'm sure some coach will want him to play college ball. Oh, maybe it won't be a big, well-known college, but a smaller one willing to invest in him."

"So he thinks he can still play football?"

"Absolutely. Once his donor marrow starts working, he'll be cured and go on with his life."

"You're a brave girl, Julie. Not every girl your age would take on such a marriage and its possible problems."

Julie shrugged. "I love him." She swirled the spoon through the half-melted remains of her ice cream. "I wish tomorrow was over. His surgery scares me."

"He's young, and that's in his favor. Plus

the doctors wouldn't operate if they didn't think it would help."

They returned to the room, where Luke's mother had joined him and Steve. Luke looked drowsy. "They gave him medication, so he'll sleep soundly tonight," Nancy said. "But we have to leave now."

Luke reached out for Julie. His eyelids looked heavy and his speech was slurred when he said, "The doctor said I could see you in the morning before I go into surgery. Please see me before they put me to sleep?"

"I'll come early."

"I love you."

She bent and kissed him. "I love you too."

24

Julie couldn't sleep that night, and headed for the hospital at six in the morning even though Luke wasn't scheduled to go into the OR until nine. She arrived at his room just as a nurse was giving him pre-op medication to relax him. One arm was hooked to an IV, but he held Julie tightly with his free arm when she bent over his bed. Although he smelled of medicine, he felt warm, and she longed to climb into bed with him and hold him.

"The others will be here soon," Julie said. "Everyone wants to see you before you go into surgery."

"You look beautiful," he said.

She knew how she really looked—dark circles smudged her under-eye area and she hadn't bothered to put on any makeup except for a little lip gloss. "I'll look better when you come down from recovery."

"Julie, I want to tell you some things before they operate."

"What things?"

"I want you to know I'm okay about this and I want you to be okay about it. No matter what the outcome is."

It felt as if a hand had reached into her chest and clutched her heart. "The outcome is that you'll be all right," she said stubbornly.

"I also want you to know I've done a lot of thinking about some of the things we talked about in L.A. You know, about the hereafter and all. I've been reading up on it in all my spare time." He grinned. "Heaven's a real place, Julie—a beautiful place—and if I can't wait for you at the end of an aisle on our wedding day, I'll wait for you in heaven."

"Luke, you're scaring me—"

"Please, let me finish. I don't want to scare you. I only want you to know that either way this surgery turns out, I'll be fine. I—I just want you to be fine."

"I can't think about losing you. Don't make me."

"You're the best part of my life and I will always love you."

Tears had sprung to her eyes. Behind her, she heard others come into the room, and she knew that his mother, her parents, and Steve and Diedra wanted to be with him too. She felt panicked, afraid of letting go of his hand. "I'll see you in a few hours," she said through gritted teeth.

His eyelids drooped from the sedation, but still he held on to her. "If it's possible to send a message from heaven," he whispered, "I'll get one to you."

She choked back a sob and broke her hold, then stepped aside so that the others could surround his bed. Later, in the hallway, when he was wheeled out of his room for the elevator ride down to the surgical floor, he told the orderlies to hold up. They waited while he looked from face to face of the people who loved him, reminding Julie of a man memorizing a map so that he wouldn't get lost in the dark. Finally, he grinned, handed Julie a folded piece of paper, then gave everyone his thumbs-up signal.

Julie watched as he was wheeled away, listened to the clack-clack of the wheels of his bed and the swish of the elevator doors as they closed behind him. Cut off from him, she shuddered.

"Let's go down to the surgical waiting room," her father said, gently taking her arm.

They trooped down to the area where family and friends waited for news from various operating rooms. A telephone linking the surgical floor with the waiting room would occasionally ring and tell people that their loved one had been taken to recovery and the surgeon would be down to talk to them soon. In the waiting room, Solena and Frank were already camped out on sofas. Julie tried to join them, but found it impossible to sit still.

As the hours dragged by, the phone rang several times, always for others. Every time it rang, Julie jumped. She felt taut and edgy. Around one o'clock, her father tried to get her to eat something, but she refused. She stared down at the floor, listening to the thump of her heart, the whispers of those around her.

Suddenly the waiting room door opened and she looked up to see Luke's surgeon standing in front of their group. Surprised, she glanced at the phone, wondering why she hadn't heard it ring. The doctor removed his green head covering. Julie allowed her eyes to travel the length of him and saw flecks of blood on the green paper coverings of his shoes. *Luke's blood,* she knew instinctively.

"The tumor was far more entrenched than we ever imagined," the surgeon began. "It was totally ingrown to the side of his heart."

Julie heard Nancy begin to sob.

"I'm sorry," the doctor said. "We did everything we could."

Somehow, through it all, Julie didn't lose her composure. She heard questions and answers, but the words didn't make sense. She was beyond caring what was said anyway. Slowly, she stood and removed the folded piece of paper Luke had given her only hours before. She'd deliberately not opened it, saving it for this time when she knew she would need contact with him most.

"What's in the note?" she heard a tearful Solena ask.

Numbly, Julie unfolded the paper. On it, Luke had drawn a single, perfect flower.

The day of Luke's funeral, snow blanketed the ground. Cold white drifts covered cars and fences and the sky was a dull shade of leaden gray. To Julie, riding in the funeral home's limo to the cemetery, the whole world looked black and white. Void of color.

The high school closed for the day and almost the whole city turned out to bury their hometown hero. On Main Street, traffic lights blinked yellow and a police escort led the long, lonely precession to Luke's final resting place. Julie wore black, including a black mantilla over her long blond hair. She sat in the car sandwiched between Nancy and Steve. In the limo's other long seat were Diedra and her parents. The trip seemed slow, endless.

"I never thought I'd have to do this again," Nancy said tonelessly, and Julie knew she was remembering her husband's funeral so many years before. Luke's mother stared through the window. "Who will ride with me when it's my turn?"

No one answered, and Julie tightened her hold on the edge of the car seat. Inside, she felt as dead as the world outside the car window seemed. As empty as the stretches of snow between the headstones of the cemetery.

At the burial site, hundreds had gathered, all dressed in shades of black and gray. The car stopped, and attendants helped Julie and the others make the walk to the tarpaulin-covered pit where Luke's casket would be placed. Because the ground was frozen, a special machine had been used to dig the hole. Julie could still see its tracks in the packed snow. She heard the crunch of snow beneath her boots, felt the sting of frigid air on her face.

Julie watched as Frank led the pallbearers—all members of the football team and wearing black armbands—toward them. A mantle of flowers, each one as white as the snow, cascaded down the sides of the steel-gray casket. The petals of the flowers were frozen, singed by ice, brittle and stiff. Unbidden, Luke's long-ago words came to her. *"Someday, I'll dress you in flowers,"* he had said. Instead, it was he who had been wrapped in blossoms.

She hardly heard the brief ceremony. She felt isolated and cut off from reality, not caring what was said. No words could make a difference. Luke was gone and nothing could bring him back. Her movements were mechanical, like an elaborate puppet's. She went through the motions, but in her heart, she was hollow and empty. And cold. So very cold.

Once the ceremony was over, Julie's parents urged Nancy to receive friends at their home because it was so much more spacious. People arrived steadily all day, bringing food and flowers and small gifts. Nancy, ever gracious and kind, accepted every expression of grief over the loss of her son. But Julie felt removed from the ritual, abhorring it. Still, she knew it meant a great deal to Luke's mother, so she tolerated it.

Late in the afternoon, as it grew dark and colder, Diedra found Julie in the backyard, huddled against a leafless and barren oak tree. "Steve and I are leaving for the airport," she said gently. "We have to go home to L.A."

"Good-bye," Julie told her. How far away and long ago L.A. seemed.

"You should come in the house, Julie. It's cold and you'll get sick."

"So what?"

Diedra smoothed Julie's hair, flecked with snow from the blackened branches of the tree. "Please come visit us this summer. Will you promise me you'll come?"

Julie traced her fingers along the roughened bark of the old tree trunk. "See our initials? Luke carved them for us when he was twelve." The letters looked scarred and shrunken by the cold. She brushed them lightly with gloved fingers.

"You're breaking my heart, Julie. Please tell me you're going to be all right."

"Luke used to bring me flowers."

Steve called to Diedra from the porch.

"I've got to go, honey." She hugged Julie,

who stood motionless. "Don't forget—we're expecting to see you this summer."

Julie didn't answer; she only brushed her fingertips over the worn initials as Diedra left.

Later, when her house had emptied and her father was taking Nancy home, Julie wearily climbed the stairs to her room. She stripped, dropping her clothes in a heap onto her floor, pulled on a flannel nightshirt, and climbed into her bed.

After knocking lightly, her mother opened the door and entered the room. The light flooding in from the hallway blinded Julie, and she turned away from its glare. "Julie . . ." Her mother halted beside her bed. "Honey . . . if there's anything you want . . ."

"I want Luke," she said without emotion.

"Honey . . . please . . . I'm sorry . . . so sorry . . ."

"Good night," Julie said, then curled into a tight ball and pulled the covers over her head. Minutes later, she heard her mother leave the room. "Luke," she whispered into the darkness. "Why have you left me all alone?"

25

"Julie, your mother and I are very concerned about you." Bud Ellis sat on the side of Julie's bed, looking helpless, his big hands folded in his lap.

"I'm fine, Dad."

"You're *not* fine," Julie's mother interjected. "You don't eat, you don't go to school, you don't see your friends. Julie, you've lain in that bed for over a month. You've lost so much weight we hardly recognize you. Please, honey, snap out of it."

Julie peered dully up at her parents. Why didn't they leave her alone? Food had lost its taste and appeal. And she'd tried to go back to school after Luke's funeral, but she couldn't concentrate and she couldn't keep up in her classes. All she wanted to do was sleep. Because when she was asleep, she could forget how much she hurt. "I'll try to get up later," she said in an effort to placate her parents. "Right now, I'm too tired."

She saw her father glance up at her mother. He sighed and touched her shoulder through her bedcovers. "I miss him too, Julie. Every day, I think about him. But what you're doing to yourself isn't right. You can't curl up and die too."

Curl up and die. The idea didn't sound so bad to her. Without Luke, she certainly couldn't think about *living.*

"Why don't you get up, get dressed, and come into school with me," her father said.

"I'll make you late." Her bedside clock read eight-thirty. Usually, he was gone by seven-thirty.

"Who cares? I'm the coach, remember? Besides, first period is my free period this semester. Come on—drive in with me."

"Not today. You and Mom go on without me. I'll rest and maybe when you get home this afternoon, I'll feel better."

Her father rose, but her mother kicked off her shoes. "If you're staying home again, I will too."

Julie was mildly surprised. Her mother rarely missed work, and now that second semester had begun, more and more kids would be seeking her services at the high school for help with college applications. "You don't have to stay home. I'm just going to stay in bed today." Her thoughts grew fuzzy.

Julie heard her parents whispering at her door. Then her father left and her mother came back to her bedside. "Solena called last night. She wants to come over after school."

"I don't think I'm up to visitors. Tell her I'll call her later."

"Julie, you've been putting her off for days. She's your best friend and she calls every day asking about you."

Julie felt tears brim in her eyes. All this conversation was confusing her, upsetting her. She sniffed and turned over to face the wall. "Please, not today. I—I just don't want to have to see anybody today."

Minutes later, she heard her mother softly close the bedroom door, and soon afterward, Julie fell into the welcoming arms of a deep, dark, dreamless sleep.

Afternoon sunlight streamed through Julie's bedroom window, awakening her. Someone had pulled up her window shade, and the winter sun cut a path across her bed and pillow.

She buried her face under her covers, but the light was relentless. Who had done such a thing? she wondered.

She sighed and realized that the only way to shut out the sun was to get up and pull down the shade, but her arms and legs felt almost too heavy with exhaustion to move. She forced herself upright, staggered to the window, leaned over her desk, and fumbled at the cord for the shade.

From the kitchen below she heard her mother moving around and smelled the aroma of simmering chicken soup. Normally, the aroma would make her mouth water, but today it made her feel nauseous. She yanked down the shade and returned to her bed, then buried herself under the covers until she heard her mother come into her room.

"How about supper in bed?" her mother asked cheerfully, setting down a tray laden with soup, crackers, milk, and green Jell-O. When Julie was a small child, green gelatin had been her favorite.

"I'm not hungry."

Her mother sat on the bed and pulled Julie's covers from off her head. "Look at me, Julie."

Julie struggled to focus.

"This has got to stop. Your father and I can't bear to see you wasting away like this."

"Please, Mom, don't—"

"No. You listen! I've talked with our doctor, and he says that the way you've been grieving is cause for alarm. When I told him how much weight you've lost, he said it might be necessary not only to get you counseling, but to hospitalize you and put you on an IV."

Julie wanted to be angry, but she didn't have the energy for it.

"So sit up and eat or I will drive you to the hospital personally and check you in."

Wearily, Julie obeyed. "I'm up, but I still don't want to eat."

"You have a visitor," her mother announced without preamble.

"Tell Solena to come back tomorrow."

"It isn't Solena."

The bedroom door inched open, and Nancy peeked into the room. "Hi, Julie. Can I come in?"

Julie hadn't seen her since the funeral, and seeing her now caused fresh pain to stab at her heart. Still, although Nancy looked tired and she'd lost weight, she also looked serene. "Sure. Come in."

Pat Ellis moved so that Nancy could take her place on the bed. "Your mother tells me you're not doing so good."

Feeling betrayed, Julie glared at her mother. "I'm tired, that's all."

"You're depressed," Nancy corrected. "I've been depressed too, but not like you." She placed her hands on Julie's. "I lost my only son, Julie. I'll never get over the pain. But I will get on with my life."

"What do you mean?"

"I'm moving out to L.A. Steve's offered me a job. He and Diedra are starting a small production company and they need an office manager. Luke talked to him before the surgery and asked Steve to take care of me." A wistful smile turned up the corners of her mouth. "Just like Luke—to be worried about me. Anyway, I'm going where there are no memories to haunt me every day."

The news jolted Julie. Her last link with Luke was being broken. "When will you go?"

"Just as soon as my house sells."

Tears filled Julie's eyes. "I'll miss you."

"We've been through a lot together through the years. Frankly, I've grown to love you like a daughter. That's why it hurts me to see you harming yourself this way."

Julie dropped her gaze, unable to speak around the lump in her throat.

"Luke wouldn't have wanted you to do this to yourself, you know. He wanted the best for you. He wanted you to be happy."

"How can I be happy without him?"

"I don't know . . . all I know is that someday, you will be. You'll be happy"—she paused—"and you'll fall in love again."

Julie shook her head adamantly. "I'll never love anybody the way I loved Luke. I won't risk being hurt again."

"Love is always a risk. Just like Luke's surgery." Nancy smoothed Julie's tangled hair. "Just before he went back to the hospital, the bone marrow donor program had found him a match."

Julie gasped. "They did? Why didn't he tell me? Why didn't he get the transplant?"

"Because even if the transplant had worked, the tumor wasn't going away. He made the decision to risk the surgery and do the transplant afterward."

"Are you saying that he knew he might not live through the operation from the start?"

"Yes."

"But why?" The information tortured her.

"Because in his mind, the benefit out-weighed the risks. With the tumor gone, the bone marrow transplant had a better chance of working."

"But if he'd had the transplant first, maybe he'd still be alive. He took the risk for nothing."

Nancy shook her head. "He told me that life is full of risks and that if a person doesn't take them, life is very shallow. And he said to me, 'Mom, dead is dead.' Luke hated dying by degrees. He told me that he'd rather have dying over with all at once than have it happen bit by bit."

Julie felt no consolation. "What am I going to do without him?"

"You're going to live your life. You're going to honor him by doing the things you would have done if he'd never gotten sick and died."

"How can I?"

"The same as all of us—one day at a time." Nancy put her arms around Julie and held her for a long time. Finally, she pulled away, saying, "I'll let you know when my house sells. Please come see me before I move. And once I settle in L.A., I want you to visit me there. Please take care of yourself, Julie."

When she was gone, Julie flopped wearily back against her pillow, going over the meaning of Nancy's words in her mind. *Luke had known he would probably die, but he had the surgery anyway.* She saw his face, his thumbs-up, his broad, sunny smile as he disappeared behind the OR doors.

Her mother stepped forward, holding the food tray. She set it on Julie's lap and picked up the bowl of soup, stirring it, until the aroma and warmth filled the air. "Listen to Nancy, Julie. She knows what she's saying. Life is for the living."

Julie felt an unbearable weight of sadness press against her chest, but her mother looked so expectant, Julie reached for the soup spoon.

"No," her mother said softly. "Please, let me help you."

Their gazes locked, and Julie saw a tenderness in the depths of her mother's eyes that shook her. "All right," Julie whispered.

Then her mother smiled, ladled soup into the spoon, and held it to Julie's lips, feeding her slowly and expertly, as she hadn't done since Julie was a tiny child.

It took Julie another three weeks to regain her strength and begin putting on lost pounds.

She also began studying at home, attempting assignments, doing take-home tests. She began to talk to her friends again and decided to return to school the first of April.

Her return was bittersweet. Luke's presence haunted the halls, and sometimes she could swear she saw his baseball cap bobbing through the crowds as they moved between classes. But kids were genuinely glad to see her, stopping her, talking to her, sharing memories of Luke with her. Her mother helped her tremendously with makeup work and arranged special tutoring for the classes Julie was too far behind in to catch up with on her own. She structured a summer tutorial program, so that even though Julie wouldn't technically graduate with her class in June, she would at least be able to receive her diploma at the end of the summer.

One Saturday, Julie was reading on the back deck in a patch of sunlight, a blanket thrown over her lap, when her father rushed out the door. "Honey, quick! Come with me!"

Startled, she gawked at him. His eyes were glowing, his expression excited. "What's happening?"

"I can't tell you. I have to show you. Come on."

"Dad, I really don't want—"

He tugged her to her feet. "You have to come with me to the football stadium and see this with your own eyes. You're not going to believe it, Julie. But you have to see it."

26

Julie hadn't thought about the new football stadium in many months. And she didn't want to see it now, but her father was so excited, she couldn't refuse him. At the stadium, he screeched to a halt, leaped from the car, and hurried to open her door. "You need to get up high," he said, taking her hand. "Then you can see it better."

Julie climbed the cement bleachers obediently, forcing herself not to think about all the times she'd come to the stadium with Luke.

When they were about a third of the way up, Julie had to stop and catch her breath. "Sorry," she told her father. "I'm out of shape."

"No problem. This is high enough anyway. Look." He pointed down toward the field.

She turned and let her gaze follow his finger. A fine stubble of wild grass blanketed the rough, rutted field with green fuzz. But there was something else sprouting in the center of the field. Green stems, arranged in neat rows, were emerging from the caked earth. She squinted. "What's growing?"

"Tulips."

"Why would you plant tulips in the middle of your football field? You told me it had to be smoothed out and sodded."

"I didn't plant them."

Slowly, the truth dawned on her. "Luke?"

"I'm sure of it," her father said. "It'll take a couple of weeks until they're all up and blooming, but once they're finished, I think you'll see a pattern of some kind. Like a design he planned out."

She remembered Luke's words: *"If it's possible to send a message from heaven, I'll get one to you."* Tears blurred her eyes. "But how? When?"

"Tulips have to be planted by October, or November at the latest, before the ground freezes, so I figure that's when he must have done it."

"Right after he went back on chemo."

"Probably so."

She clapped her hand across her mouth to

stifle a sob. Her father pulled her into his arms. "Julie-girl, it's all right. Go ahead and cry. He meant this for you, honey. He did this even though he knew he might not be here to share it with you."

She imagined Luke arriving in the dark of night, digging holes in the hard ground, dropping each bulb into each hole, and covering it over so that no one could tell what he'd done. The bulbs had lain dormant beneath the snow all winter long until the gentle fingers of spring had awakened them. Like the thawing snow, she felt her grief begin to soften, her terrible pain begin to melt.

Every day afterward, Julie returned to the stadium, climbed the steps, and watched Luke's testimony of tulips bloom in a rainbow of spring colors—red, yellow, purple, hot pink. The stems stood tall and straight, one series arranged in a single line, another in a crudely shaped heart, the final one in the shape of the letter U. *I love you.* Just as Luke had carved on the oak tree in her backyard the summer before.

Late one afternoon, while she waited for her father down on the field, a bulldozer roared to life and rolled through double gates at one of the end zones. "No!" Julie cried, bolting toward the big yellow machine.

Suddenly, her father emerged from one of the stadium tunnels and parked his large body squarely in front of the dozer. "What do you think you're doing?" he yelled up at the driver.

"Got a work order, buddy," the driver shouted over the noise of the engine. "I need to level the field so the sod trucks can come in and get it planted tomorrow."

"Daddy, don't let him," Julie begged.

"Not yet," Bud Ellis told the dozer driver. "It's not ready to be leveled yet."

"But this work order—"

"I'm the football coach at this school, and I'll take responsibility for changing your order."

The driver looked doubtful. "I don't know . . ."

"Not today," Julie said boldly.

"Okay. So when?"

"When the tulips finish blooming."

"What?" The driver looked at her as if she were insane.

"You heard the lady," Bud Ellis said. "When the tulips are gone."

She left them arguing about it and walked out onto the field, where she knelt next to a row of colorful flowers and gently fingered the waxy petals.

In her mind's eye, she saw Luke's face, his playful grin, and she smiled back at him.

"So, you're still sending me flowers," she said to his image. "Do you think you can fix *everything* with flowers?"

In the hazy sunlight, his image nodded, gave her a thumbs-up, and faded away into the spring air.

Julie blinked, glanced around, and realized that she was standing by herself in the middle of a football field blooming with tulips. Luke was gone. But he was waiting for her some-where. Somewhere, on the other side of all her tomorrows.

I'll Be Seeing You

For Christy Brown,
a real winner

"He has made everything beautiful in its time."

(Ecclesiastes 3:11)

One

"Give it a rest, Reba!" Carley Mattea said. Only her friend Reba Conroy could get excited about a new patient admitted to their floor. "We're not Knoxville General's social committee," Carley added. She balanced on her crutches, flipped the gears on Reba's electric wheelchair, and guided it backward toward Carley's room. Her new friend was an incredible optimist. Carley couldn't understand it.

"I heard his name's Kyle Westin," Reba reported. "I asked a nurse and she said he's from Oak Ridge, like you. Maybe he even goes to the same high school. Wouldn't that be a fabulous coincidence? You come to the hospital but end up making friends with a cool boy."

"You're all the new friends I want to make while I'm here, Reba." Carley tried to smile sweetly. Reba was too much, talking about boys. A few days before, Carley had undergone surgery on her leg for a nasty break that had occurred the day after Christmas. An infection had landed her in the hospital on IV antibiotics. Carley wasn't so sick that she was confined to bed, but she'd been bored stiff. Then Reba had rolled into her room and started a conversation. Now it seemed as if they'd known each other forever.

"I like making new friends," Reba volunteered. "It's fun."

Carley had a totally different attitude about meeting new people. Actually, the only place she felt comfortable was in the hospital. People were used to kids with problems, so they didn't stare at her as much. Sure, a broken leg was a common enough thing to see, but her face—*that* was a different matter.

Carley propped her crutches against a

chair and struggled up onto her hospital bed, where she punched the TV remote control button. "Oak Ridge High School isn't so small that I wouldn't remember a guy named Kyle Westin, and I've never heard of him. Besides, I'm sure we'd never end up in the same crowd."

"Would you please turn that dumb thing off? We have strategy to discuss."

"Strategy?"

"Sure. Like how we can meet him . . . get to know him."

Carley rolled her eyes. "I don't want to meet him. He probably doesn't want to meet anyone either."

"He's just been admitted. Give him a day or so. He'll loosen up."

"From the back he looks perfectly normal," Carley said, turning up the volume with the remote control. "Believe me, Reba, normal guys aren't interested in girls like me."

The eighth floor of the giant hospital was reserved for adolescent patients with a variety of medical problems. With his face turned to the wall and his covers pulled up to his shoulders, there was no guessing what might be wrong with Kyle Westin.

Reba looked crestfallen, and Carley momentarily regretted dashing the fourteen-year-old girl's good spirits. *It's for her own good*, Carley told herself. Carley had learned early on that if she didn't set her expectations too high, she didn't get hurt. "Look, I didn't mean to rain on your parade. I'm sure Kyle will become one of the 'gang' once he realizes that he's a prisoner and there's nothing he can do about it." She leaned forward conspiratorially. "Unless, of course, he makes a rope out of his bedsheets and lowers himself out the window."

Reba giggled. "You're so funny."

"Sure, a real comedienne," Carley said without humor.

She liked Reba. The girl had been born with a type of spina bifida. She had a dwarflike appearance and used a wheelchair. But she had an effervescent personality and a sunny disposition. She had been hospitalized for corrective surgery to her abdominal area.

"Once Kyle gets to know you, Carley, I bet he'll like you."

"I told you, guys don't like girls who look like me." She almost used the word *freak*, but stopped herself.

"Maybe dumb, immature guys. My dad says that beauty is in the eye of the beholder."

"Reba, get a grip. In the years between twelve and twenty, guys don't think with their brains. Or see with their eyes. They see through the eyes of all their friends. And of their friends' friends."

Reba laughed. "Well, maybe Kyle will be different. Maybe he'll like you for who you are."

"Sure . . . and if cows could fly, we'd all be wearing football helmets."

Afternoon sunlight filtered through the large window of Carley's room, which looked out on the expressways of the large city. Flecks of snow clung to the outside windowsill, and although it was the second week in January, faint smudges of the words *Merry Christmas* could still be seen on the inside of the glass.

Reba fiddled with the controls on her chair. "You've got to stop putting yourself down, Carley. Sure, your face is messed up, but at least you're alive."

"That's what my mother tells me," Carley said dryly. "It didn't help when I was twelve. It doesn't help now."

A nurse stuck her head through the doorway. "There you are," she said to Reba. "We've been looking everywhere for you. It's time for afternoon medications. Come on back to your room."

Reba made a face. "Do I have to?"

"Yes, you have to." The nurse stepped into the room and tugged at the wheelchair. "You can visit Carley later. Your doctor wants you on bed rest before your surgery."

"Go on," Carley told Reba. "I'll come down to your room after they deliver dinner."

When she was alone, Carley switched off the TV. She elevated the head of the bed until she was sitting upright, crammed the bed pillow against the small of her back, and sighed. She'd start physical therapy (PT) on her leg soon. The process would be painful, but she could endure it. No use having two parts of her body messed up. Yet it didn't seem fair to her that they could fix her leg but not her face. They could never fix her face.

Carley's phone rang. "Hey, Sis," the voice on the line said. "Are you driving the doctors and nurses nuts yet?"

"I consider it my sacred duty."

Janelle laughed. "Listen, Jon is driving me over tomorrow after school. I've got a *ton* of work from your teachers."

Carley had an instant image of her pretty eighteen-year-old sister and her boyfriend dragging in boxes full of homework. Today was Wednesday. "Don't they ever let up? I'm stuck in the hospital. Who has any energy to study?"

"Getting your leg healed and functioning again isn't a round-the-clock process," Janelle kidded. "I'm sure you can find an hour or two to hit the books. Oh, Mom said that she and Dad will be over Saturday morning to visit. Is there anything you want me to bring when Jon and I come?"

Carley was looking forward to seeing her

family. Her home in Oak Ridge was sixty miles from the hospital. With the distance to the hospital and everybody's work and school schedules, daily visits were hard to fit in. "Could you bring new batteries for my cassette player? And some more of my Books on Tape. They help pass the time."

"You should make friends while you're there. Don't clamp on that headset and ignore everybody."

"I'm in the hospital. How many friends can I make in a place like this?"

"You never know."

"Believe me, I know."

Just as Janelle hung up, the supper trays arrived. After eating, Carley went down the hall to visit Reba, whose room was full of relatives. Carley ducked away before anyone could see her and stare or ask questions. She hobbled back to her room as quickly as she could on her crutches. She watched TV and finally drifted off to sleep.

Carley awoke sometime in the night from a bad dream and lay wide awake, staring up at the ceiling. She couldn't recall the dream, only that it had left her heart pounding and her body damp with perspiration. She took slow, deep breaths to calm her heart but knew sleep wasn't going to return anytime soon. She decided to walk down the hall to the nurses' station at the far end. She was too antsy to stay in bed.

The corridor was quiet, and as usual for the night shift, it was dimly lit. She hopped out of her room and paused at the door to the room next to hers. It was the room of the boy Reba was so eager to meet, Kyle Westin. She wondered if he really was a hunk and where he went to school if he did live in Oak Ridge.

Carley didn't know why she nudged open his door. She saw in the dim light that Kyle lay in the bed, still turned toward the wall. Carley wondered if he'd even moved since his check-in. Was he paralyzed? she wondered. The night-light, mounted on the wall at the head of his bed, was on.

She edged closer, the rubber tips of her crutches squeaking. She realized she had absolutely no right to be in his room, but she stopped beside his bed and leaned over, hoping to catch sight of his face. Unexpectedly he flipped to his back and cried out, "Who's there? Who is it? What do you want?"

Carley was so startled, she dropped one crutch and attempted to hide her face with her open hand. She needn't have bothered. In the soft light she saw that large gauze pads covered Kyle's eyes. The pads were taped snugly to his temples and cheeks, and strips of gauze were wound around his forehead.

Kyle Westin couldn't see her. He was blind.

Two

"Who's there? What do you want?" Kyle repeated.

"Don't panic," Carley whispered hastily. "I—It's just me. I'm your neighbor. In the room next door. You know, a patient like you."

"What are you doing in my room?"

She didn't want to confess that she'd been acting nosy. "I thought I heard you make a noise as I was walking by toward the nurses' station. I was checking to see if you were all right."

He turned back toward the wall. "I'm not all right."

Nervously she chewed her bottom lip.

Leave, she told herself, but for some reason she couldn't. "Do you want a nurse? I could push your call button. I mean in case you couldn't find it since your eyes are bandaged." She felt stupid mentioning the very thing he was surely most sensitive about. She hated it when small children pointed at her and asked, "Hey! What's wrong with your face?"

"I don't want a nurse," Kyle said. "A nurse can't help me."

"Well, I'm sorry if I scared you." She bent down to pick up the crutch that had fallen, then repositioned it under her arm. "So, I'll just excuse myself—"

"What time is it?" He acted as if she hadn't spoken.

"Um—it's three o'clock."

"Is it afternoon already?"

"Three in the morning."

He rolled over to face her. "And you're out roaming around?"

Although his eyes were bandaged, Carley saw that light brown hair spilled over the tops of the gauze strips wound around his forehead to help hold the eye pads in place.

His cheeks were broad and high, his jaw square, his complexion smooth. He was as good-looking as Reba had hoped he'd be. "Couldn't sleep," Carley answered. "I had a bad dream."

"I can't sleep either."

Silence filled the room, yet Carley still couldn't make herself leave. He seemed so helpless, bewildered and lonely. She remembered when she was twelve, how terrified she'd been alone in the hospital. With doctors poking and prodding and machines and medicines that frightened her or made her sick. With pain in her face so intense, it had made her scream. "The nurse can give you something to help you sleep," Carley told Kyle kindly.

"I don't want to sleep."

She understood that part too. She, too, had once been afraid to fall asleep. Afraid that if she did, she wouldn't wake up. "Sometimes, it's best just to give in and take extra pain medication," Carley said. "It helps you stay mellow."

"Who said I needed pain pills?"

"Just a guess."

"I don't want any pain pills. I hate the way they make me feel."

"I know—like you're in 'la-la' land. Sort of dopey and spaced out. But sometimes that's not so bad because it helps make the time pass faster."

He kept turning his head, as if fixing on her voice. She stepped closer so that he wouldn't have to work so hard. "What's your name?"

Carley hesitated, then realized that to her he had form and substance, but to him she was only a disembodied voice floating in a dark void. He was blind. He couldn't see anything. She was safe. "Carley Mattea," she said.

"I'm Kyle Westin." Awkwardly he held out his hand. Too high, but she managed to reach and clasp his palm. He didn't let go. "You're right, Carley. I hurt a lot, but I don't want any pills."

"It's okay to take them when the pain's really bad."

"But I want to hurt."

"You do? Why?"

"Because the pain reminds me that I still have eyes."

Goose bumps appeared along her arms. The image of his strong male face without eyes unnerved her. "That's an odd thing to say. I figured you did. I mean, why wouldn't you? If you want to tell me," she added hastily. She hated to be asked about her scarred, lopsided face.

"Some friends and I decided to make our own rocket fuel. You know, just to see if we could. It exploded in my face. Burned my corneas and my chest." He pulled back his hospital shirt and she saw large bandages across his upper body.

She smelled ointments and cotton padding and winced, knowing how badly even a sunburn hurt. "Will the burns be all right?"

"They don't think I'll need skin grafts."

"That's good."

He paused. "But they're not sure if I'll ever see again."

She heard his voice catch and felt waves of pity for him. When she'd been younger, she'd suffered with headaches so severe that she'd passed out from the pain. And when the doctors had discovered a tumor in her left nasal cavity pressing against her brain, she'd had to have immediate surgery.

At the time, she'd overheard her parents talking in soft, frantic whispers to her doctor. They'd asked, "What's the worst that could happen?"

And he'd answered, "It could be malignant and she could lose the left side of her face."

She asked Kyle, "When will they know about your sight?"

"The eye specialist said that the corneas have to heal, and that can take two to three months."

"So you have hope. That's good."

He sank back against his pillow. "I don't feel real hopeful. I—I hate being blind."

By now Carley had settled herself on the edge of his bed in order to take the weight off her leg, which was throbbing. She knew what hopelessness felt like too. It was waking up from surgery knowing that she'd been cut across the top of her head from one ear to the other and down the front of her face. It was knowing that in order for the tumor to be removed, she'd had to lose parts of facial bones, which could never be replaced. It was learning that although her left eye and her mouth had been left intact, her face was permanently disfigured and scarred.

Feeling grateful that she wasn't blind, Carley said, "But you may still get your eyesight back. Don't give up."

Kyle took a deep, shuddering breath. "Yeah. Sure."

"So," she asked, "should I get lost now and let you try to get some sleep?"

His hand tightened on her wrist. "Don't leave. Please. I—It helps to talk."

"No problem." His hair looked soft and she wanted to touch it.

"Why are you in the hospital?" he asked.

"I got Rollerblades for Christmas and managed to fall and break my leg really bad. The doctor set it, but it wasn't healing just right, so they decided to operate and put the bones back together with pins and screws. That was two days ago, but when they got in there, I had an infection, so I have to stay in the hospital awhile. They dump antibiotics into me through an IV four times a day, but whenever I'm unhooked, I grab my crutches and wander around."

"Will your leg be all right?"

"Eventually, but I have to begin physical therapy soon, then come back for more once I check out and go home. I'll be glad to lose these crutches. I mean, I can't sneak up on *anybody.*"

For the first time she saw him smile. "I think that's what I heard. The tips of your crutches squeaking. I guess it's true what they say about a person's other senses getting sharper when one of them is missing."

"Don't tell me that. I have a teacher who's deaf as a post and I sure don't want his eyesight any sharper. He may catch me reading the novel I prop behind the text for his class."

Kyle smiled again. "You're funny."

She wanted to tell him that her sense of humor was a by-product of living with her facial deformity, but then realized that there was no reason to divulge what he couldn't see. "A sense of humor helps," she said. "Laughing makes hurting less painful."

"So when I start hurting, I should find something to laugh about?"

"Well, there are degrees of pain. The very worst requires pain pills—a topic we've already covered. But the not-too-bad pain can be helped with a good laugh." She didn't add that *emotional* pain was a whole separate matter from the physical kind. Or that laughing and making jokes about her face over the years was her way of putting others at ease, no matter how much it hurt her.

She continued. "Think about it. Before your accident, you knew nothing about making rocket fuel. Now I'll bet you could write a term paper on how *not* to make the stuff."

She saw his expression work through the tragedy to the black comedy of his situation and was rewarded by his wry smile. "I see your point."

"And that's another thing. Do you know how many times we use the words *see* and *look* when we're trying to tell somebody something? Now you have the perfect excuse to say, 'No, dumbo, I don't see, and I can't look.' " She held her breath, hoping he wouldn't take offense, and was rewarded by another smile.

"What are you, a philosopher?"

"No way. I prefer art to philosophy."

"I used to prefer chemistry," he said.

She applauded. "Great, you're catching on already. 'Used to prefer chemistry'—get it? That's black comedy if ever I heard it."

"I won't let one feeble joke go to my head." He shifted in the bed, but hung on to her arm. "You like art. Do you draw?"

"Some. Mostly I like to design. You know, like clothes and fashion stuff. And I'd like to start with these stupid hospital gowns."

"So where do you go to school?"

She hesitated, not wanting to tell him. If they did attend the same school, it meant that he'd expect he might run into her in the halls if he ever got his sight back. And she knew she didn't want him to see her as she really looked.

Just then his room door opened and a nurse entered. She stopped stock-still and blinked at the two of them. "Good grief, Carley, what are you doing in this room at three o'clock in the morning?"

Three

Carley scrambled off the bed and grabbed her crutches. "I couldn't sleep and came looking for company."

"Maybe other patients would like to sleep," the nurse chided.

"It's okay," Kyle interjected. "I asked her to stay and talk to me. I couldn't sleep either."

The nurse pursed her lips. "I don't think your doctors would approve of your late hours. It's time for vitals. Go back to your room, Carley, before we all get into trouble."

Vitals meant the process of taking blood pressures and temperatures, which the nursing staff did routinely round the clock. "I figured I'd save you the trouble of waking me up," Carley said, starting toward the door.

"Carley?" Kyle called out to her.

She turned. "Yes?"

"You were right about pain being easier to take if you laugh some. You've helped me feel better. Thanks for that. Will you come back and visit me in the morning?"

She felt her heart do a flip. No boy had ever expressed an interest in her. But then Kyle couldn't see how ugly she was. "If you want me to."

"Anytime," he said.

"Shoo," hissed the nurse at Carley good-naturedly.

Carley angled her way out the door, looking back to see Kyle raised up on his elbow. His white bandaged eyes were turned in her direction, as if she were the center of the universe and her return the most anticipated event in recorded time.

"You met Kyle in the middle of the night? That's just so cool! Tell me, what's he like?"

Carley wasn't prepared for Reba's visit. After she'd left Kyle's room, she had returned to her own and promptly fallen into a deep, dreamless sleep, which had ended at eight A.M. with the clanking arrival of breakfast trays. She was eating when Reba rolled into the room, but Carley was groggy and in no mood to play Twenty Questions. "He's had a chemistry accident and burned his eyes and he's not sure he'll get his sight back again. So he's not having a very good time," she mumbled between bites of soggy cereal.

"That's awful." Reba's eyes grew wide with sympathy. "Is he nice? Do you like him? Was I right—is he cute?"

"Slow down. My brain's only half awake."

Impatiently Reba nudged her wheelchair closer to where Carley sat on her bed with her tray table positioned over her lap. "Well, hurry and wake it up. They're taking me down for X rays soon."

Carley smiled at Reba's zealousness. "And I've got to go to PT at ten. Yes, he's nice. Yes, I like him. Yes, he's cute."

"Do you realize that this could be the start of a major relationship? And to think you met right here in the hospital."

"He was scared and alone last night. We

talked. But I don't think he's ready to make me his girlfriend."

"Well, I want you to introduce me to him. Will you do that?"

"Of course I will. But he's probably sound asleep, and besides, I'm sure he'll be here for days."

"Yes, but by this time tomorrow I'll be down in surgery, then in Recovery and ICU. It may be days before I'm up and rolling again."

Carley shook her head in defeat. "All right, let's go next door and pester Kyle."

She poked open his door cautiously, not wanting to wake him if he were sleeping. He was sitting up in bed patiently pressing the TV remote from channel to channel, pausing to listen for a moment before moving on.

"We're here to rescue you," she said, moving into his room and holding the door for Reba.

"Carley!" He sounded so pleased, it made her heart skip a beat. "Who's 'we'?"

"This is my friend Reba."

Reba rolled up alongside Kyle's bed and touched his arm. He groped with his free hand until he caught her hand. "I'm in a wheelchair," Reba said. "It's electric, so if you hear a whirring sound, you'll know it's me."

"I'm hearing sounds I never noticed when I could see."

Carley didn't want him to get depressed about his eyesight again, so she changed the subject. "Reba here is sort of the social coordinator of the floor, but she's got a date with her surgeon tomorrow and she didn't want you to get checked out before she recovered enough to be back on the job."

Reba giggled.

"I'm here for probably a week," Kyle said. "An ophthalmologist is keeping tabs on my eyes and another doctor keeps a check on my burns. As soon as they heal enough, I can go home."

"I hope it works out for you," Reba said.

"What about you? Will your operation get you out of your wheelchair?"

"No. They can't fix what's wrong with me. But the operation will make me more comfortable."

Kyle's expression was one of shock that

Reba couldn't be "fixed." Carley wondered how he would have reacted to Reba if he'd been able to see her. Or to Carley. She felt insulated and safe so long as he couldn't see either of them.

"I—I'm sorry." Kyle's fist balled up among the covers. "It's so frustrating not being able to see anything. I feel like a nonparticipant. I can't even get out of bed without someone to help me. I hate asking for help all the time."

"I can help out a little," Carley said. "If you want something—even company—call my room."

"I can't dial the phone."

"Sure you can." Carley came closer, picked up the phone, and placed it in his lap. "Take the receiver and feel the numbers pad." She watched his fingers trace over the raised buttons. "I'm in Room eight-twenty-eight, so you dial a seven plus eight, two, eight. Get a mental picture of how the pad looks and let your fingers locate the numbers. Now push them." She pressed his fingertips from number to number and dialed her room. "Each key has a different tone, you know. Pay attention and pretty soon you'll be able to dial area codes, seven-digit numbers, even foreign cities."

Gingerly he experimented, listening attentively to each electronic tone. He was rewarded by the sound of a phone ringing from next door. His face broke into a grin. "All right. I did it."

"A piece of cake," Carley said. "If I'm in my room, we'll talk. And if you want something, I'll come hopping over."

Kyle asked, "How do you know so much about dialing the phone 'blind' if you can see?"

"I can tell your parents have never put you on phone restriction." Carley patted his shoulder as if she were indulging a small child. "Why I've learned to slip this sucker under the covers at night, dial in the pitch-dark, and not misdial a single digit."

Reba clapped.

From the edge of Kyle's bed Carley performed a mock bow. "Thank you. Thank you."

Kyle laughed. "I can tell I'm in the presence of a true genius in devious maneuvers. I'm impressed."

Carley felt a twinge of guilt. Would he consider her failure to tell him about her scarred face devious? She gave Reba a sidelong glance, but Reba was looking raptly at Kyle, so it didn't seem as if she thought anything was amiss in Carley's purposeful omission.

"Did you know that you and Carley both live in Oak Ridge?" Reba blurted out.

"No. Why didn't you tell me, Carley?"

She felt her cheeks flush, then realized he couldn't see her embarrassment. She shot Reba a look that said, *Blabbermouth!* Reba shrugged innocently. "I was going to, but we got interrupted last night," Carley explained.

"Where do you go to school?"

Her heart began to pound. More than anything, she didn't want them to be students at the same high school. She took a deep breath and named her large public high school. "I started in September as a sophomore," she said. "But I don't do any after-school stuff—you know, clubs and things."

"I go to Webb." It was a prestigious private school. "I'm a junior. And I used to belong to the chemistry club."

Carley breathed a sigh of relief. At least that hurdle was crossed. "I'm sure your membership won't be revoked due to your mishap."

"And I go to middle school, but not in Oak Ridge," Reba offered, as if the only important information was their schools. For Carley the most valuable information was that she'd never have to meet Kyle in the halls and have him stare or, worse, turn his head away in distaste.

Two white-coated doctors and a nurse's aide swept into Kyle's room. "Good morning," one of them said, glancing at the three of them. Carley automatically dipped her head to allow her long brown hair to sheild the left side of her face. "Kyle, it's Dr. Goldston and Dr. Richmond. Are we interrupting anything? We've come to take you down to Ophthalmology and change your bandages."

"It has to be done in the dark," Kyle explained to Carley and Reba. "My eyes are real sensitive to light."

"We've got places to go." Carley assured him, hustling to pick up her crutches.

In the hallway Reba stopped her chair and said, "Kyle sure is nice. And good-looking too. It must be terrible to be blind. I feel sorry for him, don't you?"

"Of course."

"Well, I'm betting he gets his eyesight back," Reba said firmly. "Don't you think he will?"

"No way of knowing." Carley was aware that a small, perverse part of her was glad that Kyle couldn't see. She felt bad about it, but also knew that his blindness was her safety net. So long as he couldn't see her, he would think she was normal.

And for Kyle Westin, normal was what she wanted to be.

Four

Carley returned to her room, where she was hooked to an IV for her dose of antibiotics. By the time she was unhooked, it was time to go down to PT to begin rehabilitation on her leg. An aide took her down in an elevator in a wheelchair, along a covered walkway, to a separate building. Inside, a large and spacious physical therapy room was filled with equipment and tables. Therapists were working with patients of all ages.

"My name's Linda Gallagher and I'll be your PT." The woman who stood in front of Carley was slim and youthful, with long hair that hung down her back in a French braid.

"I'll be working with you twice a day thirty minutes per session in a series of exercises to get your leg functioning perfectly again. You'll be off those crutches in no time."

"What? Give up my crutches? How will I fight off my admirers?" Carley didn't bother to hide her face from the physical therapist. She figured the woman was used to seeing deformity.

Linda grinned. "So, I have a comedienne for a patient. Believe me, you're a welcome departure from the kind who grumbles all the time." She helped Carley out of the wheelchair, boosted her up onto a low table, and started examining her leg, which was held rigid by a cast. "What happened?"

Carley told her about the accident.

"And this was the day after Christmas?"

"Yes, but after I'd spent almost two weeks in the cast, X rays showed that it wasn't going back together just right, so Dr. Olson told us he'd have to operate and reset it."

"And, according to your chart, that's when they discovered the osteomyelitis."

"The what?"

Linda smiled. "The infection."

"Whatever. Anyway, I have to stay in the hospital until it goes away."

"It'll give us time to establish your therapy."

Carley kept waiting for Linda to ask about her misshapen face. Linda didn't. Instead she started right in explaining about the therapy. "We'll start with simple stretching exercises. Your chart states that you sustained tendon damage around your knee and ankle too."

"My doctor said he may have to operate on the tendons again." She understood the severity of her break and how concerned her parents had been about it. But considering her medical history, she refused to get too agitated about a broken leg. It would be fixed. However, she regretted losing her Rollerblades over it.

After the leg had been set the first time, her mother had said, "Those Rollerblades are going in the garbage."

Carley had protested, "But Mom, they're brand-new. I just got them!"

"I don't care. Don't you realize that because of them you could walk with a limp for the rest of your life?"

To which Carley had replied, "I'd look like Quasimodo in *The Hunchback of Notre Dame*, wouldn't I?" She leaned over, curled her lip, and dragged her leg which was now encased in plaster.

"That isn't funny, Carley," her mother said.

"Why not? Bum leg and weird face. I think it's funny."

Linda, the PT, interrupted Carley's thoughts. "You'll also start riding the stationary bike and in about ten days you'll begin partial weight-bearing exercises. I'll start you out with two-pound weights, take you to four, and eventually get you to where you'll once again have full ROM—that's range of motion."

"Will I be able to drive?" Carley had taken her road test in October, on her sixteenth birthday.

"Not right away," Linda said. "But it is your left leg, so if you've got an automatic shift, it shouldn't be too long before you can drive. Just be careful. You don't want to rack up the other leg."

"That's for sure. I hate being stuck in the hospital."

"We'll get you out as soon as we can," Linda said cheerfully.

Carley thought about Kyle, lying upstairs, a prisoner of his darkness. "Do you work with blind people?"

"No, I don't. But we have people on our staff who do. Why?"

"There's this guy on my floor who's blind, and I was wondering what you all did to help somebody like him."

"First his doctor has to authorize it, but basically, in the beginning, he'll have to be trained to move around safely. Plus he'll need to be counseled from a psychological perspective. Blindness is a big emotional adjustment."

Carley understood perfectly about adjusting to the emotional aspect of a catastrophic event. When she'd been told that the tumor removed from her face had been cancerous and that nothing could be done to reconstruct her lost bone and tissue, she'd gone into a deep depression. She'd wept for days, even though her doctor had tried to console her with the news that he'd cut out all of the tumor and that after chemotherapy treatments she shouldn't have to worry about the cancer ever returning.

At the time, they'd shaved her head, operated, and stitched her up so that black sutures ran in long lines over the top of her head and around her nose. With time, her hair grew back and the suture lines faded. But the deformity remained. Her face looked sunken on the left side, her nose scrunched, her eye half closed. She was ugly—no doubt about it.

"Well, I'm hoping his doctors can fix up this guy so that he won't be blind," Carley told Linda, forcing herself away from painful memories.

"I hope so too," Linda said.

Carley started her therapy thinking more about Kyle and his problems than her own broken leg. She wanted the best for him. She just didn't want to be in his line of vision when, and if, his bandages came off.

———

"Hi, Sis. Whatcha doing?" Janelle breezed into Carley's hospital room, shopping bags in each hand, her purse slung over her shoulder.

"Bowling."

Janelle laughed. "I see you haven't lost your sense of humor."

Carley was sitting in a recliner chair, her leg outstretched. She tossed down the magazine she was reading. "Where's lover boy?"

"Jon's coming; he stopped down at the snack bar." Janelle plopped the bags on the floor, leaned down, and hugged Carley, then grabbed another chair and pulled it closer. The bag tilted and spilled books onto the floor. "You've got homework in every subject."

"That brightens my day."

"Tell me what's happening. Mom and Dad want a full report."

Carley described her physical therapy session.

"Did it hurt?" Janelle asked.

"Like crazy. But you know what they say: No pain, no gain."

"Jon says that all the time."

"Remind me never to use that phrase again."

Janelle eyed Carley narrowly. "Be nice."

"Do I have to?"

"Why don't you like my boyfriend, Carley?"

Carley didn't know exactly how to answer. She hadn't meant to sound so caustic. She hedged. "Jon's okay."

Before Janelle could press for more of an answer, Jon walked into the room. He carried a sack from the snack bar in one hand and a giant cup of cola in the other. "How you doing?" he mumbled toward Carley, careful to avert his eyes from her.

"Doing just great," she said.

"You want to sit by us?" Janelle asked.

"No," he answered, much too quickly. "I'll just drag a chair over here." He indicated the small table on the other side of the room. "Mind if I turn on the tube?"

"Help yourself," Carley told him.

"I thought you came to visit." Janelle sounded irritated.

"You girls want to gab. I'll stay out of your way." He opened the sack and extracted a hamburger, fries, and a pile of ketchup pack-ets. He switched on the TV.

Janelle turned toward Carley and shrugged. "I'm sorry. I thought he'd be more sociable."

"I'm used to it."

"What's that supposed to mean?"

"Nothing. I'm just saying it's all right if he does his own thing. He's *your* boyfriend. I wouldn't expect him to get excited about coming to the hospital to see me."

Janelle frowned as if she knew something wasn't quite right, but since Jon was in the room she couldn't make Carley talk about it. "Have you heard from any of your friends from school?"

"I don't have friends like you do, Janelle."

"What about that Dana girl?"

"We haven't been friends since Thanks-giving."

"I didn't know that."

"When the guys started noticing her, she dropped me like a hot potato."

"Well, that was mean of her."

Carley sighed. Janelle was wrapped up in her own social life. Not that Carley blamed her. Janelle was in her senior year and planning on college. Plus, she was pretty and popular and outgoing. "I've forgiven Dana. Why should she be saddled with a social liability like me?"

"She's petty. And you're *not* a liability."

"She's normal," Carley corrected.

"Well, have you made any friends here? A few days ago you were still groggy from your surgery, but surely you've poked around by now."

Carley told her about Reba and Kyle.

Janelle sucked in her breath when she heard that Kyle was blind. "I'd hate to think of a guy with his whole life ahead of him being blind," Janelle said.

"His blindness may not be permanent. His doctors aren't sure yet."

"That's a relief." Janelle tipped her chin forward and studied Carley thoughtfully. "Do you like him?"

"Of course I like him. Why wouldn't I?"

"No, I mean *like* him, like him."

Carley blushed under her sister's keen scrutiny.

"You do, don't you?"

"I hardly know him. We've had maybe two conversations."

"So what? I knew I liked Jon the first time I laid eyes on him."

"Well, Kyle's never laid eyes on me. And believe me, if I have my way about it, he never will."

Five

That evening Carley had just finished supper when her phone rang.

"It's me," Kyle said.

Her pulse fluttered crazily. "Hello, 'me.'"

"I dialed the phone just like you taught me. Got it right on the first try."

"I'd applaud, but I'm holding the receiver."

He laughed. "Doing anything?"

"Counting the flowers on the wallpaper."

"Want to come visit me?"

Her heart skipped a beat. "Sure. Let me grab my crutches and hop over." He wanted to be with her! She forced herself to calm down. After all, he was trapped in the hospital and didn't have anything else to do. Plus, he'd never seen her face.

She went to his room and found him sitting in a vinyl armchair at the small table in the corner of his private room. "You've made progress. You're out of bed."

"Yeah. You missed all the excitement. I spilled my lunch tray all over the floor. My mom was just walking in the door when it happened and she pitched a fit because no one was helping me. I told her that the nurses were busy and I shouldn't have gotten impatient. Besides, I don't like being fed like I'm some kind of baby."

Carley was sympathetic to his feelings. She said, "*Being* helpless and *feeling* helpless are different things."

"Exactly. Anyway, Mom nailed my doctor and he sent someone who works with the visually impaired to see me. She taught me some things about how to negotiate in a seeing world."

"Like what?"

"Come sit over here and I'll show you."

She watched him fumble for another chair. "I'll get it," she said.

"No." His voice was firm. "I need to learn how to handle things like this."

Slowly, he caught the arm of the second chair, stood, and pulled it out from the table. His movements looked choppy, but he did get the chair for her. She lay her crutches aside and sat down, propping her broken leg on another chair. "I'm impressed," she said. "The last time a guy pulled a chair out for me was in seventh grade."

She didn't add that it had been done as a cruel joke. As the boy had pulled it out, he'd turned to his buddies and said, "Freak alert." They'd all laughed and she'd felt humiliated.

"Okay, so I might not have offered if I wasn't trying to show off," Kyle admitted.

"I'm glad you've learned some things to help you take care of yourself. Nobody likes to feel useless."

"I guess you would understand."

"What do you mean?" She caught her breath. Had someone told him what she looked like?

"Your broken leg. I guess people are always rushing to help when you want to learn to do things for yourself."

She let out her breath slowly. "That's right. I've had to knock people over with my crutches in order to get them to let me do things for myself."

His brow furrowed, then he grinned. "You're joking."

"Must not have been much of one."

"It's just that it takes me longer to catch on to things because I can't see people's faces and read their expressions."

"I didn't think of that."

"This being blind is hard stuff. My doctors are saying that if the chemicals that burned my eyes were acids, then I have a good chance of recovering my sight. But if they were alkaline, I may never get it back."

"Don't you know what chemicals you used to make the fuel?"

"I've been trying to remember, but my friends and I were mixing lots of stuff that afternoon." He shook his head. "All I know is that I want to see again. I have to, Carley. I just *have* to."

She heard passion in his voice. She, too, had felt that same kind of longing. She craved to have a normal appearance, but no amount of wishing for it could restore her looks. Beauty was for other girls. It couldn't belong to Carley. "Well, until you can," she said cheerfully, "at least you'll know how to manage."

Kyle leaned back in his chair, his palms flat against the table. She wondered if touching something made him feel grounded, more connected. "One of the worst parts is being bored," he told her. "TV is a waste. I tried to listen to one of my favorite shows, but I couldn't make sense of it."

"I can see and I can't make sense of most of them."

He rewarded her attempt to lighten his mood with a smile. "I realized that a lot of the show's humor depended on visual gags, on the actors' expressions. Anyway, I had a hard time following, so I turned it off."

She had a sudden inspiration. "You need to borrow some of my Books on Tape. You have a cassette player, don't you?"

"Of course."

"Then I'll loan you some of my books."

"What kind of books?" He sounded skeptical. "Not romances, I hope."

"I have those, but I won't force them on you. I also have mysteries, thrillers, fantasies —in fact, if you have any lit books you need to read for school, I could probably find a few of those titles too. Sort of like Cliffs Notes for the ears."

He laughed. "How about chemistry and physics books?"

"Get a grip. I'm talking entertainment here, not instant tranquilizer."

"You wouldn't mind loaning me some of your tapes?"

"I offered, didn't I? You'll like them, and listening to them will take you right out of this place."

"You can't imagine just how much I'd like to be out of here."

She recalled wishing the same thing when she was going through her facial operation. Once they told her that removing the malignant tumor would leave her face deformed, all she wanted to do was run away, escape. She said to Kyle, "Don't you wish you had the power to turn back time? To go back to before your accident and start fresh and avoid the things that led up to it?"

"Yes," he said, his voice barely a whisper. "I can't believe how much you understand stuff, Carley. It's as if you can read my mind."

"It's easier to understand something once you've experienced it."

"You mean about your leg? Like you'd turn back the clock to before your accident and not do the same dumb stunt that led to breaking it?"

She was referring to her sense of loss over her looks, but of course he had no way of knowing about that. "Sure, I mean my leg. Who wants a broken leg with an infection in it?"

"And if I could start over with that rocket fuel, I would do things differently. I'd at least have put on safety glasses."

"Why don't you leave rocket-fuel con-cocting to NASA?"

"I will from now on."

She gazed at him in open admiration. Kyle was tall, good-looking, easygoing and, more than likely, popular—just the type of boy she'd always sneak peeks at in the halls at school. Just the type of boy who'd never notice her existence. Or worse, turn away in revulsion once he saw her face. But here, in the hospital, with his eyes bandaged, the scales of social acceptance were balanced. He couldn't loathe what he couldn't see. She could be at ease with what she couldn't change.

"Carley? Are you okay?"

She started. She'd been so deep in her thoughts, she'd almost forgotten they'd been in the middle of a conversation. "Whoops— sorry. I guess I had a temporary brain freeze. My mind wandered." She whistled, snapped her fingers, and called, "Here, mind, here, mind. Come back now."

Kyle broke into hearty laughter. "You're *so* funny. Most girls I know don't crack jokes like you do. Give me your hand."

"I'm still using it," she kidded, but held her hand out toward him.

He reached, caught her palm, and laced his fingers through hers. "There, that's better," he said.

She stared in fascination at their entwined fingers. "How do you mean?"

"I wanted to touch you. Hold on to you. You don't mind, do you?"

"No," she said, hoping the word hadn't tumbled out as fast as her heart had begun to beat. "I mean, it's fine with me."

"Can I ask you something personal?"

"How personal? My IQ is a closely guarded secret."

"Do you have a boyfriend?"

Caught totally off guard, Carley was momentarily speechless. No one had ever asked her that question before.

"Um—not really."

He grinned. "That's good."

She squirmed self-consciously before realizing that he couldn't see her discomfort. "How about you?" she asked boldly, not sure she wanted to hear his answer. "Any special girl?"

He shook his head. "Basically I'm shy," he said. "I can't ever get up the courage to talk to girls. My tongue gets all tied in knots and I come off sounding like a jerk."

She found his confession hard to believe. "You don't seem shy to me. You talk to me."

"You're different."

If only you knew how different, she thought. She asked, "So, what makes me different?"

"I don't know exactly. But when you wandered into my room and started talking to me, I knew you were different. You really understand what this is like for me . . . this . . . this being blind."

"I know it's got to be tough."

"My doctors keep preparing me for being impaired. And so did the woman who worked with me this afternoon. Even if my sight comes back, it probably won't ever be the same."

Carley didn't know what to tell him. She didn't want him to think his situation was hopeless, but she didn't want to ignore the seriousness of it either. "Well, don't dwell on the downside. Just work hard at becoming self-sufficient. It'll make waiting around for the outcome easier."

He squeezed her hand. "You have a way of saying the right thing to me." Suddenly he pushed back from the table. "What time is it?"

Carley glanced at the clock on the wall.

"Almost seven." She was amazed at how the time had flown since they'd been together. "Why?"

"My parents are coming any minute now. I want you to meet them."

Panic gripped her. She couldn't let them see her. "Oh, I can't." She grabbed for her crutches.

"But why not? What else is there to do around this place?"

She thought fast. "Reba," she said, struggling to her feet. "Remember, she's got surgery tomorrow and I've got to go visit her and make sure she's all right."

He nodded in understanding.

Carley bolted for the door, moving as fast as she could on her crutches, afraid to glance down the hall toward the elevators in case Kyle's parents might be headed her way. Afraid they might see the girl with the twisted face leaving their son's room and ask questions about someone he thought was normal.

Six

Carley didn't visit Reba because her friend's room was crowded with relatives. So she marked time in the visitor's lounge, keeping her head ducked so that her long brown hair would help conceal the left side of her face. When it was after nine o'clock, she cautiously returned to her room and quickly shut the door. She called Reba and said she'd be pulling for her during her surgery.

"You still friends with Kyle?" Reba asked. She'd been given medication to help her sleep and her voice sounded slurry.

"We talked for a couple of hours tonight."

"That's nice. Did you mention your face?"

"No way. I'm enjoying him thinking I'm a regular girl."

"Someday he might see you."

"Not if I can help it. Think about it. Once my infection clears up, I'll go home and he'll make friends with someone else. If he's even still here."

"So you won't see him again when he's out of the hospital?" Reba's voice drifted.

"No," Carley said. "I won't see or talk to him again." She paused, sensing that Reba was fading fast. "Go on to sleep," she told her. "I'll see you as soon as they put you back in your room."

" 'Honesty is the best policy,' " Reba mumbled.

"What?"

"My . . . grandfather says . . . that . . ."

Carley sighed. "I'm changing the policy. Good night."

She hung up and lay staring at the ceiling until the nurse came to hook her up for her evening dose of antibiotic. With her thoughts on Kyle, she drifted into a dreamless sleep long before the medicine was finished dripping.

The next morning Carley gave several of
her Books on Tape to Kyle. "Can you stay?"
he asked.

"I'm on my way to physical therapy." She
was feeling guilty. Maybe Reba was right.
Maybe she should tell him everything.

"Can we talk more later?"

"I don't want you to get sick of me."

"It's all right if I do. We're in a hospital."
The gauze pads concealing his eyes made
it difficult to know if he was teasing. "It's a
good thing I have a sense of humor," she
offered cautiously.

He grinned. "I made a joke and you
caught on to it. I'm getting better at this humor stuff, huh?"

"Don't let it go to your head, buster." She
said goodbye and went out into the hall,
where an orderly took her down in a wheelchair for her PT appointment.

Once her session was over, Carley returned to her floor and asked about Reba at
the nurses' station. "She came through with
flying colors," a nurse told her. "She's down
in Recovery, and we expect she'll be sent up

here by late afternoon. But no visitors except family today."

"No problem," Carley said, feeling greatly relieved that Reba had done so well.

"By the way," the nurse said, "your lunch tray's been delivered to Kyle Westin's room. He told us you knew all about it."

She didn't, but she faked it with the nurse and hobbled down the hall to Kyle's room. He was sitting at the table, his tray in front of him. Another covered tray had been placed on the table facing an empty chair. "Are you eating your lunch and mine too?" she asked.

"Carley! Come sit. I thought we could have lunch together. I had to make the nurse think you had preapproved the idea. Do you mind?"

How could she mind eating lunch with a guy like Kyle? "Your company's much better than that exercise lady on TV at noon." She propped up her crutches and sat down. "What is this stuff?" she asked, lifting the lid. "It looks like roadkill."

"It tastes all right. Soup's good."

She watched him encircle the soup bowl

with one hand, pick up the spoon, keeping it low, lean far over the warm bowl, and ladle soup into his mouth. She felt grateful all over again that she had her eyesight. "Not bad," she told him.

"The soup or my table manners?" he asked.

"The way you maneuver," she explained. "The soup's dreary."

He laughed. "I've been practicing hard at learning how to feed myself. Every meal, I spill less and less. You know I'm feeling brave if I got up the nerve to invite you to have lunch with me."

"You seem to have a knack for it. Feeding yourself, I mean."

"The therapist taught me to touch all the food first, position it on the tray so that I'd know exactly where everything was, and keep my hands low when I come at it. It works."

Fascinated, she watched him for another minute. She'd been taught that it wasn't polite to stare, and she hated it when people stared at her, but Kyle couldn't see her studying him, so she didn't think she was be-ing rude.

"I'm still not very fast at eating, though," he apologized. "It's made me realize how quickly I scarfed down my food before."

"Don't we all," Carley said.

"So how's Reba doing?"

"I hear she's doing fine, but it'll be an-other day before I check on her personally."

"What're you doing tomorrow?"

She stirred her fork through a gloppy mound of mashed potatoes. "Well, after I check out the Saturday morning cartoons, my parents are coming for a visit."

"They don't come during the week?"

"They would if I was in bad shape," Car-ley explained. "They own a bookstore in Oak Ridge and they put a lot of time into running it. It's hard for them to get away. But on Saturdays they have extra help." Carley didn't mention her sister to Kyle or that both of them worked there most week-ends, Carley almost always in the back un-packing and pricing stock. She didn't like working with the public because people stared and asked dumb questions. Once, a small child had seen her face and had screamed in fright.

"What's the name of the store?" Kyle asked. "I'll drop in when all this is behind me."

She didn't want him doing that. She had meant what she'd told Reba—once she was out of the hospital, she didn't want to run into Kyle again—whether or not he could see. The hospital acted as a safe harbor, a place where they were on equal footing. Reluctantly she told him the name of the store, telling herself that if he should ever drop by, she could have family or employees tell him she wasn't there. Soon he'd stop coming.

"Is that why you have so many Books on Tape?" Kyle asked. "Which, by the way, are pretty cool. I'm partway through a murder mystery."

"I get the tapes from the store, but I've always loved to read, so it's just another way to 'read' a book as far as I'm concerned."

"When I read, it's chemistry and physics. Quantum theory. Stuff like that."

"That side of my brain doesn't work,"

Carley said with a laugh. "I'm a total waste when it comes to math and science, but I guess you have a reason for that."

He nodded. "I want to attend MIT— Massachusetts Institute of Technology—and take up engineering and maybe someday work for NASA. The one thing I've always wanted to do was learn how to fly a plane. I have an uncle who owns a small plane. He operates a business flying around real estate agents and advertising banners."

"I've seen those signs. They say Eat at Joe's and stuff like that."

"He's busy during football season flying over UT stadium with ad messages. He takes me up with him sometimes. He's even let me man the controls." Suddenly he grew quiet. "I want to be a pilot. At least I did. Until this happened."

He sounded so despondent that Carley was sorry she'd opened the door to the conversation. "I want to go to the Chicago Art Institute," she inserted quickly, hoping to get his thoughts off his situation. "Who knows, maybe I'll shake up the fashion industry with my 'innovative designs.'" She

emphasized the last to make it sound comi-
cal, like words from a TV commercial.

"I'd ask to see your work, *but* . . ." Kyle
said without humor.

Carley regretted her remark. Trying to
cheer him up had backfired. "It's not much
to see, really. Let's talk about something
else."

"Why not? Talking seems like all I can
do."

She stabbed her fork into a piece of chocolate cake on her food tray. "We could talk
about dessert," she said. "It's chocolate and
maybe older than both our combined ages."

He offered a half smile, but pushed his
tray away. "I'm not hungry anymore. Everything's cold by now anyway."

"It's because I got you to talking instead of
concentrating on lunch."

"It's because I'm blind," he blurted. "It
isn't fair!" He shoved the tray again, and
Carley had to grab at it to keep it from skid-
ding off the table.

"I—I'm sorry," she said softly. He was
breathing hard and she wasn't sure if he
might want to cry. "I know it isn't fair, but

sometimes we just have to live with what can't be changed."

"How would you know? All you have is a broken leg. Bones heal."

Of course she couldn't tell him how she knew. "I should be going," she said, reaching for her crutches. "Time for my afternoon antibiotic hookup."

He said nothing.

She headed for the door, the rubber tips of her crutches squeaking on the floor. She paused at the doorway and gazed back at him. "Bye."

"Bye," he said without moving.

Brilliant afternoon sunlight played across his golden brown hair and spilled across his gauze-bandaged eyes. But she knew that inside the bandages, he was alone in the dark. And there was nothing she could do about it. Not one single thing.

Seven

On Saturday morning Carley's parents came to visit, laden with a bag of books and tapes. "Your doctor says you'll probably be out of here early next week," her father said after kissing her on the forehead. "He says you're responding well to the antibiotic, and according to your X rays, your leg looks to be knitting properly."

"Good. I'm ready to blow this place." Carley joked, but she knew she'd miss Reba and Kyle. Most of all Kyle.

"Of course, you'll still have to come in for physical therapy," her mother said. "But that can be as an outpatient."

"My therapist seems to think I can drive,

so I can bring myself in for the sessions. No need for you or Dad to take off from work."

"Janelle can bring you."

"Sure—my sister's going to cut into her social life to usher me to therapy three times a week." Carley was thinking about Janelle's red-hot romance with Jon.

"She can just rearrange her priorities," Carley's mother said. "Your leg is more important than any of her extracurricular activities."

"Mom, it's no big deal," Carley insisted. "I can drive myself."

"We'll cross that bridge when we get there," her father said. "No use arguing about it now. Let's get you out of the hospital and home first."

Carley shrugged. Her dad was right. Why argue now? There was plenty of time to argue later. "So, how are things at the store?"

"Well, we're gearing up for Valentine's Day," her mother said. "We rearranged our magazine racks to make room for a line of greeting cards. I figure they'll sell really well. You know how business is: We start on back-to-school the first of August, fall merchandise in September, Christmas by October—"

"Even earlier these days," her father interjected.

"Anyway," her mother continued, "I'm redoing some displays with lots of red and white ribbons and lace and cute little Victorian-style cupids. And some of the romance publishers are putting out special Valentine titles, so we've got plenty of new displays with the holiday theme."

"My favorite holiday," Carley muttered unkindly under her breath.

"Valentine's Day is a wonderful holiday," her mother said, glancing at her husband, who gave her a wink.

Sure, Carley thought. *If you're normal.* Frankly she'd always thought some sadist invented it. Valentines and syrupy sentiments of love were a cruel joke. She'd learned early on that Valentine cards only went to pretty, popular girls. Janelle practically waded hip deep in them every year. "The best thing about Valentine's Day is that boxes of chocolate are half price on the day after," Carley said.

Her father laughed. "I see you haven't lost your wit."

"I don't want to be witless," she quipped, making him laugh again.

Her parents stayed until late afternoon, then hugged her goodbye and left. Once they were gone, Carley felt blue. She liked her family and she considered herself fortunate to have such supportive parents. All during her ordeal with the cancerous tumor, they had been by her side, and when she'd been permanently disfigured, they'd sent her to counselors and did everything possible to help her adjust to her lifelong disfigurement and build up her self-esteem.

She was deep in thought, when someone rapped on her door.

"It's open," she called.

Kyle entered her room, feeling his way cautiously along the wall as he went.

She scrambled toward him, wincing in pain over the sudden movement, but fearful that he might bump into something. "Let me help," she blurted.

"I can manage," he said. "Just tell me if anything's in my path."

"My room's exactly like yours," Carley told him. "Just flip-flopped." She watched him inch closer. "Does a nurse know you're trying to navigate on your own?"

"I didn't think I needed a guide. Or a red-tipped cane just yet."

Eventually he made it to the small table near her window, where he groped for a chair. She itched to help him, but sat quietly, since she knew he wanted her to. When he was finally seated, she let out a deep breath. "You're here," she said.

He grinned, his expression looking pleased. "Maybe I'm not so helpless after all." He rubbed his shins. "A little black and blue maybe, but not helpless."

"To what do I owe the honor of this visit?"

"I wanted to apologize for the way I acted yesterday."

"You were angry. I understood."

"I didn't have to take it out on you."

"I didn't take it personally . . . honest."

He shifted in his chair and leaned forward, holding out his hand in a gesture that asked her to take hold of it. Heart pounding, she slid her hand into his. "I—I think you're a really nice person, Carley. I can't imagine how I would have made it these past days without your help."

"That's me. Carley the Helpful One. How do you suppose that translates in Chinese?" She was babbling, but couldn't stop herself. She felt totally flustered by his sincerity. Absolutely unsettled by his attention.

"Um—I'd really like to ask you something."

"You can ask."

"I don't want you to think I'm weird or anything."

"This must be serious." She tried to sound lighthearted, but her palms were sweating. She hoped her hand didn't slip out of his.

"Not too serious." He tipped his head and his brown hair spilled over the gauze wrapped around his forehead. "I've just been wondering what you look like, that's all. I mean, you know what I look like and I haven't a clue as to what you look like."

Her heart wedged in her throat. How

should she answer him? "I look like a girl," she finally said. "Hair, arms, legs—the usual stuff."

He laughed, but she hadn't meant it to be funny. She didn't want to be discussing her looks with him. A sudden thought unnerved her. What if one of the nurses had alluded to the fact that she was less than perfect-looking? That something was wrong with her?

"But tell me about yourself. Are you tall, short, athletic? What color's your hair and your eyes? I'm not trying for your vital statistics, just a mental picture."

"Well. . . ." She drew out the word, stalling for time. "What do you think I look like?"

"That's not fair. No matter how I describe you, you can agree or disagree, whether it's true or not."

"I won't. Tell me, what's your mental image of me?"

He squirmed, and she knew she'd put him on the spot. But he'd put her on the spot too. "All I have to go on is your voice."

"How does my voice make me sound?"

"Your voice makes you sound friendly.

And nice." He appeared more comfortable with this third-person approach—this pretense that her voice was a separate personality.

"And what about the color of my hair? Can my voice give you a clue about that?"

"Blond?"

"Dark brown."

"Straight?"

"Like a board."

"Long?"

"Long," she confirmed. "And what color does my voice say my eyes are?"

"Um—blue."

"Brown."

"I like brown eyes. My favorite color." He grinned gleefully, caught up in the game.

"Oh, puh-lease . . ." she drawled dramatically.

"You don't believe me? It's true. In the first grade I had a crush on a girl named Trianna Lopez. She had the most beautiful brown eyes."

"Fine. Sit there and talk about another girl in front of me." Carley pretended to be miffed.

She didn't fool him. Kyle laughed and said, "She was only six!"

"I forgive you."

"I'll bet you're tall."

"Only five foot three. I'd never make the basketball team."

"That's all right. I've never had a thing for jocks." He toyed with her fingers still nestled in his hand. "I'll bet you're thin too."

"Average."

"There's nothing average about you, Carley."

She felt her face blush crimson. If only he knew how *un*average she really was. "So now are you satisfied? Do you have a picture of me?"

"Sort of."

"Well, here's what I've learned about *you*, mister," she said, poking him playfully with her forefinger. "You're attracted to tall, willowy blondes with blue eyes and straight hair. I, on the other hand, am a not-so-tall brunette with brown eyes and straight hair."

"One out of four isn't bad for a guy in my situation," he insisted.

For a second she thought he might get melancholy remembering that he was blind. Quickly she said, "All right, one out of four is good."

He sat still, his face turned fully toward her. For an eerie moment she thought he might be able to see through his bandages. "What now?" she asked.

"There's another way I could satisfy my curiousity a little bit. If you're willing, that is."

"How?"

"You could let me touch your face. You know, explore it with my fingers."

Eight

❖

Kyle wanted to touch her face. But if he did, he'd know for certain something was wrong. Carley got an instant picture of his fingers tracing along the caved-in area between her left eye and nose and recoiling in horror. He'd ask, *"What's wrong with you?"* and she'd have to tell him that she was a freak. That just like Humpty Dumpty, all the plastic surgeons and medical geniuses couldn't put Carley Mattea back together again.

"I know you're still here," Kyle said, "because I'm still holding your hand. What's wrong? Did I upset you?"

"No," she said, a little too quickly. "I had

a shooting pain in my leg. I was gritting my teeth until it went away."

With those words Carley realized that she'd crossed a subtle barrier. Before, she'd simply avoided telling him the truth by not divulging certain details. Now she'd told him two outright lies. Truthfully she *was* upset, and there was no pain in her leg.

"I'm sorry," he said. "I thought maybe I'd offended you by asking to touch your face. I don't know why I asked. Maybe because the woman from blind services encouraged me to explore the world with my sense of touch. She said it would help me 'see' things. Forget it."

"It's all right. I—I really don't mind." *Another lie!* "But you know what I think would be better?"

"What?"

"I think it would be better to wait until you can actually see my face for yourself. Yes, that's what I want. I want to greet you face-to-face once your bandages come off."

He didn't say a word right away. He only held her hand and brushed his thumb repeatedly across her knuckles. "Even when the bandages come off, there's no guarantee I'll be able to see again."

"But I think you will," she insisted. "And because I think so, I want you to wait until you can see me with your own eyes."

"And if I can't?"

"Then you can touch away."

He slumped back in the chair.

She disliked bringing Kyle's mood from happy to glum; it wasn't a nice way to treat him. But she'd been desperate to take his mind off the idea of exploring her face with his touch. What a disaster it would have been. She didn't understand why it was so important to her that he maintain his illusions about her looks, but it was.

"Do you know what?" she asked brightly. "The orderly will be here any minute to take me down to PT." She told him another lie. She wasn't scheduled for another PT session until Monday morning.

"I'll go back to my room." Kyle stood.

"Let me walk with you."

"How? You're on crutches, remember?"

"We'll manage."

"Then let me take your elbow and follow

about a half step behind. That's the way I was taught to have someone lead me."

Carley let him grasp her right elbow and slowly she began to take small steps with her crutches so that he could keep up. Back in his room again, he climbed into the bed. "I think I'll listen to another one of those books you loaned me. I'm not much good at doing anything *but* listening."

"I have more," she said, eager to make up for any distress she might have caused him. "Mom and Dad brought me a bunch of new ones today."

"Will you come visit me later?" he asked.

"Absolutely."

"My parents are coming this afternoon. I'd like for them to meet you."

"Um—all right," she declared, knowing full well that she'd find something to keep her busy and away from her room so that she wouldn't have to meet them.

Carley returned to her room, grateful to be out of her awkward situation. How had she gotten herself into this mess? Was it wrong of her to want to protect herself from his discovering what she really looked like?

Was it wrong to want him to believe that she was normal, even pretty?

Later, when she figured Kyle's parents might be on their way up, Carley went to visit Reba. The girl was still recovering from her surgery, but fortunately she was alone in her room. IVs hung by her bed, and tubes leading from her stomach were partially concealed by bedcovers.

"For drainage," she explained to Carley.

"Are you in pain?" Carley might have felt revulsion if she hadn't been through so much medical trauma herself.

"Not much," Reba said. Her voice sounded soft and she spoke slowly, but at least she was lucid. She nodded toward a small machine next to her bed with its IV line threaded into her arm. "Morphine dispenser," she said. "If I start to hurt too bad, I can make the drip come faster."

"How long before you're able to get up?"

"Don't know." Reba's eyes closed, but soon opened again. "Talk to me. Take my mind off this stuff."

Carley told her about Kyle's visit and him wanting to touch her face.

"Wow," Reba mumbled. "Close call."

"Tell me about it. It's getting harder and harder to keep my secret."

"What if he asks one of the nurses about you?"

"Don't think I'm not worried about it. But they're professionals. So if one does tell him about me, I hope she'll be kind and won't say, 'Carley? You mean the dog-faced girl?' "

Reba grimaced. "No one would ever say that about you."

"You're wrong, Reba. Someone did say it."

"Who?"

"Jon, my sister's boyfriend."

"That's so mean!"

Carley patted Reba's arm. "Don't get worked up about it. It happened months ago. I was cutting through the gym at school and I heard some guys talking and heard one of them mention Janelle's name. Naturally I stopped and eavesdropped. They were telling Jon how lucky he was to have a babe like Janelle for a steady date. And too bad she didn't have a sister. And Jon said, 'She does —it's Carley, the dog-faced sophomore girl.'

"Then I heard a couple of the guys make

barking noises and Jon say, 'Man, I can hardly stand to look at her, she's so ugly.' I stopped listening then. I ran out of there as fast as I could. I didn't cry until I got home, but to this day I can't stand to be around Jon."

Reba's eyes grew wide as Carley talked. "Did you ever tell your sister?"

" 'Course not. It's too babyish to whine about it to her. I mean, what am I going to say? 'Your boyfriend called me a dog. I think you should dump him.' I need to be tough, Reba. Kids are always saying mean things about me. Dumb things. They don't know what it's like to look at this face in the mirror every day. People who are normal haven't got a clue about how badly words hurt. Worse than rocks sometimes."

Reba nodded. "Why can't people understand that no one likes being different. But people who are different still have feelings."

Carley realized that Reba, most of all, understood what she was saying. All her life Reba would be confined to a wheelchair. She was simply somebody that medical science couldn't make normal. A lump of tears lodged in Carley's throat. Tears for Reba. Tears for herself.

"I've been trying to figure out why I've let this whole thing with Kyle get out of hand," Carley said slowly. "I mean, why didn't I just come clean with him from the beginning? You told me to." Tears swam in her eyes.

"What do I know?" Reba offered a smile.

"You knew more than me. I guess it was just so nice to have a boy *like* me. And he liked me in spite of the way I looked. And now I can't seem to stop pretending with him."

"You could if you wanted to."

Carley shook her head. "No. I don't want to. I keep thinking that soon I'll get out of here and get back to my life."

"But once he gets out, he might come looking for you."

"But if he can't ever see me, it won't matter."

Reba blinked. "Do you hear what you're saying, Carley? It's almost as if you don't want him to get his eyesight back again."

Carley bowed her head. What Reba had said was true. She dreaded Kyle regaining his vision. And yet it was wrong to wish him confined to a lifetime of darkness simply because she didn't want him knowing she was disfigured. "He's the first guy who's ever been nice to me, Reba. The *only* one since before I was twelve."

"And you don't think he'll be nice to you once he knows what you look like?"

"No," Carley said miserably. "I live in the real world. And in the real world guys don't stick around for girls who look like me."

Just before bedtime Carley's phone rang.

"Where were you tonight?" Kyle's voice sounded hurt. "I told you my folks were coming and that I wanted you to meet them. Why did you run off?"

"I went to visit Reba. I hadn't seen her since her surgery and I didn't want her to think I'd forgotten about her," she explained quickly.

"Oh." His voice lost its edginess. "How she's doing?"

"Pretty good."

"Carley, I didn't mean to sound off at you. It's just that I've been talking about you to my friends and parents a lot. I've been telling them about this terrific girl I've met and they want to meet you too. Except that you're never around, so everybody thinks you're a figment of my imagination. Or worse, that I'm a liar."

Recalling Reba's admonition to come clean with Kyle, Carley took a deep breath. "Kyle, I think we should talk. I need to tell you something."

"Can you tell me tomorrow? The nurse just gave me a sleeping pill," he said, stifling a yawn.

"Sure . . . tomorrow's fine." She felt relieved. She really didn't want to confess everything tonight.

"Listen, my two best friends are coming tomorrow afternoon and I want them to meet you."

She wondered if this fetish of his to introduce her to his friends and family was ever going to end. "You're putting me on the spot, Kyle."

"Why? Just because I want my friends to meet the person who's making this whole ordeal bearable for me?"

She didn't know what to tell him and she didn't want to argue about it on the phone either. "We'll talk about it tomorrow."

"Tomorrow," he said, sounding drowsy. "But I promise we'll be next door to see you, so don't run off. Because if you do, we'll go looking for you if we have to search every floor of the hospital."

Nine

"You want *what?* Are you out of your mind?"

Carley bit her lip, not wanting to lash out at Janelle, who stood in the hospital room wearing an incredulous expression. "Don't get all hyper on me," she said as soothingly as possible. "I'm not asking you to rob a bank or anything."

"It's a dumb idea, Carley, and I won't do it. I won't pretend to be *you!*"

Janelle's stubborness was testing Carley's patience. Didn't her sister realize that she was desperate? And that desperate times called for desperate measures?

Carley had come up with the scheme late

the night before and called Janelle first thing Sunday morning. "Please come see me right away," she'd begged. "Don't even go to church first, just come straight here."

But when Janelle arrived and Carley revealed her plan for what she wanted Janelle to do later in the afternoon, Janelle adamantly refused. Carley glared at her sister, whose chin jutted out obstinately. "I never ever ask you for a favor, and the one time I do, you act as if I asked you to murder somebody."

"This is more than a favor, Carley. It's an out-and-out lie. I can't pretend to be you just so that you can impress some boy."

"This isn't some stupid kid prank, you know. I have good reasons for Kyle's friends to think that you're *me*. Kyle and I've become good friends. I really like him and I don't want his friends to tell him that I'm some kind of freak."

"You're not a freak!" Janelle stamped her foot. "And if anyone says you are, I'll deck 'em."

"Thanks for the show of loyalty." Carley sighed. "But I can deck people if I choose to.

The one thing I can't do is look normal. You're my sister and I need you to help me out here."

"You really like this guy?"

Carley nodded vigorously. Was her sister about to cave in?

"Then be honest with him. Tell him about yourself; he'll understand."

Carley exploded with "That's easy for you to say. You've never had people stare at you. Or call you names. Don't you see? I don't want to take the chance that he'll 'understand.' I want him to think I'm pretty. And if his friends meet *you*, then that's exactly what Kyle will think."

Unable to look Carley straight in the eye, Janelle sagged into a nearby chair and glanced down at the floor. "This is emotional blackmail."

"No. It's a favor. From one sister to another."

Suddenly Janelle sat upright, a gleam in her eye. "There is this small thing of your broken leg. Or do you expect me to throw myself down the stairwell?"

"I've already thought about that," Carley

said, holding up her hand. "If you roll into Kyle's room in a wheelchair with your leg stretched out and a blanket over your lap, no one will know that your leg isn't broken. Kyle's friends will see a pretty girl who says that her arms were hurting from using crutches. And Kyle won't see anything at all. I'm telling you, Janelle, this will work if you put a little effort into it."

"What will work?"

Both girls whipped around in the direction of the voice that had interrupted their discussion.

"Jon!" Janelle jumped up from the chair and went toward him. "What are you doing here?"

"I got to church and your mother said you'd come here instead, so I left and came looking for you. What's up?" He avoided looking at Carley.

Carley groaned and flopped back onto her pillow. Just what she needed—Jon to muddy up her plan. And just when she'd almost had Janelle persuaded.

"What's up is that my sister has some

harebrained idea about me impersonating her for this guy she's met in the next room."

Jon looked confused.

"He's temporarily blind," Carley interjected, none too kindly. "So he's never seen my face, and most likely never will. But his friends are coming to visit him this afternoon and he wants them to meet me and see what a 'babe' I am. But we all know that's not the case, don't we?"

Jon's face colored, but he still shook his head. "I don't want any guy coming onto my girl." His arm snaked around Janelle's waist possessively.

"Oh, puh-lease. . . ." Carley rolled her eyes dramatically. "Think of it as a temporary loan."

Even Janelle looked exasperated with him. "Cut the Neanderthal routine, Jon. I'm a person, not your property."

"But you're *my* girl!"

"And Carley's my sister."

"You're not seriously thinking about doing this, are you?" Jon sounded angry.

"What if I am?" Now that Janelle was on

the defensive, Carley decided to keep quiet and let the two of them argue it out. Maybe Jon's attitude was just the push Janelle needed to send her into Carley's camp on this issue.

"Because it's dumb, that's why."

"Yes, it's dumb, but Carley *is* my sister, and she wants my help."

"If she asked you to jump in front of a moving car, would you do it?"

"That is so lame. Just the kind of thing you'd tell a two-year-old. Which I'm not!" Janelle whirled around and started for the door. "I'm going to buy myself a Coke. Cool off, Jon!"

She grabbed her purse and flounced out the door. Jon glared after her.

"Not much fun to be called names, is it?" Carley asked him when they were alone.

Jon gave her a sullen glance and crossed to the window, where he stood with his hands thrust into his pockets and scowled.

Carley sat forward and swung her legs over the side of the bed. "It wouldn't kill you to cooperate, you know. We're talking a fifteen-minute visit that won't mean anything to you, but will mean everything to me. And to Kyle."

"It's just not right," Jon answered.

"Lots of things happen that aren't right. Like getting cancer when you're twelve and turning into a permanent sideshow. You know, someone's idea of a joke."

"What's that supposed to mean?"

"Woof-woof." She saw the back of his neck and ears flush red. He turned slowly and their gazes locked. "I'm sorry you don't like me," she said. "But I can't help the way I look. And I don't like people making fun of me."

"Who says I don't like you?"

"It's written all over your face every time you look at me. Or rather, *don't* look at me."

She was surprised when he said, "I really care for Janelle. She means everything to me. Are you going to ruin it for us?"

Carley felt a sense of power and for a minute wanted to see him squirm, but the feeling passed when she remembered how urgently she needed Janelle's help. No use causing a scene simply to get revenge. "Wrecking people's lives isn't my style," she told him. "But I would appreciate a good word from you. It would help this deal go down much more easily."

Before he could respond, Janelle swept back into the room, a can of diet cola in her hand. "The vending machine hardly had anything good," she grumbled.

Jon took a deep breath and stepped in front of her. "I've been thinking while you were gone."

Carley resisted the urge to blurt, *"That's what you smell burning—Jon's brain."*

"I think you should help Carley."

Janelle glanced from Jon to Carley and back again to Jon. "I was gone less than ten minutes. How did she persuade you so quickly? Especially when she's been working on me for an hour."

"I overreacted. What she wants is really sort of harmless." He glanced toward Carley. "Sort of like wearing a mask for Halloween. This guy will be happy. Carley will be happy. No one will know it's you. And then that's the end of it."

Carley ignored Jon's bad humor and nodded eagerly. "I told you, Sis, it'll only take a few minutes, and you don't ever have to do it again."

Janelle's shoulders drooped. "I hate it when people gang up on me. Especially people I care about."

Carley felt a twist of guilt and vowed she'd make it up to her sister sometime. "I'll be grateful forever."

Her phone rang and she grabbed the receiver. It was Kyle. "Hi," she said cheerfully.

"You're in your room."

"You sound surprised."

"You usually run off."

"Now, now," she chided.

"Listen, my friends Steve and Jason are here. They were cohorts in my infamous rocket-fuel stunt, except that they didn't get hurt. Anyway we want to come by and say hello."

"Don't do that!" Carley cut her eyes to Janelle and Jon, tucked the receiver beneath her chin, and pointed frantically at the wheelchair she'd confiscated earlier from the nurses' station. "What I mean is, why don't I come to your room? It's a mess here and I don't want strange boys around." Janelle rolled her eyes. "I can be there in five minutes," Carley added, ignoring her sister.

"Sure, no problem," Kyle told her. "Come soon."

"I can't stay long," she warned. "I have visitors coming too, and I want to be in my room when they arrive."

"No problem. Stay ten minutes. Stay an hour. I only want my friends to meet you." She heard a smile in his voice. "I only want them to meet the most special girl in the whole world."

Ten

"I really hate this," Janelle whispered as Jon helped her into the wheelchair.

Carley limped over with a blanket from off the bed. "But I need you to do it so much. And I'll never forget how you helped me. I'll be grateful forever!" She pumped up the area with a pillow and tossed the blanket across Janelle's lap.

Jon leaned down and adjusted the footrest so that Janelle could prop her leg in a thrust-out position. "You know how to work one of these things?"

"I can manage," Janelle snapped.

Carley fussed with the blanket, making

sure that it covered Janelle's lap and leg completely. "Just tell him—"

"I know what to say." Janelle pushed herself toward the door, paused, and scowled back at Carley and Jon. "What about my voice? Do you think he's clever enough to hear a difference?"

Carley's stomach constricted. She'd forgotten about her voice. "You can do a pretty good imitation of me. You always did when we were little and you wanted to get me in trouble with Mom."

"We've grown up since then. At least, one of us has."

Carley gritted her teeth. Janelle certainly wasn't being agreeable. "You're going to do just fine," she said. "And you'll never know how much this means to me. Never, ever."

Janelle rolled out into the hall while Jon and Carley peeked around the doorframe. When Janelle knocked on Kyle's door, Carley ducked backward. "She's in," Jon said. "Now what?"

"Now we loiter in the hall by his door and maybe we can hear something."

Jon looked at her as if she were nuts, but he tagged along when she hopped out on her crutches. She rested her back on the wall beside Kyle's door, and Jon leaned his shoulder against the wall next to her. She strained to hear through the slightly ajar door, but only snatches of words and mumbles came to her. She whispered, "I sure wish I could hear better."

Jon arched his eyebrow at her. "If only we'd thought to put a tape machine in her lap, she could have gotten the whole conversation."

She flashed him a hateful look. All at once her knees started shaking as it dawned on her that she was manipulating people's lives! She was working so hard to protect *herself* that she was forcing her sister and her sister's boyfriend to conform to her will. And she was deceiving Kyle and his friends by misrepresenting herself to them. She felt a wave of guilt and remorse. And fear. If Kyle found out about her now, he really would hate her. And she couldn't blame him. But she felt as if she'd gone so far with her charade that she couldn't drop it now. She couldn't tell him the truth at this stage.

Kyle's room door swung open and Janelle rolled out in the wheelchair, waving good-bye over her shoulder. Carley ducked under Jon's arm and headed in the opposite direction down the hall, fearful that one of Kyle's friends might stick his head out the doorway and see her. When she felt it was safe, she returned to her room. Janelle and Jon were preparing to leave.

'She shut the door fast. "So what happened?"

"Nothing happened. I was charming and sweet."

"Did Kyle say anything?"

"He said he'd call me later." Janelle picked up her purse and slipped on her coat. "But of course, he thinks I'm *you*."

"You don't have to leave yet. We could watch an NBA game on TV, or maybe some old movie." Now that the charade was over, Carley didn't want to be left alone. She wanted her sister to stay. She wanted to get back into Janelle's good graces.

"I've got a Lit test tomorrow and I need to study for it." Janelle started for the door with Jon.

"Janelle," Carley called. "Thanks."

Janelle didn't smile. "You're welcome. We'll walk down the stairwell to the ground floor," she said. "Less chance of being seen by Kyle's friends."

Then Janelle and Jon were gone and Carley was alone. All alone.

"My friends were suitably impressed." Kyle was eating dinner in Carley's room. Their trays were spread out on the small table near the window, and the TV played softly in the background.

"That's nice," Carley said, grateful that he couldn't see how little she was eating. She didn't have much of an appetite tonight.

"What did you think of them?"

She started. Why hadn't she pressed Janelle for more details? "They seemed nice."

"Nice?" Kyle cocked his head. "Steve practically fell over your chair. Did he hurt your leg?"

"No. I'm fine."

"Is anything wrong?" His expression looked puzzled.

"No. Why do you ask?"

He touched his meat loaf, gave the plate a small turn, and cut off a piece with his fork. Carley realized he'd become quite adept at feeding himself despite his blindness. "You— um—sounded funny today."

"Funny ha-ha or funny peculiar?" She tried to laugh off his observation, but her heart began to thud.

"I don't know. Your voice sounded different to me this afternoon. Not like your usual self. I've grown used to your voice and the way it sounds. I like it."

"How does my voice sound?"

"Sort of sexy."

She giggled with pure pleasure. Her voice was hers alone, and he liked it. She didn't have to speak through her sister's mouth. It was Carley's voice Kyle heard. "Sexy? Me?"

"That's what I said." He grinned. "When all you have is someone's voice to go on, you notice the smallest change. And today you just didn't sound like yourself."

"Um—I had a little allergy attack right before I came by to see you. Maybe that made me sound different."

"Maybe so." He still acted perplexed, but she didn't pursue it and decided to change the topic to get his mind on something else. "So, have you heard how much longer you'll be locked in this place?"

"My doctor hasn't said. How about you?"

"The antibiotic is working fine—no fever for days. I'll get another X ray tomorrow."

"So you may be leaving sooner than me."

"I've been here for over a week and I'd like to leave. Wouldn't you?"

"Sure." But his tone was hesitant. "It's a little scary, though, thinking of going outside these walls when I still can't see."

"Will someone be with you when you go home?"

He shook his head. "Both my folks work, so I'll have to be on my own for most of the day. It wouldn't be so bad if I could see. I'm behind in all my schoolwork and I'm in accelerated classes. I'll probably never catch up."

"Are we having a pity party?"

"You're not going to let me feel sorry for myself? Not even just a little?"

"It won't help." Carley toyed with her fork. She wasn't being insensitive to his plight, but she knew how senseless it was to sit around complaining about what couldn't be changed. Life went on whether a person participated in it or not. "But I know how it feels to be swamped with schoolwork. That's enough to give anybody a downer."

He laughed. "Well, I'm not ready to learn braille and I don't want to spent the summer in school, so I'm not sure how I'll catch up."

"Why don't you have Steve or Jason tape your class lectures for you? Maybe then you wouldn't fall so far behind."

He straightened in the chair. "Why didn't I think of that?" He sounded amazed that something so obvious could have eluded him.

"You don't have a brain as devious as mine?" she offered playfully.

"Carley, that's a great idea. My dad could arrange to have all my classes taped and I can keep up that way. Why, I might even be able to take tests orally."

She tapped his hand. "I charge big bucks for advice, you know."

"I'll pay." They laughed together, but soon Kyle grew quiet, thoughtful. "Can I tell you something?"

She nodded, then realized that he couldn't see her. "Sure," she said for emphasis.

"I like you."

She felt her mouth go dry. "I like you too."

"Once we both go home, can I call you? Visit with you?"

So long as you're blind, she thought, but she said, "Oh gosh, once you get back to regular life, you'll forget all about me."

Kyle grabbed her hand and held it tightly. "Not so, Carley. I'll never forget you."

She felt a wave of fear. There was no way they could have a relationship once they were both out of the hospital. Sooner or later someone would see her and tell Kyle the truth. Certainly there would be no way she could ever persuade Janelle to impersonate her again. How could she put him off without hurting his feelings or telling him

more than she ever wanted him to know?
"Why don't we wait and see how things go
once we blow this place?"

"You don't want me to keep in touch, do
you?" He looked dejected.

"I didn't say that."

"But it's what you meant. Is it because I
could be permanently blind? Is it because
you don't want to be stuck with a guy who's
blind?"

"No way," she started to protest.

Kyle interrupted. "Steve and Jason told
me how pretty you are. I can't figure out why
you don't have a boyfriend, unless you're so
beautiful that you can pick anyone you
want. If that's the case, I don't stand a
chance."

In her heart she longed to tell him that he
was handsome, smart, nice—the most wonderful guy she'd ever known. And that having him for a boyfriend would be the greatest
thing that ever happened to her. But of
course she couldn't. She could never let him
know how she truly felt. "I think we should
not talk about this stuff," she said quietly. "I

think we should have fun right now and not talk about tomorrow."

"But—"

"Please," she begged. "Let's just be friends as long as we're here."

"If that's what you want. . . ." He tried to keep the hurt out of his voice.

"It's what I want."

Eleven

"You're going home? Lucky you." Reba gave Carley a wistful look. "I sure am going to miss you."

"I'll call you," Carley said, feeling sorry for Reba, who was still recovering from her abdominal surgery. "And before you know it, you'll be headed home too." Home for Reba was a small town in middle Tennessee, at least four hours from Knoxville and the hospital.

"When are you leaving?"

"My mom's packing my stuff and filling out the paperwork right now."

"I'm glad you stopped by to tell me. Have you told Kyle?"

Carley shook her head. "He's my next stop." She didn't let on how much she was dreading it.

"What have you decided to do about him?"

"Nothing. I figure that once he goes home, he'll get on with his life."

Reba dismissed the idea with a wave of her hand. "I think you're dreaming. I think he's going to want to see you."

"Don't say that. You and I both know it's impossible."

"Wrong. You *think* it's impossible, so you won't change your mind about telling him the truth."

Carley squealed, "Will you stop it already! I know what I'm doing."

Reba shook her head in exasperation. "Never mind. It's like talking to a brick wall." She grinned. "Anyway, keep your promise and call me. I know we haven't been friends for long, but you're my best friend ever and I want things to work out for you. You know, Carley, in spite of the way your face looks, you really do have a shot at being normal."

"Just how do you figure that?"

Reba's gaze led to the wheelchair parked near her bed. "I wish my face was the only thing messed up about me."

Impulsively Carley leaned down and hugged her. "I'll be in touch." She positioned her crutches under her arms and retreated from the room.

She stopped at Kyle's door, took a deep breath, and knocked. When he called, "Come in," she did.

"I got my walking papers," she told him without preamble.

His bandages couldn't hide his disappointment. "I'll miss you."

"That's what Reba said. Maybe I should start a fan club. Charge a fee." Carley kept her voice light and breezy.

"You said you'd be back for PT. Will you come up and visit with me?" he asked.

"You bet. I'll even bring you some new Books on Tape."

He held out his hand and she reached out and grasped it. His grip felt warm and strong and she wished she didn't ever have to let go. "You take care of yourself," he said.

"You too."

"You did mean what you said the other night about staying friends, didn't you?"

"I meant it." She was telling him what he wanted to hear and only hoped he wouldn't hate her when he figured out the truth—that she had no intention of ever seeing him again.

Without warning, Kyle reached up and caught the side of her face with his hand. She gasped, but then realized he was cupping the right side, the normal side. "Don't be mad," he said softly. "I've wanted to touch you for the longest time."

Just so long as his fingers didn't venture to the left side of her face, she didn't mind. "It's all right," she said, glad she had crutches for support because her knees had gone weak with anxiety and emotion.

He smoothed his thumb along her cheek, brushing the fringe of her eyelashes and the bridge of her nose. *Too close!* her mind warned. Carley pulled back. "Please don't," he whispered. "Can I touch your hair?"

She gulped. "Okay."

His fingers moved upward until they stroked the tips of her thick, dark hair. He wound strands around his hand, tugging them gently, tenderly. He rolled long clusters between his thumb and fingers, as if testing the texture. As if tasting it with his sense of touch. He reached higher, combed his fingers through the thickness, and said, "Very soft. I figured it would be."

Her breath caught in her throat and she could scarcely breathe. Tears stung her eyes. She longed to have him kiss her. If only . . . *if only.*

He withdrew his hand and brought his fingers to his nose and sniffed deeply. "Smells like flowers. And sunshine." He turned his face toward her, and she touched the corners of the bandages on his eyes. They were the barrier that held him prisoner, yet protected her. "I've noticed that scent every time you've come into my room. I've wondered if it was your hair or some perfume."

"New shampoo. The ad campaign said it would drive guys wild," she joked, hoping to make him laugh and break the tension.

He smiled. "Funny girl. But you don't always have to make a joke."

Humor was the only way she knew of dealing with intense emotional moments. "I've got to go." She stepped backward.

"I'll be seeing you, pretty Carley."

She winced because his words had stung. "Goodbye, Kyle."

She hurried next door, where her mother looked up from the suitcase she was packing. "There you are. I wondered where you ran off to." She paused and eyed Carley narrowly. "Are you all right? You look like you're crying."

"I'm fine, Mom. I was just saying goodbye."

Her mother shook her head, bemused. "You never cease to amaze me. You've always said you hated hospitals, and now you're crying because you have to leave this one. I'd have thought you'd never wanted to see the inside of this place again."

"I don't, Mom. Call the nurse and tell her

I'm ready for the wheelchair ride downstairs." She turned to the mirror and stared at the twisted half of her face, then jerked her hair back into a ponytail. Suddenly she didn't want anything to obstruct her true image, her real self. She didn't want to forget that what Kyle had made her feel was an illusion. She would never be normal. Or pretty. She mustn't ever forget. *Never!*

At home Carley moped around the house for the rest of the afternoon, unable to shake a case of the blues. She missed the routine of the hospital. Most of all, she missed Kyle. The next morning Janelle asked, "You want a ride to school? Jon's picking me up."

"I'll catch the bus," Carley said. "The sooner I get back into my regular routine, the better."

"Mom wants me to take you to PT tomorrow afternoon. Trouble is I have ensemble practice every day after school. State competition is in March, and if we don't practice every day, we'll never get a superior rating."

"I can drive myself."

"Tell that to Mom."

"I'm telling you, I can drive. There's nothing wrong with my right foot, and that's the one that controls the car."

"You'll have to clear it with Mom," Janelle said.

"How will you get home if I persuade her?"

"Jon will bring me."

"I forgot about lover boy."

"Be nice. I'll give up ensemble practice on the days you have PT if Mom says you can't drive yourself."

"You shouldn't have to do that."

Janelle shrugged. "I hate practice."

But Carley could tell that her sister really did want to practice. It was her senior year and her final opportunity to earn a superior rating at state chorus competitions. "Let me talk to Mom."

At school she felt as she always did—a nonparticipant, on the outside looking in. Her classes weren't a struggle; schoolwork came easily to her. But blending into the social scenery was something else again. A few kids spoke to her, asked her how her leg was doing, but most looked past her. Or over her. Or through her as if she hardly existed. She couldn't wait for the bell to ring, marking the end of the day, so that she could go home and forget all about high school and how she didn't fit in.

She told herself that in a few days she'd toughen up and it wouldn't matter. But the truth was that someone—Kyle—had treated her as if she were pretty and desirable. Now she had to return to being the ugly duckling, and it was difficult.

She was deep in thought, fiddling with the combination lock on her locker after school, balancing books and crutches, knowing she had to hurry if she was going to make it to her bus stop, when her notebook slipped from her hands and spilled on the hall floor.

Kids pouring out of rooms scurried past, stepping all over the binder. She could only watch helplessly, for she was unable to stoop down and rescue her notebook for fear of being trampled. All at once a boy's voice said, "Let me get that for you, babe."

She spun, forgetting to shield her face. Her rescuer was tall with dark hair and brown eyes. He was smiling, but as he caught sight of her face, his smile faded, and shocked surprise took its place. "I'll get it," she snapped, and struggled to hold her crutches with one hand while she bent over.

Then another male voice intervened. "Problems, Carley?"

It was Jon. He stooped and gathered up her notebook and scattered papers. He stood and glared at the other boy, still standing, staring. Jon snarled, "What's your problem? If you're not going to help, get out of the way."

The boy darted off.

"Dumb jerk," Jon muttered under his breath.

Carley straightened, her body burning with humiliation. "Thanks for retrieving my stuff," she said, grabbing for the notebook.

Jon held it back. "Wait."

"I've got to hurry or I'll miss my bus." She couldn't bear to look him in the eye. Couldn't stand knowing that he'd seen her humiliated by a stranger's look.

"I'm hanging around waiting for Janelle. Will you wait with me?" Jon asked.

"I can't."

Jon reached out and took her arm. "I want to talk to you, Carley. There're some things I need to say. Some things I *have* to say. You can get a ride home with Janelle and me, so don't run off. Hear me out. Please."

Twelve

The second bell rang and Carley sighed. "Well, I don't have much choice, do I? I'll never make it in time to catch my bus now."

Jon took her books and stacked them atop his. "Come on," he urged.

"Where to?"

"To the atrium."

The high school was built in the shape of a wheel, with the atrium at its hub and halls poking outward like spokes. With benches, potted plants, and a large overhead skylight, the atrium became an indoor student gathering place between classes and before and after school hours. Once there, Carley settled on a concrete bench emblazoned with the school seal. Jon sat down beside her and gestured toward the Fine Arts hallway. "Janelle has to come this way, so she'll see us."

Carley looked at her watch. Janelle wouldn't be out of practice for another forty-five minutes. She didn't think she and Jon could fill up the time simply talking, but she had no choice. "All right," she said, folding her hands in her lap, "What do you want to say to me? Ask suggestions for a Valentine's Day gift for my sister?"

"Buying Janelle presents isn't ever a problem."

Carley hadn't figured it would be. Pretty girls like Janelle always got gifts for Valentine's Day. "So then what can lowly little me do for you?"

"First off, I'm really crazy about Janelle."

"So tell me something I don't know."

"I also know you don't like me very much and I want to tell you that I don't blame you. I've acted like a real jerk."

Amazed by his confession, Carley stared at him. "Well, we do agree on some things."

In spite of her put-down, Jon smiled. "You do have a way of delivering a line, Carley."

"Don't you know? Comedy is my forte."

He rubbed the palms of his hands over the fabric of his jeans, and she could tell that he was nervous. "I know that you could have ruined things between Janelle and me if you wanted to."

"Why would I do that?"

"Some girls might have done it. If . . . if they overheard their sister's boyfriend saying rude stuff he didn't mean."

Carley shrugged, remembering the day in the gym when she'd heard him call her a dog. "It's ancient history, Jon. No use dredging it up."

"It was dumb of me. I didn't know you were there that day, and I was smarting off for the guys, acting like a big shot. I'm really sorry because I know it hurt you."

He looked miserable, and she almost felt sorry for him. "I've heard worse," she said. "When a person doesn't look normal, she hears a lot worse."

"I haven't been able to forget it," he said.

"Especially now that I know you better. And now that I know how much Janelle cares about you."

"She does?" Carley was mildly surprised. She'd always thought of Janelle as somewhat self-centered and too focused on her own life to have much interest in Carley's.

"She's like a bulldog sometimes. Nobody dares say anything mean about you, 'cause if she hears about it, she marches right up to them and makes them apologize. She tells them what a hero you are to have survived cancer and show up in school every day in spite of the way the doctors left your face. I heard her go off on someone once, and after five minutes of talking about how brave and special you are, she had the girl in tears."

Carley couldn't have been more shocked if he'd told her Janelle had sprouted a second head. "Janelle? My sister?"

"Don't you know how much she protects you?"

At a loss for words, Carley shook her head.

"Well, she does. She's changed my viewpoint about people who are handicapped. Or at least, people who aren't normal. And after getting to know you better, I agree with her. You're all right, Carley. You kept my secret when you could have ruined things between me and Janelle."

She blinked, and turned her head, over-whelmed by both his apology and his revela-tion about her sister's fierce loyalty toward her. "I wouldn't try to break up the two of you."

"You know that thing she did for you at the hospital with the guy next door—pre-tending to be you—was hard on her."

"I know she hated to lie for me."

"It was more than that," Jon said. "She told me later that sitting in that wheelchair gave her a new perspective on the world. She told me that she thinks it should be mandatory for every healthy teenager in the country to go around in a wheelchair for one day so that they can see what life's like for people who are maimed or deformed. She said that the world looks different when you're eye level with a person's waist and helpless."

Carley saw admiration stamped all over

his face and realized that she'd been as guilty of prejudice toward Janelle as others often were of *her*. How had she been so oblivious of her own sister's thoughts and feelings? "I'm glad you told me," Carley said. "I *think* I am . . . geez, now I'll have to really be nice to her."

Jon grinned and stood up. "I've never felt about any girl the way I feel about Janelle. I mean, she's pretty and all, but she's also special in other ways."

"You're a real cheerleader, Jon."

His face reddened. "Look, I didn't mean to go on and on. And I'd appreciate it if you didn't go telling her that I turned into a slobbering puppy over her."

"Well, as one dog to another, I think I can keep your secret," Carley said with a straight face.

Jon looked startled. "I told you I was sorry about saying that."

"I'm kidding," she said with a smile. "Lighten up."

He grinned sheepishly. "Thanks for understanding."

"Your secret's safe with me."

Just then Janelle came sauntering up the hallway, books balanced on her hip. "Hi, you two." She glanced from one to the other. "Boy, you look deep in conversation. Am I interrupting anything? What's up?"

"Nothing," Carley and Jon said in unison.

Janelle eyed them suspiciously. "It doesn't look like nothing."

"You're out early," Carley said, switching gears.

"Only fifteen minutes. I thought you were taking the school bus home."

"I changed my mind."

"I asked her to ride with us," Jon explained.

"So, let's get home." Carley stood and retrieved her crutches. "I have homework to do."

"I've got your books," Jon said. "I'll carry them to the car."

Quickly he and Carley took off side by side, leaving a befuddled Janelle to tag along behind.

It wasn't until the next afternoon when Janelle was driving Carley to her PT appointment that Janelle brought up the incident again. Their mother had categorically refused to allow Carley to drive herself. At least not until she was farther along in her therapy.

Janelle said, "When I came up yesterday, the two of you were totally engrossed in conversation. And when I said hello, you both acted as if I'd intruded on some clandestine meeting."

"You want to talk about this now?"

"Why not? I think the two of you were up to something and it involved me."

Carley felt her cheeks color. "Not true. We were just talking."

"Let's not argue. Just tell me what you and Jon were talking about."

Carley thought fast. "Um—Valentine's Day. He was asking my opinion on what to get you."

"I know you don't care for Jon." Janelle ignored the whole Valentine's Day story.

"He's all right."

"You said that before, but you didn't mean it."

"I've changed my opinion."

"Why?"

Carley sighed, and fiddled with the buttons on the radio. "I've gotten to know him and there's more to him than I once thought."

"Such as." Janelle repositioned the car's rearview mirror.

"He's not a total loser."

"Thanks for the endorsement."

"I didn't mean it that way. I wasn't sure Jon liked me. It seemed as if he was always avoiding me, and I figured it was because he couldn't deal with my looks."

"Jon's not that way." Janelle defended him.

"I know that now. I'm just not around guys very much, so sometimes I don't know what to say. Or how to act."

"You do all right with Kyle."

"You know he's different."

"Are you going to visit him today after your PT appointment?"

Carley stared out the window. The Tennessee countryside looked brown and stark, making her realize what a long, dreary month January could be. "I'm not sure I should."

"Why not?"

"Why prolong the agony? Once I left the hospital, I made up my mind to forget about him."

Janelle pulled into the parking lot adjacent to the physical therapy building attached to the Knoxville hospital. She put the car into park and turned off the engine. "I think you're making a mistake," she said quietly.

"How could it be a mistake to keep some guy who thinks I'm beautiful from learning the truth?" Carley leaned her head against the seat headrest and looked up through the windshield into the blustery gray sky. Without the engine to keep the heater going, the car's interior was chilling fast.

"Because you've got a rotten perception of physical beauty and its importance," Janelle said. "Because, believe me, being pretty isn't all it's cracked up to be. In fact sometimes it's the most awful burden in the world."

Thirteen

"I find that really hard to believe," Carley said after a few minutes had passed in silence. "How can being pretty be a handicap?"

"Because when a person's pretty, that's all people expect her to be. She isn't appreciated for anything except her physical appearance."

"What's so horrible about that?" Carley wanted to know. "I think it would be nice to have somebody look at me and say, 'She's pretty,' instead of 'Look, a freak.'"

"Anybody who puts a value on another person just because of his or her physical attractiveness is pitiful." Janelle's hazel eyes fairly crackled with conviction. "I don't want people hanging around with me because I look good, but because they *like* me."

"Get a grip," Carley insisted. "That's just not the way things are in the real world. All my life I've heard kids make fun of other kids because they were different—even before this happened to my face. I remember in the fifth grade there was this fat girl in my class. She wore thick glasses, too, and everybody made fun of her. Sometimes to the point of making her cry."

Carley dropped her gaze as she spoke, recalling the girl with clarity. "I'm sorry to say I teased her too. In fact after my surgery I wondered if leaving me deformed was God's way of paying me back for being mean to her."

Janelle recoiled. "You can't believe that! God's not that way. What about all the others who teased her? Did they get cancer and get left scarred?"

"Not that I know of." Carley stared hard at her hands as if they might hold some answer. "But why did this happen to me? Why did I have to get left with half a face?"

Janelle reached over and squeezed Carley's

shoulder. "Nobody has that answer. And trying to come up with one could drive you
nuts."

"As if I'm not already."

Janelle wagged her finger. "Only when it
comes to guys."

"And guys are the worst. You wouldn't
know because you've always had to beat
them off with a stick, but they only go after
girls who are pretty. Cripes, you've had a zillion boyfriends."

"A zillion?" Janelle rolled her eyes. "I've
dated a few, but most of them hardly see me
as a person, just someone they can show off
to their friends."

Carley wasn't the least bit sympathetic.
She said, "I'm sixteen years old and I've
never had a date." Old hurts welled up inside her. "Why do you suppose that is?
Could it be because I'm not pretty? Why
isn't my wonderful personality taken into
consideration?"

"Now you're being sarcastic."

"No. I'm being realistic. I'm never going
to have a date. No guy's ever going to ask
me out or take me anywhere out in public."

Janelle sighed heavily. "I know it seems that way now."

"You bet it does."

"Kyle might just be the one if you'd give him half a chance."

"So long as he's blind and so long as we don't have to mingle with the rest of the world, Kyle and I can have a thing for each other. But the minute his vision clears, or his friends meet the real Carley, it'll be over between us. Trust me. I know what I'm talking about."

Janelle balled her fist and pounded the steering wheel. "You are *so* stubborn and bullheaded."

Carley quickly brought her fingers up to either side of her head like horns and snorted.

Janelle shook her head while trying to suppress a smile. "I give up. But someday you'll find out I'm right. Looks aren't nearly as important as you think they are." Janelle pointed toward the hospital. "Go on and keep your PT appointment before we have to fight about this."

Carley grasped the car door handle. "What are you going to do? It's too cold to sit out here in the car."

"I'm going into the hospital cafeteria and have a cup of hot chocolate." She reached into the backseat and grabbed a book. "And study for an American History test." She made a face.

"I'll come there after I finish."

As Carley was fishing out her crutches, Janelle asked, "So what did you tell Jon?"

"About what?"

"About what to buy me for Valentine's Day."

Now it was Carley who grinned. "I told him to think gold and pricey."

Janelle returned a smile and nodded. "Good advice, little sister."

Together they walked to the Rehabilitation building, where Janelle took the covered walkway to the hospital and Carley went inside the PT center. When she'd completed her therapy, she ventured over to the hospital, but not to the cafeteria. Instead, she took the elevator up to her former floor, and, with heart thudding, she ambled down the hall to Kyle's room. The door was ajar and she halted in the doorway.

In the room she saw Kyle down on all fours, methodically feeling the floor in a circular pattern. Fascinated, she watched, realizing he was searching for something. Under the bed she spied the small foam rubber baffle that fit over the end of an earplug for comfort when wearing a headset, and she knew that's what he was trying to find. She wanted to shout, "I see it!" She wanted to rush in and pick it up for him. Yet she did nothing but watch him pat the floor and grunt in frustration.

Pity for him flooded through her. If he didn't regain his sight, he would spend the remainder of his life learning to adjust to living blind in a seeing world. If he remained sightless, he'd never get to realize his dreams of working for NASA or of flying an airplane.

Feelings of guilt twisted her insides like a sharp knife. To protect his illusions of her, she'd wanted him never to be able to see her. How unfair! No one deserved to be confined to a world of darkness if it was preventable or correctable. Just because she was limited to a less than normal life was no reason to selfishly wish the same sentence on him. Silently she pleaded to be forgiven for her attitude. *Let Kyle get his sight back*, she begged with all her heart.

All at once Kyle reared up and sat stock-still. "Who's there?" he asked.

Caught off guard, Carley pressed her back to the door frame. She should speak up. But she didn't.

"Hey, I know somebody's in the room with me. Tell me who."

Still she kept quiet.

"You're being rude, you know. I can't see you, but I know you're there. Why don't you say something?" His brow furrowed and his voice sounded angry.

Why don't I say something? Carley couldn't believe she was behaving this way. Couldn't understand why she was provoking him. But her vocal cords refused to respond. It was as if they'd been cut; she was helpless to reveal herself.

"Talk to me!" Kyle shouted.

She backed out of the room, desperate to be gone. One crutch caught on a corner of the door and she almost went sprawling, but she managed to regain her balance without making any noise. She spun and barreled down the hall toward the elevator. Tears almost blinded her, and her breath came in rapid gasps, half sobs.

Behind her she could hear Kyle calling, "Whoever you are, you're a stinking coward! You have no right to sneak up on a blind person, then run away. Do you hear me?"

Carley jabbed frantically at the elevator button, terrified that a nurse would hear Kyle and discover her trying to escape. The elevator came and she flung herself through the opening doors. Mercifully it was empty and she sagged against the side, heaving great breaths of air. Her hands shook and her knees wobbled, but she'd escaped without him knowing who'd been in his room.

She finger-combed her hair and tried to regain her composure during the ride to ground level, where Janelle was waiting in the cafeteria. "You must be seriously deranged," she told herself shakily under her breath. Kyle was right, only a coward would have refused to face him. Why hadn't she greeted him? Stayed for a visit? Why had she gone up in the first place when she'd told Janelle she wasn't going to? When she had sworn to herself she would never see him again?

"You're horrible, Carley Mattea," she muttered to herself. *You upset Kyle and ran off. You were mean and hateful.*

Janelle called out to her, gathered up her book, and hurried over. "What took you so long? Hey, are you okay?" She squinted at Carley. "You look discombobulated." The expression was a longtime favorite of their Southern grandmother.

"I'm all right." She clenched her hands hard around the grips of her crutches. "Tell me, what does 'combobulated' look like?"

Janelle ignored Carley's attempt to divert the conversation. "Did your physical therapy hurt?" Automatic sympathy flooded her pretty features.

"A little," she lied.

"They overworked your leg, didn't they?"

"As Jon says, 'no pain, no gain.'"

"Well, I'm glad I'm driving so that you can relax."

Carley didn't want to relax; she wanted to forget she'd ever met Kyle Westin and experienced what it was like to be thought pretty and normal. Whoever said "ignorance is bliss" was correct. Before, she could only speculate what it would be like. Now that she knew, she hated it. The feeling was painful and sad. Like a taste of some wonderful fruit that a person could savor only once and then never forget.

In the car she reclined the seat and closed her eyes, hoping that Janelle would get the message that she didn't want to talk. Because there was no way she could ever explain that it wasn't her leg that hurt. It was her heart.

Fourteen

Two days later Carley still hadn't figured out why she'd behaved so foolishly at the hospital. Deciding that she had to get it off her mind, she called the hospital, dialed Kyle's extension, and heard the voice of a stranger. Kyle had checked out and returned home. She hung up, glad he'd been released, but disappointed that she hadn't been able to talk to him.

She told herself it was for the best. No contact was the best thing. Now she could get on with her life, and he could get on with his.

Her mother took off from the bookstore to drive Carley to her appointment with her orthopedist, Dr. Olson. "If he says it's all right for me to drive, will you let me?" Carley asked.

"If he agrees, yes," her mother answered.

Dr. Olson had his technician take X rays of Carley's leg, and once the film was developed, he put the various views up on a light-board and studied them while Carley and her mom looked on. "Your bone looks good. The pins are holding fine and the infection is entirely cleared up. I know you didn't want to be in the hospital for ten days, but it was the best course of treatment for you. The IV antibiotic really did the job."

There was no way to tell him just how much of an impact the hospitalization had had on her life, so Carley simply asked, "How much longer will I have to wear this thing?"

He looked at her chart. "Let's see—surgery was three weeks ago, at the beginning of January. It takes six to eight weeks for a bone to knit, so maybe as early as mid-February."

"She would have been out of the cast sooner if it hadn't been for the infection,"

Carley's mother observed, making it sound as if the doctor was somehow at fault.

"Osteomyelitis isn't common, but it can happen." Dr. Olson said good-naturedly. "The important thing is that Carley's well on the road to recovery now."

"Time flies when you're having fun," Carley interjected. She saw no reason for her mother to blame the doctor for something that was nobody's fault.

"And what about her tendons? You told us that she may have to have further surgery on them."

"Let's see how she does with PT once the cast is off. Maybe further surgery is avoidable. In the meantime if you want to hang up your crutches, you can."

"I can manage without them," Carley said.

"But," her mother said doggedly, "her infection had nothing whatsoever to do with the fact that she once had cancer, does it?"

"Absolutely nothing," Dr. Olson assured her. "The infection could have happened to anyone."

Carley saw her mother look relieved, and until then she hadn't realized the cancer issue had been weighing on her mind. It certainly hadn't weighed on hers. Later, when they were driving home, Carley said, "Mom, my cancer was four years ago, and the oncologist only sees me once a year. He told you I was cured. If the doctors aren't worried about it, why are you?"

"I'm not worried," her mother contended. "I believe you're cured. I just don't want us to be blindsided like that again. I mean, who expected headaches to turn into a cancerous tumor?"

"And who expected the 'fix' to leave my face like this?" Carley finished quietly.

"It was the only way to save your life." Her mother glanced over at her. "We never talk about it. You seem so well adjusted and all. You crack jokes. You forge ahead with life. And when I look at you, I don't see it anymore."

"How could you *not* see it? My face is deformed!"

"Not to me. To me I see my beautiful little daughter who's alive."

Carley sighed. "Well, the rest of the world sees a girl with a messed-up face."

"Do you tell people what happened? Do you let them know how you got this way?"

"Oh, sure, Mom, right! Just what I want to do—deliver my life story to everyone who stares at me."

Her mother fiddled with the heater controls, partly out of being flustered, Carley figured, because the car was plenty warm. "Well, people like that are insensitive and callow. People can't help the way they look, just the way they act."

Her mother's view of the world seemed simplistic to Carley. And naive. But perhaps a person needed to live with something before she understood it. "I've made up my mind that everybody would be better off if people wore paper bags over their heads. You know, with little cutouts for eyes and mouths. That way we'd all be on equal footing when it comes to a social life."

Her mom smiled. "It seems you've been giving everything a whole lot more thought these days. Don't think I haven't noticed the way you've moped around the house ever since you came home from the hospital. Care to tell me why?"

"No reason," she said, turning to gaze out the window. She couldn't tell her mother about Kyle and the emotions he'd stirred up in her. Emotions that might have never surfaced if he could have seen her face. She caught sight of her face in the side mirror and purposefully turned so that she didn't have to look at her own reflection.

"Maybe I've forgotten how traumatic high school can be," her mother mused, half aloud, watching Carley from the corner of her eye. "I think it's time we started making the rounds to plastic surgeons again."

Carley shrugged listlessly. "We did that, remember? They told us there was nothing they could do to fix me."

"But things change in medicine every day. There are new technologies, new break-throughs. They do things now they couldn't do a few years ago. I think we should check it out again."

"Do you think they can make me look normal?"

"I think we should go ask. Do you want

me to set up an appointment? Do you want to think about it for a while?"

Carley didn't have to think about it. She wanted it more than anything. She wasn't being unrealistic; she knew she might never be pretty no matter what they did to her face. But she had to look better than this. Otherwise, what kind of future did she have other than joining the circus as a sideshow exhibit?

"Sure, Mom. Let's do it. Let's see if all the smart doctors can put Carley together again."

On Saturday Carley went to work in the bookstore, her first day of work since before her accident. She arrived with Janelle before the start of the business day, and while her sister set up the register and readied the counter area for customers, Carley walked along the aisles, inspecting the shelves.

"Boy, Mom sure has the place junked up," she said over her shoulder.

"She's a sucker for Cupid," Janelle said. "Every time a publisher offers a new display, she makes room for it."

Carley leaned over to examine one lavish cardboard unit colored with vivid red hearts, nosegays of violets, and embossed ribbons of white Victorian lace. She stuck out her tongue.

"That's not nice," Janelle said, coming up beside her.

Carley blushed, but pretended she wasn't embarrassed about her childish antics. "Sorry, but I think Valentine's Day is a waste."

"Hush. You'll hurt Cupid's feelings."

"Let the little dirtbag suffer."

Janelle giggled. "Does this mean you're not going to send anybody special a card?"

"Who would I send a card to?"

Janelle crossed her arms and tapped her toe and waited patiently for Carley to figure it out.

"Kyle?" Carley squealed. "Are you implying I should send one to Kyle?"

"And why not?"

"He's blind. He couldn't see it anyway."

"That's rude, Carley."

Instantly she felt ashamed. "I . . . um . . . just don't think I should send him one. It's a dumb thing for a girl to do. Guys are supposed to send cards, not girls."

"What rock did you crawl out from under? If you like somebody, you should let him know. What could it hurt to send the guy a little Valentine? It might even make him feel good."

Carley started to list all the reasons why not, when the phone rang. Janelle hurried to the front desk and answered it. She cupped her hand over the mouthpiece and held it out to Carley. "It's for you."

"Me? No one ever calls me here. Who is it?"

"Your personal Cupid."

"Kyle?" Carley felt her mouth go dry. "Tell him I'm busy. Tell him I'm not working today." Her heart began to thud with panic.

"She's on her way to the phone," Janelle said sweetly into the receiver. "Give her a minute to get here."

Carley shot her a threatening look, but she came forward and took the receiver. She pretended it was Janelle's neck and squeezed it extra hard.

"I'll be in the back," Janelle said, breezing away.

Carley took a deep breath and said hello.

"Hello yourself. Remember me? Your friendly next-door hospital neighbor?"

"Of course. How goes it?"

"I thought you were going to call me."

"I did, but you'd checked out."

He was quiet for a moment. "I left my phone number with the nurses. In case you asked."

"I—I didn't think of asking."

"I asked them for yours, but they said it was against hospital policy to give out the information. Then I remembered about your parents' bookstore."

"So, here I am." She forced herself to sound perky.

"I was going to call you last week, but I wanted to wait until after my checkup on Friday."

Her heart hammered harder and she half dreaded, half hoped for what she knew he was about to tell her. "How did it go?"

"I can see, Carley. I'm going to be all right."

Fifteen

"That's wonderful, Kyle." Carley tried to control the tremor in her voice.

"Oh, my vision's not perfect. I've still got a long way to go."

"What do you mean?"

"Well, I'm real sensitive to light. But when he took my bandages off, I could see shapes. Everything was really blurry and my eyes watered like crazy, but things are looking clearer and sharper every day."

"So no more gauze pads?"

"I've graduated. I have to wear dark glasses if I go outside. Or even if I'm inside and the lights are bright. And my doctor still wants me to keep my left eye covered with a black patch for a while, but for the most part I can see again."

Carley twirled the phone cord around her finger. She knew she should keep asking him questions and be happy for him, but both were difficult for her to do when she had so much at stake in his answers. "How long before you're one hundred percent?"

"It may be weeks yet. And they still don't know if my vision will ever be twenty-twenty or not. I just wish I could lose this stupid eye patch. I look and feel ridiculous."

"Like a pirate, huh?"

"Worse. People come up to me all the time and ask me about it. Seems kind of rude to me, but still they ask."

She understood completely. "People are nosy. You have to ignore them."

He gave a short laugh. " 'Course my friends Steve and Jason tell me to consider the plus side."

"Such as?"

"It's a cool way to meet girls."

"Whatever works."

"But I told them I've already met the perfect girl."

Her hand had grown clammy on the receiver and she was having trouble keeping it tight on the slippery plastic. "That's nice of you to say."

"That's why I want to get together with you."

"Well I—"

"Not right yet," he added hastily. "I'd like my eyesight to clear up a little more so that I can see you. I'd like to ditch the patch too. I mean, when you can only see out of one eye, there's no depth perception. Uncool. I can't judge how close or how far away something is, which makes me fumble around a lot. But it sure beats not seeing at all."

"I'd guess so."

"Anyway, I want to meet you. See you with my own eyes. Steve and Jason are still talking about you."

She couldn't think of anything to say, but she was desperate to keep a meeting from happening.

"Listen to me," Kyle said apologetically. "I'm going on and on about me and I haven't once asked how you're doing. How's the leg?"

"I've ditched the crutches. And my doctor says I might be able to shed the cast by the middle of next month."

"Maybe in time for Valentine's Day?"

Carley's eyes darted to the calendar posted on the wall behind the desk. Sure enough, February fourteenth was pretty much in the middle of the next month. "Maybe."

"Well, whether you're in a cast or not, I'd like you to go to our school's spring dance with me. It's on the weekend after Valentine's Day."

"I don't dance."

"I don't either, but so what? We'll just go together, sit, and watch the others. It's being held at the big Marriott downtown; there'll be a banquet and everything. It's going to be really nice. Of course, I can't drive because of my eyes, but we'll go with Jason and Steve."

"I won't know anybody."

"You'll know me. Plus, you've met Jason and Steve. Their girlfriends are pretty nice. We'll all have a great time together."

Just then the door of the bookstore opened and a customer walked inside. "Uh

—can we talk about this later? Business is starting up and I have to go to work."

"You bet. But don't hang up without giving me your home phone number."

Quickly she told him, then said goodbye. Janelle came behind the counter as she was hanging up the phone. "Thanks a lot for making me take that call." Nervous perspiration caused Carley's bangs to stick to her forehead.

"I'm not going to lie for you. I did that once and I hated it." Janelle smiled at the customer who was browsing the stacks. "What did Kyle want?"

"He can see again and he wants to meet me. He wants to take me to some dance his school's having." Carley sagged into a chair behind the counter. "Not me of course. *You.*"

"And who's fault is that?"

"I'm not in the mood for a lecture." She glanced around to see if the customer had his back to the front desk. She hated the idea of the man staring at her once he saw her face. "I'm going into the back room and start unboxing and cataloging."

"I wish you'd been honest with Kyle from the very beginning."

"Well, I wasn't, so start helping me figure out a way to keep this face-to-face meeting from ever happening."

Janelle threw up her hands and backed away. "Oh no, baby sister. You're on your own this time."

"Aw—come on."

Janelle ignored her plea. "I'm going to see if this man needs help." She swept from behind the counter and hurried over to the browsing customer.

Carley hauled herself to the backroom, where boxes of new books were stacked and waiting. She lowered herself onto a nearby chair and stared gloomily at the floor. Life wasn't fair! For the first time in her life, she'd been asked out on a date. And by the one boy she'd give anything to go out with. Except that she couldn't because the girl he thought was her, wasn't. And the girl he thought was pretty, was not.

She should have been honest with him from the start. Except that if she had been honest, he would never have wanted to see her in the first place. And the days that she'd known him in the hospital had been wonderful, because for just a short time she'd been treated as if she were a normal girl.

Carley sighed and told herself to get to work. Thinking about Kyle was only depressing her. She'd think of some reason to keep him from meeting her. After all, she'd been able to fool him and his friends once. She'd have to do it again. She'd have to come up with something that would end her relationship with Kyle once and for all. There was no choice. She'd shut the door on their friendship forever.

That night Carley did something that she hadn't done in years. She took the family photo album off the shelf and retreated to her room, closed the door, climbed onto her bed, and spread it out in front of her.

She started with her baby pictures. She turned the pages and saw herself transform from cute, chubby, and bald with a broad, toothless smile into a gangly seven-year-old with front teeth missing and lank dark hair in braids. By the time she was nine, the teeth were back and the hair was brushing her shoulders.

Her fifth-grade school picture was the last one ever taken with her face in one piece. Carley stared long and hard at the grinning photo. At the perfect symmetry of her nose and eyes. At the full, dimpled cheeks and the smooth, flawless complexion. At her forehead uncluttered by bangs. Why, by anybody's standards she had been cute, even pretty in a childlike, innocent way.

She ran her fingertips over the photograph, as if by touching it she might somehow absorb her former self into her present self. How wonderful it would be if she could align the two faces and superimpose the younger one onto her current one. How good it would be to fill in the sunken places of her "now" face with her "then" face.

She had been born whole and complete. At age twelve she'd been held hostage by cancer. And robbed of normalcy. No clever cosmetic makeover could ever make her look whole again. So, how did she mourn for this lost piece of herself? This missing part from the inside of her body that so affected the outside?

Carley sighed and shut the photo album. She caught sight of her reflection in the mirror over her dresser, but did not turn away. No need to ask, "Mirror, mirror on the wall, who's the fairest of them all?" Her mirror couldn't lie. The truth was stamped within its frame just as surely as it was stamped upon her face.

Now she resembled a piece of modern art—a painting by one of those artists who liked to paint people in the shapes of cubes and squares. Her face was right out of a futuristic drawing, lopsided and off-center. When she smiled, it caved in more tightly, like a flower turning in upon itself.

The phone call from Kyle had been wonderful and she was happy that he was able to see. But she was more determined than ever that he shouldn't ever see her. For the girl he'd created in his imagination was the girl she wanted him to think of as Carley. She still wasn't sure how she was going to get him out of her life once and for all, but she was determined to do so. No matter how much it tore her up to do it. No matter how badly it broke her heart.

Sixteen

"I'm ready to meet you, Carley. It's all I've been thinking about."

Kyle's words on the phone ten days later caused Carley's heart to skip a beat and her stomach to constrict. She'd taken the call in her room on the portable phone and lay across her bed, clutching it to her ear. Her leg in the cast felt as if it weighed a ton— almost as heavy as her heart felt in her chest. "I've been thinking about it too," she said.

"And the dance? Will you go with me?"

"I can't."

"Why not? I told you I don't care about dancing. I just want to be with you. I want to show you off."

"I'm not a prize cow, you know."

"That's not what I mean and you know it." His voice sounded hurt. "I miss you, Carley. I miss talking to you. Visiting with you. I even miss your Books on Tape. I have a bunch to return, you know."

"Just keep them. I can get more."

"What's wrong? Why don't you want to see me?"

Her heart was thudding so loudly that she was afraid he might hear it through the receiver. "I have something to tell you."

"Tell me. Please."

Her gaze fell on a photograph of Janelle and Jon taken over the Christmas holidays. They had their arms around each other and Jon was wearing a Santa hat. Inspiration flooded through her. "Remember in the hospital when you asked me if I had a boyfriend?"

"You said you didn't."

"Well, that wasn't exactly the truth."

"You have a boyfriend?"

"Yes. Jon and I've been going together for over a year, but we had a big fight before Christmas and sort of broke up."

"If you broke up—"

"But now we're back together," she added hastily.

"And the whole time you were in the hospital he never paid you a visit?"

"He was away on a skiing trip with his parents."

"At the start of the new semester?"

Carley chewed on her bottom lip. This wasn't going as well as she'd hoped. "What is this, Twenty Questions?" she asked. "Take my word for it, he and I had a fight but we've made up and we're together again."

"Why didn't you tell me this in the hospital?"

"I—I didn't know how."

"Simple. You say, 'Kyle, let me tell you about my boyfriend.' I remember asking you if you had one."

"Sorry. I didn't."

"And so you met my friends and let them think you liked me."

"I *do* like you." She began to squirm. "It's possible to like you *and* still have a boyfriend, you know. I really thought we had broken up for good when I met you in the hospital. But now that I'm back in school and all—well, I realized I still liked him." Lying to Kyle was difficult, but she felt she was in too deep to turn back now.

He didn't say anything for such a long time that she wondered if he'd put the phone aside and walked away. She asked, "Kyle?"

"I'm here."

"I—I'm sorry."

"I still want to meet you."

"What?" She couldn't believe he was being so insistent. "Why?"

"Carley, when I was in the hospital, you helped me more than anybody. The talks we had, the visits, the phone calls—all those things kept me from climbing the walls. I want to meet you. I want to see you for myself. I want to tell you thanks to your face."

"Jon's jealous," she blurted. "He doesn't like me seeing other guys."

"Couldn't he understand this one time? I'm not asking for much. After this one meeting I'll drop out of your life. I promise."

Her head was spinning, desperate to find a

way out of her dilemma. She didn't want him out of her life, but the need to protect herself was far more intense than her willingness to tell him everything. Suddenly an idea came to her. "Okay, all right, fair enough. I'll let you see me. But it has to be from a distance."

"How far? North Carolina?"

The sarcasm in his voice made her cringe. "I don't want Jon to know about you," she explained. "Please. If you care about me, you'll do me this favor."

Again there was a long pause. "All right. Whatever you want." She sagged with relief. "Where can I see you?" he asked.

She realized she had no place to tell him because she'd never been anyplace on a date. *Where would Jon take Janelle?* she wondered. She remembered her sister telling her about the Mudpie, a coffeehouse that had opened in September and had quickly gained favor with the older high school crowd. She asked Kyle if he'd heard of it.

"I've been there once. Before my accident."

"Well, that's where I'll be Friday afternoon with my boyfriend. That's when you can see me."

"What time?"

"Four-thirty."

"All right."

"But, Kyle, you can't come over and speak to me. You have to hang back. I—I wouldn't want Jon to know. He wouldn't like it."

"I won't embarrass you." His voice sounded emotionless. "Steve will be with me because he has to do the driving, but I'll make certain he keeps out of the way too."

"I—um—probably won't wave to you, or acknowledge you in any way." Carley nibbled on her bottom lip nervously.

"I understand the rules."

"I wish things could be different."

"You're the only one who can make things different."

She knew he was right. "I can't," she said softly into the phone. "I just *can't.*"

Carley cornered Jon in the atrium the next afternoon while he was waiting for Janelle to finish ensemble rehearsal. When she told him her plan, he balked. "Are you crazy? I can't do that."

"And why not? All I'm asking is that you take her to the Mudpie Friday afternoon and buy her coffee or a soda. I'll even pay for it."

Jon shook his head. "There isn't enough money. If she suspects anything, she'll kill me and disown you."

"Believe me, being disowned is preferable to your not helping me."

"Don't pressure me. I won't do it."

Tears of frustration welled up in her eyes. It wasn't easy for her to beg. "Kyle promised he'd keep out of the line of vision. He swore that all he'd do is look, then leave. You've got to help me, Jon. Please."

"Don't cry." He glanced nervously toward the hallway, where Janelle was soon to appear. "If Janelle sees you, she'll have to know why. Have you asked her if she'd do it for you?"

"She won't. I know she won't. And once she knows the plan, she'll never go to the Mudpie with you. No, it's better to take her, let Kyle slip in and see the two of you, and disappear. He'll see her, and Steve will tell

him it's me, and he'll think I'm beautiful.
Nobody will get hurt."

"Nobody?"

"All right—*I* won't get hurt. What's so
terrible about that?"

Jon looked pained, indecisive. Carley felt
as if he wanted to help, but was scared.

"This will be the end of it, Jon. Once Friday is over, the door will be closed and I'll
never ask a favor of you again. Please help
me."

On Friday Carley had a makeup test after
school and missed the bus. That left her no
choice but to accompany Jon and Janelle to
the Mudpie, which worked out better because, with Carley along, even if Janelle
happened to see Kyle and Steve in the coffee
shop, she wouldn't be suspicious—Janelle
knew Carley would never run the risk of
bumping into Kyle. Her sister would never
suspect that *she herself* had set up the meeting.

The three of them sat in a booth in the
far back of the small coffee shop. Carley told
them it would make her feel self-conscious if
she sat anywhere else, and of course Janelle

believed her. She fidgeted, watching the clock constantly. At exactly four-twenty she excused herself to go to the bathroom. There, in the small, protected hallway, Carley could peek around the corner without being seen.

The coffee shop was crowded with tables and booths filled with teens and groups of twenty-somethings preparing for weekend fun. A sofa, two easy chairs and a coffee table toward the front gave the place a homey atmosphere. Green plants hung on cords from the ceiling, and the aromas of exotic coffees and sweet-scented vanilla and cinnamon spiced the air. Carley would have enjoyed herself if she hadn't been so nervous.

When she saw Kyle come in the door, she caught her breath. He wore a wheat-colored cable-knit sweater, jeans, and dark glasses. Another boy was with him; she assumed it was Steve. Her heart wedged in her throat as she watched Kyle scan the room. She watched as Steve nudged him in the ribs. Kyle stared toward the booth where Jon sat with Janelle.

Janelle, oblivious to her surroundings,

leaned toward Jon, her face animated and smiling. Jon held her hand across the table, took a dollop of whipped cream from atop his cappuccino, and offered it to Janelle's pretty red mouth. Kyle watched the scene without expression. Knowing she was hurting him, Carley felt a terrible heaviness. She squeezed her eyes shut, and when she opened them again, Kyle and Steve were gone.

She gazed longingly at the space that had held him. At the sunlight playing through the glass window and leaving bright patches on the floor where he had stood. He was gone, just as he had promised. Her charade was over. She was safe, yet inside she felt no elation, no satisfaction. She felt hollow and empty.

Goodbye, Kyle. His dark glasses had hidden his eyes, and with a start she realized that she had never once looked into their depths. She didn't even know what color they were. And now she never would.

Seventeen

"Hello, Carley. I'm Dr. Chaffoo."

"Hi," she said, shaking the hand of the plastic surgeon. She took a seat beside her mother on the leather sofa in the doctor's plush office.

The doctor was good-looking, with a wide, generous smile, blue eyes, and brown hair flecked with gray. He didn't wear the white lab coat so typical of other doctors she had known, but instead was dressed in a well-tailored navy suit, crisp white shirt, and a colorful silk tie. Her mother had assured Carley that he had come highly recommended, and together they'd driven the thirty miles into Knoxville to meet with him about the possibility of reconstructing her face.

"I've obtained your medical charts and read through them," Dr. Chaffoo said, leafing through a thick manilla folder on his gleaming mahogany desk. "I've also talked to your oncologist and have a very thorough picture of what you went through four years ago."

"The question is," her mother interjected, "can you help my daughter? Can anything be done to give her a more normal appearance?"

"Is that what you want, Carley?"

"More than anything." Carley felt both anxious and excited. She was afraid to get her hopes up, yet she longed for him to tell her she was "fixable."

Dr. Chaffoo stood, came around his desk, raised her chin with his forefinger, and scrutinized her face. It made her feel self-conscious. She disliked anyone staring at her too intently. Gently he smoothed his thumb along the sunken contours of her cheek, eye, and nose, then returned to his chair. "In a few minutes I'm going to take you into another room where I have an imaging computer and a camera set up. But first let's talk about the realities of reconstructive surgery. No matter how much plastic surgery you have done, you'll always have a scar on your face and some residual effects of your cancer surgery. I can't make you perfect."

Carley felt her hopes sag. No one could help her.

"However," the doctor continued, "I can make you look a whole lot better."

"Tell us," her mother said.

"What plastic surgeons try to do with this type of malformation is add symmetry back to your face. As it is now, anyone who sees you is automatically drawn to the defect because your face is out of proportion. If we fill in the caved-in areas, your cheek can look fuller, your eye can be elevated to align with the other, and your nose can be reconstructed to give you a more normal appearance."

Her mother asked, "But bone and tissue were removed during her cancer surgery.

They told us it can't regrow. It's gone forever."

Carley looked straight at the doctor. "What do you use? Silly Putty? Paper and paste? Play-Doh?"

Dr. Chaffoo laughed heartily. "Good suggestions, but your body would reject such foreign substances. No . . . whenever possible I'd use your own body tissue, fat, and bone. Some silicone plastic if necessary."

"My tissue? How?"

"First I'll send you to a radiology lab and have a three-dimensional CAT scan made of your head. This type of X ray will help me see you on the inside before I operate. It will give me exact dimensions of your nasal and cranial areas and offer me a model to follow for rebuilding. An old photograph of you will also be used for comparison."

"Like *The Terminator?*" She remembered her photo as a twelve-year-old, and a movie she'd once seen about a robot made to look human.

He laughed again. "I'll be able to see the extent of the area needing work, and that will help me gauge the amount of material I'll need to harvest for your surgeries."

"How many surgeries?" her mother wanted to know.

"Probably three. Each one about six months apart with two to three hours in the operating room and one to two days in the hospital for recovery."

Carley's hopes dipped. She hadn't expected it to take so long. "But that could take over a year and a half. I'll be a senior by the time I look acceptable."

"But you're so young," the doctor said. "Over the course of a lifetime what's eighteen months?"

My entire life in high school, she thought, but didn't say it. A normal social life would still elude her. And being able to meet Kyle face-to-face was a dream gone up in smoke. Secretly she'd harbored the hope that fixing her face might take less time and therefore give her another opportunity to work something out with him.

"You said you could use tissue from my daughter's own body. Tell us about that part." Her mother didn't even sense Carley's disappointment, but pressed the doctor for more details.

"I can take cartilage from behind your ear to replace nasal cartilage." He tugged on his ear to demonstrate flexibility. "Your ear will be fine and look perfectly normal."

"But what about bone? Could you take some from my leg?" She held up the leg in the cast. "I'm sure there's plenty to go around."

"Actually I'd use a calvarial bone graft— that's bone taken from your skull and grafted into existing bone in your cheek to provide a floor for fat I'd take from your abdomen or buttocks. The fat will plump out the area."

She stared at him. "You're going to take a chunk out of my head?"

"The skull's thick. You won't miss the fragment I'll take." She remembered what it had been like to be bald from chemo. It had taken years to grow her hair long again. As if reading her mind, Dr. Chaffoo said, "Don't worry, I won't have to shave your head. I'll take bone from in back of your hairline. You can brush the rest of your hair over the area. I'll insert the bone through an incision in your gum line." He raised his lip and pointed to the area above his upper teeth. "And the bone to enhance your eye area can be inserted through an incision under your eyelash line." He ran his finger along the lower lashes of his left eye.

Carley thought the whole idea sounded bizarre and creepy, and it made her stomach feel queasy. She glanced at her mother, who didn't look especially pleased with his descriptions either. "Sounds like fun," Carley said drolly. She recalled how horrible she looked following her surgery for the removal of the cancerous tumor.

"The stitches are exceedingly fine. I do them with a microscope." The doctor stood. "Come with me, Carley. I want to show you something."

In another room he took color photos of her, front and side views, and sent the picture electronically into a nearby computer. Her image popped up on the screen and she grimaced. She thought she looked ugly.

"Well, Mom, if the FBI ever puts these on the walls of the post office, I'll sue," she quipped.

"Watch this," Dr. Chaffoo said.

Carley leaned over his shoulder and watched as he moved the computer's mouse on its pad. Every few seconds she heard it click and slowly watched her face transform on the computer screen. With wonder she saw her left eye shift upward and the space between her nose and eye socket fill in. She watched the bridge of her nose swell and smooth, until her nose looked straight and perfectly formed. She saw her cheek plump and fill in like a round, full apple.

Minutes later Dr. Chaffoo leaned back in his chair and said, "Well, there you are, Carley. This is how I can make you look."

Beside her she heard her mother's breath come out in small sobs. And seeing the transformed image, Carley could scarcely catch her own breath. "I—I look all right. I look like a regular girl," she whispered. Slowly she raised her hand and touched the glass of the monitor. She traced her fingertips over the screen, over the full-faced view of her picture. For the first time in years Carley Mattea was pretty.

Through a mist of tears she said, "Please make me look like that. Please give me back my face."

She decided to begin her series of surgeries over the upcoming spring break. "My teachers are accustomed to my spending time in the hospital," she told her family. "Why break the pattern? If everything goes okay, I can have the second surgery over Christmas and the final one next summer."

Dr. Chaffoo scheduled her CAT scan for the end of February, but now that she knew she could look normal, she was anxious to begin the process, in spite of her dread of the actual surgeries.

Carley was working in the backroom of the bookstore on a Saturday afternoon with Janelle. Together they were unboxing books and chatting about Carley's upcoming transformation. "I think it's super," Janelle told her. "Too bad you had to wait so long."

"It's a little scary," Carley said. "And I sure don't look forward to more hospital time. Maybe they'll give me a discount. What do you think?"

Janelle giggled. "It's doubtful. Listen, I'll do your makeup when it's all over. Better yet, I'll treat you to a makeup artist."

"You will?"

"Absolutely. Only the best for my kid sister."

Carley dragged a box of books to a nearby shelf and, with her back to Janelle, began to stack the volumes on the shelf. "I'll be glad when this cast comes off too. Dr. Olson says another week—on Valentine's Day if you can believe it. You know, Janelle, this is the first time I've looked forward to Valentine's Day in years. Because once it's behind me, I can go for that CAT scan."

"Carley?"

She heard Kyle's voice from the doorway and froze. She heard Janelle pause before saying, "No. I'm Janelle, Carley's sister."

"But I thought—"

Carley's heart pounded and her knees quivered. Silently she prayed that Janelle would send him away. But even as she prayed, she could feel his gaze on her back.

Janelle said, "I know what you think. But it isn't true." Janelle took an audible breath. "That's Carley over there."

Carley gripped the side of the shelf to keep her knees from buckling. Then she heard Janelle leave the room and close the door quietly behind her.

Eighteen

Carley kept her back to Kyle and her gaze locked onto the covers of books inches from her nose. Her spine felt rigid. She heard him move across the room and stand directly behind her.

"Carley? Is this really you? Why did you introduce your sister to me and my friends and tell us it was you? I didn't even know you *had* a sister! What's going on? Tell me."

"Why did you come?" She ignored his deluge of questions. "You told me you would leave me alone after you came to the coffee shop."

"I wanted to see you," he said simply. "I figured if I came to the bookstore while you were working, your boyfriend wouldn't be a problem." He paused, then added, "But that guy in the coffee shop wasn't really your boyfriend, was he? He's your sister's boyfriend."

She saw no way around telling him the truth. "Yes. Jon is Janelle's boyfriend."

"Would you please turn around and talk to my face?"

She refused by shaking her head. "Would you please go away and leave me alone." It wasn't a request, but a demand.

"I won't go without talking to you face-to-face."

"There's nothing to say, Kyle."

"Why won't you look at me? I know it's you. I can smell your hair, all clean and sweet, like flowers. I'll never forget the way your hair smells. Please turn around."

She felt as if a knife was twisting in her heart. She had come to the end of the road. There was absolutely no way to avoid the inevitable any longer. No way to continue to hide the truth from him. She tasted the bitterness of defeat. Softly, with voice trembling, she asked, "Why do you think I don't want to look at you, Kyle?"

"I have no idea. But it's driving me crazy."
She felt his hand on her shoulder.

"Do you think my sister's pretty?"

"Sure, but— Is that what this is about? You think you're not pretty?" He sounded incredulous. "I don't care what you look like."

"Really," she declared. Then slowly she turned, until she was looking him in the face. He was inches taller, but she raised her head so that he could see her fully. Slowly he removed his sunglasses. His skin looked pink around his eye area, and moist with an ointment of some kind. His lashes and eyebrows, which must have been burned off in his accident, were beginning to regrow in a dark stubble. His eyes were a shocking shade of intense blue.

As Kyle peered down at her, his expression was first one of shock, followed by disbelief and stunned silence. He took a step backward. "What happened to you?"

She clenched her fists, digging her nails into her palms, hoping that the physical pain would replace the emotional pain and keep her from crying in front of him. She'd thought she'd prepared herself for such reactions, but she wasn't prepared. She remembered all the times he'd taken her hand and his face had lit up with a smile. But now he was seeing her in all her ugliness, all her deformity. "Cancer. When I was twelve. They cut it out, but left me looking like this."

"Cancer? Are you all right now?"

"I'm free of cancer," she said, but knew she'd never be "all right" in his presence again.

"But why didn't you tell me? Why didn't you say something while we were in the hospital?"

"I couldn't think of a good way to work it into the conversation."

His expression clouded, and anger formed lines around his mouth. "You should have told me."

"I liked having you think I was normal. It was a nice change for a boy to talk to me and treat me as if I were a real person. Instead of a freak."

"You aren't a freak," he said sharply.

"I'm hardly material for a modeling career, now, am I?"

"Why do you have to handle everything like it was a big joke? This isn't funny, Carley. You lied to me. Worse—you carried off a sneaky scheme to keep me from the truth. If I hadn't come here today, I'd have gone the rest of my life thinking you were somebody you weren't!"

She understood his anger, but she had no tolerance for it. "It was *my* face. My life. I didn't owe you anything. Stop criticizing me."

"You made out like we were friends. Like you cared about me."

"I did care. I—I just didn't think my physical appearance was any of your business."

He stepped closer and she felt the bookshelf against her back. "You didn't trust me," he snapped. "You figured that what you looked like would determine if I liked you or not. That wasn't fair!"

"I've seen the way guys look at me, Kyle," she fired back. "Can you believe that not one of them has ever looked me in the face and asked to be my friend? Or my *boy*-friend?"

He took her by the shoulders. "Well, I'm not like other guys."

"Right." She twisted out of his grasp. "If Steve and Jason had actually seen the real me that day in the hospital and said to you, 'Man, that girl is ugly,' what would you have done? Would you still have wanted to hang out with me? Would you still have asked me to your school's dance?"

He glared at her. "We'll never know, will we?"

She pulled herself up to her full height. "*I* know. Tell me, aren't you the tiniest little bit disappointed that I'm not the 'babe' you thought I was? Isn't there some small part of you that isn't totally shocked and disappointed? Remember, I saw your face just a while ago when you first looked at me. And I remember all the times you told me you thought I must be pretty." Now *she* was angry, and tired of being defensive about what she'd done. Kyle would never understand, *could* never understand what it had meant to her ego to have him believe she was attractive.

"All right, so long as we're finally being honest, yes, I'm disappointed. I'm sorry you're not what you wanted me to believe you were. I'm sorry you had cancer and that your face is messed up. I'm sorry I said things in the hospital to make you think your looks were important to me."

His words brought her no satisfaction. What had she expected him to say? "Then I guess we both got something out of this whole thing, didn't we? For a while you got to think I was pretty and I got to think some guy liked me. Too bad illusions can't be real life."

He glared at her without speaking, but she didn't care. As far as she was concerned, their discussion was ended. There was nothing left to say. Slowly Kyle slipped his sunglasses back onto his face. She wondered if the glare of the overhead lights had begun to hurt his eyes, started to ask, but thought better of it. No use letting him know how much she still cared about him. Better to make a clean break and put him out of her life once and for all.

He asked, "Do you know what I learned

when I was blind, Carley?" She shook her head, not trusting her voice. "I learned how to see. Corny, huh? I learned that vision can be a handicap because it allows us to make judgments based on what our eyes show us.

"Don't get me wrong, I'm very happy I have my vision back. I'm not sure I could have made it through a lifetime in the dark. But in some ways it would be good if everyone could spend some time without their vision. It teaches you what's important."

"Just like being disfigured teaches you," she countered. "But I'd rather have read the lesson in a book than experienced it."

He ignored her barb. "Do you know what blindness taught me about you?" He didn't wait for her to answer. "It taught me to see you from the inside out."

"Ugh—with all my blood and guts?" She'd tried to crack a joke.

He refused to be diverted. "I didn't come here today to embarrass you or to hurt your feelings."

"So why did you come?"

"All I wanted was to say thank you for helping me through my time in the hospital.

And to see your outside and how it fit with your inside."

"I'm sorry the match-up didn't work out," she said.

"You're right, it wasn't what I expected." He turned toward the door. "It wasn't what you led me to expect."

Tears stung her eyes, but she refused to let them escape. "I'm not sorry," she insisted. "Not one bit sorry that you once thought I was pretty. It was the first time in my life someone did."

"Well, I'm sorry," he said, pausing at the door. "I'm sorry you didn't trust me enough to tell me the truth."

She raised her chin, willing it to stop trembling. "When you tell Steve and Jason the truth, what will you say? How will you describe me? Don't answer. I know what you'll say. It's what everyone who ever sees me says. You'll tell them that my face is a wreck."

"Can a plastic surgeon fix your face?"

"Just this past week I met one who thinks he can. Funny, huh? If you and I had met two years from now, I'd be much more acceptable. Bad timing, Kyle."

He pulled open the door.

"By the way," she called. "I release you from your invitation to your school's Valentine dance. Believe me, it wouldn't be much fun for you with everyone staring at your date."

"It wouldn't be any fun being with a girl who didn't want to be there," he tossed back.

"This isn't my fault," she said stubbornly. "I gave you what you wanted: a pretty girl who kept your mind off your pain and problems in the hospital."

"You haven't even got a clue about what I want, Carley. And the sad part is that no amount of my telling you will make you know."

"Go away," she said. "I don't want your pity. And I don't need your charity."

He nodded curtly, stepped through the doorway into the busy bookstore, and was gone.

Nineteen

Carley moped for days after Kyle's visit. Secretly, deep in her heart, she hoped that he'd call. Not that she'd given him any reason to call her, but nevertheless she still held on to the hope that he might. But as the week passed and he didn't call, she abandoned hope.

She experienced a profound sense of nostalgia as the middle of February crept closer. She missed her days in the hospital when Kyle had "seen" her through the eyes of imagination. She thought about Reba and called her.

"How're you doing?" she asked.

"Wonderful!" Reba fairly bubbled into the

receiver. "I was thinking about you and wondering how you were doing. Did you and Kyle ever connect once you got home?"

Carley couldn't bear to go into the whole mess, so she simply said, "No. But I told you before I left the hospital nothing would come of us."

"Too bad. He was a nice guy and I thought he liked you a lot. I went to visit him after you went home, and all he did was talk about you."

The news twisted like a knife in Carley's heart. "But he'd never seen me," she reminded Reba. "Seeing me would have spoiled all his notions about me. Don't forget, Reba, love and beauty go together."

"Maybe not. I have a boyfriend and I'm no beauty."

"You do!" The news drew Carley up short. "Tell me about him."

"His name's Mike and he has cerebral palsy. We met at school, in our special ed. class. He's really super and he likes me, Carley. He's come over to my house and he's coming on Valentine's Day too. We're going to watch a video."

Carley felt a twinge of jealousy. Reba was in a wheelchair and she had a boyfriend. Jealousy quickly passed as she recalled what Reba's life was like. She said, "I think that's terrific," and meant it.

But after she hung up the phone, Carley felt more alone than ever. *Wait till I get my surgery*, she told herself. But it didn't help much. It might be two years before she looked more normal and by then high school would be over. And Kyle would go away to college. Their paths would never cross again and he would never get to know her without her scarred face.

What does it matter? she asked herself. She'd ruined any chance they might have had anyway. Still, she knew she would never forget him. Never. He was the first boy who'd ever treated her as if she were attractive. He was the first boy she'd ever loved.

Janelle was especially nice to Carley on Valentine's Day. She bought her a big box of chocolates in the shape of a heart. And her parents gave her a card with a gift certificate to her favorite department store. *But so what?* she thought. They were family and they always tried to make her feel better about the one holiday of the year she hated most.

Even Jon came through with a card for her. She told him thanks, but decided that he'd only done it to rack up brownie points with Janelle. Jon gave Janelle a dozen red roses, two cards, and a gold bracelet with a miniature gold heart dangling from it. It was pretty and Carley told Jon so when she sat with him and Janelle in the atrium during lunch break.

Students milled around the sunlit garden area waiting for the class bell to ring. "Want to come with us to the Mudpie after school?" Janelle asked.

"Mom's taking me to get this cast cut off," Carley reminded her. "Tomorrow I have to go to Rehab and really start working to get my leg back in shape." Carley was glad to turn down Janelle's offer. The last thing she wanted to be was a third wheel on Valentine's Day with Jon and Janelle.

Jon leaned back on his elbows. "No more Rollerblades?"

"Naw. I'm switching to bungee jumping."

Jon and Janelle laughed.

As they walked out of the entranceway door, they saw a crowd of students. "There's a plane buzzing our school," someone called.

"No way!" a boy shouted back.

"I'm not lying. It's dive-bombing us."

"Get on out here," Janelle called to Carley.

Carley sighed and hobbled along.

"I don't see anything," Jon said.

"He's coming around for another pass," a boy reported. "Just wait a minute."

"If this is your idea of a joke . . . ," someone else said.

"I'm telling you, the plane'll be back."

Carley heard the buzz of a small engine moments later. She gazed heavenward, and all at once saw the single-engine plane swooping down from the west.

"There it is! See, I told you," the boy shouted.

Fascinated, Carley watched along with the crowd of students as the plane dipped lower and lower.

"What's that guy doing?" Janelle asked.

"Beats me," Jon answered.

Carley continued to watch along with everyone else. Trailing behind the plane, she now saw, was a sign in big red letters.

"He's got a sign," Jon announced. "What's it say?"

"This must be some dumb advertising gimmick," another kid said in disgust.

As the sign unfurled behind the small plane, Carley couldn't believe her eyes. " 'Carley, Be Mine. K.W.' Who's Carley? Who's K.W.?" someone asked.

Carley's heart skipped a beat. She remembered what Kyle had said about his uncle and his own love of flying. Had he somehow persuaded his uncle to buzz the high school and fly the banner? Was Kyle in the plane with him? She read the banner again and laughed as she heard a girl say, "That's the most romantic valentine I've ever seen or heard about!"

On the other side of her she felt Janelle take her elbow. "You hate Valentine's Day? Kyle and you are through, huh? My, my, baby sister, remind me never to believe anything you tell me again!"

Carley stood speechless, watching the plane pull the long sign across the sky directly over the school.

"Are you saying this is the work of that guy, Kyle, from the hospital?" Jon asked, unable to disguise his disbelief.

"And very good work it is," Janelle cooed. She turned to Carley. "So what do you say now?"

Carley couldn't speak. A lump the size of a fist was clogging her throat. Kyle truly cared about her. Why else would he have gone to so much trouble and expense? Why else announce to the world he wanted Carley as his valentine?

"Actions speak louder than words," Janelle said in Carley's ear. "If I were you, I'd make one very important phone call as soon as you get home from the doctor's office."

Behind them Carley heard someone ask, "Who's Carley?"

She wanted to shout, "I'm Carley! Me! The girl with the messed-up face." But of course she didn't. The whole school would discover the identity of Carley. Janelle would see to that.

Elated and overwhelmed, Carley managed to answer Janelle, "I think I will make that call. I'd hate to leave the guy hanging."

Janelle groaned over Carley's bad joke, but Carley scarcely heard her. She looked up to see the plane cut a wide circle, dip its wing as if in greeting, and head off. The sign fluttered behind it in the wind, the large crimson letters stamped across the face of the sky, bright as the flare of a rocket.

A Rose for Melinda

This book is dedicated to
Trevor Clark McDaniel, a lamb of God.

My deep appreciation to Dr. Mary Duffy—
thanks for sharing your expertise!

Blossoms

❧

WELCOME TO MRS. BARBER'S
1ST-GRADE CLASS
ROOM 105, BEN FRANKLIN
ELEMENTARY SCHOOL

RULES:

1. Raise your hand to ask a question.

2. Take turns.

3. No hitting, no shoving, no talking.

4. Bring notebook to school every day.

5. Be kind to each other.

September 7

Dear Melinda Skye,
   Thank you for sharing your snack.
You are very pretty.

Signed,
your friend,
Jesse Rose

September 7

Dear Jesse Rose,
   Thank you. I have new shoes. Do you
like them?

Your friend,
Melinda Skye

October 1

Dear Melinda,
   I don't like school. But I like you.
Do you like me?

Your friend,
Jesse

October 1

Dear Jesse,
   I like you. But I like school. Reading is
the best part.

Your friend,
Melinda

October 2

Dear Melinda,
   The best part of school is seeing you.

Your very good friend,
Jesse

P.S. I like baseball. I want to play for the Braves. They are my favorite team.

October 3

Dear Jesse,
   I like ballet. I take classes and want to be a real ballerina. I will be famous.

Your friend,
Melinda

October 21

Dear Mr. and Mrs. Rose,

I'm afraid that Jesse must be placed on an "in-room" suspension from recess for the next three days for fighting on the playground. Although he has assured me that he "only socked Toby Gillman in the nose because he shoved Melinda Skye off the swing," as his teacher, I can't allow physical attacks on fellow students to occur. Please understand that I think Jesse is a good child. He has never disrupted the class until this unfortunate incident. As you are aware, this school system has a zero-tolerance policy regarding physical violence, and therefore Jesse must be punished for his aggressive act toward another student. Please call our principal if you have any questions regarding Jesse's suspension. Be assured that Toby is receiving the same punishment for shoving Melinda.

Sincerely,
Nancy Barber

October 22

Mrs. Barber,

*Jesse has told his father and me that he will not hit
Toby again "UNLESS Toby hurts Melinda." We've
always tried to instill a sense of right and wrong in
our son, and he knows that hitting others is wrong.
For some reason, Jesse has formed an attachment to
Melinda and feels a need to defend her—like some
kind of mini-Lancelot. We understand and accept his
punishment and are confident that he will behave in
the future if Toby behaves.*

Sincerely,
Ann Rose

Dear Jesse,
    Thank you for punching Toby for me.
I am sorry you have to miss recess,
but I will sit with you at lunch all next
week because you are my hero.

Friends forever,
Melinda

December 4

Dear Melinda,
   I made this picture for you. It's me playing baseball and you watching. Do you like it?

Jesse

December 5

Dear Jesse,
   I like the picture a lot!!!!! I put it in my room.

Melinda

An Invitation
To: Jesse Rose
From: Melinda Skye
Date: December 16, Friday
Time: 7:30 P.M.
Place: Memorial Auditorium

Jesse—Melinda wants you to come watch her dance in the "Nutcracker Suite" next weekend. She is one of the cherubs in the dance company and will be in the front row. Perhaps your parents will bring you, and after the performance, you can all come backstage and say hello.

Elana Skye (Melinda's mom)

[Transcript from the VCR of Leonard and Elana Skye. Scene of backstage bedlam as girls dressed in tutus and leotards scurry around shrieking and giggling.]

OFF-CAMERA VOICE OF LEONARD SKYE: Slow down, Princess. There's somebody here to see you.

[Camera swings around to show Jesse and his parents. Jesse walks over to Melinda, hands her a pink rose wrapped in tissue.]
JESSE: I liked . . . I mean, you danced real good. I stayed awake the whole time!

MELINDA [giggles]: A rose? For me? **[Glances up at camera]** Look, Daddy, Jesse brought me a rose. A rose from a Rose. **[Giggles again]**

ELANA *[Steps into camera shot, bends down]:* This is just beautiful. How thoughtful, Jesse. *[Looks up]* Thank you for bringing him.

[Camera swings and shot widens to include Jesse's smiling parents.]
ANN ROSE: He saw that on television . . . you know, the part about giving an actress, or dancer in this case, a bouquet of roses after the final curtain. He insisted he bring roses for Melinda.

JOHN ROSE: I took him to the florist and he bought it with his own money.

VOICE OF JESSE: That's why there's just one. They cost a whole lot!

[Camera swings around and zooms in on Jesse's face as all adults laugh off-camera.]
ELANA: What do you say to Jesse, honey?

MELINDA: Thank you a whole bunch. *[Throws arms around Jesse and kisses him wetly on the cheek. Adults laugh. Jesse's eyes widen. Camera pulls back and kids wave at lens.]*

[Fade to Black]

Happy Valentine's Day

BE MINE, VALENTINE

GUESS WHO?!?
XXXXX

Happy Valentine's Day

Let's Swing, Valentine

Your friend, Me!!! P.S. I knew which card
was from you, Jesse. Thank you for
the candy hearts—YUMMY!

Memo
To: All Parents
From: Nancy Barber
Date: May 20

To commemorate the end of the school year, we will hold a small "graduation" ceremony on Friday, the last day of classes. All family members are invited to this ceremony, which will be held at 3 P.M. in the cafeteria. Please plan to attend if at all possible. I am proud of each student and want everyone to have a sense of a job well done!

Report cards will go out within two weeks of the end of classes. Have a wonderful summer!

May 23

Dear Melinda,
   I will miss you very much all summer. I will write to you, OK? My mom said it is all right with her if your mom says I can. Will you miss me too?

Jesse

P.S. Can I be your boyfriend? Like a REAL boyfriend, not just a boy who is a friend?

May 23

Dear Jesse,
   Yes, I will miss you. Yes, let's write. I am
going to dance camp in July. I am going
to visit my Grandma in Florida in August.
I love her bunches and bunches. See
you next year!

Melinda

P.S. My mom says I have to wait longer
before I can have a real boyfriend.
But thank you for asking.

P.P.S. If I could have a boyfriend, I
would pick you!

Dear Mr. and Mrs. Skye,
   Melinda has been a pleasure as a student. She's
bright and outgoing with a delightful sunny disposi-
tion. Her love of reading and writing points to her
being a stellar student with great success in the
classroom. She is well able to express herself in
writing, and if her dream of being a dancer doesn't

pan out, I think she'll make a wonderful writer someday!

Sincerely,
Nancy Barber

Dear Mr. and Mrs. Rose,

Jesse is a kind and thoughtful boy with a big heart and a well-honed sense of caring. His test scores indicate that he's a very capable student, and I expect him to do well in the remainder of his school years. Although he can sometimes be shy and reserved, he knows what he wants and works hard to achieve his goals. I must say, he certainly has note-passing down to a science!

Sincerely,
Nancy Barber

June 12

Dear Elana,

Since school ended, Jesse has been bugging me to invite Melinda over so they can play. He says he misses her and doesn't want to wait until school starts before *he sees her again. Can I pick her up Wednesday morning? Or, if you'd like, come for coffee around ten, and we'll have a visit while they play. I so enjoyed your company in our shared room-mother duties last year and would like to catch up and talk about next year. Some changes are in the wind for the Rose family.*

Ann

June 15

Dear Ann,

After our visit and talk the other day, I strongly wanted to write you some words of encouragement. Also, it's so difficult to talk with the kids hanging around, and as you said, you really don't want Jesse to know what's going on just yet.

First of all, every marriage has problems, so don't think that the situation between you and John is hopeless. I'm glad you've found a good counselor. Perhaps, in time, John will join you in therapy. Few problems get solved unless a couple works hard on them together.

Your getting a job when school starts seems like a good idea. I know it isn't easy to return to the workforce when you feel "underqualified and undereducated," but as you noted, we don't always get to do what we want.

Jesse is bright and so very nice. He'll weather the change. And Lenny and I will be circumspect about you and John around Melinda so that she doesn't ask Jesse questions he can't answer.

Remember, I'm here for you. Lenny and I will help however we can.

Elana

August 10

Dear Jesse,
Today we went to Walt Disney World. It's really fun, but I wish you were here to go on the rides with me. You'd like my grandma too. She's been sick, but she is feeling better now. Please don't be too worried about your mom and dad.

Parents argue. It's normal. I'll be home
before school starts.

Melinda

You're Invited!!!!

Who: Melinda Skye, age 8
What: A Birthday Party
When: August 31, 3:00 P.M.
Where: Melinda's house

(Jesse, please come to my party
because you are my best friend.)

Dear Jesse,
   The music box you gave me is my
favorite thing. Thank you a whole
bunch. I know it must be tough, but
don't let Toby tease you about coming
to my house after school now that your
mom is at work. I know it isn't much fun
for you when I have dance class, but
that's only three days a week. The

other days we have lots to do. I'll get better at Nintendo. Maybe even beat you someday! Your idea of building a tree house is great. My dad said he would help us. And he will, too, because he always keeps his promises.

Melinda

September 12

Thank you for the baseball cards for my birthday. I did not invite you to a party, because I did not have one. Life is not very happy around my house. Coming to your house after school is great for me because it's fun. I am glad we are still best friends. I wish my mom and dad were happy like your mom and dad. You made my birthday a good one anyway. Thanks, Melinda.

Jesse

Greetings from the Atlanta Skyes!

Another year finds us all well and happy. We'll begin with Lenny, who continues to earn seniority at America South Air Lines and rack up the miles as a pilot. We can't believe he's flown the equivalent of twice around the earth in the few years he's been with the airline. For fun, he continues to terrorize local golfers with his formidable swing, and he says that his goal in life is to play every major course in the states before he's fifty. (Golfers of America, you have been warned!)

I continue to chase after Melinda, who keeps me on the go with her ballet classes and school projects. Between helping sew costumes at the dance studio and running publicity for the upcoming presentation of *The Nutcracker* (in which Melinda will dance in the corps), I haven't had time to catch my breath this fall. I also chaired the autumn auction and fund-raiser for the local children's hospital. I'm pleased to say we met our goal! In fact, they've asked me to chair the event again next year, and of course I said yes.

As for Melinda, she's loving school, dance and more dance. We never dreamed she'd stick with it the way she has, but she's been fanatical about becoming a ballerina since she was five, so what can we do except support her?

My mom, in Florida, continues to decline in health, but she won't move into a care facility no matter how much I beg. She says, "I don't want to live in one of those. They're full of old people."

Sure hope this finds all our friends and family happy and healthy and ready to take on the New Year. Peace on Earth!

The Skyes

March 12

Dear Jesse,

I am very sorry you fell out of the tree house and broke your arm. Mom says that we can't play Batman and Batgirl up in the tree anymore. I guess we should have waited for my dad to tie the rope on the branch, because our knot wasn't a good one. My mom will make you good lunches while you stay at my house so your mother can go to work, and I'll bring your homework every day until you can come back to school. I think your cast is kind of neat. Thanks for letting me be the first to sign it. Please don't let Toby sign it. He's mean.

Melinda, your (Bat) friend

Elana and Lenny,

How can I thank you enough for all the help you've given me this school year? I wouldn't have made it without you, and neither would Jesse. He talks about Melinda and both of you constantly. You are so kind to include him in your family outings. And your offer to let him spend the summer at your house while I work is overwhelmingly generous. With my family way out in California, and John's in New York, I really don't have anyone to watch my son, and a day care center isn't where he wants to be.

As you know, John and I are separating. I'm not sure what I'll do when third grade begins in the fall,

but something will work out one way or another. I feel
blessed that you are so generous and kind to us.

As ever,
Ann

November 2

Dear Grandma,
   Third grade is fun. Lots more
homework, but I like my new teacher.
My friend Jesse and I are in different
classrooms this year, but he still comes
over after school and we do our
homework together. Guess what? Jesse
now can sleep over when his mom goes
out of town, because Mom fixed up
the room in the basement. Jesse's mom
went to California this week, so
Jesse's staying with us, and it's fun to
do homework and go to school
together. He's better than a brother,
I'm sure.
   Here's really good news! Mrs. Houston
picked ME to dance the part of Clara
in The Nutcracker this year. You know

how much I love to dance. Someday I
will be a famous ballerina, so stay
healthy so you can come see me when I
get to dance on the great stage.

For Halloween, me and Jesse dressed
up like Frankenstein (Jesse) and Miss
Piggy (me). Mom stuffed my leotard
with foam padding and Dad made a
pig snout for me. Mom took pictures and
said she'll send some to you. Jesse and I
cleaned up in the candy department.
We got a ton. But don't worry, I won't
eat it all (at once ... ha-ha). Did a lot
of kids knock on your door? I still like
little bags of chocolate kisses best.

Well, I guess that's it for now. I'll write
again real soon.

XXXOOO
Melinda

P.S. I LOVE the diary you gave me for
my birthday, and I write in it every
night. When I've filled it up, I'm getting
another one! It feels great to write
down my feelings.

Seasons Greetings

Dear friends and family,

It's hard to begin a holiday letter on a sad note, but I must. After eleven years of marriage, John and I have agreed to split. This has not been an easy decision for either of us, but it is a necessary one.

Our house is on the market, and over the holidays Jesse and I will be moving to Santa Cruz, where we will live in the house I grew up in. I'm so glad I didn't sell it after my dad died last year. It should be a good place to resettle, and I have plans for us once we're there. I will work and also attend college so I can earn credits toward a degree in education. John has already moved out. He's taken a position with a company in New York.

Our new address is on the envelope of this letter and on the enclosed sheet. Our e-mail address remains the same. Please keep us in your thoughts. I must admit, Jesse is having a very hard time with all of this. But what child wouldn't? Maybe next year life will look brighter for us.

We still send our best wishes for a happy holiday!

Ann and Jesse

TO: Ballerina Girl
Subject: New Home

I am in California, but I don't like it here. I miss my dad. I miss my old friends, I miss my house, and most of all, I miss you and your mom and dad. I don't like my new school, and I have to go to an after-school program now. I don't like that either. I think about the fun we used to have, my special room at your house, and how great you and your parents were to me. I feel so lucky because I have those memories. I wish things were the way they used to be. I hope you will e-mail me A LOT!

How are things for you? How's school? When you are a famous ballerina, please don't forget me. Please.

Jesse

Name: Melinda Skye
Date: September 10
Mrs. Garner, 6th grade

What I Did on My Summer Vacation

This summer was a dream come true! I went to dance camp in Tampa for two whole weeks! My ballet instructor in Atlanta, Mrs. Houston, learned that prima ballerina Petrina Milicoff, who once danced with the Bolshoi Ballet in Moscow, was offering summer classes to promising students. Mrs. Houston recommended me! My mother sent in my application plus a videotape of me performing. I received a letter of acceptance in June, right after school was out. I was so excited that I didn't sleep for days.

When the date finally arrived, Mom and I flew to Tampa, where I spent the hardest (and best!) two weeks of my life in a dance studio with Ms. Milicoff. Twenty-five girls were invited. Only three of us were twelve years old. Ms. Milicoff said I have "the look of a dancer" (which is not too tall or too short, long neck, long legs, and small bones). She encouraged me to continue my training in Atlanta and said that when I turn sixteen, I should try out for the corps of a troupe that travels to Europe during the summers. Sixteen seems like a long way off when I want something as much as I want this!

The other thing that happened this summer is I made a new friend. In August, the house across the street was sold (it's been empty for ages!) and Bailey Taylor—who is exactly my age (her birthday's July fourth!)—moved in with her parents, her twin half sisters (six years old), a dog and two cats. When I found out she was coming to Rosswell Middle School, I promised to be her friend. Bailey doesn't dance; she plays the flute (but she hates to practice). She reads tons of teen magazines and knows all the latest fashion news.

That's most of what happened to me over the summer. It's changed me some. If possible, I want to be a ballerina more than ever.

Melinda,

I'm in boring English and decided to write to you instead of taking boring English notes. I mean, who wants to know about Louisa May Alcott and her boring book? Besides, I already read one of her books at my school in Virginia. When we walk home today, let's stop off at the Jiffy Store and buy some teen magazines so we can figure out what's hot this fall. I have five dollars that I got for baby-sitting my bratty sisters.

Oh, before I forget, do you know Richie Manetta? He keeps staring at me and I don't want to let him know it matters. Unless, of course, he's really cool. Then I want to let him know it matters. But if he's totally a brick I will ignore him. Your word is the law!

Bailey

MELINDA'S DIARY

November 16

All Bailey talks about is getting a boyfriend. She asked me if I've ever had one and I told her I have a friend boy—a best friend who moved away but keeps in touch. That's Jesse, of course! He's not a boyfriend in the romantic sense. At least not for me. (He still sends me birthday and Christmas cards *from California.) OK, so maybe I'm being a little dishonest, but Bailey asked a hundred questions, so I dug out my memory box and showed her pictures of him. (Good thing he sent his school picture this year!)*

Bailey said he is really cute (which he is, but I never thought about it). And then she started pumping me about whether I'd ever kissed him and stuff like that. I told her I didn't want to get too personal, but she was like a dog with a bone and told me all about the boys she's kissed and blah-blah-blah. More information than I wanted. But it has made me think about being kissed. I wonder what it feels like? And as long as I'm thinking about it, I guess I'd rather kiss Jesse than any of the guys at school. Not that I'll probably ever see him again. Still, it's fun to think about. . . .

Not that I have time for a boyfriend. Ballet and school take up almost every minute of my life . . . except for the small part Bailey takes up asking dumb questions!

Hi and Merry Christmas!
Thanks for the photos you sent on the Web. You look really pretty in your ballet dress, and I know you must have danced really great in The Nutcracker this year. I still remember the time I

went backstage when we were in first grade. I thought you were pretty then too. I hope you remember.

I'm into skateboarding big-time and I'm in a competition in March, so I'm doing a lot of practicing at a park near my house where all us boarders hang. Mom's still in school and working. The other big news is that my dad remarried and now I have two stepbrothers. Dad wants me to visit them this summer in New York. I don't really want to go, but I'll have to. He tries to keep in touch, but now that he has a new family the divorce seems even harder on Mom.

I'll send you postcards from the city. Maybe we can e-mail each other too while I'm there. I know you'll probably be going to some dance school this summer, but I still think about the fun we had when we were kids. I sort of miss it. You have the best family and I used to wish my dad was more like yours. Instead, I have a dad that's like mine.

Your e-mails to me make me feel good. Have a good holiday and give a special hi to your great parents. Mom may take me up to the mountains to ski for a Christmas present!

Jesse

February 21

Jesse,

We had to make an emergency trip to Florida because my grandma is dying. I'm freaked. I really love her and I can't imagine never seeing her again. I'm so sad. So sad.

This is in two parts because Grandma died yesterday. The funeral is the day after tomorrow. I can't stop crying. More later.

Melinda

To all your family,

Jesse and I are so sorry about the loss of Melinda's grandmother and your mother, Elana. We both send our love.

With sympathy, Ann and Jesse Rose

Hi friend,

I'm so glad you're home from Florida and I'm so sorry about your grandmother. I was almost five when my grandpa died, but I remember it like it was yesterday.

Mom and Dad had just divorced and Dad had dropped out of our lives (whereabouts still unknown). Mom cried a lot. I was scared because I thought she might die too and then who was going to take care of me? Instead, she married Bill and had Brenda and Paula and talked about how much Grandpa would have loved seeing them and how they'd grow up and never get to know him. Which hurt my feelings because she never once mentioned how much he liked ME, or how much fun Grandpa and I used to have together.

Well, I didn't mean to go on about myself. Here's some happy news: My cat Bubbles is going to have kittens. Do you think your parents will let you have one? If so, you can pick out any one of the litter you want. Sort of in memory of your grandma.

Bailey

Bailey!
Mom said I can have the kitten! And I will always love her and take care of her. You are a true friend!

Melinda

MELINDA'S DIARY

April 4

I love my kitten! She's pure white except for a black mask around her eyes, like Zorro. Jesse tells me I should name her Zorita because she's a female. Zorita sounds pu-r-r-rfect, so that's her name.

<Melinda> How are you, Jesse?

<Jesse> I'm fine. How's Zorita?

<Melinda> Cute as ever. There's somebody here I want you to meet.

<Bailey> Hi, Jesse. This is Bailey. I'm over at Melinda's house and we're IM'ing you together.

<Jesse> Hi, Bailey. Melinda says you play the flute.

<Bailey> That makes me sound so nerdy, and I'm not. I'm a real babe!

\<Melinda\> Yes, she's Bailey
the Babe. All the guys at school
think so. Ouch! Bailey just
slugged my arm for telling you
she's popular with the boys.

\<Jesse\> Don't slug Melinda! I'll
be forced to polish you off like I
did Toby Gillman. That's a story
you can ask Melinda to tell you
sometime.

\<Bailey\> Who's Toby? Someone
tell me!

\<Melinda\> I just told her he was
my tormentor in first grade.
Now she's really impressed
because you defended me. You
were my hero!

\<Jesse\> That was then. What
about now?

\<Melinda\> You still are!

\<Bailey\> Oh p-u-l-ease! I know

when I'm being shut out. Nice
to meet you J. Adios.

<Melinda> Write me when you
get back from New York. Okay?
I'll keep my fingers crossed that
you like your "new" family.

<Jesse> I hope so too. . . . Bye.

TO: Ballerina Girl
Subject: My New York Trip

The visit is over and I'm glad to be home. Because NY could never be home for me. The first week was awkward, everyone being extra polite and all. My stepbrothers, Richie and Darrin, didn't know how to treat me. They played games on their computer until Dad chewed them out for ignoring me. Neither one is very athletic. Dad got all over them, but it didn't make them want to hang with me at all. If we did do something together, it was just to be polite. His new wife, Donna, was nice to me, but she works, so she was not there during the day much.

Dad took ten days off work and we took trips into the city and out to some woods for hiking. That was okay. Sight-seeing highlights included the top of the Empire State Building, the ferry to Staten Island and the Statue of Liberty. One day Dad took us all to Yankee Stadium for a ball game, but it rained! We sat around for an hour waiting for it to clear up.

Truth is, Dad and I don't have much to talk about. We're strangers. That really hurts. When he put me on the plane home, we just stood there looking at each other. He said, "If you ever want to spend a summer here, just say the word." I know he wanted me to hug him, but I didn't want to. So I just said thanks and got on the plane. When I was younger, I used to dream about him begging me to come live with him and I would say no, hoping to hurt his feelings real bad. I still feel he shouldn't have left me and Mom. He shouldn't have. Your parents are so perfect. Maybe this is hard for you to understand—but thanks for being there to let me get it off my chest.

Jesse

TO: Ballerina Girl
Subject: Happy Birthday to my most Beloved Daughter!!!!

Sorry I must be away on your actual B-day, Princess, but I promise to make it up to you when I return. Paris is a beautiful city and I really want to bring you and Mom here for vacation. You'd love it! Of course, you usually find some ballet school to run off to during the summers, but maybe you can work in some vacation time with your parents. What do you think? There's a ballet to attend here and I'd be sure we'd get tickets.

I'll see you the day after tomorrow, so think about where you'd like to go for your birthday. Ask Mom for ideas too. You're thirteen! I can hardly believe it. I'm the father of a teenager! Love to my two favorite women!

Dad

MELINDA'S DIARY

September 6

School's barely started and I've already got a pile of homework—ugh! I wrote a long e-mail to Jesse trying to encourage him about his family troubles. It must be hard. He feels torn between his parents, but of course, he's really devoted to his mom. I wish I could see Jesse again, up close and personal. I really like him, but falling for someone who lives across the country doesn't make sense. Wish I were like Bailey and could find someone at school, but no one interests me the way Jesse does. Maybe someday, some boy will. Until then, Jesse is the one! I can't believe I've known him so long and we're still close. What or who could break that tie up?

Atlanta School of Ballet

April 7

Atlanta School of Ballet
4325 Peachtree Blvd.
Atlanta, GA 30021

Dear Ms. Skye:

We are pleased to confirm your acceptance by the Washington School of Classical Dance for its summer training program, beginning June 14. This opportunity, offered only to approximately one hundred dancers in the country, will require you to live in the dorms and attend classes three times a day, six days a week. A packet from the Washington School will arrive shortly with all data pertaining to your scholarship. Once again, congratulations, and we look forward to your return to our school in the fall.

Sincerely,
Madeline Houston
Director

P.S. Melinda . . . we're so proud of your accomplishments. I can't think of a more deserving student than you. Congratulations! M. H.

MELINDA'S DIARY

April 8

I made it!!!! I can't believe it, but the letter came today confirming my acceptance into the best classical-dance training program in the whole country!!! Mom and I shouted and screeched and danced all around the kitchen when I read the letter to her.

In June, Mom and I fly up to Washington, D.C. Then Mom comes home and I stay up there two whole months doing the hardest, most disciplined work of my life! I'm excited, but scared too. I'll miss seeing Bailey every day. I'll miss Zorita's soft purr. I'll miss e-mailing Jesse. The competition will be fierce, but I've always wanted this.

I know that getting into the corps of a good ballet troupe is so very competitive that some of the girls would push you down a flight of stairs if they thought it might eliminate competition and better their chances. (What I just wrote sounds hateful, but it's the gospel truth!) Gosh, I hope I don't make any enemies.

Stop it, Melinda!!! (Sometimes I have to be stern with myself.) Just go and dance and learn!

"Hello, Melinda. It's me, Jesse."

"No way!"

"Way."

"You're calling me? From California? Is—is everything all right?"

"Of course. When I got your e-mail about being accepted into the Washington program, I asked Mom if I could call you and she said I could, so here I am."

"Oh, Jesse . . . this is so sweet of you. Really. I—I haven't heard your voice in years."

"How do I sound?"

"Great."

"You too. I'm kicked about your getting picked. I mean, I know how much you love ballet."

"But it's going to be hard, Jesse. I mean this is a whole different level."

"You scared?"

"A little."

"You're going to be the best."

"I just hope I don't embarrass myself. Some of the girls are sixteen and seventeen and ready to go off to real dance troupes. Dance masters come to watch us and pick the best and dismiss the others. Imagine, training all your life only to be told you're not 'suitable.' It's a crusher."

"That won't happen to you, Melinda. When you're sixteen, they'll fight over who'll get you."

"I hope! But enough about me. What about you, Jesse? Are you going to New York to see your father again this summer?"

"I can't get out of it."

"Promise me you'll give them another chance, OK?"

"I'll give them another chance. Um . . . Mom's making signs at me to hang up, so I've got to go."

"Thanks for calling. It means a lot to me."

"Write me from Washington. If you have the time, I mean."

"I'll find the time. Goodbye, Jesse."

"Bye. You know what? I miss you . . . even after all these years."

June 23

Dear Melinda,

I miss you like crazy! But I know you're loving it. Boy, from your letter, it sure sounds like you're really working hard. I can't believe you're not feeling good. What a pain to be up there competing with all those prima donnas and not feeling good.

Listen, I'm gonna bust if I don't tell you something. I was saving it till you got home, but I can't wait another minute. Here goes. I went to the mall last Friday and ran into Peter Keating. (Remember, I had a thing for him in September, but he was in high school and my parents squashed it.) Anyway, Pete asked me to go to the movie playing at the mall and I said "Sure." Inside it was practically empty and the theater was totally dark, and then Pete slid his arm around me and the next thing I knew he was KISSING me! Wow, I thought my nail polish would melt. It was SO hot! (And I don't mean the temperature.)

So now Pete and I are "on" again and he's coming over this Saturday while I baby-sit the twins and Mom and Bill go shopping. My plan is to lose the twins (temporarily) and practice kissing Pete. Gotta run now. More after Saturday!

Hugs,
Bailey

P.S. Sure wish you were going to be here for my birthday!

July 4

Dear Bailey,

First, HAPPY BIRTHDAY!!!! This is our only day off, so I'm answering your letter before classes begin again in the morning. That's how great a friend you are! Careful with Pete. Don't practice too much kissing because it might lead to something else. Sorry if I sound like your mother, but I only want you to BE CAREFUL.

I think I'm trying too hard. My timing's off and the dance master embarrassed me in front of the whole class yesterday. I just couldn't keep up and she really snapped at me. Some of the girls giggled (competition, you know). I could have sunk through the floor. I've got bruises all up and down my legs too, probably from too much barre work. I've been putting on stage makeup to cover the purple blotches, but my bunkmate noticed them last night and said I should tell our trainer. Fat chance! I'm not about to whine and complain about a few bruises.

Have you been to my house to visit Zorita? You said you would, so don't get too focused on Pete that you forget my poor lonely cat (who I'm sure misses me and wonders why I don't sleep in my bedroom every night).

Well, we're heading into town to listen to Pops in the Park and watch the fireworks show over the Potomac River. I plan to sleep in the van all the way there and back! Write soon!

Melinda (who wishes she felt better!)

TO: Lenny
SUBJECT: 911

Honey, I know you're 40,000 feet over the Atlantic right now, but you'll pick this up when you land. I've received a call from Washington. Melinda has collapsed and has been taken to Georgetown University Hospital. The doctors think it's exhaustion. I'm on my way to the airport and I'm frantic. I can't get to Washington fast enough. Call the hospital as soon as you get this. I don't care about the six-hour time difference. Dear God, I hope she's all right. I hate that she's alone until I get there.

Elana

Roses

MELINDA'S DIARY

July 8

This has to be the MOST embarrassing thing that's ever happened to me! One minute I was in class doing a plié, my arms arched, my back perfectly aligned: the next minute, I woke up on the floor of the dance studio. Thinking back, I did feel dizzy and light-headed, and suddenly everything went to spinning. I felt hot all over and the music sounded like it was coming through a tunnel, then my stomach felt funny, and then came the floor and people screeching and the master holding my hands and rubbing my face. Someone stuck a wadded towel under my head and someone else lifted my feet. And voices kept saying, "Call an ambulance."

By the time the medics arrived, I was sitting up and feeling better, but I had to go to the ER and get checked out. The hospital called Mom, who came all the way up from Atlanta, and now I'm in a hospital room and she's huddling with some doctors in the hall. She said Dad's on his way back from Paris. I'm mortified! But I'm tired too. I'll bet I'm anemic, like Patti Johnson was last year. The doctors kept asking me questions in the ER and now it occurs to me that they were trying to find out if I'm a bulimic

UGH! How gross . . . sticking a finger down your throat to make yourself throw up just to lose weight. But I am losing weight. (I sort of fudged to the doctor when he asked my normal weight.) But I'm NOT bulimic. No way!

And the worst part of all is that everybody's conspiring against me to make me go home! I don't want to go home! Don't they understand? If I leave the school now, I'll never get asked back! This isn't fair. I've wanted this all my life and now it's going to be snatched away all because of a little fainting spell I had during class. I CAN'T STAND IT!!!!!!

TO: All Concerned
Subject: Melinda

I've created a special address heading—All Concerned—to keep everyone in our circle of family and friends updated about Melinda, and either I or Elana will give you information. PLEASE DON'T CALL THE HOSPITAL. We flew home with Melinda yesterday and checked her into Emory University Hospital, where she'll undergo tests for the next few days. She's running a fever, but she doesn't seem to have an illness—baffling. At the least, she's very anemic.

Elana is blaming herself for not catching Melinda's weight loss, bruising and excessive tiredness before Melinda took off to Washington. But our girl's never had a sick day in her life beyond those due to the common cold, so why should we have been suspicious?

We have great confidence in her doctors, especially her hematologist, Dr. Jan Powell, who we've been assured is one of the best in her field.

Melinda, Elana and I appreciate your prayers and thoughts, and as soon as we know what's going on, we'll let you know. In the meantime, keep praying.

Lenny

"Hi . . . is this really you, Melinda?"

"Bailey? Where are you?"

"The lobby. They won't let me upstairs to see you."

"Mom's turned into a real watchdog. She told the nurses' desk not to let anyone in. She's down in the cafeteria having dinner or she'd never have let me take this call."

"That's so mean!"

"She's not being mean, Bailey. She's just being Mom. It's good to hear your voice. . . ."

"Now don't start crying, or I will too. Can you tell me what's going on? I haven't got long to talk."

"How did you get here anyway?"

"Pete drove me. Now, tell me, what's happening?"

"I—I feel like a pincushion. They've drawn blood about a hundred times and sent me down for a CT scan—"

"A what?"

"It's a test—a full-body X ray."

"Oh. Did it hurt?"

"No . . . but *all* the needle sticks are awful!"

"When can you come home?"

"I don't know."

"Your mom asked me to take temporary custody of Zorita. She's being a good cat but she misses you."

"I miss her too. I miss everybody. Will you do me a favor?"

"Anything."

"E-mail Jesse. He's probably not on Dad's e-mail list. Jesse still thinks I'm in Washington."

"I'll e-mail him today. Now, don't cry or your

mom will pump you and you'll have to confess that I came here and talked to you. And my parents will *kill* me if they think I got into a car with Pete without their permission."

"Thanks for taking the chance, Bailey."

"Don't you know? 'Chance' is my middle name. I really want to see you."

"I'll beg Mom to bring you next time she comes. Maybe we'll know something by then. And . . . and thanks for telling Jesse for me."

TO: All Concerned
Subject: Tests

I'm letting those of you we love know all that is happening. They took Melinda down for a bone marrow aspiration today. I stood by her bed holding her hand while they told her about the procedure. It's horrible! They stick a long needle into her lower back between her vertebrae while she's curled into a fetal position. She'll only have a local anesthetic to numb the skin and she has to lie stone-still. One of the nurses said that Melinda could hold her hands and squeeze as hard as she wanted. She said that Melinda could yell or cry—anything except move. I begged them to let me go along, but Melinda wouldn't have any of it. She looked at me and said, "Mom, I'm not a baby." I watched them roll her away while I cried. Doesn't she know? She's MY baby. Please keep praying. We don't know what else to do but wait and hope.

Elana

TO: Jesse Rose
Subject: Melinda

Hi—

This is Bailey, Melinda's friend. Remember me? Well, it doesn't matter. What does is this: I'm writing you because Melinda asked me to. She's in the hospital. Now, don't freak. We still don't know too much about what's wrong with her. It's got something to do with her blood, because that's what they keep testing. Here's what happened. She fainted in ballet class in D.C. and got rushed to a hospital. Her mother went to Washington and flew back with her to Atlanta, where Melinda got checked into another hospital.

There she lies until the doctors figure out what's wrong. I've talked to her and she sounded scared. Just as soon as I know something, I'll e-mail you—you can contact me anytime. The important thing is that we help Melinda get through this really bad time, because we're her two best friends in the whole world. That's what she told me once.

Bailey

MELINDA'S DIARY

July 11

They stuck a needle in my back today. I couldn't see it, but I really felt it . . . like it was sucking out my insides. It hurt so bad. I tried not to cry. I squeezed the nurse's hands so hard that she yelped and I felt bad even though she said it was okay. I wished I'd let Mom come with me for the test, but I didn't want her any more upset. She looks like she's going to cry all the time. Dad looks like he hasn't slept in days. I hope whatever's wrong with me isn't bad. Please, God, don't let it be bad.

TO: Ann
Subject: Apology

I am so sorry you were inadvertently left off our e-mail news list. Please forgive us. Lenny and I have been distraught over Melinda and we're not thinking clearly. The second I heard Jesse's voice on our answering machine, I realized what had happened. Poor kid! He sounded upset. I had forgotten how long he and Melinda have been friends. Of course the news hit him hard. Melinda said she'd asked Bailey to get the word to him.

Well, you're in the e-mail loop now and just as soon as we know something, we'll send out the word. I hate the worried look on her doctor's face. I know that whatever is wrong, it's serious—much more than a case of severe anemia like they'd first suspected.

Tell Jesse that Melinda will be in touch, because they have computers here at the hospital and patients can use the Internet and e-mail. We just found this out today.

Elana

UNIVERSITY PATHOLOGY CONSULTANTS

121 East 18th Street, Suite 318
Atlanta, GA 30020
Phone: (800) 555-4567 Fax: (800) 555-4568

BONE MARROW PATHOLOGY REPORT

Referring Physician: Janet Powell, M.D.
Specimen Number: JL01-99437
Hematology Associates
Emory University Hospital, Suite 2010
Atlanta, GA 30020

Date Collected: 7/11
Date Received: 7/11
Date Reported: 7/12

Diagnosis: Acute Lymphoblastic Leukemia

Gross Description
The specimen consists of 5 slides and 2 additional aliquots of 3 cc each, labeled "Bone Marrow Aspirate, Melinda Skye."

Microscopic Description:
The bone marrow aspirate demonstrates extensive hypercellularity with normal bone marrow elements essentially replaced by infiltrating lymphoblasts. There are multiple mitotic figures seen. The lymphoblasts demonstrate a high nuclear/cytoplasm ratio and clumped nuclear chromatin. Some nuclei display a folded appearance. Scattered among the abnormal cells are small numbers of erythroid, myeloid, and megakaryocytic cells.

Flow cytometric immunophenotypic studies demonstrated a

population of beta lymphocytes, which expressed the CD19 and CD20 antigens, and were weakly positive for CD10 (CALLA) antigens.

Cytochemistry was positive for TdT, further corroborating a lymphoblastic process and poor prognosis.

The findings are consistent with acute lymphoblastic leukemia.

Stephen R. Jones, M.D.
Pathologist

TO: Jesse
Subject: The Final Word

Hi. . . . I'm writing this from a hospital computer. My fingers are shaking and I'm crying. Dr. Powell gave us the results of my tests today. She told us what's wrong with me. I have leukemia, Jesse. I have cancer.

Melinda

TO: My Ballerina Girl, Melinda
Subject: Sad

Ever since Bailey sent me the e-mail telling me you were in the hospital, my worried imagination has been going crazy. I thought about all the things that could have made you sick—really bad flu, or some weird disease. I never thought it could be cancer. You're too young to get cancer! I know cancer isn't contagious: it can't be "caught" like a cold. But why you, Melinda? It shouldn't happen to someone as wonderful as you!

Mom says you have a good doctor and that you'll get the best care in the world. PLEASE write me often—every day if you feel like it—and let me know how you're doing. I think of you every minute of every day.

Jesse

P.S. I'm sending you something to cheer you up as soon as I get the money together!

TO: Jesse
Subject: Just to Talk

I don't know why I got cancer, and don't think I haven't asked! The doctors don't know, Mom and Dad don't know. Maybe it's just bad luck. But whatever it is, I sure do hate it. This doesn't seem real. I keep thinking this is a bad dream and I'll wake up any minute. But I don't wake up. And I have to take chemo treatments, which scare me to death. Gee, did I really mean to write "death"? Oh, Jesse, I wish I could see you. . . . I wish this wasn't happening to me. . . . I just want to go home and have everything the way it used to be.

Melinda

TO: All Concerned
Subject: Doctor's Report

Now that we know the worst, we're hoping for the best.

First of all, thank you for all the cards, notes and gifts you've sent Melinda since we learned the news. Her hospital room looks like an annex for a boutique! Really, your generosity is much appreciated and has cheered Melinda greatly.

Melinda has been transferred to All-Children's Hospital, where she'll be supervised by a team of physicians in a state-of-the-art complex associated with St. Jude, the famous children's cancer research hospital in Memphis. She has a hematologist, an oncologist, a psychiatrist (for adjustment to the diagnosis), a nutritionist, a social worker—in short, a whole team of people to help her cope with her cancer (the latest concept in treating the patient as a whole, not piecemeal). A good idea, I guess, but there are a lot of new people in our lives, the kind that parents hope they never have to meet under circumstances we never think we'll face.

Melinda had a blood transfusion to elevate her red cell count and she looks and feels much better. She's also on antibiotics to deal with the bone marrow infection and is fever-free for the first time in days. Tomorrow she'll begin her first round of chemo, which her oncologist, Dr. Neely, hopes will put her into remission. Once they adjust her levels of chemo, which is pretty potent stuff, she'll get to return home. Then she'll go onto outpatient status. She'll have to come in for more treatments (the doctors call them protocols), be hooked up to an infusion pump for a few hours at a time and have more chemo dumped into her via IV, but at least we'll be able to take her home after each treatment.

The goal is to get her into remission and keep her there. Some patients never have a relapse. Others can have one after being cancer-free for a few years. A patient is considered "cured" if there are no relapses after five years. Frankly, there's so much to learn and adjust to that we're all overwhelmed. I asked Dr. Neely how we'll get through this and he said, "The same way everyone else gets through it—one day at a time."

More later,
Lenny

MELINDA'S DIARY

July 15

  The chemo started today. IVs in my arm, wads of pills in my mouth, a whole schedule of stuff that is poisonous. Dr. Neely says it has to be strong enough to kill the cancer cells. I hope it doesn't kill me along with it.

I asked him if I was going to lose my hair. He said, "Maybe not." I sure hope he's right. I imagine a bald ballerina and I start to cry. The doctors told me that I can return to dancing as soon as I'm in remission and feel up to it. They want me to be physically active. But no one understands how hard dance is and how far behind I'll have fallen. Where will I ever get the energy to compete again? I'm sick to my stomach and have to stop writing. WHY IS THIS HAPPENING TO ME????

TO: Jesse
Subject: Melinda, of course

I wish I could answer the questions you ask me, but I can't. Yes, she's really sick. Yes, she's really unhappy. I don't know about the dying part, but I won't even THINK that! I did get to go up and visit her and she looks pretty good. Skinnier and paler, but still like Melinda. Just to prove it, I'll bring a camera next time I go and take some pics of her and her hospital room and I'll send them to you. I'll be your eyes and ears, Jesse. I promise!

Bailey

━━━━━━━━━━━━━━━━━━━━━━━━━━━━━━━━━━━━

Elana's Journal

Midnight

I bought this journal today because I have to start writing things down...private things that I can't share in coast-to-coast e-mails, not with Lenny, certainly not with Melinda. I see my daughter, my dear child, writing in her little diary that she puts away and locks if anyone comes into the room while she's writing in it (as if I'd ever read her personal and private diary!). I know it's a release for her. The psychiatrist, Dr. Sanchez, was pleased when she learned that Melinda has the habit of keeping a diary. She told me that "journaling" is therapeutic. God knows I need such therapy myself, so I'll give it a try.

I can't believe this is happening to our child. Cancer. The word alone sends shivers of pure terror through me. But Melinda is such a brave little soldier. She goes through every treatment without complaint. I believe it's due to years of discipline from ballet. Ah . . . her ballet. She gets upset with me if I even mention it. Competing and losing a part to another is one thing; having your dream snatched away so cruelly is quite another. She doesn't deserve this.

I must stop thinking negatively. Melinda WILL dance again. She WILL beat leukemia. She absolutely, positively WILL. I can't afford to think otherwise. Lenny has his job to keep his mind occupied. But my job, my joy, has always been Melinda. How ironic that in my "volunteer" mode, I chaired events that raised thousands for this hospital. Now our Melinda is a recipient of all that effort and money. And me? I feel "out of work." How can I let Melinda know that I want her to need me as much as I need her?

MELINDA'S DIARY

July ??? (Lost track of time, but it seems like forever.)

I felt pretty good today. No nausea, and the food even tasted all right. (Some of the meds I take give food a funny—like peculiar, not ha-ha—taste). I can't believe all the presents and flowers and cards I've gotten! My friends from school, dance class, relatives . . . Mom had to take stuff home. Dad sent me a HUGE bouquet. Bailey gave me a white teddy bear with a red heart sewn into its fur. But my best present is a whole dozen pink roses from Jesse. They are so beautiful. His card said, "Roses go to the prettiest flower of all. From a Rose (admirer)." Isn't that sweet? I'd like to see him face to face . . . (before my hair falls out—if it does).

Bailey says she and Jesse e-mail each other regularly to "discuss" me. I'm not sure I like that too much. But it sounds petty to say anything about it, because both are my friends and I know they just want to help. Bailey brought me pictures of Zorita and I got a big lump in my throat because I want to go home and be normal again.

Will I ever be normal again?

Felt rotten today. Threw up all my supper. Refused ice cream for bedtime snack. Sleep is all I want.

Mom practically lives here at the hospital with me. Sometimes I wish she'd just go away. Other times, I want to crawl in her lap like a baby with a boo-boo. I haven't written Jesse in days, because I just don't feel like it. He probably hates me.

A new horror started today—sores inside my mouth from the chemo. They hurt so bad, I can't eat anything. I HATE my life!

Some therapist visited today. She taught me about imaging. I'm supposed to imagine my white blood cells "eating" the cancer cells. Tonight I played a video game with some super-graphic, kick-butt woman wiping out a nest of robotic aliens. I pretended she was ripping through my bloodstream destroying cancer cells. I got the second-highest score according to the chart of those who've played the game in the past month. Hail, Melinda!

Woke up this morning and found a huge clump of my hair on the pillow. I cried. I guess I won't be one of the "lucky ones" who keep their hair. Mom said that because my hair is so thick it's hardly noticeable, but I notice it! I told her I want it all cut off.

Mom brought her hairdresser, David, to the hospital today and he sat me in a chair and cut my hair into a super-short pixie cut. I look so different. But at least now if it all falls out, I'll be used to seeing it short. Plus, now there won't be as much to fall when it leaves my head.

Bailey came up and went on and on about how "cute" I looked. She said the new cut makes my eyes look huge. I told her thanks. I think it makes me look like a refugee from a concentration camp. Maybe that's because I've lost twelve pounds in two weeks. But I just can't eat anything!

July 30

Dear Melinda,

   I've given up sending you e-mails because you never answer them. The only news I get is from Bailey. Even your dad's stopped sending e-mail updates. I can't stand being cut off. Please don't abandon me.

Jesse

MELINDA'S DIARY

July 31

I'm ashamed of myself. I've been thinking about myself and what was happening to me so much that I forgot to really look around and see everybody else stuck in this hospital. Mom rolled me out into the halls in a wheelchair (THAT sure felt weird, rolling instead of walking), and I saw so many others with cancer like me—some a whole lot younger and a whole lot worse off!

The little kids are the saddest to see. Most of them are bald and they look so thin—I call it "the chemo look." One boy who's maybe four or five was sitting in the children's rec room coloring. There he was, an IV hooked to his arm, another to his chest, his little bald head bent over a coloring book. The crayons were spread all over the table, his tiny hand was holding a brown crayon, and he was coloring as if it was the most normal thing in the world. I just sat there and watched him and felt tears sliding down my face. It made me so sad. He's like any other little kid, except he isn't. He has cancer. Like me.

I went back to my room and cried for an hour.

TO: Jesse
Subject: Apology

I got your card and note and I'm sorry I've not been a very good friend. So much has been happening to me that I lost sight of some of the things in my life that really count. You're at the top of that list. I had Mom bring your framed picture from my dresser to the hospital and now I can see you every day and remind myself that what's happening to me is also happening, in a way, to my family and friends.

Dad uses words like "brave" and "courageous" when he e-mails people about me, but that's not really true. I'm neither of those things. I'm scared and angry and very unhappy. I don't know why anyone wants to be around me, because I'm so mean to people—especially the people who matter the most to me, like you and Mom and Dad. Even Bailey has been "busy" lately. Oh, she calls and has come to visit a couple of times, but the truth is we don't have much to talk about these days. My world is so small now. Hers is normal.

Dancing, the thing I once did that made my life

mine, lies in ruins, like a crumbled wreck. I'd better stop writing because I'm getting melodramatic. I won't stop writing you ever again. That's a promise.

Melinda

TO: Jesse
Subject: Friendship

OK . . . to answer your latest e-mail accusation: I AM NOT ABANDONING MELINDA. (I'm shouting this answer to you.) For starters, I have to baby-sit my twin sisters (HALF sisters!) this summer while Mom and Bill work, so I don't have much time to go to the hospital and back. The hospital is miles from here and when traffic's bad (which is almost all the time in Atlanta), it takes almost an hour just to get there. That leaves me only weekends to visit her. Most of the time, Mom and Bill have other things to do on weekends, so they can't take me and it's a rare day they let me get into a car with teen drivers (like Pete, my boyfriend, whom they don't like me dating, but that's another story!).

So you see, crabbing me out for not visiting

Melinda more often isn't very fair. Yes, I know, now that I've explained everything, you're sorry.

Apology accepted.

Friends(?),
Bailey

MELINDA'S DIARY

August 1

Mrs. Houston brought Tanya and Kathi for a visit today. They looked SO good! So healthy. I wanted to crawl under the covers and hide because I do not look good or healthy. They kept talking about how much everyone missed me and how poorly they do in class without me there to "push them to perfection." I know they're just giving me a line to make me feel better, but it was good to hear anyway.

Mrs. Houston says that just as soon as I'm able to resume classes, she'll work extra with me so that I can get back into shape more quickly. She said that she's saving a part in this year's Nutcracker and that dancers from the Denver Dance Company will be a part of our production. And that includes Natalie Blackbird, one of the best ballerinas in the country! I promised all of them that I'll be back real soon. I mean it too! I will!

Elana's Journal

August 1

It's 2:30 a.m. and I'm sitting in the hospital chapel because I can't sleep. I've stayed in the room with Melinda most nights (there's a large chair that makes up into a bed, a lumpy bed), but once she falls asleep, I lie there wide awake. I come here because it's open around the clock and I find it quiet and peaceful. The room feels like a refuge to me. Behind the altar area is a beautiful stained-glass window of healing hands touching through a rainbow. The window's lit artificially from behind so that it looks as if it's never dark outside. It helps offset the darkness inside my heart.

Melinda's been here two weeks already and still no remission. I thought it would happen more quickly. She's getting the newest drugs, the most powerful weapons science has against leukemia, but remission remains elusive. Her cancer still lurks, like a crouching lion, in her blood tests. How do I fight an enemy I can't see? How do I balance being Melinda's mother and her guardian? I know I hold on too tight. I can't help it.

I come here to pray. For strength. For healing. For wisdom. Sometimes the night seems endless and the days too rushed. Oh, what I'd give to go back to my mundane life of schlepping my daughter to dance rehearsals, of grocery shopping, summer cook-outs, and busywork. I miss Lenny when he flies out for days at a time. I miss my life. I want Melinda well and whole. And home.

Yes, I want her home!

MELINDA'S DIARY

August 4

I promise to be nicer to Mom. It's not her fault I'm stuck here (unless leukemia turns out to be genetic, then it IS all her fault! A little humor). I don't know why I take it out on her. I can see how it hurts her, but I'm nasty anyway. Bad ME! But I will do better. I swear!

Melinda Skye's case continues to prove stubborn. I'm adjusting her protocols and will introduce SGX-243. It's experimental, but she fits the parameters of suggested use and I believe her case calls for it. Will monitor her closely for the adverse side effects mentioned in the drug studies. Her family continues to be supportive and open to treatment options. Melinda is a strong-willed girl with above-average intelligence that will serve her well during the difficult months ahead. Submitted: 8:10 P.M., August 4

MELINDA'S DIARY

August (whatever!)

I absolutely, positively, categorically WILL NOT spend my birthday in this hospital. I told Dr. Neely this morning to either fix me or cut me loose, because I want OUT. He said he's trying something new. I hope so, because I'm so sick of this place I could scream.

Elana's Journal

August 5

Dr. Neely told us that he wants to try a new drug on Melinda because he's not getting the "required results" from other drugs. The new medication is part of a clinical trial and, according to him, results have been promising. It's a hard choice to make. Lenny's more daring than I and he wants to give the go-ahead. I'm more hesitant.

The side effects sound grim—weight gain, bleeding gums, sudden nosebleeds, brittle bones. The

brittle bones part scares me the most. Doesn't anyone realize that she can't ever dance if her bones
begin to break? Lenny reminds me that these are
potential side effects, and that Melinda may not
experience any of them. Dr. Neely says she'll be
closely monitored and that once remission is
achieved, the dosage will be decreased and eventually he will wean her off of it and onto a more
standardized regimen.

My foot-dragging has caused friction between
Lenny and me. I don't like that, because we really
need to lean on each other. I don't know what to
do. Lenny wants it. Dr. Neely wants it. Melinda
wants it. I'm the only holdout. I want Melinda
well, but at what cost?

MELINDA'S DIARY

August 10

That Bailey is such a nut! Today she brought a
stack of teen magazines and her entire brand-new
school wardrobe to model for me. She had drawn
up a chart listing the clothes and three columns:

Consider It, Burn It, Buy It. *As she modeled each piece, I checked off my opinion. Then she said she'd go shopping for me and get the things I liked best. That way, I'll have new clothes for school without ever setting foot inside a store. And of course, they'll be "of the moment" because Bailey's so hip about fashion.*

It really perked my day. Even Mom got into it and offered her opinions. She said she'd give Bailey the money to get whatever I wanted. What we didn't say out loud is that I won't be starting school on time. I'm trying not to think about that because we have to "wait and see" until I know how I handle my treatments. (Or is it how they handle me?)

I started the new drug combos today and I think I feel better already. (That's the power of positive thinking!) Mom finally caved, but I know she's not thrilled about it. Dad and I ganged up on her— unfair, but necessary. It's MY body and MY disease. I said, "Experiment on me. Please. Just get me out of here!"

It looks like I won't be shaving my legs for a long, long time. "Chemo hair loss" means more than saying goodbye to the hair on top of my head. My eyebrows are gone and so are my eyelashes (not to

mention body hair in very private places!). Dr.
Neely says it'll grow back when chemo's over, but
for now I look smooth and round as a pumpkin. I'm
glad I'm in the school's homebound program and
everyone can't see what a freak-a-zoid I've become.
I refuse to go to school until I look better NO MAT-
TER WHAT.

TO: Ballerina Girl
Subject: New Meds

I'm betting this new drug will be the one! I just
feel it deep inside me. I've got my fingers
crossed for you.

Got a long letter from my dad saying how much
he wants me to be a part of his family. He says
that Donna's boys are like sons to him, but I'm
his REAL son and that makes him proud. I want
to say, "Well, how about my REAL mother?
She's half of me too." He can't just take the part
he wants and forget the part he doesn't want.
Life doesn't work that way. I haven't written him
back because I honestly don't know what to say.
He expects to walk back into my life after all this
time and pick up where we left off. It can't be

done. I'm not seven anymore. And he's a different person than the one I worshiped back then.

Write soon,
Jesse

I know what you're saying. There was a time when I thought Mom and Dad knew everything, but now I know they don't. Sometimes they look as scared as I feel. That rocked me the first time I realized it. Mom still sleeps here at night. Can you believe it? I've told her it's okay for her to go home and come back the next day. She won't. Then it hit me: She can't make my leukemia go away and this is all she has to offer me. Her presence. So I've stopped telling her I'm fine without her at night. She needs to be here for reasons of her own.

Maybe your dad needs to feel like he's still a part of your life instead of the parent who checked out and missed all those years of you growing up. Maybe he's trying to make up for what he can't go back and change.

Forgive me. I've been talking to Dr. Sanchez (the shrink) too much! I see deep meaning in everything. Too much time to lie around thinking . . . that's all.

Philosophically yours,
Melinda

Audio Transcription by Dr. Neely for Insertion into Medical File of Melinda Skye:

Latest labs indicate that SGX-243 is working for Melinda Skye. There's a dramatic turnaround. Her spinal fluid is clear, her white blood count is near normal, and healthy red cells are proliferating. While I'm heartened by the results, I know the treatment can't be repeated. Let's hope it holds. Submitted: 10:07 P.M. August 20

TO: All Concerned
Subject: Success!

Finally. The new drug is turning the tide and we've achieved remission, so it looks as if she'll be able to come home before her birthday. This is a banner day. Elana and I can't wait to get our little girl out of this place, and Melinda can't wait to leave.

We've got a schedule set up for continued chemo over the next six months, but maybe the worst is over and future tests will show that Melinda's cancer-free. I believe she's weathered the storm and permanent remission will be achieved. She's suffered enough and now it's time to pick up our lives, which have been on hold ever since this nightmare began.

Thanks again for your prayers. Keep it up!
Lenny & Elana

MELINDA'S DIARY

August 25

I can't believe I'm sitting in my own bedroom writing this. Everything looks just the way I left it before I took off to Washington, but it's kind of unreal too. I'm so used to the hospital, the nurses' comings and goings, the other kids, the smells of the halls, the rattle of the food carts, the doctors dropping by twice a day. The gang on my floor threw me a little party before we left—very sweet. There were balloons and cupcakes and there was a clown to entertain the little kids. I was the only teen up there and the younger kids looked up to me. Keisha, who's six, even cried, but I promised to visit when I return for my treatments. (Maybe she'll be out by then, I hope, I hope.)

Zorita was sitting on my bed when I got here. Bailey had tied a bow with a bell around her collar and she looked really cute. I think she's forgiven me for leaving her for so long, because she curled up on my pillow like she used to do.

When I think over the last two months, they seem like a bad dream. But they weren't. I know they really happened, because there's a shunt in my chest for the upcoming chemo treatments. It's ugly, but I can hide it under my clothes. I'm tired now and I'm going to bed with my cat.

Elana's Journal

August 25

This will be quick. Part of me is elated to have my baby back in her room down the hall. The other part is scared witless. At the hospital, nurses were close at hand, so if Melinda had any problems I could run and get them. Here, it's only me and Lenny. Maybe only me because Lenny travels so much.

Lenny programmed all the important phone numbers into our telephones and I have lists of emergency measures to take if something I can't handle happens, but still it's frightening to be the sole one in charge. I think Melinda senses my fear and ineptitude.

I pray that everything goes well. Melinda's been through so much ... TOO much for a girl who'll be fourteen in a few days. She's changed since June, and seems older, more stoic. I miss my little girl.

TO: Ann

Subject: Melinda's Birthday

When I asked Melinda what she wanted for her birthday, she said, "I'd like to be cancer-free, go to Paris with a dance troupe, have boobs bigger than apricots, and see Jesse Rose." At this time, the first three things on her list are out of reach. But seeing Jesse isn't. If you're willing to let him come, we'd love to fly him to Atlanta for a visit. As Lenny says, "A lot of things in Melinda's life are out of my control, but a nonstop flight across the country for one of her friends isn't one of them!"

I know school might have started (it has here and Melinda cried because she couldn't go), but if you'll let Jesse come for even a few days, Lenny and I will be ever so grateful. Please think about it and call us. If the answer's yes, we'll arrange everything.

Elana (with fingers crossed)

TO: Elana and Lenny
Subject: Melinda's Birthday

How could I say no to such a heartfelt request? Besides, if I did, my son would never speak to me again! Plus, he might stow away on a plane and go anyway!

Yes, school has started, but so what? Jesse's had a terrible summer. He talked about Melinda constantly and so wanted to see her. He had little to do after returning from New York and I felt really sorry for him moping around while I worked. Don't tell Melinda, but he sold his skateboard and some of his baseball card collection to kids here at the apartment complex in order to send her flowers and the few presents that he's bought for her birthday.

I wish I could make arrangements for the flight myself but I could not financially afford for him to do this. He can stay up to a week, but don't let him wear out his welcome. And thank you. This visit will mean all the world to him.

Ann

MELINDA'S DIARY

August 30, 11 P.M.

Seeing Jesse again after all this time has been strange and wonderful at once. I've been a nervous wreck ever since Mom and Dad announced that he was coming. I was glad, but not thrilled, and I only wished they had asked me first instead of surprising me with the news. Not that I didn't want to see him—I did. But let's face it: I'm not at my best. Chemo has left its ugly mark. After weeks of being sick and burpy, I'm now swinging the other way: F-A-T. Dr. Neely told me this might happen (I still take a handful of pills every day plus the sucky chemo treatments), but I really didn't think I'd look so freaky.

My face looks like a Moon Pie—round and flat, really gross. Bailey says I'm overreacting, but she's not the one swollen up like a toad. Then I learned that Jesse was coming. I wanted to put a bag over my head. What was Mom thinking?

I was so nervous going to the airport tonight to meet Jesse's plane that I was sick to my stomach. Dad parked the car and we walked into the terminal. The monitors flashed that Jesse's flight from LA had landed, so we waited near the security entrance. My mouth was so dry I couldn't even swallow. I saw him coming, because he was holding a really big teddy bear. He looks like his pictures, but taller, and his eyes are still so very, very blue. When Jesse saw me, his face turned beet red. (He was probably wishing he could get right back on the plane and head home!) We just sort of stood there staring at each other like a couple of stupid cows, then Mom started gabbing blah-blah-blah—all the way through the baggage claim, the walk to the parking lot and the whole ride back to the house! There we sat in the back of her SUV, me hugging one car door, and Jesse the other while Dad drove and Mom talked. I thought I was going to scream, "Please be quiet!" but I bit my tongue. She was ruining everything! Just talking and talking, and me and Jesse embarrassed because we really didn't know what to say to each other—not that we had much of a chance with Mom's mouth running. Jesse and I had "talked" through cards and e-mails, but suddenly, in person, we were strangers.

Just as I was considering opening the door and hurling myself into traffic, I felt Jesse reach across

*the seat in the dark and his fingers touch mine. I
felt frozen in place, but his fingers warmed mine
and soon I started to relax. We sat that way for the
rest of the ride to the house, Jesse's hand holding
mine and Mom blabbering about everything and
nothing. But by then, I didn't care. Jesse was here.
And I was with him.*

    \<Bailey\> I know it's late, but I'm
looking out my window and I
see that your bedroom light's
on. Is your computer on? Can
you e-mail me right back? Is
Jesse there?

    \<Melinda\> Yes, I'm here and
totally awake. I heard my
computer e-mail bell ding and
was glad it was you. . . . Yes,
Jesse's here in his old room in
the basement. He said it was
like coming home.

    \<Bailey\> Tell me EVERYTHING!
What's he like? Do you still like-
like him? Details, I want details.

<Melinda> He's cute and a little shy. Not that I blame him. Mom practically talked our ears off from the airport to the house. Then when we got here, she sat us in the kitchen for cookies and milk! Can you believe it? Just like we were in grade school. I wanted to crawl under the table, I was so embarrassed. Finally, Dad said it was time to "turn in" . . . another embarrassing moment. He marched Jesse down to the guest room. Doesn't he know that Jesse's like three hours behind us and probably isn't one bit sleepy? Good thing there's a TV down there.

<Bailey> What are you and Jesse going to do tomorrow on your birthday?

<Melinda> Mom and Dad are taking us to Six Flags (where I plan to lose them in the crowds).

<Bailey> Can I bring your
present over in the morning?
And meet Jesse?

<Melinda> Come around 9:30,
or you'll miss us.

<Bailey> See you tomorrow!
And happy birthday in advance.
Night, now. (And NO sleepwalking
down to Jesse's room.)

Elana's Journal

August 30

11:30 p.m.

I got under Melinda's skin tonight with my in-
cessant talking from the second Jesse arrived. She
kept giving me furtive looks and I knew I was
overdoing it, but I couldn't seem to control my
mouth. Even Lenny mentioned it to me when we
were alone, saying he felt "sorry for the boy" because of my verbal bombardment. Maybe it's the

strain of the past weeks, but I vow I won't do it again.

Seeing Melinda and Jesse together again brought back memories of the two of them in grade school. They were both so cute and practically inseparable. I loved having him around and so did Melinda. So many memories . . .

She's grown up so fast. My daughter, my child . . . so pretty and smart. And burdened with cancer. It's not fair!

HAPPY BIRTHDAY!
To the world's best daughter . . . with all our love, Mom and Dad
P.S. There's a little surprise for you in the garage.

MELINDA'S DIARY

August 31 (My Birthday!!!!!)

This has been the best day of my life (so far)! At breakfast, I got Mom and Dad's card and let them blindfold me and lead me out to the garage. When Mom removed the blindfold, I almost fainted.

They'd had the garage converted into a dance/ exercise room for me! Air-conditioning, heating, a partial wooden floor, a mirrored wall and a barre so that I can work out on my own. Also, a treadmill and StairMaster to build up my endurance. This is wonderful! Now I can go at my own pace and return to the studio when I'm in better shape. I just screeched and hugged them both. I asked Dad, "But what about the cars?" (He's been known to obsess about his little BMW.) He said, "A little exposure to the elements never hurt a car." And Mother said, "He's been thinking of trading it in anyway for something more suitable for a man in his forties." And they gave each other a little look that said they were pleased to have surprised me so totally.

Jesse tried the treadmill and the StairMaster, but he said he'd leave the barre work to me. Then Bailey came over and we had to go through the squealing and excitement again. She met Jesse and pronounced him "really cute" to me when he wasn't around to overhear. I don't know why I care what Bailey thinks of him, but I do. She gave me a really cool top and a beaded bracelet for gifts.

We went to Six Flags, but I was really wiped out, so I wasn't much fun. Mom wanted to take me home, but I absolutely refused, so Dad and Jesse went on the rides together. Mom got some good pics of them and they both looked like they were having a good time. When we came home, I threw up (sure don't want Jesse to know that part), then I crashed and slept until about seven o'clock. I crawled downstairs and they were waiting to eat. I voted for pizza, and after it came I ate a piece and felt better. Mom brought out a cake (angel food with white coconut icing, my favorite) and lit candles, and Mom, Dad and Jesse sang to me. I still can't believe he's really here!

Jesse and I finally got to be alone at about ten o'clock. We sat out on the porch in the swing watching fireflies.

Jesse asked, "Do you know why fireflies light up?"

"No," I said.

"It's the way they tell each other that they're available," he said.

"Nice trick," I said.

"See?" he said, pointing into the darkness where the bugs kept glowing on and off. "That one's saying, 'Find me, find me.' And another is saying, 'Here I am, here I am.' "

Jesse took my hand and my heart started to pound like a drum. He reached under the swing and brought out a box. (I must have been asleep when he put it there.) He said, "Happy birthday."

I unwrapped it and held up a beautiful ballerina figurine. She's perfect and very fragile.

"It's made of porcelain," he said. "That's supposed to be nice stuff."

I told him how much I LOVED it. I wanted to hug him, but I was too shy. Good thing too, 'cause Mom came out and said it was time for a snack (our code for "time to take more pills").

The ballerina is on my dresser, in the place of honor she deserves, and I see her whenever I look up.

I've known Jesse forever . . . I wonder if what I felt for him tonight is l-o-v-e? Mom would say I'm too young to be in love, but I don't know. . . . He's very special to me. He makes me glow.

Elana's Journal

August 31, 11 P.M.

Tonight, as I looked at Melinda and Jesse together, I saw a woman inside my child. And I saw how Jesse looks at her, with adoration, pure sweet adoration.

He doesn't appear to see the effects of her cancer

on her, which is a miracle, I think. I'm grateful that he has been so kind to her. How awful it would been if he had acted like a jerk and rejected her. How would she have accepted his rejection? It would have crushed her. If he chooses not to stay in touch once he returns to California, I'll understand. But until that happens, I bless that boy.

If I could put the joy of this day in a bottle and save it, I would. It helps balance out those days in the hospital when all seemed bleak and lost. My child is growing up . . . and as her mother, I'm torn between wanting it and dreading it. I wish my mother were still alive and that I could talk to her.

Happy birthday, Melinda, my daughter, my child. I love you so very much.

===

TO: Mom
Subject: My Visit

===

I'm using Melinda's computer to write this while she's napping. Her mom said it's OK, that my tapping on computer keys won't wake her. I like being here and seeing her again. I was afraid during the flight that she'd think I was some nutty kid from a past life she'd HAD to invite just to be nice. I was afraid she didn't really want me here but had agreed to my visit so she wouldn't hurt her parents' feelings. She's told me though that she's glad I'm here, and that she hopes we can be friends forever. Nice, huh?

I like her mom and dad as much as I ever did (although her mom talks a lot, but DON'T tell her I said so). You should see the way they fixed up their garage so that Melinda can begin dancing again! BTW, her dad's taking us all to a Braves game Friday night (if Melinda feels like it). He's on flight duty now, but he'll be home tomorrow.

Hope you aren't missing me too much. I'll fly home next Saturday and will send the schedule once Mr. Skye sets it up. Wish I could stay longer.

Jesse

═══════════════════════════════

MELINDA'S DIARY

September 1

Tomorrow is Labor Day, and we're going out on the lake in the sailboat. Jesse's never sailed before even though he lives in California. He leaves Saturday and I'm really going to miss him, but I'm glad he won't be around to witness my further decline. I'm getting fatter by the day and the new meds make me really tired and cranky. I have a chemo session next Friday and will begin the homebound program next Monday. Not looking forward to either!

Bailey says school's boring (her usual take on school), but that she's been looking around for a new boyfriend because Pete's going to the community college and doesn't have time (or interest) for her these days. Poor Bailey—she wants a steady boyfriend so much. Hope she gets one soon.

I keep trying to stay dance-fit. Going up on pointe is killer! My feet are so out of shape. I have *to build up the calluses again, and no matter how tight I wrap my little footies, they still hurt. My toenails began to bleed from the pressure of toe work. Jesse wanted to get Mom, but I grabbed him. "She'll make me stop," I said. "I have to keep going."*

He said, "Maybe you should stop."

"I'll never get into shape if I don't toughen up," I said. "No pain, no gain."

We were standing real close and that's when he saw the shunt taped to my chest. I was mortified. I explained that it has a shut-off valve but is connected to a portal vein, and that it's there so the doctors won't have to find a vein every time I go for chemo. Veins often collapse because the chemo is so strong. I was afraid he would be grossed out, but he only asked questions and studied it. He made me feel that wearing a shunt is the most normal thing in the world.

He told me that science is his favorite subject, especially biology (he's in some kind of accelerated program in his school and he attends a few classes at the community college. This was news because he's never mentioned it before). I told him, "Way to go," and he grinned (which almost stopped my heart). I thought I knew everything about him, but now I know that I don't. Which is fine with me. It's sort of like digging through a box and finding something unexpected that makes you feel happy.

<Melinda> While you get to
hang with Jesse, I am stuck in
classes. Not that I'm jealous.
Anyway, big news: Pete is
definitely history and I've
tumbled for Kerry Robinson. I
should have mentioned sooner
that he and I have been flirting
in class (we have two together!)
and hanging out in the halls, but
I wanted to wait until it was a
fait accompli (see, I AM learning
something in French class).

<Bailey> Kerry is totally a jock
and totally popular. I'm so happy!

<Melinda> Congrats on landing
Kerry. What happened to Allison,
his main squeeze from last year?

<Bailey> She got preggie! Kerry
swears not by him.

<Melinda> And you believe
him? They were joined at the
hip all last year.

<Bailey> Sure I believe him.
Why shouldn't I?

<Melinda> Don't get offended.
Just be careful. Actually, I feel
sorry for Allison. Don't you?
She's only fourteen and "with
child." What will she do? Do
you know?

<Bailey> I don't know anything
about Allison's story. Don't
worry, I'll be careful. How about
you? Are you and Jesse still
"just good friends"? Any mouth-
to-mouth action yet?

<Melinda> When something
exciting happens, I'll tell you. I
have to go now. Movie about to
start on the VCR for Jesse and
me. Popcorn, sodas, ice
cream—no wonder I weigh a
ton. But NO parents hanging
over us. Mom and Dad went out
for the evening.

MELINDA'S DIARY

September 2 (Labor Day)

We had a good breeze on Lake Lanier, and the sailboat skimmed along like a waterbird. Jesse was impressed. I told him that sailing is the best way to ride the wind and he agreed. Dad showed him how to trim the sails, swing the boom, and tack to move the boat across the lake. Mom packed a picnic and we dropped anchor in the middle of the lake and feasted. I had to cover up most of the day and slather on the sunscreen because some of the meds I'm taking interact with the sun. I really didn't mind since I didn't want Jesse to see me in a swimsuit in my present blubbery condition.

Later, Dad and Jesse went swimming off the boat and I went below and took a snooze. (Will I ever feel 100 percent again?) We headed home right before sunset. Jesse and I sat on the bow of the boat and watched as it cut through the water like a knife. He slipped his hand over mine and it was like we were in perfect sync with each other, like we had one heart beating between us.

When we got home, Dad made ice cream and Jesse and I watched the fireflies come out. He said, "You want me to catch some in a jar for you?"

I said, "Sure."

And he said, "Did you know that scientists pay for these bugs? I catch them out where I live and stick them in the freezer. When I've got a bagful, I take them into the science department at the university and they pay me thirty-one cents a gram for them—nine dollars an ounce."

"They don't look like they weigh much," I said.

"It's a way to earn money," he said. "And I'm helping a scientific cause."

As usual, Jesse's knowledge surprised me, so I urged him to catch a hundred fireflies and stick them in our freezer, but when he brought the jar to me and I saw the flies trapped inside, their little lighted bodies going dim, I started to cry.

"What's wrong?" he said.

"It's sad," I said. "They don't hurt anyone. They're so gentle. And now scientists are going to experiment on them."

Jesse said, "They're insects. They have no nerve endings or higher brains."

I kept crying and said, "I don't care. It just doesn't seem fair that they should die."

Jesse said, "They don't have to die." Then he unscrewed the lid and let them all go.

I felt stupid because I'd made him throw away spending money. I said, "I'm sorry."

And he said, "I promise I will never catch fireflies again, because they should never be held against their will, or frozen and dissected, even if it is for the good of science."

I wondered if he was poking fun at me for being so silly about an insect, but when I looked into his beautiful blue eyes, I saw that he was serious. He'd held the power of life and death over them but had released them, allowing them to live on, to please me. And while we watched them fly off into the night, I got the feeling that we weren't really talking about fireflies at all, but about mercy and kindness and doing something nice just because you can.

September 7 (one of the worst and BEST days ever!)

We took Jesse to the airport today at noon. When we came home, I locked myself in my room and had a good cry. I'm going to miss him so much! I already feel like there's a big hole inside me because he's gone. I think he might like me too. (I hope.)

Here's exactly what happened. Mom dropped us off and went to park the car so that Jesse could check in. We waited in line together, and after Jesse checked in, we hung around the terminal, because we both knew that once he went through the metal detectors it was really goodbye. (Mom had told me she'd park and come inside to look for me at the check-in counters.) Jesse held my hand and I tried to act cheerful and not to cry even though there was a lump in my throat the size of a tennis ball.

He said, "I really had a good time."

I said, "Me too. Thanks for coming."

He said, "Can I come again someday?"

I said, "Will you? Maybe next summer. You think?"

He said, "Maybe."

A tear trickled down my cheek and he wiped it off. He said, "I'll e-mail and write. You too?"

All I could do was nod, because I didn't want to bawl like a baby.

He headed toward security to wait in line and pass through. The line was moving slowly, but not too slow for me, because I didn't want him to leave. He was almost at the front of the line when he turned and hurried back to me. I stared, wondering what was going on. He said, "I forgot something."

"What?" I asked.

Then he grabbed me and kissed me right on the mouth! Before I could react, he turned and raced back to security, threw his backpack on the conveyor belt, and went through the detectors without *setting off any alarms. Except for the one inside my heart. It was ringing like crazy. Everyone around us was watching, and I know I must have turned twenty shades of red. Here I was, standing in Hartsfield Airport with hundreds of people heading off to their flights, and I, Melinda Skye, fourteen for only a week, had experienced my first real kiss in front of God and everybody.*

Today, Jesse kissed me, fast and hard, and it felt wonderful. Best of all, he meant it with all his heart. Tomorrow, I'll tell Bailey. Tonight, it belongs to just me.

MELINDA'S DIARY

Friday the 13th

Chemo sucks. It took an hour and it hurt. The only thing that saved the day was visiting my old floor and saying hi to the kids. Keisha has gone home. But I saw three new faces of kids who've checked in since I left.

Cancer sucks too. Especially when it picks on little kids. I'm tired now and don't feel much like writing.

TO: All Concerned
Subject: Outpatient Chemo Begins

This has been a hard week for our little girl. Her friend Jesse Rose returned to California, she started homebound schooling, and her outpatient chemo treatments began. The protocols are two weeks on (three days a week) and one week off, for the next three months. Once chemo is over, she'll be tested frequently over the next six months and if she remains cancer-free, she'll return for semiannual checkups over the next few years. If the drugs do their part, she should be out of the woods in five years (by the time she's eighteen and heading off to college, this whole ordeal should just be a really bad memory).

I told her I'll take her to Paris to celebrate when her chemo treatments are over. She said, "Dad, save your money . . . I'm going with a dance troupe." What a girl! She never forgets her dreams and goals. Elana and I are so proud of her. Elana has dropped all her outside activities, except tennis, which she says she needs to "vent" and blow off stress. I use golf for the same purpose.

Thanks again for all your concerns. I'll only post if there's something meaningful to say.

Lenny and Elana

MELINDA'S DIARY

September 20

Jesse wrote to say he really liked the B-day gift I sent (it's getting harder to think up good things to give him anymore—hey, maybe I'll mail him ME!). I keep thinking about him kissing me. I wish it could have been in private, because now I wonder if he did it just to say thanks for the good time, or if he meant it from his heart. I finally told Bailey how it happened and she said it was "really romantic," because he was almost through security and had to make a special effort to come back to kiss me. I tried to play it down because I know she's been kissed lots of times. And me? Well, who wants to kiss a girl with cancer except for a best friend, like Jesse? (Who may just feel sorry for me.)

He says he wants to come visit again next summer. I'd like that, IF I'm looking like my regular self and IF I don't have an invitation to dance school again.

Homebound school isn't too bad. I get the work done easily, but I miss going to school. I miss seeing friends in the halls, the smell of chalk dust and, yes, even the cafeteria food. Bailey (the nut!) took a video camera to school and made a tape for me she calls "A Day in the Life of . . ." She had that camera running all day. She interviewed our friends, teachers, even the principal. Everyone says they miss me and want me to hurry back. Some of the guys on the soccer team sing to me. Very cute (and very bad singers). I've watched it sooo many times. It makes me laugh. But it also makes me cry because I can't be there.

Elana's Journal

September 25

Now that life has settled more into a routine, I can be reflective of the past few months. What can I say? For so long, I was in "emergency mode"—sheer panic over what was happening to Melinda. Now I feel as if we're treading water. Our lives revolve around her chemo treatments and their aftermath. Some days she's too sick to even sit up. Others, she endures the treatment just fine. There's no predicting. As it drags on and I watch her push herself, I want to insist that she rest and take it easier. But it makes her angry if I meddle. It's dance that drives her.

Last week, we got caught in traffic and she became tense because she knew she was going to be late for class. (An unpardonable sin most of the time although Mrs. Houston has given Melinda great leeway with the studio "rules.") Still, Melinda holds herself to a high standard and refuses to "cave," as she calls it, to bend or break studio protocols. In short, she won't allow herself any special privileges no matter what.

Anyway, we got caught in traffic after chemo and by the time I pulled into the parking lot, she was extremely upset. She opened the car door and discreetly vomited. It broke my heart to see her heaving, knowing I could do nothing to help her. When she was finished, she dug out a bottle of mouthwash she keeps in her dance duffel bag and rinsed her mouth, took a few deep breaths and got out of the car. I said, "Honey, do you have to go?"

And she said, "Yes, I have to go."

I watched her toss her gear bag over her shoulder and march into the studio. I cried ... for her, for my helplessness, for all the things I can't change.

MELINDA'S DIARY

October 4

Mrs. Houston reminded us that Natalie Blackbird will arrive next week with some of the Denver dancers to begin rehearsals and to lead our advance class. So now I have a goal. Be in competitive shape for the experience AND get picked for a role in this season's Nutcracker. And boy, do I ever have a long way to go.

October 10

I found a few hairs growing on my body today! My eyebrows look as if they're coming back and maybe I can chuck the false eyelashes in another few weeks. Knowing how to put on stage makeup and fake hair and lashes has been a real plus. At least I don't look like a plucked chicken when I go to the trouble to paste it all on.

TO: Jesse
Subject: This and That

I hope you don't mind resuming our e-mail talks. I thought you'd like to hear about Melinda from an observer like me, one who cares about her as much as you do. (OK, maybe not in exactly the same way, but just as much in a best friend way.) She's really doing pretty good. The other day I went with her for a chemo treatment. She sat in this chair that looks like a big recliner and a nurse hung a bag of liquid, hooked it into the shunt in Melinda's chest and said she'd check on her in a bit.

I tell you, my eyes were riveted to that gizmo, and for a minute, I felt all queasy in my stomach. But Melinda never noticed. She said, "Let's play Scrabble," like it was the most ordinary thing in the world. So we played (she tromped me), then we watched some TV (each little private chemo room has an overhead TV). Finally, the nurse came back. The bag was empty, so she unhooked Melinda, took some vital signs and said, "See you in a couple of days."

Melinda looked pale, but she got up. We rode down in the elevator, met her mother in the lobby and drove home. M. just rested against the seat and listened to a CD while we maneuvered through traffic. Jesse, it was as if this was the most ordinary way to spend an afternoon instead of the most ghoulish. She's so brave!

B

TO: Bailey
Subject: Melinda

Thanks for writing to me. You're right—I only hear good stuff from M. Nothing bad. I know chemo is hard, because a woman in my mom's office is being treated for breast cancer and Mom's dropped some info about what a hard time the woman's having. So I figured M. can't be breezing through it like she sometimes pretends. It's really hard for me to be so far away while she's going through all this. I guess it's no secret that I care about her. Really care.

My school is having some dumb fall festival dance and a girl asked me to take her. Beth's nice, but I don't feel about her the way I feel about M. I decided to go to the dance, but I'll be thinking about M. the whole time. She's all I think about most of the time anyway.

Jesse

Melinda's Diary

October 18

The nurse talked to me (again!) about joining the teen cancer support group. They meet on the second Friday of every month at seven o'clock in the hospital auditorium. I tried to be polite, but I have no intention of EVER going to those meetings. I don't want to hang around with a bunch of kids with cancer. I want to hang around with regular kids—kids who aren't sick, who've never been sick. Maybe that's selfish of me, but it's the way I feel. I WON'T GO!!!!!

TO: Ballerina Girl
Subject: Control

I don't blame you for not wanting to go to cancer support meetings. Mom suggested I go to a kids of divorced parents group that meets on her college campus, but I nixed that idea as soon as it was out of her mouth. Who wants to sit around with a bunch of strangers and dis their parents' divorce? Not me.

Dad's putting pressure on me to fly to NY for Christmas. That's not going to happen. What would Mom do? Spend the holiday alone! No way. She said it was all right with her if I went, but I could see by the look on her face she didn't mean it. I'm not bailing on her the way he did.

I won a blue ribbon in a skateboard competition last Saturday (Mom got me a new one for my

B-day—state-of-the-art, a fine piece of work-manship). I've lined up a job in a sporting equip-ment store for the Christmas break. Just a few hours a day, unloading stock and stocking shelves, but it's a paycheck.

Wish I could see you for Christmas.

Jesse

<hr />

MELINDA'S DIARY

October 22

I'm sad tonight. Bailey let it drop that Jesse is go-ing to a dance with some girl named Beth from his school. B. acted all embarrassed once she'd spilled the news. She said she was sorry, that she'd never meant for me to know. I'm not sure if I'm mad at her or not. It hurt because my feelings for Jesse are mixed up. But it's not fair for me to expect him never to look at another girl. Unrealistic too. He's more than a thousand miles from here. I guess I'm lucky he still thinks of me at all.

It would have been better if he'd never kissed me. I wish B. had kept her big mouth shut.

MELINDA'S DIARY

November 15

Jesse's never said a word about the dance or the girl he took. I've pumped Bailey, but she swears he's never mentioned it to her in his e-mails either. She said she even asked, but he didn't answer. I asked her why they're e-mailing each other in the first place, and she said it's because she feels like they have a lot in common—me, of course, but also divorced parents. She says I can never understand what it's like to feel rejected and unwanted by a parent—which is different from Jesse's situation because both his parents want him. Still, Bailey thinks they're "kindred spirits."

Yikes! What's wrong with me? B. is my friend. And so is Jesse. The real problem is this girl, Beth. I wonder, is she pretty? Is she sexy? Whatever she is, I'm sure she doesn't have cancer. I'm so mixed up. I wish B. had never told me about Beth and Jesse! What was she thinking?

December 15

Chemo's over. I feel like a person let out of prison. They removed the shunt too and I'm sure not going to miss THAT sucker! I'm learning so much with Ms. Blackbird. She's worked individually with me and says I'm inspiring. She says I should audition for the Denver ballet group when I'm sixteen because they take young dancers for summer internships. I can't believe it! She thinks I'm good enough to become a part of her company's dance corps! Of course, if I'm accepted (fat chance!) and can really join a troupe full-time after graduation, I'll have to forgo college . . . at least for a while. I don't know how Mom and Dad would take the news. I know they have a college fund for me, and Grandma left me a chunk for college too. But dance supersedes college in my book! I won't be able to dance forever and I can always go to college.

Our Christmas performance will be at the Fox Theater Friday night. I've been dancing in The Nutcracker *since I was a kid, but I'm more excited about this one than I've ever been about others. Dad says we can buy a copy of the tape PBS is shooting of the performance and we'll send it to Jesse for a Christmas present. I wonder if he'll care (now that Beth is in the picture).*

TO: Bailey
Subject: Third Degree

Why do you keep asking about Beth in your e-mails? There is NO me and Beth. I took her to a dance because she asked me to. I have no plans to date her. She's OK, but not right for me. Please don't ever tell Melinda about Beth. I don't want her to think any girl means more to me than she does. And that's the truth. Thanks for keeping my secret (which I never should have dumped on you).

Jesse

MELINDA'S DIARY

December 20

I spent the evening consoling Bailey because Kerry broke up with her. He's such a RAT! He dumped her right before Christmas—probably because he's too cheap to buy her a gift! I reminded her that he'd done the same thing to Allison and she's pregnant! I think B. knows deep down she's better off without him. According to B. he was mak-

ing too many demands on her anyway. I can guess what "demands" she means too.

It's hard for her, though, because she's the kind of girl who always thinks she needs a guy. I've never been able to figure out why. She's a great person, fun to be with, always ready to do anything for a friend. I wish she could see herself through my eyes.

I realize she's a little bit of a drama queen too. She tends to blow everything way out of proportion until it takes on gigantic importance. Good thing she wasn't the one who got leukemia. How would she have coped with that?

"Merry Christmas, Melinda."

"Jesse? Is this really you?"

"No . . . it's my evil twin. Just kidding. . . . How are you?"

"I—I'm fine. And you?"

"Fine. Listen, I called to thank you for the tape. And the Braves shirt. They're both perfect."

"You're welcome. . . . Thanks for the rose pendant. I'm wearing it now."

"I'm glad you like it. The tape is my favorite thing. You look so . . . so real. I've replayed the Chinese dance part so many times I can hum the music in my sleep."

"Tchaikovsky would be pleased to know that."

"You, um . . . looked beautiful. Even prettier than that famous ballerina you like so much."

"I don't think so, but thanks for saying it. So . . . what did you get for Christmas?"

"My father sent a video camera. Said that if I won't come to him, then the least I can do is send tapes of my day-to-day life. It's a pretty good idea, actually. I can send you tapes too."

"Would you?"

"I've taped our apartment and me and Mom opening presents this morning."

"How's your mom? We didn't get a Christmas letter from her this year."

"She's all right. Wrung out because she's taking an extra course this term. So tell me, is everything still okay with you?"

"I guess so. My latest blood counts were normal. I'm going back to school in January. You know—back into the classroom. I'm excited, but sort of scared about it too."

"Why?"

"I've been out ever since last May. Everybody's so far ahead of me. Not with studies and class work, but with friends and cliques and all the social stuff. Know what I mean?"

"Bailey's there. She'll make sure you fit right in, won't she?"

"She'll help, but I may be a total social retard. I'll have to see how the kids treat me."

"You didn't plan on getting cancer. They should be nice to you."

"We'll see, won't we?"

> **<Melinda>** When Jesse and I talked, I really wanted to ask him about Beth.
>
> **<Bailey>** You didn't, did you!?!
>
> **<Melinda>** No. I bailed. Lost my nerve.
>
> **<Bailey>** Whew! So glad you didn't, because I wasn't supposed to tell you about her. If he finds out I did, he'll never tell me anything again!
>
> **<Melinda>** Then I'm doubly glad I didn't. He tells you things he

doesn't tell me. It hurts my feelings.

<Bailey> Back up, girlfriend. Why would he tell you about another girl? Poor strategy.

<Melinda> Do you think he really likes Beth but is only being nice to me for old time's sake?

<Bailey> NO WAY!!! He's not a jerk like Kerry who's telling everybody that he and I did IT (which is a total lie, if anyone says anything to you. Sure he pressured me, but I held him off and now am I ever glad I did!). I can't wait until high school. Maybe the guys will be more mature.

<Melinda> News flash, Bailey . . . you've already dated high school guys and didn't like the way they treated you.

<Bailey> So maybe I won't date anybody. Most guys are jerks anyway.

<Melinda> Bailey without a boyfriend? I won't believe it until I see it. Not to change the subject (OK, changing the subject), want to come over New Year's Eve and stay up with me and watch the ball drop in Times Square on TV? I'm going to call Jesse and say happy New Year at midnight. You can wish him the same thing.

<Bailey> New Year's Eve sounds fine. Patti's having a party, but I don't want to go because Kerry's going to be there with his new airhead girlfriend. Who wants to be subjected to seeing them do the kissy-face thing all night long? Not me! And yes, I'd like wishing Jesse happy New Year. You know, he may be the only nice guy left on the planet.

<Melinda> Bring brownies, the ones you bake with the M&M's in them. I'll cover the popcorn and soda. We'll have fun. And Jesse will be so surprised. Yikes! I just thought of something. What if he's at a party with Beth?

<Bailey> Then he'll hate himself because he wasn't home when you called. Trust me.

December 30

My Confession

 I am pond scum. Puppy piddle. Turtle turds and beetle dung. And every other nasty thing I can think of! Why am I all of these loathsome things? Because I've fallen in love with Jesse Rose. And the only reason I'm writing it down is that there's no one I can tell. Especially my best friend in the whole entire world, Melinda. And if I don't tell someone, I'm going to burst. So this piece of notebook paper becomes my "confessor" and the keeper of my awful secret.

 Jesse treats Melinda like she's a queen. I want a guy to treat me the same way. But no boy does. Things start out good between us, but once we get used to each other and the goo-goo feelings fade, we drift apart. Most of the time, I get pressured to do things I don't want to do with the guy. If I don't cave, he walks. That's the way it was with Kerry.

Except I did let him go a little too far (not all the way, but almost!). So now he's spreading rumors, and there's nothing I can do, because kids at school want to believe him—Mr. Cool Jock. Now other guys are asking me out because they think I'm easy—which I'm NOT!

I never want Melinda to know any of this. Especially how I feel about Jesse. What kind of friend wants her best friend's guy? Especially a best friend who's sick with a terrible disease? Also, I know the truth about Jesse and Beth (that Beth is nothing to him) and I don't tell Melinda. Still I let Melinda think the worst.

See how worthless I am? I hate me. But not enough to stop loving Jesse.

Signed,
Bailey Taylor
Prisoner of Dark Secrets

P.S. I feel better after writing this. Tomorrow night I'll hear Jesse's voice on the phone. It'll break my heart *because I know he only cares for Melinda, but I want to hear him so much. Love hurts. Oh yeah . . . it hurts big-time.*

MELINDA'S DIARY

January 3

Returned to school today. Scared, but happy to be back. I'd forgotten how loud the halls can be after all the time I've spent alone at home. I stood at my locker and soaked up the atmosphere like a sponge. Some kid almost ran into me and I nearly panicked because I sure don't want to get injured and end up back in the hospital. I've had enough of hospitals to last me the rest of my life!

In homeroom, everybody was friendly, but I knew they were talking about me. "She's the girl with cancer," a girl whispered (loud enough for me to hear). "Is she bald?" "Is she wearing a wig?" others asked. I wanted to yell "No," but I wasn't supposed to hear them, so I kept my mouth shut and kept smiling. Don't they know it hurts to be talked about? What's wrong with people anyway?

Mom got permission from the superintendent of schools for me to carry a pager at school. If I ever get sick, I can page her and she can come get me. But I won't use it because it's so lame, and besides, it makes me feel even more like an outsider. I ate lunch with Bailey (lucky we have the same schedule!) and got eyeballed by the football players. Bailey says that they're shunning her. Why is Kerry being so mean to her? I'm glad I know someone like Jesse, who's never been mean to me.

P.S. I think he's over Beth, because on New Year's Eve, he said he was sitting alone by the phone wishing he could hear my voice. If Beth were really important to him, he'd have been with her. That's what I think, anyway.

February 14

Jesse is so cute and original! He sent me a beautiful bouquet of flowers for my desk for Valentine's Day. My desktop on my computer, that is. His virtual roses arrived in this morning's e-mail and I've had them up and running since I got home from school. I can change their color and their size whenever I want. I put them right in the middle of my screen and every time I look at them, I smile. He makes me so happy!

February 14

Dear Self,

This is the first Valentine's Day that I haven't had a boyfriend since I can remember. No matter. Jesse's the only boy I like. And I know he'll never like me in the same way.

Maybe I'll become a nun.

(Sister) Bailey

May 23

Dear Lenny and Elana,

No, you're not seeing things. There really is a graduation announcement enclosed in this envelope. Isn't it beautiful? I never thought this day would come, but I graduate from the Santa Cruz College School of Education on Friday. I can hardly believe it myself! I've even impressed Jesse—which is a hard thing for the mother of a teenage boy to do, don't you know! I only wish you all could attend the ceremony and share my happiness.

Now comes the challenge of finding a job. I've sent out résumés to high schools throughout the area and already have four interviews scheduled. Jesse wants us

to return to Atlanta, of course. Naturally, I know why.
He's still smitten with Melinda, even after all these
years. Goodness knows I've tried to make a life for the
two of us here, but he still yearns for what he can't
have. I've told him that he can apply to any college he
wants, and frankly his grades are good enough that I
know he'll qualify for scholarship money somewhere.
He tells me he wants to study medicine. Can you
imagine? My son, the doctor!

Thank you for your encouragement over the years.
Friends like you are few and far between.

Ann

TO: Melinda
Subject: Summer Vacation

There's no getting out of it. I have to spend most
of the summer with my dad in New York. Mom
and I had a fight about it, but she says her
hands are tied, there's nothing she can do to
keep me from having to go. She says I have to
do what he says until I'm eighteen. It sucks.

Jesse

<Melinda> I was online when your e-mail arrived, so don't go away.

<Jessie> Hey! Why are you up so late?

<Melinda> Term paper due tomorrow and I'm behind. I'm feeling tired and I crash as soon as I get home instead of getting right to my work. 'Nuff about me. Sorry about your messed-up summer, but you just might have a good time. It wasn't nearly as bad as you thought it would be last time you went. Remember?

<Jessie> But I only had to stay a few weeks last time. This is for the whole summer. What will you be doing?

<Melinda> Dad surprised me and Mom with plans for a six-week vacation to Europe. We leave on June 11. I was

planning on taking extra dance classes this summer (since I missed out on Washington this year), but that's out now. I've always wanted to see Europe. Of course, I thought it would be with a dance troupe instead of with Mom and Dad, but Dad made me a promise when I was in the hospital.

<Jessie> Your dad's the best! Will you have e-mail?

<Melinda> Yes . . . Dad's taking his laptop. Give me your New York snail mail and e-mail addresses, and I'll keep in touch. Well, I've got to get back to my paper, but it's been really nice talking to you.

<Jessie> It sure has! I wish I could see you this summer. Even though my visit last summer wasn't under the best conditions, at least I got to see you. Just

wait until I'm eighteen . . . I'm
moving to Atlanta.

<Melinda> I'll hold you to that!

June 25

*Hello, dear Melinda. I hope this finds you well
and happy. I am writing you this brief note because
I wanted to tell you that I have spoken to our director, Jeremy McAllister, about your considerable talent. He is most curious to see your audition videos,
so when you can, please send your tape to the address on the front of this envelope, to my attention. I
will see to it that Jeremy views it immediately. Who
knows, perhaps he will offer you a summer apprenticeship!*

*As you well know, the world of ballet is most com-
petitive, and with companies folding continually
for lack of funding, spots in a good company are
difficult to earn. However, I do believe you have a
chance of achieving your goals. Work hard this
summer, and I'll look for your package for Jeremy.*

Ciao,
Natalie Blackbird

Dear Jesse,

Paris is awesome. So far, we've visited the Eiffel Tower, Notre Dame, the Arc de Triomphe, lots of shops and two art museums—the Musée du Louvre and Musée d'Orsay. Just walking through the galleries made me feel a part of history. When I saw the Mona Lisa, I got goose bumps, but when I saw some of the original Degas ballerina series, I cried. The paintings seem to glow and the dancers look as if they might stand or turn or smile at any moment. I was surrounded by the ghosts of greatness and long-dead images of once-living people. It was eerie.

M

Hey Bailey,

You would absolutely LOVE Paris! A paradise for a fashion diva like you. The teens are très chic like nothing I've ever seen before. I look so totally frumpy by comparison. Biggest turnoff for me is that they all smoke. I'm not kidding; kids 11 and 12 *years old stand at bus stops with cigarettes, puffing away. Ugh. And little motor scooters dart around with girls holding on to some guy who's driving. No helmet laws either. I bought you a present at the cutest little boutique (the salesgirl said Madonna shops there). You must come to Paris someday (maybe to visit me when I dance here one day in the future!).*

Hugs, M

Jesse,
Arrived in Madrid yesterday. Today it rained and we spent the day at the Prado. More art treasures to see. I guess this might be boring to most American teens, but not to me. Dragging around with my parents can be a bore—honestly, they are so CONSTANT—but still I'm having a good time. It would be more fun if you and Bailey were along on the trip, but I can't have everything. Hope you're surviving your stay in New York.

M

P.S. Will try for e-mail hookup 8 P.M., July 4 (six-hour time difference should catch you at 2 P.M.).

<Melinda> Are you there?

<Jessie> You bet! Didn't get your postcard until yesterday though.

<Melinda> I mailed it ten days ago! Talk about s-l-o-w. . . . What's going on?

<Jessie> Fireworks tonight at Shea Stadium after Mets game. How about you?

<Melinda> We've toured most of Spain. Loved Granada and Seville best. No fireworks here because no one cares that it's America's birthday. It's funny being in a foreign country for one of our holidays. Anyway, last 4th I was in D.C., and my troubles began. Hard to believe it's been a year since my diagnosis. Sure glad it's all behind me.

<Jessie> Me too. Where are you headed next?

<Melinda> We leave for Germany tomorrow and then we'll take a tour of what Dad calls "the blond countries" (cute, huh?) . . . you know, Sweden, Holland, Denmark. I'm having fun, but I'm getting homesick.

<Jessie> I guess you're not dancing.

<Melinda> No. And I feel stiff and fat from nonmovement. Oh, before I forget, today's Bailey's birthday. I sent her an electronic card, but it would be nice if you e-mailed her and wished her a happy birthday. OK?

<Jessie> Will do. When will you be home?

<Melinda> August 1. Europe's nice, but there's no place like home. (Didn't someone named Dorothy say that?)

<Jessie> It depends on where your home is, I guess. Mine is definitely not in New York! Keep writing. Your postcards keep me going.

MELINDA'S DIARY

August 3

I'm glad to be home, but I'm so jet-lagged that I haven't even unpacked. While we were away, Dad had a gazebo built in our backyard as a surprise for Mom. She's always wanted one and it is really cool. I'm looking out my bedroom window and seeing her sitting there with her morning coffee and the newspaper. The lawn service planted vines around the base, and by next summer, it'll be covered with flowers. It'll be so romantic!

Bailey loved her B-day gift from Paris and had a fit over the things I brought back from all the countries we visited. My big project before school starts will be a scrapbook full of photos and ticket stubs and programs. I'll call it "Europe on $500 a Day," which Dad thinks is very funny (and accurate, according to Mom, because Dad spared no expense!).

Bailey has gone all summer without a boyfriend—some kind of record for her, I think. She says she's not hooking up with any guy who doesn't treat her good (the way Jesse treats me, she says). She told me he sent her a B-day e-mail, but she seemed kind of disappointed when I told her I'd suggested it to him. Probably my imagination.

Back to the studio on Saturday, and boy am I ever rusty. Sooo glad I have the mini-studio in the garage to work out my kinks before Mrs. Houston sees me. But I am looking like my old self again. All hair has made a complete comeback. Weight's gone. Boobs no bigger. Oh well. . . . Two out of three ain't bad.

August 3 (night)

Mom sorted through stacks of mail held at the post office and gave me the note from Natalie Blackbird. I almost fainted! And I can't believe it arrived just AFTER we had left on vacation. What bad timing! Anyway, we'll get a package together tomorrow and send it off FedEx. Mom said she'd write a note explaining why it took so long for us to respond. I hope the delay won't count against me!

TO: Ballerina Girl
Subject: Can I Visit?

You'll never believe what my dad says he'll do for me. He's willing to route my return trip to California through Atlanta with a weekend stay-over if it's okay with your parents. All your postcards and e-mails made him curious about you (yes, he does remember you from our first-grade class and the night of the *Nutcracker* performance), and he was surprised that we've kept in touch all this time.

I told him about you and how I stayed with your family so much right after his and Mom's divorce, and about how I used to wish your dad was MY dad. I really dumped on him. He got all teary, almost broke down, said it had been hard on him too with Mom moving to California and him not being able to watch me grow up. He said he was sorry, that divorce is always hard, but that his and Mom's marriage hadn't been good from the start. I told him I didn't want him dissing Mom and he didn't. He just said, "The past is the past. We all made mistakes." He said he only wants to start fresh with me because he loves me.

Anyway, we cleared the air and I guess I can see both sides of their divorce now. Donna and Dad get along real well and I can tell it makes a difference when two people really care for each other. Then he offered to route me through Atlanta to visit you. I really want to come. Can I? I promise not to be a bother. I want to see you again.

Jesse

TO: Jesse
Subject: Your Trip

Yes, you can come! I'll be at the airport to meet your flight. And this time, Mom promises not to talk!

M

August 17

This is one of the worst nights of my life. I look across the street and see a light glowing on Melinda's porch and I know she's outside in her yard in the gazebo with Jesse. She told me she was making them a picnic supper and they were going to "dine under the stars." I acted excited and even helped her pick out music for her CD player and candles for her big evening with him. But inside, my heart was breaking. I want to be the one with Jesse under the stars. I want him to hold me and kiss me.

But she's my best friend and I could never make a move for him. It would be traitorous. Plus, I know the truth: Jesse loves Melinda. Therefore, he'll never love me. If only I could find a guy like Jesse. If only my brain would turn off and I could stop thinking about them and feeling sorry for myself. If only I could give up this impossible dream. If only . . .

MELINDA'S DIARY

August 17

Years from now, when I think of this night, I will count it as one of the best of my life. And for the first time ever, my dream of becoming a profes- sional ballerina slipped into the background. Why? Because tonight Jesse kissed me. Not the quick kiss- and-run of last summer, but a real kiss, one that left my knees shaky and my heart racing.

I can still taste the peppermint of his tongue and smell the lemony scent of his skin. I can still feel the warmth of his body and the touch of his hands on my arms and around my waist. I can hardly hold the pen straight as I write this. But I will try to write it down just as it happened, so that I will never forget what it felt like. . . .

In the afternoon, Jesse played at my computer and swore not to peek while Bailey and I got things ready for a special backyard picnic for me and Jesse. Bailey helped me pack a basket and choose special music. We made chicken salad and cut up some watermelon. "And here is a bag of M&M's," Bailey said before shutting the lid of the hamper basket.

"You look sad," I said to her. I had noticed that

she'd been awfully quiet while we worked—not typical for Bailey.

"No," she said. "Just green with envy."

"You'll find the right guy this year," I told her.

"Maybe," she said, looking like she was going to cry.

"For sure," I said.

Maybe I should have been a better friend and pressed her to tell me why she was so sad, but I didn't because all I could think about was my evening with Jesse. (I'll make it up to her after he leaves.)

After the food was ready, Bailey helped me spread a blanket on the floor of the gazebo and place big squishy cushions all around. We set thirty-six votive candles on the railings and Mom's silver candelabra on a tray in the center of the blanket. I put my CD player on a bench.

"It looks beautiful," I said to Bailey.

"Yes," she said. "Like a fairyland."

"You think?" I said.

"You're so lucky," she said, and hugged me, then jogged away before I could even say thank you. Strange.

Mom and Dad went to dinner and a movie (very nice of them) and later, when the stars came out, Jesse and I walked together from the house to the *gazebo. He carried the picnic basket and at the gazebo he stood for a minute looking at all the flickering candles (which I'd lit minutes before), and he said, "You did all this for me?"*

"For both of us," I told him. "Do you like it?"

"I like it," he said. "Very much."

We ate and talked and told each other our life plans. We've been friends for years, and I know a lot about him, but not everything. He told me that he really does want to become a doctor and I asked, "Since when?"

"Since you got sick," he said. "I want to make people well. Especially kids."

"It takes a long time to become a doctor," I said.

"I don't care how long it takes," he said. "It's what I want to do."

After a while, we didn't say anything; he just leaned against the big cushions and pulled me to his side and we gazed through the candles at the stars. There was no moon, just a million stars winking down at us and a CD playing Clair de Lune. Jesse nuzzled my ear and whispered, "I love you, Melinda."

I turned my face toward him and his lips touched mine and it was like a rocket went off inside my head and my heart. I said, "I love you too, Jesse," because I really, really DO love him. I asked,

"When did you know it?" (Because I was curious about how friendship turned into love for him when we live so far apart and he has another life way out in California.)

He said, "Maybe on the first day of school in first grade, when I saw you standing in the doorway. I remember you were dressed in a yellow dress. You looked like sunshine and you lit up all the dark places inside me."

I laughed and told Jesse that he had quite a memory. Grandma had given the dress to me along with shiny yellow patent leather shoes.

He said, "I thought you were a princess." Then he looked into my eyes, and my heart picked up speed again. "My happiest memories are of those afternoons when I came to your house and we played together," he said. "Even when I fell out of the tree and broke my arm, I was happy, because it meant I could stay at your place and I didn't have to listen to my parents fight."

I felt sad for him. And happy that our family had given him a place to belong.

Jesse reached into his pocket, dropped something small into my hand and closed my hand around it. He said, "Will you take this? It's a birthday present, but I want to give it to you now. I bought it in New York before I came."

"What is it?" I asked before I opened my hand.

"A birthstone ring," he said. "But it's also a promise ring, because I want you to promise that someday you'll take a real ring from me and wear it forever."

I held the ring up and the green stone twinkled—almost as if it was winking at me. I put the ring on my finger and started crying. Jesse kissed me again. And then again. And again. And again. Within the gazebo it was as if we were the only two people in the universe and the stars had left the sky and rained their fire into my heart.

I belong to Jesse and he belongs to me. He leaves tomorrow. How will I ever get through the rest of the year without him to hold me?

September 25

Dear Melinda,

I've decided to start writing letters to you because I might want to say something that's too personal for e-mail that anyone might be able to read. (You know who I mean—parents!) I'll also keep up the e-mail, but today it's a letter, because I haven't stopped thinking about our time under the stars. Next summer, I'm coming to Atlanta if I have to hitchhike all the way. I can get a job there just as easily as here. And Dad will just have to understand any cutback on my visit to NY so that I can spend more time with you. I don't know where I'll stay, or how I'll manage all the details, but I'm coming. So be prepared.

I love you and I want to be with you. Nothing's going to get in my way.

Forever yours,
Jesse

P.S. Mom is substitute teaching but will take over for a middle-school teacher going on maternity leave in January. She thinks it will lead to a full-time position, which means she'll never leave California. But I will.

October 1

Dear Jesse,

I loved getting a letter from you and I've tied it up with a red ribbon and stashed it in my memory box (along with your other notes and cards from first grade till now). I hope you don't think this is silly—the memory box, I mean. It holds all my most treasured possessions, and your correspondence ranks right at the top of my favorite-things list. So there!

Having you around all summer would be a dream come true. My mind keeps playing back the night of our picnic like a videotape (except unlike a tape, it doesn't wear out). I will never forget a single minute of that night. Never! In class, I find myself staring down at my ring instead of listening to my teacher. It's like I share a secret with the ring. The ring knows and I know that you and I love each other. I haven't even told Bailey anything more than that we had a good time.

And speaking of Bailey, she still hasn't found a special guy. I feel sorry for her (which is another reason I don't talk to her much about us. I don't want her to think, "Melinda has a boyfriend and I don't and she's rubbing it in." Know what I mean?).

Keep writing. I miss you every minute.

Love always,
Melinda

Hey M

Here I am in study hall with time dragging. Thank God Christmas break starts on Monday. I'd love to go with you and watch you dance in The Nutcracker this Friday. Thanks for asking me, but please don't think I'm a charity case just because I don't have anyone in my life like you do. After my bad experience with Kerry, I've reevaluated myself and decided that until I can have something as special as you do with Jesse, I'd rather have nothing with anyone. Don't be shocked. . . . I know what I'm saying.

Any word on your dance internship for next summer? What will you do about Jesse coming if you get an invite to Denver?

Bailey

B—

I don't know. I want both—Jesse and a dance apprenticeship. First I have to see if Jesse can really stay and work in Atlanta, which will help me decide about the other. I've heard nothing from Denver, so I guess my audition tape and the influence of Ms. Blackbird wasn't enough. It was a long shot anyway.

Oh . . . don't come over after school. I feel like I'm coming down with the flu. Wouldn't you know it? Just when the holidays are coming. Oh, about Saturday, let's hit the mall early. I want you to help me pick out the perfect Christmas gift for Jesse. Two heads are better than one and I need to get it in the mail ASAP.

Thanks for being my friend. I don't know who I'd talk to if it weren't you!

Hugs . . . M

MELINDA'S DIARY

December 25

Christmas Day and it actually snowed in Atlanta! One whole inch! Bailey and I made pathetic little snowballs and threw them at each other. The snow was wet and sloppy and it hurt when it hit. I have a huge bruise on my arm and another on my leg, but one of my snowballs hit poor B. right in the face. I hope she doesn't bruise like I did.

Jesse called and hearing his voice was like magic. I miss him so much. He sent me a charm bracelet with a single gold rose on it. I told him I'd never put a charm on it that didn't come from him, and he laughed and said that we both may be graduating from high school before he can afford to add another.

Bailey's Diary

December 25

Melinda gave me this for Christmas and so I feel obligated to write in it. I'm not like her, though, and I can't imagine keeping this up every day like she does. But she's my friend and I said I'd give it a try. Besides, it's cute, with drawings of dresses and shoes on the cover.

Melinda showed me her charm bracelet from Jesse and I said it was beautiful, because it is. Jesse loves Melinda and she loves him. End of story. But I have to say that taking a vacation from having a boyfriend has helped me see some things. So far, I've picked a lot of losers. But no more! Here's my New Year's resolution: When classes begin, I'm going to look more closely at the less high-profile guys (the ones who aren't so cocky and stuck on themselves. Guys who are NICE to me).

I guess this is it for my first entry (and maybe my last). EOM (end of message). I saw that in a movie once.

MELINDA'S DIARY

March 17

I feel punky today. Too tired to write. Performed horribly in dance class. Got a C on a history test and shouldn't have. Just an all-around bad day.

March 30

I have to go for a bone marrow aspiration. Geez, I hate them so much!!!!! But Mom dragged me to *our family doc, who did a blood test and said my white count's up (which totally freaked Mom, because it could signal the end of remission). He said I could just have a cold or maybe mono (it's going around at school) but that I should get another aspiration just to make sure. Easy for him to prescribe. He doesn't have to have one. So no dance class. Half day at the hospital. This really stinks!*

The Denver Dance Theater

April 4

The Denver Dance Theater
1234 Yates Drive
Denver, CO 80202

Dear Ms. Skye:

After carefully reviewing your dance tape and your credentials along with the strong verbal recommendation of Natalie Blackbird, I am pleased to offer you a summer apprenticeship with the Denver Dance Company. Your expenses to Denver will be paid, along with room and board for the summer, plus compensation for your performances.

If this is satisfactory, a contract will follow for

you to sign and return, as well as a complete schedule of performances. Congratulations! We look forward to working with you as a member of our dance corps.

Sincerely,

Jeremy McAllister
Director
Denver Dance Company

MELINDA'S DIARY

April 4

Long horrible day at hospital, seeing doctors and getting needles shoved in me. I'd almost forgotten the horrors of chemo, but they all came back today. It's only been a little more than a year since I went through this. Thought the day was going to be a bust. Then the letter from Denver came and I about fainted. THEY WANT ME!!! I can't believe it. A whole summer as a professional dancer. Mom looked dazed and said we should wait until Dad's back home before we "firm up any plans."

Now that I've had time to think, I'm feeling very mixed up. Just when I thought Jesse and I might spend the summer together, the letter came. I want to do both—spend the summer with Jesse AND dance with the Denver company.

I took a time-out because Bailey called, and I told her what had happened. She said Jesse's plans weren't set in stone and I should tell him about the offer because she was betting that Jesse, being Jesse, would tell me to take the dance offer.

This just isn't fair! I've wanted to be a dancer all my life, but now I want other things too. Why does it all have to be so complicated? Whatever happened to a straight course? I can't imagine not dancing. But now I can no longer imagine my life without Jesse either. I love him so. . . . What am I going to do?

UNIVERSITY PATHOLOGY CONSULTANTS

121 East 18th Street, Suite 318
Atlanta, GA 30020
Phone: (800) 555-4567 Fax: (800) 555-4568

BONE MARROW PATHOLOGY REPORT

Referring Physician: Janet Powell, M.D.
Specimen Number: JL01-99438
Hematology Associates

Emory University Hospital, Suite 2010
Atlanta, GA 30020

Date Collected: 4/04
Date Received: 4/04
Date Reported: 4/05

Diagnosis: Acute Lymphoblastic Leukemia

Gross Description
The specimen consists of 6 slides and 3 additional aliquots of 3 cc each, labeled "Bone Marrow Aspirate, Melinda Skye."

Microscopic Description:
The bone marrow aspirate demonstrates extensive hypercellularity with normal bone marrow elements essentially replaced by infiltrating lymphoblasts. There are multiple mitotic figures seen. The lymphoblasts demonstrate a high nuclear/cytoplasm ratio and clumped nuclear chromatin. Some nuclei display a folded appearance. Scattered among the abnormal cells are small numbers of erythroid, myeloid, and megakaryocytic cells.

Flow cytometric immunophenotypic studies demonstrated a population of beta lymphocytes, which expressed the CD19 and CD20 antigens.

Cytochemistry was positive for TdT, further corroborating a lymphoblastic process. The findings represent a relapse of acute lymphoblastic leukemia in this patient. **Prognosis poor, after so brief a remission.**

Stephen R. Jones, M.D.
Pathologist

Fallen Petals

I cried when I heard your news. I know it isn't macho, but I couldn't help it. Later, I went to the tennis courts and pounded the fuzz off a ball on the backboards. I hit the ball until I couldn't lift my arm and then I smashed the racket on the concrete. It didn't help. I'm still angry.

It's not fair that you're still fighting leukemia and that you have to go through chemo all over again. I'll call you so we can talk.

Jesse

TO: All Concerned
Subject: Melinda

This is one message I never wanted to write. According to Melinda's doctor, our daughter's cancer has returned. Apparently when this kind of leukemia recurs after such a brief remission, chances for another remission aren't so good. She begins a new round of chemo, but the magic drug they used before can't be used a second time. It's too toxic. What do they consider uncontrolled leukemia?

We ask you once again to keep our daughter in your thoughts and prayers. We'll keep you posted.

Lenny & Elana

Elana's Journal

April 10

I'm out of the habit of writing in this thing. . . . I got lazy, confident I'd not need to write in it. But now I turn to pouring out my feelings here once more because I am confused and, yes, angry too. We did exactly as we were told. Melinda endured months of chemo, but now it seems that those months were for nothing. Her disease has returned, and this time her doctors don't act enthusiastic about her recovery. I'm smarter now. Before, I accepted all they said with a child's innocence. Now I know that medicine does not have all the answers. I know that doctors are not gods and that victims aren't just statistics.

Her doctors don't always look me in the eye when we talk. I think it's because they've thrown everything they have in their arsenal of drugs and potions at Melinda, and they've come to discover that her cancer is still stronger than their chemical weapons.

Lenny and I feel helpless. We watch her go through the same courses of drugs again. They didn't work before. Why would they work now? We have not yet told Melinda about the grimness, because she's struggling hard to endure the course. I can't rob her of hope. Neither can I consider the alternative.

MELINDA'S DIARY

April 25

I feel like I'm locked in a time warp. Didn't I just go through all this torture? I really thought it was over, but it isn't. The doctors come at me with terrible drugs that make me so sick. Stronger doses and longer treatments. And this time, I have to stay in the hospital 24/7. Still, my enemy doesn't retreat.

I've given up school. Too sick to even think about dance and the Denver offer. A dream come true and I'm too sick to consider it. Mom says I can make up school this summer, but that would mean not dancing in Denver.

Sometimes I think Mom and Dad are keeping secrets from me. What could be more terrible than this? If it wasn't for Jesse's constant e-mails, I would go insane.

Bailey's Diary

April 27

I think it's my fault that Melinda's sick again. I've wished so hard and long for Jesse to be mine that the dark side of the universe heard my secret thoughts and allowed her sickness to return. Now I'm begging for her to get well and never be struck with cancer again. I have given up my hopeless love for Jesse (cross my heart). I would give up anything else I have if only she would get well. Please, please, let Melinda be all right.

May 3

We miss you, dear Melinda. The class is less lively, less competitive without your spirit of excellence to spur us on. Please know that we think of you every day and that all your friends and classmates look forward to your return to health and our studio. Keep up the fight. We're on the sidelines cheering for you.

All your friends at the Atlanta School of Ballet

May 15

After speaking with your mother tonight, I know you will not be coming to Denver next month. I am sad for you, for your family, for our dance company, and for the world of ballet. But once you have beaten this monster, tell me and you will have another opportunity at an apprenticeship. I promise this. Your talent is pure and bright, and on the stage of life, you shine like a star.

With affection,
Natalie Blackbird

Elana's Journal

May 25

Dr. Neely brought Lenny and me into his office today to say what we already know. Nothing is working for Melinda. "What now?" Lenny asked.

"A bone marrow transplant may be her only hope," Dr. Neely said.

"Tell us more," I said.

And he did. He said that the best transplants are usually between siblings, but that because Melinda has no brother or sister, a parent could be considered. He suggested that both Lenny and I be tested to determine who would be the best donor. Naturally, Lenny and I agreed to be tested immediately.

But Dr. Neely also warned us that the procedure is risky, especially in Melinda's weakened condition. He told us that her immune system must be totally destroyed, leaving her vulnerable to even the normally most harmless germs, but that unless her immune system is taken out, her body will reject the transplant automatically. Even if the new bone marrow takes hold, she will have to take anti-rejection medications for the rest of her life. In short, there is great risk in this procedure, but he feels it is our daughter's only chance.

We have not told Melinda yet about the transplant possibility. Lenny is withdrawn and remote, and we are both frightened by our choices. Destroying Melinda's immune system is a huge risk. Yet not doing the transplant seems to be a bigger one. How can we gamble with our daughter's life?

MELINDA'S DIARY

June 1

How much longer am I going to be stuck in this hospital? I feel like an animal in a cage. I want out. I want to go home.

June 3

Jesse called again and just hearing his voice made me feel better. He said he's got a job bagging groceries six days a week because he wants to save up all the money he can. I thought about his plans to come to Atlanta this summer. I think about a lot of things these days. I have nothing else to do. I can't concentrate on reading books, and daytime TV is pathetic. I'm the only person my age up here, so there's no one to talk to except Mom. Sometimes Bailey comes, but I know she wishes she wasn't here. I can't blame her. I wish I wasn't here either.

Elana's Journal

June 3

Blood work results came back and it looks as if I'm the better match for the transplant. I want to tell Melinda, but Lenny says to wait until he returns from Europe, because he has something to talk about. I'm relieved about the test and for the first time in months, I feel hopeful. If my marrow takes, then Melinda really can be cancer-free.

June 6

Lenny and I had the worst fight we've ever had. While in Geneva, he looked into a special cancer clinic where extreme cases of the disease are treated. He talked with the head of the facility and now wants to transfer Melinda to Switzerland. I'm horrified. How can he even consider such a thing? I don't want our child treated by potential charlatans and quacks with hocus-pocus herbs and questionable medical procedures.

"And this way is better?" he shouted.

"Bone marrow transplants are proven cures," I shouted back.

"If she doesn't die getting the treatment," he yelled.

We stood staring at each other because that's the first time either of us had used that word in a sentence: DIE. Melinda might DIE.

MELINDA'S DIARY

June 6

Something's going on between Mom and Dad. Something bad. They hardly speak to each other and I can cut the tension with a knife when they're in the room together. This is my fault. They're having problems because of me and I don't know what to do about it.

I told Jesse and he said he thinks my family's one of the strongest he's ever known and I'm worrying for nothing. I hope he's right.

Elana's Journal

June 7

Dr. Neely is negative about the clinic idea, because he feels that it's the wrong choice medically. I told Lenny that Melinda must be told of her options—the transplant or the European clinic. Lenny wants us to decide, because Melinda's still a minor. But I don't feel that way. She's almost sixteen and should have a say-so. I also feel that the choice is the only power she holds over her illness. Lenny doesn't agree with me.

While Lenny and I are at this impasse, Melinda's losing ground. A decision needs to be made ... and soon!

MELINDA'S DIARY

June 7

Dr. Neely brought a woman named Jennifer to meet me today. She's twenty, but she had leukemia when she was eight and underwent a bone marrow transplant when she was twelve. Today, she is well and fine, goes to college and plays serious tennis. She really impressed me and after she was gone, I asked Dr. Neely if he thought a bone marrow transplant might work for me. He said, "It's a possibility."

I asked Mom and Dad about it and that's when I found out what's been going on between them. "You're fighting over what I should do?" I asked. "Don't you think I should be consulted?"

Dad told me about the clinic in Switzerland. I know exactly what each one of them wants me to do, but I told them I'll decide. I know they mean well, but I'm so mad at them for not talking to me sooner! It's my body.

June 8

Talked to Dr. Neely this morning and he explained how my immune system would have to be destroyed before the transplant—three days of radiation and ten days of chemo. The worst part is that I'll have to go into isolation! Ugh! I don't like that idea. But isolation will cut down on the risks of secondary infection, he says, which is very dangerous. Only medical staff and my parents can come see me, and everyone will have to be "de-germed" before they can come inside my room. He told me Mom will be my donor.

He also cautioned me that the transplant may take, or it may not. There are no guarantees that it will work, or that I really will be "cured" of leukemia. Most of the time, a BMT improves a recipient's life immensely and does produce a cure, but not always. This bothers me. To go through all this torture and have my cancer return would be the nastiest trick life could play on me. But if it works . . . well, I could dance again. I could be with Jesse.

Anyway, I've got lots to think about. I'll e-mail Jesse and talk to him about it.

TO: Ballerina Girl
Subject: Transplant

Just get well. I want to hang around with you for the rest of my life.

Jesse

TO: Melinda
Subject: Transplant

Isolation? What's wrong with that? Can I join you? Seriously, friend, I know it's a big decision, but if the transplant works, then all this medical stuff will be over. That will be a GOOD thing, don't you think? Besides, if you go off to Geneva, I'll never see you. Here, I might be able to wave at you through a window!

Bailey

Elana's Journal

June 11

I talked with a woman today who had been a marrow donor for her brother. She told me what to expect from the procedure. I'll be under a general anesthetic and doctors will remove a pint or so of my marrow (which the doctor says I won't miss, because my body will step up production immediately to replenish my supply). They take it from my hip bones, and afterward I'll be sore, but back on my feet in no time. As soon as they harvest my marrow, they take it to Melinda for infusion. The downside is that I can't be with her during the infusion, because I'll still be in recovery. Lenny will hold her hand.

I asked Dr. Neely if there's anything I can do to make my marrow "better" for Melinda and he said, "No. You're not responsible for whether it takes or not, either. It either does or it doesn't."

Can I accept knowing my marrow didn't work if it doesn't take? That would be very hard for me. Knowing her chances are lowered because I'm not a "perfect" match is also hard. A sibling would be so much better, but Lenny and I could never have another baby after Melinda. We always wanted more children, but it never happened. Now Melinda's life is in jeopardy and a brother or sister would be such a blessing. Still, Dr. Neely assures me that unrelated donors help cancer victims all the time. I pray my marrow does the job for her.

TO: All Concerned
Subject: BMT

June 12, noon

Melinda's decided to go ahead with the transplant. Elana will be her donor and I'll be around to support both of them. I'd give anything to do more. In a few days Melinda will go into isolation, where they will begin giving her drugs to destroy her immune system. We're all scared silly.

Lenny

TO: Ballerina Girl
Subject: I'm coming!

June 13

Mom and I are coming to Atlanta BEFORE you begin the BMT process. When I came home from work last night, she gave me your dad's e-mail message and said she has a little money saved up and that she's going to spend it on the trip. She's reserved a room for us at a residence-type hotel that's near the hospital.

I hugged her big-time. I called my dad and told him I won't be coming this summer. When I explained about you, he offered to send us some money to go toward the trip. I was shocked. My parents haven't said two words to each other since the divorce, but now they're banding together to give me something I want more than anything else—a chance to see you up close and personal. One miracle down (my parents) and one to go (you getting well).

Jesse

TO: Jesse
Subject: Trip

Come as soon as you can! There's no time to spare.

MELINDA'S DIARY

June 13

Dr. Neely's not happy, because I want to wait a couple of days before he begins "killing" me—all right, maybe that's an overstatement. But I can't go into isolation until Jesse's here. Dad got Jesse's and his mother's fares comped by the airline, and they'll be here tomorrow afternoon.

Mom and Dad are throwing me a party here on the pedi-floor on Saturday. Besides Jesse and his mom, I've invited Bailey, Mrs. Houston, four girls from my dance class and three friends from school. Dad will videotape it and we'll have pizza, Cokes, ice cream and cake. I asked if I could have a pony brought up (ha-ha).

I'd love to spend some time alone with Jesse, but I can't figure out how or when. I'll think of something, because I WILL NOT go into isolation until the two of us can be together away from parents and nurses.

Dr. Neely showed me my "new" room. You get to it through an air lock, and anyone who's allowed to come in must wear a sterile gown, a hair covering and a mask. It's a bedroom with no decoration, but at least there's an intercom and a large window that looks out onto the hall, where people can stand, look in and talk to me. I can pull a curtain for privacy. It's kind of creepy knowing I have to stay inside the room while my immune system's down. I hope I don't go postal.

I'll have a TV to watch, but anything that comes in from the outside must be decontaminated. I'll be able to keep books and, of course, my diary, once all are "cleansed." I'm not looking forward to this one bit.

Elana's Journal

June 14

I can't believe the way Melinda looked when Jesse walked into her room. She fairly glowed! Ann looks wonderful too. She and I went down to the cafeteria to talk, but mostly to let the kids be alone together. Over coffee, Ann said, "They're in love, you know."

I said, "Yes, I know. Who'd have thought it would last so long. Ever since first grade!"

"He's never cared for another girl," Ann told me.

"I urged him to date others, but he wouldn't. He told me that Melinda was the only one for him and that someday they would be together."

I said, "I used to think that nothing would ever stand in the way of her dancing, but I forgot about love."

Ann said, "I've warned him about affecting her life plans for professional dancing. He said he'd stand beside her all the way."

"Cancer's in her way right now," I told Ann.

Ann reached over and patted my hand. "The transplant will change that," she said. "You'll have given your daughter life twice. Not many parents get that honor."

I'd never thought of it that way before, but it comforted me.

"I've missed you, Jesse."

"Same here. Can I hug you?"

"I'm not in isolation yet . . . hold me. Oh, Jesse, I'm scared."

"Me too. But I've read up on BMTs and there are plenty of success stories. Yours will be one too. When do you start?"

"I go into the Chamber, as I call it, on Sunday. Radiation starts Monday."

"Then we only have the rest of today and to-morrow to be together."

"That's right."

"We'll stay up all night. Can you do that?"

"Sure. The doctors and nurses are pretty understanding of my situation. Of course, they'll pop in to check on me occasionally, so we have to be on guard."

"How about your parents?"

"They know how hard this is going to be, so they won't hang around. Besides, I'll have plenty of time to sleep once I go into the Chamber. And Mom gave up her habit of sleeping here every night. But she gets here pretty early every morning."

"I just want to spend every minute I can with you."

"Me too."

"The party's a good idea. But is there any place we can go to be by ourselves?"

"I think so. I'll let Bailey help me work it out. She's clever and devious."

"I'll just bet. Know what I think?"

"I think you should kiss me before our mothers come back."

"You mean like this?"

Bailey's Diary

June 15

I know there are more blank pages in this book than there should be, but I forget about writing in it most nights. But not tonight. I need to "talk" to someone/something. Seeing Jesse again and remembering the way I once felt about him was odd. Actually, I thought stirring up the old feelings would hurt more than it did. I never want Melinda to know how I've felt about Jesse. She's still the best friend I've ever had and I wouldn't hurt her for anything. The way I've felt about Jesse is my secret and I'll take it to my grave.

That said, I redeemed myself (in my own eyes) when I helped Melinda and Jesse be totally alone after the party.

I arrived in the afternoon, just before five, and the hospital offices were closing. I snooped the upper floors and found a lounge area with a couple of chairs and a sofa where I guess staff can relax. While staff people were leaving for the day and not paying attention to me, I pretended I belonged up there and unlocked the lounge door from the inside.

I showed up at the party (a good one too). Just a few people came. Melinda's dad showed a couple of videos: one of their European vacation (boring) and one of Melinda's dance career (much better). The clip of her and Jesse from the first grade really got to me. They were both so small and adorable. Even then, Jesse had the bluest, prettiest eyes. And Melinda was precious. I know more than ever that Jesse and I never could have worked out. He and Melinda belong together.

After the party, when everyone had gone home, Jesse and I helped Melinda sneak up the stairwell. She was wearing jeans, so she didn't look like an escapee, and we were lucky not to run into anybody climbing the stairs. The climb wasn't easy for Melinda, but we rested when she needed to, and with Jesse helping her, we got there without a problem. The floor was quiet; no one was around. I took them to the lounge. At the door, Melinda hugged me and said, "Thank you."

"How long have you got before you're missed?" I asked.

"An hour or so," she said. "I told a nurse on the floor that Jesse and I wanted to be alone for a little while and she said she'd save my room for last on eleven o'clock rounds."

"Thanks for helping," Jesse said.

My heart felt really tight in my chest, but I shoved the two of them inside, shut the door and dashed to the elevator. In the lobby, I met up with Patti, one of the girls from school who'd come to the party and who was driving me home.

She was miffed because I was so late. "Where've you been? You said you were just going to say goodbye and come right down."

I got teary-eyed. "Give me a break. It's not easy saying goodbye to your best friend. She's going to be locked up for weeks and weeks with the transplant and all. Maybe months."

Patti backed off.

Here I am alone in my room and all I can think of is Jesse and Melinda and how lucky they are to have each other. I have to stop writing now. I'm crying and the page is so blurry, I can hardly see it.

MELINDA'S DIARY

June 17, Morning

I'm in the Chamber, looking out my window at my world—a corridor in a hospital isolation care unit. They irradiated me from top to bottom (painless) to begin the immune shutdown sequence. Another dose tomorrow and the next day, then the chemo—the worst part.

I'll write about my evening with Jesse some other time, because I never want to forget a minute of it. We barely made it back in time for rounds, and we didn't sleep a wink, but our time together was perfect.

He tells me he'll be outside the window as much as he's allowed, and I told him to beat on the glass if I'm asleep, because I want to see his face as much as possible. We belong to each other. I understand now that I will never love anyone again the way I love Jesse. We are soul mates.

June 23

Killing a person's immune system without killing the person is tricky stuff. The radiation left me sick, but it was nothing compared to what the chemo is doing. I didn't know I could be so ill and still be alive. Dr. Neely says it's normal—hope I'm spared abnormal. Everything else I've gone through seems like it happened in another lifetime. Except for Jesse. Seeing him at my window every day gives me the strength to endure. He presses his palm against the glass. I raise my hand and press my palm against his. The glass between us is hard and cold. But if I wait long enough, the glass warms slightly from the heat of his body. My body has no heat. I am cold all the time. I hold my hand against the glass for as long as I can stand up. And I imagine he is touching me. Really touching me.

June 25

The days are endless, the nights even longer. I asked Mom to hang a pair of my pointe shoes outside my window so I can see them. They dangle, all new and shiny pink satin and strong ribbon to wrap around the ankles. I want the shoes to remind me of the world I left behind, of the life I long to have. Ballet and Jesse, no cancer . . . this is what I want more than anything else.

Elana's Journal

June 27

Today Melinda asked me to forgive her for "being so crabby." I didn't know what she was talking about, because she's always been the world's best daughter. She said, "You and Dad are the best and I'm so glad I got to be your child."

She scared me in a way because it was almost as if she was saying goodbye.

TO: Our Closest Family Members
Subject: Update

I never imagined she would be so sick. I feel helpless. And useless. I am a father without a family. Elana hardly goes home, remaining at the hospital day and night. We eat silently in the cafeteria. I asked Elana to go out to dinner just to get away for even a few hours. She refused. I've been abandoned by wife and daughter. Orphaned by this disease that consumes our lives. I'm not complaining, because this is just the way things must be right now. Yet I'm on the outside looking in, unable to help either of the two people I love most.

Lenny

Elana's Journal

June 27

Melinda reminded me that her friend Bailey's birthday is next week and asked if we would please see to it that Bailey gets a card. How can she think of others with what she's going through? Remarkable. Ann returned to California yesterday. Lenny and I agreed that we could not let Jesse leave with her. He'll stay until this is over or until late August, whichever comes first. He sleeps at the house in his old room, hangs at the hospital all day with me. He and Melinda touch by placing their *palms against the glass window. It breaks my heart to see them stare into each other's eyes. Sometimes I wish the glass would dissolve, but then I remember, if it does, germs will invade and Melinda has no way to fight.*

TO: Jesse
Subject: Nightmares

I'm glad we can "talk" via Melinda's computer. I want to hear every detail about her, but I can't bear to go down and look at her every day like you do. She's so thin and fragile-looking. Like she might break and shatter. I keep last year's school photo of her on my bedside table and I talk to her. I tell her she's beautiful and smart and going to get well. You are the glue that holds her together now. I'm so glad she has you to love her.

Tell her that I've decided to transfer to tech high school and get a diploma in design. I want to go into the fashion business. I've been a crummy student for years, but Melinda's commitment to ballet has inspired me. Plus, she often looked at my dress doodles and said, "Bailey, you should

design clothing. You're so good at it." I'll never
have another friend like her. Please tell her that
for me, Jesse!

═══════════════════════════════

Elana's Journal

July 7

Melinda's feverish. Despite all precautions, she
has become sick! We can't believe it. Dr. Neely is
throwing massive doses of antibiotics into her, hoping to subdue any illness before it gets a toehold.

July 9

No change. Lenny and I sit by her bedside. Jesse
waits at the window.

July 11

Viral meningitis! How could this have happened?
We were all so careful. Dr. Neely says her weak-

ened immune system has left her vulnerable. We watch our child waste away. We go nowhere, do nothing except stay by her side. She asked us to give Zorita to Bailey. I said, "No, Zorita's ours. She'll be waiting for you when you come home."

July 12

Melinda lies on the bed without moving, tubes running in and out of her. Antibiotics pour into her. Monitors and constant checks reveal no progress.

July 13

Lenny and I hold on to each other's hands and talk to her. The nurse said hearing is one of the senses that still works despite comas. Did I just write that? She's slipping away from us right before our eyes. Oh, God...how can this be happening?

July 14

Dr. Neely let Jesse dress in a sterile gown and come into the room. Jesse took her hand, kissed her palm and stroked her face. He spoke not a word, but I saw tears sliding down his cheeks. I put my arms around him and together we cried over Melinda and told her how much we love her.

July 14

I'm writing this because you can't. You're really sick, and all of us are scared. Your eyes fluttered open once yesterday and my heart jumped for joy. For a minute, I thought you were looking inside me. You looked as if you were saying "I'm sorry." As if you were apologizing because you haven't the strength left to fight. I begged you not to give up. But your eyes closed and you drifted away.

Where are you, Melinda? Are you safe and warm? Do you know we're here, on the other side of your consciousness? Come back to us . . . to me. Please don't leave.

Jesse

Audio Transcription by
Dr. Leigh Neely, Oncologist,
for Insertion into Medical
File of Melinda Skye:

Received emergency call at 11:10 A.M. from ICU nurse who witnessed a seizure in this 15 y/o leukemic patient with recently diagnosed meningitis. Upon my arrival, patient was unresponsive and hypotensive. Blood pressure continued to drop despite rapid infusion of IV dopamine. Respiratory arrest ensued at 11:21 A.M. shortly followed by asystole on cardiac monitor. CPR was begun and patient was intubated. She received multiple doses of epinephrine and atropine. She briefly regained a pulse after 10 minutes of resuscitation, but went into ventricular tachycardia. Sinus rhythm could not be restored with IV lidocaine, and multiple shocks were administered via defibrillator. She remained in cardiac arrest. CPR was continued for more than 30 minutes to no avail. The patient never regained a heartbeat and was pronounced dead at 11:58 A.M. I met with family members standing by in the ICU waiting room and notified them of

unsuccessful resuscitation efforts. Body
will be taken to hospital morgue pending
funeral arrangements by the parents.Submit-
ted: 12:15 P.M., July 16

Dear Mom and Dad,

I'm writing this the night before I go into the Chamber. I gave it to Bailey to put with my special box in my closet, because I know that you'll find it someday. Maybe next week, or even years from now when I've moved away and you've decided to clean out my room, but whenever you find it, I want you to know how much you both mean to me.

I know the procedure is a gamble. If it works, I'll be the happiest person in the world. If it doesn't . . . well, at least I didn't go down without a fight. Remember that. I wanted this chance. Mom, thank you for your bone marrow. Thank you for staying by me day and night (even when I was thirteen and not so very nice to you. I didn't mean to be hateful). I was so angry about having leukemia! Why me? Why did I have to get sick? I had so many plans. I was going to be a prima ballerina. I was going to dance all over the world. Instead, I was sick, on chemo, bald and hideous-looking. Dad, thank you for taking us to Europe. Thank you for letting me pursue my ballerina dreams.

This time around, I know that it's not all about ME. It's about making the best of whatever time I'm given. And about family and friends and leaving them good memories.

Thank you for being the two best parents in the

world. I've always felt sorry for Bailey and Jesse because they never had the kind of family I have. Not
their fault either. It's simply the way life worked out
for them.

Cancer isn't the worst thing that can happen to a
person. And neither is dying young. Taking life for
granted, living badly—these things seem far worse
to me. In many ways—ways that count—I'm the
luckiest girl in the world. Here's something I wrote
when I was thirteen.

The Things I've Learned from Having Cancer

by Melinda Skye

1. Be GLAD for every new day.
2. It's okay to cry.
3. It's okay to feel sorry for yourself (but
   not too sorry).
4. Good friends are good medicine.
5. Love is the best medicine of all.

I love you both with all my heart. And I always
will.

Melinda, your loving daughter

Elana's Journal

July 17, midnight

I went into Melinda's room and found her memory box on her closet shelf. On top was a letter addressed to me and Lenny. I held it for a long time before I found the courage to open it. The letter comforted me greatly when I read it. After Lenny reads it, I will make a copy and put the original into our safe-deposit box. It will be the thing I treasure most now that she's gone. Passages are already branded into my heart.

Her box held so many keepsakes important to her. I found a sealed letter with Jesse's name on it. I wanted to tear it open and read it, but I knew I couldn't betray her that way. I'll give it to him in the morning...the day of her funeral.

I found her first pair of ballet shoes from when she was five. Were my daughter's feet ever that small? I held them to my nose and could still smell the baby powder she used before she put them on. I cried so hard, I stained the satin.

Dearest Jesse,

If you're reading this, I didn't make it through the whole bone marrow transplant thing. You see, I wrote this letter before I went into isolation, and I gave it to Bailey to put in my memory box where Mom would find it and give it to you . . . just in case. I want you to know how sorry I am life didn't work out for us. We've grown up together, but we won't grow old together. Too bad. I'd have liked to see you become a doctor.

I found a piece of paper in my memory box with the class rules from the first day of school. I can't even remember why I kept it, but I did. The last rule was the best: Be kind to each other. Jesse, you have always been kind to me. I'm not sure why. I'm very ordinary . . . just a regular girl with a few dreams and some bad luck (leukemia . . . go figure). Here's something you should know: Having you in my life made me very happy. And that matters a lot when I had to cram a whole lifetime into just fifteen years.

Please don't miss me too much. Please don't be too sad. Find someone else to love, because you have much love to give and it's a gift that shouldn't be wasted. You, Jesse, were the rose that made my life sweet.

I will wait for you in heaven.

Melinda Skye

TO: Bailey
Subject: A Favor

I want to leave one final message with Melinda. I want to slide it under her hand in her casket, and I don't want anyone to find it and take it away. I want it to be with her for all time. If you can distract anyone who's standing by her casket when I come up for a final goodbye, I'd be grateful. Will you help?

Jesse

TO: Jesse
Subject: Re: A Favor

Yes. I'll help.

Bailey

It may be a lifetime before I see you again on the far side of time. Wait for me. Look for me. Please don't forget me, Melinda Skye, because one day I will come to you. I will come.

Jesse Rose

Lurlene McDaniel began writing inspirational novels about teenagers facing life-altering situations when her son was diagnosed with juvenile diabetes. "I saw firsthand how chronic illness affects every aspect of a person's life," she has said. "I want kids to know that while people don't get to choose what life gives to them, they do get to choose how they respond."

Lurlene McDaniel's novels are hard-hitting and realistic, but also leave readers with inspiration and hope. Her books have received acclaim from readers, teachers, parents, and reviewers. Her bestselling novels include *Don't Die, My Love; I'll Be Seeing You; Till Death Do Us Part; Hit and Run;* and *Prey.*

Lurlene McDaniel lives in Chattanooga, Tennessee.